MW00715113

Charles Smith

Steam Using or Steam Engine Practice

Charles Smith

Steam Using or Steam Engine Practice

Reprint of the original, first published in 1885.

1st Edition 2022 | ISBN: 978-3-36826-033-0

Verlag (Publisher): Outlook Verlag GmbH, Zeilweg 44, 60439 Frankfurt, Deutschland
Vertretungsberechtigt (Authorized to represent): E. Roepke, Zeilweg 44, 60439 Frankfurt, Deutschland
Druck (Print): Books on Demand GmbH, In de Tarpen 42, 22848 Norderstedt, Deutschland

STEAM USING;

— OR —

Steam Engine Practice,

BY

CHAS. A. SMITH, C. E.,

Professor of Civil and Mechanical Engineering at Washington University, St. Louis, Mo.; Member of the American Society of Civil Engineers, the Engineers' Club of St. Louis, and Associate Member of the American Association of Railway Master Mechanics.

CHICAGO:

THE AMERICAN ENGINEER, 182-184 DEARBORN STREET.

1895.

PUBLISHERS PREFACE.

It is believed that some knowledge of the circumstances attending the publication of this work, "STEAM USING," as well as its companion volume, "STEAM MAKING," will be of interest to the reader.

The lamented author, Prof. Chas. A. Smith, had arranged with *The American Engineer* for the publication of the two works. While the first, "STEAM MAKING," was going through the columns of the *Engineer*, Professor Smith died, early in 1884, leaving also to the care of the *Engineer* the recently completed manuscript of "STEAM USING."

To all who are familiar with the circumstances under which the books were written—the author suffering from a mortal illness and struggling against death to thus round out his life work, only giving up to die on their completion—will appreciate and value the more highly the broad and active experience thus crystallized.

To Mr. John W. Weston, so long connected with this journal, and personally familiar with the author and his writings, has been delegated the pleasant duty of conducting these works through the various stages of bookmaking, with the result now presented. The task has not been without its difficulties, the most serious, perhaps, being the loss of the invaluable assistance of their author in the work of revision of matter and proof.

As the author died without leaving a preface to his second volume, we desire to acknowledge for him the aid which he received from various engine builders and professional men throughout the country, which the following pages will disclose

It has been the aim, as far as possible, to preserve the exact style of the author, and it is believed that the facts and features presented in both books, the heirlooms of an admirable man, acknowledged to be profound and exact in his particular lines of work, will be held to cover whatever defects of minor importance may be encountered.

THE AMERICAN ENGINEER.

CHICAGO, MARCH 1, 1885.

SKETCH OF THE LIFE AND CHARACTER OF THE AUTHOR.

Charles A. Smith was born in St. Louis, October 1, 1846. His parents were both Massachusetts people who had been still further west. From both father and mother he inherited the instincts of a sailor, and the blood of several generations of ship-masters coursed through his veins. Though he never became a sailor, he always showed a sailor's fondness for "fixing things," for using his hands, for actual construction.

While he was still an infant, his mother died of cholera in St. Louis, and he was placed in the care of his father's sister, in Newburyport, Mass. This kind aunt was his mother, and her house was his home till he had a home of his own. His mode of life was simple and plain, but young Smith made warm friends and his boyhood was happy.

I first met him in 1860, when I became principal of the Boys' High School, of Newburyport. He was then fourteen years old and a member of the second class. He was a pleasant little fellow with a frank, earnest look, and a forehead which suggested brains. When the school gave expression to its loyalty to the Union by the erection of a liberty pole and publicly celebrated a flag-raising, young Smith was selected by his schoolmates to mount the platform and haul home the stars and stripes.

The school had a very good theodolite, and when we came to Loomis' Surveying, a great enthusiasm for field work was developed, and young Smith was never so happy as when on a surveying party. He took the English course and graduated in 1862. The next spring he went into the office of J. B. Henck, civil engineer, in Boston. At that time he probably had no idea of going to an engineering school. In 1864 he was leveller on the Boston, Hartford & Erie Railway. In 1865 he became chief assistant in the City Engineer's office, Springfield, Mass. By this time he saw clearly that an engineer requires a training far beyond a high school education, and he resolved to enter the Massachusetts Institute of Technology, then first opened He had been reading ahead somewhat, with occasional help from me, so that he entered what was organized as a sophomore class. He lived again in Newburyport and went eighty miles daily on his way to and from the Institute. President Rogers was his teacher in physics, Professor Runkle in mathematics and applied mechanics, and Professor Henck in civil engineering.

He graduated in the pioneer class in 1868. I never quite understood how he managed to meet the cost of his course at the Institute. To be sure he had carefully saved the earnings of three years, and he secured for his vacations most excellent employment under the celebrated hy-draulic engineer, J. B. Francis, at Lowell, Mass. He there assisted in determining the flow of water in pipes, over wiers, the efficiency of turbines, etc. I left Massachusetts for St. Louis in 1865, so I did not follow closely his career as a student.

After a year as engineer on the Union Pacific Railway in Utah, he returned, on the completion of the road, to Boston and went into partnership with Professor J. B. Henck, as civil engineers. While there associated with Professor Henck, he took charge of a part of the Blue Ridge Railway of North Carolina, as division engineer.

At that time, in 1870, the steady development of the Polytechnic School of Washington University made it necessary to appoint an instructor of civil engineering. I took pleasure in recommending young Smith for the position, and he was appointed. For the first year he made his home in my family, and as a preparation for the work of the class room he read with me Rankine's Civil Engineering entire.

After a brief experience as instructor, Mr. Smith was appointed professor to the chair of civil and mechanical engineering, which was subsequently named in honor of William Palm. This chair Professor Smith held till June, 1883, when compelled by his last illness to resign.

Though devoted at all times to the work of his professorship, Professor Smith found time to mingle in matters of practical engineering. For five years he was consulting engineer of the Iron Mountain Railway, among other things designing the DeSoto shops, and building a new pier in the Black river. In a similar way he was associated with Messrs, Shickle, Harrison & Co., designing the arched ribs of the roof over the Chamber of Commerce, and the iron trestles of the Bessemer Iron Works. Professor Smith was engaged as consulting engineer for the construction of the water works of Hannibal, of St. Charles, in Missouri, and of Amesbury, Massachusetts. His last professional duties were in connection with the last named. The pumping works at Richmond, Va., were designed by him, his plans being entered in competition and receiving the first prize. In 1879 he spent his summer vacation as resident engineer of the Baltimore Bridge Company, building piers in the Mississippi river just below Minneapolis.

Without attempting to give a full list of the professional enterprizes of Professor Smith, I have said enough to show how tireless a worker he was, and how closely he studied the practical details of engineering. But it was in connection with the St. Louis Engineers' Club that his devotion and enthusiasm were most fully shown. He was an active member for twelve years, and the secretary for nine or ten years. The club has not always been as flourishing as it is now. It has had its seasons of depression when only the zeal and the courage of Secretary Smith seemed to hold it together. Nothing but the direst necessity compelled him to yield at last.

The fatal malady, which in the shape of a cancerous tumor, brought his life to an untimely close on the 2nd of February, 1884, was born, as he thought, of hard work, of exposure, and of physical neglect. He could scarcely stop to eat or sleep; it was work first and comfort last.

Nothing in Professor Smith's life was more heroic than the way he battled for two years against an impending fate. When too weak to stand before his class. he taught reclining upon a lounge. One of his last pupils speaks in a notice of his beloved professor of "the days of suffering spent in his study in the University, when we gathered round him as he lay on the lounge, unable to stand, and listened to his exposition of 'Economic Location,' taking as a basis the work of his friend, Arthur Wellington."

In January, 1883, he was forced to give up his class work altogether, and to keep his room. Still he was not idle. Lying on the bed, or reclining in an easy chair, he was hard at work upon his two books on "Steam Making" and "Steam Using," which are just now being issued by the *American Engineer*, in Chicago. The first was finished by the end of 1882, and arrangements were made for its publication, but the prospect for the second book was gloomy enough. Nevertheless, he worked at it with a terrible earnestness which no unfavorable symptom could diminish. Nay, though clinging to the faintest glimmer of hope of returning health, he toiled at his book with the resolute air of one who was fully conscious that his days were numbered, and that the book must speedily be finished. In spite of pain and the dark shadow of the inevitable, his mind seemed clear and his hand steady. In the spring of '83 he moved back to Newburyport, Mass., to be near his physician and his family friends. There in a quaint old house, in a quiet neighborhood of that quiet town, he finished his book, laying down his pen and the burden of life at the same time. The readers of "Steam Using" may be glad to know that the author's very life's blood went into that book; that it was the last, the most perfect fruit of a very active and noble life.

Professor Smith is a good example of a poor boy who made his own way; who fought his own battles; who earned and honored every position he took. He was always a student. Some of you will remember with what enthusiasm he studied quarternions and thermodynamics; with what zeal and success he read all that he could get on graphical statics, and how many important additions he suggested. The records of the St. Louis Club probably will show that Professor Smith has presented more papers than any other member, past or present.

As an engineer, Professor Smith was bold and trustworthy. His confidence was based upon sound theory and careful practice. He was skillful in preparing estimates and was always well informed both as regards the latest improvements in engineering, and the best methods of working the materials of construction.

These accomplishments added greatly to his value as an instructor of young engineers. His students were brought very close to engineering work. Though well read in theory, he loved to dwell on the details of practice. He never lost an opportunity to learn a new process, or to study a new machine. He used to tell how, while resident engineer on a road in

New England, he tried his hand on the engine of the construction train till he was able to "stoke" and to "drive."

Professor Smith left a wife and three children. During her husband's long and discouraging sickness, Mrs. Smith was better than a faithful nurse: she brought aid to his self-imposed labor, and hope and cheer to his fainting spirit. So well did she understand the nature of his work and his needs, and so helpful was the assistance she brought, that it is not too much to say that without her positive coöperation and encouragement the two books which he leaves behind would never have been finished.

I will not speak of personal losses. I prefer to feel that we all had much to be thankful for in Professor Smith, and the nearest had the most. Though dying in his thirty-eighth year, Professor Smith's memory may well be preserved. The world is certainly the better for his having lived in it.

C. M. WOODWARD,
Dean Polytechnic School,
Washington University, St. Louis, Mo.

St. Louis, December, 7, 1884.

CONTENTS.

CHAPTER I.

ON THE NATURE OF HEAT AND THE PROPERTIES OF STEAM:—

PAGE.

Heat—Thermodynamics—Ratios of Volume to Pressure: Regnault's Ratios—
The Carnot Engine—Making steam—Measurement of Heat Expended
—Table: The Properties of Saturated Steam—Examples in Calculation
of Heat Expended, Etc.—Table: Factors of Evaporation—Its Use—
Table: Expansion and Density of Pure Water—Entrained Water and
its Measurement.. 1— 14

CHAPTER II.

ON VALVE GEAR:—

Action of the Valve—Position of Valve with Regard to its Eccentric, Lap
and Lead—Valve Diagrams and their Application—Adjustable Eccen-
trics—The Link and Problems Connected Therewith—Gooch's Link-
Motion—Allan's Link-Motion—The Walschaert Link-Motion—Mar-
shall's Valve Gear—Brown's Valve Gear—Kirk's Valve Gear—Joy's
Valve Gear—Porter-Allen Link Motion—Herr Kaiser's Gear—The
Meyer Valve—Cut-off and Problems Connected Therewith—Ordinary
Slide Valves—Piston Valves—Poppet Valves—Double Valve—Trick's
Valve, Etc.. 15— 56

CHAPTER III.

THE QUANTITY OF STEAM WHICH MIGHT BE, AND WHICH IS USED:—

Horse-Power, Indicated Horse-Power, Effective Horse-Power, Net Horse-
Power—Examples—Curve of Expansion and its Properties—Data furnished by Experiment—Tables of Engine Trials—Analyses of Results
of Practical Tests—Internal Radiation—Analysis of Experiments Showing Effect of Internal Radiation, etc.—Tables..... .... 57— 86

CHAPTER IV.

ON THE INDICATOR, THE INDICATOR DIAGRAM AND THE DIFFER-
ENT CLASSES OF ENGINES:—

PAGE.

The Construction and Use of the Indicator—Other Devices—The Earlier
Forms of Engines—Single Acting Engines: The Westinghouse, The
Brotherhood, and the Colt Disc Engine—The Indicator Diagram and the
Effects of Internal Radiation, etc., from Actual Experiments—Com-
pounding and Indicator Diagrams in Connection Therewith—Clearance
—Forms of Compound Engines—Progress in Marine Engine Perform-
ances—Consumption of Fuel—The Value of Jacketting and Compound-
ing—Poppet Valve River Engines and Diagrams—High Service Pumping
Engine, St. Louis Water Works—Indicator Diagram from Lawrence,
Mass., Pumping Engine—Diagrams from Engines of Ocean Steamers
"Arizona" and "Aberdeen"—Engines of Mississippi River Steamer "Mon-
tana"—Engines of U. S. Lighthouse Steamer "Manzanita"—Triple Ex-
pansion Engines of S. S. "Aberdeen"—Compound Engines of S. S.
"Grecian"—Three Cylinder Compound Engines of S. S. "Parisian"—
Automatic Expansion and Governors—The Wheelock Engine—The
Porter-Allen Engine—The Rider Automatic Expansion Gear—Various
Forms of Expansion Slides and Valve Gears—The Cummer Engine
Governor—The Armington & Simms Engine—Engine of the Steam
Yacht "Leila"—The Locomotive—The Buckeye Automatic Cut-off En-
gine—The Reynolds' Corliss Engine—The Lambertville, N. J., Auto-
matic Cut-off Engine—The Porter-Allen Engine........................ 87—187

CHAPTER V.

THE EXPERIMENTS OF HIRN AND HALLAUER:—

Report on a Memoir Upon Steam Engines—Experiments with a Steam Engine—Experimental Study Comparing the Influence of Expansion in
Simple and Compound Engines...188—285

CHAPTER VI.

STEAM HEATING:—

The Theory of Steam Heating—Various systems in use in the United States
—Description of Apparatus and Experiments Used by the Author—
Project for Heating a Cotton Mill..................................... 286—298

STEAM USING;

—OR—

STEAM ENGINE PRACTICE.

CHAPTER I.

ON THE NATURE OF HEAT AND THE PROPERTIES OF STEAM.

By the term heat we understand that property of bodies by which they grow hot, and give the sensation with which we are all familiar.

Heat is produced in three ways:

By chemical action,	A.
By mechanical action,	B.
By electrical action,	C.

A.—When certain chemical elements or compounds are combined under certain circumstances, the result is a union accompanied by an increase of temperature and the development of heat; as for example, carbon or hydrogen combining with oxygen; sulphuric acid, or quick lime, with water.

B.—By the mechanical work of friction or percussion: Examples of this are continually before us.

C.—By the passage of an electric current in a conductor,—as in wires of too great resistance; or the electric arc.

The property of heat is thought by some to consist of a kind of motion or vibration of the molecules of which bodies are supposed to consist;—for solid and liquid bodies in vibration, and for gaseous bodies in the real motion of the molecules. With the arguments, pro. or con., concerning this hypothesis we have little to do further than to state that, its truth appears very probable, and in such event the production of heat by chemical combination or the passage of an electric current is simply a kind of mechanical action; in the one case, the vibration resulting from the shock of molecules attracting each other; in the other, from the setting up of a wave movement, or kind of wave, in the path of the electric disturbance, whatever that may be.

That heat was produced by mechanical means has been long known. While the identity of heat and mechanical force was suspected by Count Rumford nearly a hundred years ago, it was reserved for Joule to prove (by long continued experiment), that the same quantity of work always gave the same quantity of heat, and to Rankine and Clausius to show, theoretically, that the same quantity of heat always gives the same amount of work, which has since been proved beyond all doubt by experimental investigations.

By the labors of the two great men, Rankine and Clausius, the science of thermodynamics was created,—the application of mathematics it the laws of heat. Of this interesting and beautiful science we shall, however, only state the two fundamental principles:

First Principle—"Heat and mechanical energy are mutually convertible, "and heat requires for its production and produces by its disappearance "mechanical energy in the proportion of 772 foot-pounds for each British "unit of heat."

The British unit of heat, just mentioned, is: "The quantity of heat "which corresponds to an interval of one degree of Farenheit's scale in the "temperature of one pound of pure liquid water at and near its temperature "of greatest density (39.1°F)."

The second principle, as given by Clausius, is as follows:

Second Principle.—"Heat, of itself, never passes from a cold body to a hotter one."

Rankine states the second principle in a way that has been severely criticised by Maxwell, but which appears to mean that, a unit of heat in a cold body can do as much work as in a hot body, with the implied reservation that there must be yet a colder body into which it may pass.

Heat is converted into mechanical work through the agency of some body that is expanded by heat, such as air or water. The heat is transferred into these mediums, usually enclosed within limits of changeable volume, the expanding medium enlarging the volume against a resistance thereby does mechanical work.

It has been taken for granted that the word temperature was understood to have its ordinary meaning, and that neither the ordinary thermometric scales of temperature, nor the ordinary instruments used for measuring temperature required description; but when great accuracy was required, the use of the air thermometer drew attention to a very convenient scale. Dry air and some of the other gases increase in volume or pressure from the temperature of melting ice to that of boiling water under the atmospheric pressure as follows:

From the volume or pressure 1 to:

	Constant Volume.	Constant Pressure.
Air	1.3665	1.3670
Hydrogen	1.3667	1.3661
Nitrogen	1.3668	......
Carbonic Acid	1.3688	1.3669
Carbonic Oxide	1.3667	1.3719
Nitrous Oxide	1.3676	1.3719
Cyanogen	1.3829	1.3877
Sulphurous Acid	1.3843	1.3903

NOTE.—The above ratios are from Regnault.

With the air thermometer the change in volume of a portion of dry air was used to measure the change in temperature, and the natural result was that the temperature at which the dry gas would have no volume, if the law should hold so far, was taken as the zero or starting point of such a scale. This zero is —461° F. or —273° C., and is called "absolute zero," and temperatures measured on this scale are called "absolute temperatures." We shall give later another and better reason for this scale and its name, for we know now that all the gases above given can be reduced to liquids and solids and therefore are not perfect gases.

A perfect or "reversible" engine was devised by Sadi Carnot; and although such an engine cannot be constructed, and if constructed, could not be worked; still it is extremely useful in assisting our conceptions and in giving us a limit beyond which we cannot hope to proceed with improvements.

The operation of the Carnot engine is as follows: From a hot body, at temperature T_1, a working body receives heat at the same temperature T_1, expanding and doing work from the heat in the hot body directly. After a time the hot body is withdrawn, leaving the working body at the same temperature T_1, and it then expands by virtue of the heat which it contains until its temperature has fallen to T_2. In expanding, more work has been effected, which, of course, goes to the credit of the engine as work done. At the temperature T_2, the working body is brought into contact with a body called the "cold body," at the same temperature T_2; work is then done on the working body from the outside in compressing it to such a point, heat meanwhile passing from the working body to the cold body at the same temperature. So that by continuing the process of compression after the removal of the cold body, the working body will have just reached its first state of volume, pressure and temperature; the work expended in the two compression processes is, of course, to the debit of the engine, but there is on the whole a balance of work done by the engine.

It can be shown in this case, whatever be the working substance used: First.—That this engine utilizes more heat than can be utilized by any other kind of engine working between the same temperatures T_1 and T_2. Second.—That the work done, or heat utilized, is to the heat expended from the hot body, as the difference between the temperatures between which the engine works, $T_1 - T_2$ is to the absolute temperature of the hot body T_1. Hence the fraction

$$\frac{T_1 - T_2}{T_1}$$

where T is an absolute temperature, is known as the efficiency of the engine, and is the maximum efficiency which can be reached by theory.

The proof of the above statements is given in any work on thermodynamics, so that we shall not enter upon it here, believing it out of place in a work of a practical character.

From the properties of the Carnot engine, a scale of temperature, based upon the work done by a body when $T_1 - T_2 = 1°$, is established; and it has been shown that the scale thus established coincides in origin and amount with that of the perfect gas thermometer, which places it upon a more substantial basis.

When heat is put into any body it may either increase the agitation of its molecules, thereby heating it or raising its temperature; or it may expand it against an external resistance doing external work; or it may change its condition, overcoming molecular attractions, doing what is called internal work; or it may do two or three of these three things at the same time.

When a fire is lighted under a boiler containing cold water, the heat generated by the chemical action of combustion passes from the fire and the gaseous products of combustion to the iron of the boiler, through the iron of the boiler to the surface in contact with the water and thence into the water. The volume of the water slightly increases with the temperature, raising the level partly by its own increase in volume and partly by the increase in volume of the air contained in the water. The heat increases the molecular agitation of the water, till, usually at the temperature of 212° F., the boiler begins to make steam. If, as in many of the boiler trials, the man-head or safety valve is open; or, as in a common tea kettle, there is no other pressure than that of the air upon the water, at this temperature the water remains; and all the heat going into it is expended in overcoming the molecular attraction of one atom of water for another, and in forcing the molecules apart. In thus overcoming the molecular attraction it is doing internal work, and at the same time in lifting the atmosphere by the steam formed, it is performing external work.

When the quantities of heat which a pound of water requires to raise it from the temperature of melting ice into steam at any given pressure are measured, that which it takes to raise the temperature is not exactly the difference in the temperatures which would be required if the specific heat of water were constant, but a unit of heat raises the temperature of a pound of water a little less than one degree at the higher temperatures. When a boiler is making steam at a given pressure other than that of the atmosphere, there is a temperature at which steam forms from the water and above which the water cannot be raised. This is known as the temperature of evaporation for the pressure. It is to be noted that the pressure of the atmosphere may be partly removed and low pressure steam formed at less than atmospheric pressure.

The quantity of heat required to evaporate a unit of weight of water at different pressures, and to raise the temperature up to that of evaporation, was carefully determined by Regnault in an extensive series of experiments made at the expense of the French Government. The volume of one pound weight of steam, and, of course, its reciprocal, the density or weight of a cubic foot of steam, was determined by experiments made by Fairbairn and Tate.

From the heat of evaporation, the volume of steam, the pressure under which it was evaporated, and the volume of the water from which it was formed are computed:

First.—The external work in foot-pounds, or the product of the pressure in pounds per square foot by the difference in cubic feet of the volume of one pound of steam and one pound of water.

Second.—The external work in heat units obtained by dividing the external work in foot-pounds by 772.

Third.—The internal work of evaporation obtained by deducting from the heat of evaporation the external work found above.

Fourth.—The sum of the internal work of evaporation and the heat expended in raising the temperature,—sometimes called the total internal heat.

Fifth.—The sum of the heat expended in raising the temperature of the water, and the heat of evaporation; or, the sum of the total internal heat and the external work in heat units; or, the sum of the heat expended in raising the temperature, in internal work of evaporation and in external work, is called the total heat. These quantities may all be stated in foot-pounds, and some writers prefer to use them in this way. But, although the measurement of mechanical work is usually made in foot-pounds, all measurements of heat and steam which require measurements of temperature are best made with a thermometer, and by heat units; we shall, therefore, retain the heat units. There is also this advantage, that in computation there will be smaller numbers and less figures involved.

The measurement of the heat expended in raising the temperature of water, in the total internal heat and the total heat, are all based on a starting point of one pound of water at the temperature of melting ice. As, however, such quantities are usually used by differences, many writers give these data from 0° F. Of course this does not require any real existence to the imaginary pound of water, as water assumed in this way. It gives a little less numerical work with feed water at low temperature, but is of no help when the specific heat has varied so as to alter the heat expended in raising the temperature of the water from the difference between the temperature and 32°. We adhere to the basis of melting ice.

Most of the theoretical writers use as a base for the tables the temperature of evaporation, although others use the pressure,—a much more practical starting point for engineers. But these writers have not given the internal and external heats, have used in some cases the 0° F. starting point referred to above, and have given extended decimals. In our own table we have only given the nearest heat unit, and have given a table, not for every pound of pressure, it is true, but one in which it is very easy to interpolate the nearest unit. We believe this table to be convenient for use and sufficiently extended and accurate.

The heat of evaporation is called latent heat of evaporation, but as the term latent has now no meaning we shall not retain it.

As the Regnault experiments on steam are always considered models in every respect, and as being of unapproachable accuracy, we shall only say that they were made in all circumstances and conditions in a thoroughly practical way, and that the values reached have been computed from purely theoretical grounds; so also with densities. The table is to be relied upon, and we shall not explain the experiments or comment further upon them, but will illustrate by a few examples the use of the table here given:

TABLE I.—THE PROPERTIES OF SATURATED STEAM.

Pressure in lbs. per sq. inch above the atmosphere.	Temperature of steam in degrees Fahrenheit.	Heat above 32° F. in water at boiling point.	External work in heat units.	T'l heat above 32° Fahr. in steam.	Internal work of evaporat'n in heat units.	Latent heat of evaporat'n in heat units.	Total internal work above 32° in heat units.	Weight of 1 cu. ft. of steam in pounds.	Volume of 1 lb. in cubic feet.
—14	90			1109					
—13	121	99	62	1118	967	1029		0.006	172.0
—12	138	106	65	1124	943	1018		0.008	117.5
—11	150	118	67	1127	942	1009		0.011	89.6
—10	160	128	67	1130	935	1002		.014	72.6
— 9	168	136	67	1133	925	993		.016	61.2
— 8	175	143	68	1134	923	991		.019	52.9
— 7	181	150	68	1137	918	987		.021	46.7
— 6	187	156	69	1138	913	982		.024	41.8
— 5	192	161	69	1140	909	979		.026	37.8
— 4	196	165	70	1141	906	976		.029	34.6
— 3	201	170	70	1143	903	973		.031	31.8
— 2	205	174	71	1144	899	970		.034	29.5
— 1	209	178	71	1145	896	967		.036	27.6
0	212	181	72	1146	893	965	1074	.038	26.3
1	215	184	72	1147	890	962	1074	.041	24.3
2	219	188	72	1148	888	960	1076	.043	23.0
3	222	191	73	1149	887	958	1078	.046	21.8
4	225	194	73	1150	885	956	1079	.048	20.7
5	227	196	73	1151	882	953	1079	.050	19.7
6	230	199	74	1152	879	951	1079	.053	18.8
7	233	202	74	1152	877	950	1079	.055	18.0
8	235	204	74	1153	876	948	1079	.058	17.2
9	237	206	74	1154	873	947	1080	.060	16.6
10	239	208	74	1154	872	945	1080	.062	16.0
11	242	211	75	1155	869	944	1080	.065	15.4
12	244	213	75	1156	867	942	1080	.067	14.9
13	246	215	75	1156	866	941	1081	.070	14.4
14	248	217	75	1157	864	939	1081	.072	13.9
15	250	220	75	1158	863	938	1083	.074	13.4
16	252	222	75	1158	862	937	1083	.076	13.0
17	254	224	76	1159	859	935	1084	.079	12.7
18	256	226	76	1159	858	934	1084	.081	12.3
19	257	227	76	1160	857	933	1084	.083	12.0
20	259	229	76	1160	856	932	1085	.086	11.6
22	262	232	76	1161	853	929	1085	.090	11.0
24	266	236	77	1162	850	927	1086	.095	10.6
26	269	239	77	1163	848	925	1087	.099	10.0
28	272	242	77	1164	846	923	1088	.104	9.6
30	274	244	77	1165	844	921	1088	.109	9.2
35	281	251	78	1167	838	916	1089	.120	8.3
40	287	257	78	1169	834	912	1091	.131	7.6
45	293	263	78	1171	830	908	1093	.142	7.0
50	298	268	79	1172	825	904	1093	.154	6.5
55	303	273	79	1174	822	901	1095	.165	6.1
60	307	278	79	1175	818	897	1096	.176	5.7
65	312	282	80	1176	814	894	1097	.187	5.3
70	316	287	80	1178	811	891	1098	.198	5.0
75	320	291	80	1179	808	888	1099	.209	4.8
80	324	294	80	1180	806	886	1100	.220	4.5
85	328	298	81	1181	802	883	1100	.231	4.3
90	331	301	81	1182	800	881	1101	.241	4.1
95	334	305	81	1183	798	878	1101	.252	4.0
100	338	308	81	1184	795	876	1102	.263	3.8

Note for "Total internal work above 32° in heat units" column (rows —13 to —1): All these may be taken as 1070 in practice.

TABLE I.—THE PROPERTIES OF SATURATED STEAM.

Pressure in lbs. per sq. inch above the atmosphere.	Temperature of steam in degrees Fahrenheit.	Heat above 32° F. in water at boiling point.	External work in heat units.	T'l heat above 32° Fahr. in steam.	Internal work of evaporat'n in heat units.	Latent heat of evaporat'n in heat units.	Total internal work above 32° in heat units.	Weight of 1 cu. ft. of steam in pounds.	Volume of 1 lb. in cubic feet.
105	341	311	82	1185	792	874	1103	.274	3.6
110	344	315	82	1186	789	871	1104	.284	3.5
115	347	318	82	1187	787	869	1105	.295	3.4
120	350	321	82	1188	785	867	1106	.306	3.3
125	353	324	82	1189	783	865	1107	.316	3.2
130	355	327	82	1190	781	863	1108	.327	3.1
135	358	329	82	1191	779	861	1108	.338	3.0
140	361	331	83	1191	777	860	1109	.348	2.9
145	363	334	83	1192	775	858	1109	.359	2.8
150	366	337	83	1193	773	856	1110	.369	2.7
155	368	340	83	1194	771	854	1111	.380	2.6
160	371	341	83	1194	770	853	1111	.390	2.6
165	373	344	83	1195	768	851	1112	.400	2.5
170	375	347	84	1196	765	849	1112	.412	2.4
175	377	348	84	1196	764	848	1113	.422	2.4
180	380	351	84	1197	762	846	1113	.433	2.3
185	382	353	84	1198	761	845	1114	.443	2.3
195	386	357	84	1199	758	842	1115	.463	2.2
205	390	361	85	1200	754	839	1115	.484	2.1
215	394	365	85	1201	751	836	1116	.505	2.0
225	397	368	85	1202	749	834	1117	.525	1.9
235	401	373	85	1204	746	831	1119	.546	1.8
245	404	376	85	1205	744	829	1120	.567	1.8
255	408	380	85	1206	741	826	1121	.587	1.7
265	411	383	85	1207	739	824	1122	.608	1.6
275	414	386	85	1208	737	822	1123	.627	1.6
285	417	389	86	1209	734	820	1123	.649	1.5
335	430	392	86	1213	725	811	1127	.750	1.3
385	445	417	86	1217	714	800	1131	.850	1.2
* * *	* * *	* * *	* * *	* * *	* * *	* * *	* * *		
435	457	428	87	1220	705	792	1133	.950	1.05
485	467	440	87	1224	697	784	1137	1.049	0.95
585	487	460	87	1230	683	770	1143	1.245	0.80
685	504	477	88	1235	670	758	1147	1.439	0.69
785	519	493	88	1240	659	747	1152	1.632	0.61
885	534	507	88	1244	649	737	1156	1.823	0.55
985	516	520	88	1248	640	728	1160	2.014	0.50

Values below * * * are computed and not experimental.

NOTE.—For all values of Total Internal work below the atmosphere 1070 heat units may be taken. All decimal parts of heat units have been neglected and the last one may therefore be in error.

Example I.—How much more heat is needed to boil a pound of water at 200 pounds per square inch boiler pressure than at five pounds per square inch, the feed being at 60° F. in either case.

AT FIVE POUNDS.

Units.

Heat required to raise 1 pound water from 32° to boiling at 5 pounds pressure....... 196
Deduct heat to raise from 32° to 60° not used... 28

Heat to raise from 60° to boiling.. 168
Internal work of evaporation 882
External work of evaporation.... 73

Heat required to boil from feed at 60° at 5 pounds.. 1,123

AT TWO HUNDRED POUNDS.

	Units.
Heat required to raise 1 pound water from 32° to boiling at 200 pounds per sq. inch..	359
Deduct heat to raise from 32° to 60° not used	28
	331
Internal work	756
External work	84
	1,171

Heat required to boil 1 pound of water from feed at 60° at 200 pounds:

$$1,171 - 1,123 = 48 \text{ units.}$$

$$\frac{48}{1,123} = 4 \text{ per cent., nearly.}$$

The same result could be reached more directly.

	Units.
Total heat from 32° at 200 pounds	1,199
Total heat from 32° at 5 pounds	1,161
Difference	48

Deducting from the 1,151 the 28 units not used, from 32° to 60°, the feed being at 60°, we have 1,123 for the divisor to reduce to per cent. as before.

We advise the reader to use the former method, by preference, in his computations, as serving to keep in full view the different uses and the various amounts of heat required for them; although there is, of course, more numerical work required to do so.

The reason so much more difficulty is experienced in maintaining high pressure than low pressure steam is to be found, not in the boiling of equal weights of water, but in the fact that the high pressure steam leaves the boiler more easily. If, for example, it be employed in an engine, the engine can be made to do more work thereby. If, in running a boat, the boat going faster the engine uses more steam; if employed in heating a building, the radiators act more energetically with the higher pressure, transmit more heat, condense more steam, and the skillful attendant suits his fire to the work.

Example II.—How much saving of fuel can be made by raising the temperature of the feed-water from 100° F. to 200° F., the boiler pressure being 120 pounds per square inch.

	Units.
Total heat for 120 pounds	1,188
Deduct in the one case the units not used in raising the water from 32° F. to 100° F..	68
Required from 100° F. to boil at 120 pounds	1,120
In the other case deduct for not using from 32° to 200°	169
Required to boil at 120 pounds from water at 200° F	1,019

Difference between 1,120 and 1,019 is 101 units, or about 9 per cent.

In order to compare the performance of different boilers working with different pressures and fed with water at different temperatures, it is necessary to assume a standard pressure, temperature of evaporation, and temperature of feed-water. Various temperatures of feed-water have been used, 0° F., 32° F., 100° F., the latter about the usual temperature of feed-water for condensing engines, and 212° F., used more generally than any of the others as a standard; while for the pressure and temperature of evaporation the atmospheric pressure and 212° F. are usually taken.

Example III.—By experiment with a boiler at 160 pounds per square inch it was found that, one pound of coal evaporated 7.91 pounds of water. The temperature of the feed-water was noted at 120° F.: required the equivalent evaporation from and at 212° F.

	Units.
Total heat of evaporation from 32° F. at 160 pounds............................	1,194
Deduct from 32° to 120°, units not used..	88
Heat to evaporate from 30° at 160 pounds..	1,106
Internal heat of evaporation at 212°...	893
External work of evaporation at 212°...	72
Sum or heat of evaporation at 212°...	965

$$7.91 \times \frac{1,106}{965} = 9.06 \text{ as the evaporation required.}$$

In order to facilitate this computation the following table of factors of evaporation is given:

TABLE II.—FACTORS OF EVAPORATION.

PRESSURE IN POUNDS PER SQUARE INCH ABOVE THE ATMOSPHERE.

Temp. of Feed-water (°F)	0	5	10	15	20	25	30	35	40	45	50	60	70	80	90	100	120	140	160	180	200
32	1.187	1.192	1.195	1.199	1.201	1.204	1.206	1.209	1.211	1.212	1.214	1.217	1.219	1.222	1.224	1.227	1.231	1.234	1.237	1.239	1.241
35	1.184	1.189	1.192	1.196	1.198	1.201	1.203	1.206	1.208	1.209	1.211	1.214	1.216	1.219	1.221	1.224	1.228	1.231	1.234	1.236	1.238
40	1.179	1.184	1.187	1.191	1.193	1.196	1.198	1.201	1.203	1.204	1.206	1.209	1.211	1.214	1.216	1.219	1.223	1.226	1.229	1.231	1.233
45	1.173	1.178	1.181	1.185	1.187	1.190	1.192	1.195	1.197	1.198	1.200	1.203	1.205	1.208	1.210	1.213	1.217	1.220	1.223	1.225	1.227
50	1.168	1.173	1.177	1.180	1.182	1.185	1.187	1.190	1.192	1.193	1.195	1.198	1.200	1.203	1.205	1.208	1.212	1.215	1.218	1.220	1.222
55	1.163	1.168	1.171	1.175	1.177	1.180	1.182	1.185	1.187	1.188	1.190	1.193	1.195	1.198	1.200	1.203	1.207	1.210	1.213	1.215	1.217
60	1.158	1.163	1.166	1.170	1.172	1.175	1.177	1.180	1.182	1.183	1.185	1.188	1.190	1.193	1.195	1.198	1.202	1.205	1.208	1.210	1.212
65	1.153	1.158	1.161	1.165	1.167	1.170	1.172	1.175	1.177	1.178	1.180	1.183	1.185	1.188	1.190	1.193	1.197	1.200	1.203	1.205	1.207
70	1.148	1.153	1.156	1.160	1.162	1.165	1.167	1.170	1.172	1.173	1.175	1.178	1.180	1.183	1.185	1.188	1.192	1.195	1.198	1.200	1.202
75	1.143	1.148	1.151	1.155	1.157	1.160	1.162	1.165	1.167	1.168	1.170	1.173	1.175	1.178	1.180	1.183	1.187	1.190	1.193	1.195	1.197
80	1.137	1.143	1.146	1.149	1.151	1.154	1.156	1.159	1.161	1.162	1.164	1.167	1.169	1.172	1.174	1.177	1.181	1.184	1.187	1.189	1.191
85	1.132	1.137	1.140	1.144	1.146	1.149	1.151	1.154	1.156	1.157	1.159	1.162	1.164	1.167	1.169	1.172	1.176	1.179	1.182	1.184	1.186
90	1.127	1.132	1.135	1.139	1.141	1.144	1.146	1.149	1.151	1.152	1.154	1.157	1.159	1.162	1.164	1.167	1.171	1.174	1.177	1.179	1.181
95	1.122	1.127	1.130	1.134	1.136	1.139	1.141	1.144	1.146	1.147	1.149	1.152	1.154	1.157	1.159	1.162	1.166	1.169	1.172	1.174	1.176
100	1.117	1.122	1.125	1.129	1.131	1.134	1.136	1.139	1.141	1.142	1.144	1.147	1.149	1.152	1.154	1.157	1.161	1.164	1.167	1.169	1.171
105	1.111	1.117	1.119	1.123	1.125	1.128	1.130	1.133	1.135	1.136	1.138	1.141	1.143	1.146	1.148	1.151	1.155	1.158	1.161	1.163	1.165
110	1.106	1.111	1.114	1.118	1.120	1.123	1.125	1.128	1.130	1.131	1.133	1.136	1.138	1.141	1.143	1.146	1.150	1.153	1.156	1.158	1.160
115	1.101	1.106	1.109	1.113	1.115	1.118	1.120	1.123	1.125	1.126	1.128	1.131	1.133	1.136	1.138	1.141	1.145	1.148	1.151	1.153	1.155
120	1.096	1.101	1.104	1.108	1.110	1.113	1.115	1.118	1.120	1.121	1.123	1.126	1.128	1.131	1.133	1.136	1.140	1.143	1.146	1.148	1.150
125	1.091	1.096	1.099	1.103	1.105	1.108	1.110	1.113	1.115	1.116	1.118	1.121	1.123	1.126	1.128	1.131	1.135	1.138	1.141	1.143	1.145
130	1.085	1.091	1.094	1.097	1.099	1.102	1.104	1.107	1.109	1.110	1.112	1.115	1.117	1.120	1.122	1.125	1.129	1.132	1.135	1.137	1.139
135	1.080	1.085	1.088	1.092	1.094	1.097	1.099	1.102	1.104	1.105	1.107	1.110	1.112	1.115	1.117	1.120	1.124	1.127	1.130	1.132	1.134
140	1.075	1.080	1.083	1.087	1.089	1.092	1.094	1.097	1.099	1.100	1.102	1.105	1.107	1.110	1.112	1.115	1.119	1.122	1.125	1.127	1.129
145	1.070	1.075	1.078	1.082	1.084	1.087	1.089	1.092	1.094	1.095	1.097	1.100	1.102	1.105	1.107	1.110	1.114	1.117	1.120	1.122	1.124
150	1.065	1.070	1.073	1.077	1.079	1.082	1.084	1.087	1.089	1.090	1.092	1.095	1.097	1.100	1.102	1.105	1.109	1.112	1.115	1.117	1.119
155	1.059	1.065	1.068	1.071	1.073	1.076	1.078	1.081	1.083	1.084	1.086	1.089	1.091	1.094	1.096	1.099	1.103	1.106	1.109	1.111	1.113
160	1.054	1.059	1.062	1.066	1.068	1.071	1.073	1.076	1.078	1.079	1.081	1.084	1.086	1.089	1.091	1.094	1.098	1.101	1.104	1.106	1.108
165	1.049	1.054	1.057	1.061	1.063	1.066	1.068	1.071	1.073	1.074	1.076	1.079	1.081	1.084	1.086	1.089	1.093	1.096	1.099	1.101	1.103
170	1.044	1.049	1.052	1.056	1.058	1.061	1.063	1.066	1.068	1.069	1.071	1.074	1.076	1.079	1.081	1.084	1.088	1.091	1.094	1.096	1.098
175	1.039	1.044	1.047	1.051	1.053	1.056	1.058	1.061	1.063	1.064	1.066	1.069	1.071	1.074	1.076	1.079	1.083	1.086	1.089	1.091	1.093
180	1.033	1.039	1.042	1.045	1.047	1.050	1.052	1.055	1.057	1.058	1.060	1.063	1.065	1.068	1.070	1.073	1.077	1.080	1.083	1.085	1.087
185	1.028	1.033	1.036	1.040	1.042	1.045	1.047	1.050	1.052	1.053	1.055	1.058	1.060	1.063	1.065	1.068	1.072	1.075	1.078	1.080	1.082
190	1.023	1.028	1.031	1.035	1.037	1.040	1.042	1.045	1.047	1.048	1.050	1.053	1.055	1.058	1.060	1.063	1.067	1.070	1.073	1.075	1.077
195	1.018	1.023	1.025	1.030	1.032	1.035	1.037	1.040	1.042	1.043	1.045	1.048	1.050	1.053	1.055	1.058	1.062	1.065	1.068	1.070	1.072
200	1.013	1.018	1.021	1.025	1.027	1.030	1.032	1.035	1.037	1.038	1.040	1.043	1.045	1.048	1.050	1.053	1.057	1.060	1.063	1.065	1.067
205	1.008	1.013	1.015	1.020	1.022	1.025	1.027	1.030	1.032	1.033	1.035	1.038	1.040	1.043	1.045	1.048	1.052	1.055	1.058	1.060	1.062
210	1.008	1.008	1.011	1.015	1.017	1.020	1.022	1.025	1.027	1.028	1.030	1.033	1.035	1.038	1.040	1.043	1.047	1.050	1.053	1.055	1.057
212	1.002	1.002	1.005	1.009	1.011	1.014	1.016	1.019	1.021	1.022	1.028	1.033	1.035	1.038	1.040	1.043	1.047	1.050	1.053	1.055	1.057

Temperature of Feed-water in Degrees Fahr.

The use of this Table of Factors of Evaporation is readily seen by taking the last example. The boiler evaporating 7.91 pounds at 160 pounds per square inch from feed at 120° F., the evaporation factor from Table II. for 120° and 160 pounds is 1.146. 7.91 × 1.146 = 9.06, as before, for the equivalent evaporation from and at 212° F.

We introduce one other table here—the weight of 1 cubic foot of water at different temperatures. Very often in the trials of a boiler or engine the most convenient unit of measurement of water is the cubic foot. This will be the case when a weir measurement is made or when the water is measured by a water meter. The use of a water meter involves many precautions, the most important being the following: The meter should work under moderate head of supply and small head of delivery; it should be set in such a manner that it can be tested in place under the exact conditions of use; if a positive meter, it should be especially constructed to work freely, if it is to be used in warm water. This table is also used for estimating the weight of water in boilers, and for correcting boiler trials for differences of water level.

TABLE III.—EXPANSION AND DENSITY OF PURE WATER.

FROM D. K. CLARK AND BY RANKINE. APPROXIMATE FORMULA.

Temperature in degrees Fahrenheit.	COMPARATIVE.		Density of Weight per Cubic Foot.
	Volume.	Density.	
32	1.00000	1.00000	62.418
35	1.99993	.00007	62.422
39.1	1.99989	.00011	62.425
40	1.99983	.00011	62.425
45	1.99993	.00007	62.422
46	1.00000	1.00000	62.418
50	1.00015	.99985	62.409
52.3	1.00029	.99971	62.400
55	1.00038	.99961	62.394
60	1.00074	.99926	62.372
62	1.00101	.99899	62.355
65	1.00119	.99881	62.344
70	1.00160	.99832	62.313
75	1.00239	.99771	62.275
80	1.00299	.99702	62.232
85	1.00379	.99622	62.182
90	1.00459	.99543	62.133
95	1.00554	.99449	62.074
100	1.00639	.99365	62.022
105	1.00739	.99260	61.960
110	1.00889	.99199	61.868
115	1.00989	.99021	61.807
120	1.01139	.98874	61.715
125	1.01239	.98808	61.654
130	1.01390	.98630	61.563
135	1.01539	.98484	61.472
140	1.01690	.98339	61.381
145	1.01839	.98194	61.291
150	1.01989	.98050	61.201
155	1.02164	.97802	61.096
160	1.02340	.97714	60.991
165	1.02580	.97477	60.812
170	1.02690	.97380	60.783

TABLE III.—Continued.

Temperature in degrees Fahrenheit.	COMPARATIVE.		Density of Weight per Cubic Foot.
	Volume.	Density.	
175	1.02906	.97193	60.655
180	1.03100	.97006	60.548
185	1.03300	.96828	60.430
190	1.03500	.96632	60.314
195	1.03700	.96440	60.198
200	1.03889	.96256	60.081
205	1.0414	.9602	59.93
210	1.0434	.9584	59.82
212 by formula.	1.0444	.9575	59.76
212 by measurement.	1.0466	.9555	59.64
230	1.0529	.9499	59.36
250	1.0628	.9411	58.78
270	1.0727	.9323	58.15
290	1.0838	.9227	57.59
298	1.0899	.9175	57.27
338	1.1118	.8994	56.14
366	1.1301	.8850	55.29
390	1.1444	.8738	54.54

The use of the table of the properties of steam is more frequent in the study of engine performance and indicator diagrams than of boiler performance, but there is an important point in determining the evaporation of a boiler in which it becomes of use.

As bubbles of steam formed on the hot iron of a boiler rise through the water to the surface, breaking and scattering spray, a portion of water thus thrown up into the steam room is carried along with the steam, and unless more heat be supplied to evaporate this water it increases the volume caused by the steam condensed in the pipes in the upper portion of the boiler. This water carried with the steam is said to be "entrained" with it and is called "priming" by many writers. When the proportion of water becomes so large as to be evident in the action of the engine or the exhaust, it is usually called by engineers "foaming." The amount of such water is increased if the water is dirty and covered with scum, or if grease and alkali combine to form a soap. The amount of water which can be carried by steam in suspension is very great, but depends somewhat upon the velocity of the current of steam; if the passages are large, and the flow of steam of moderate velocity the water has time to drop out of the steam by the action of gravity. In some cases the amount of water carried in weight has been known to be three times that of the steam carrying it, although usually it does not exceed 10 to 15 per cent.

The higher the pressure of steam the greater its density and the quieter, other things being equal, is the process of ebullition and the smaller the quantity of entrained water. The amount of water thrown up in spray is largely dependent on the circulation, being much diminished by improvements in that direction. The area of surface water in contact with the steam seems to be an important matter according to some authorities, but as this varies very greatly without any apparent effect, we are not inclined to attribute much importance to it. A violent rush of steam close to the top of a body of water is to be avoided, as even a current of air would throw spray in such a case.

The accurate determination of the water entrained with steam is a matter of great difficulty and at the same time of great importance in the determination of the performance of boilers and engines.

Four methods have been devised to measure the amount of water entrained, and two of them have been used in practice.

The first method, that of M. G. A. Hirn, is the most used. It depends upon the amount of heat given out by a known weight of a mixture of steam and water and is best performed as follows:

A barrel is set on a platform scale and a known weight of water run into it. It is convenient to put in 298 lbs. of water. Steam is taken from the top of the steam pipe by a rubber hose terminated by an iron pipe capped on the lower end and perforated with holes drilled obliquely to the radii, but in the plane thereof. This pipe is placed in the barrel of water and steam turned on; the scale is loaded 2 lbs. more, and as the steam comes into the water the fluid increases in weight, and when the beam tips there is 300 lbs. of water. The temperature of the water is then carefully noted. The disposition of the jets keeps the water stirred up thoroughly, and the flow of steam into the water being horizontal only, the water remains steady. The weight is then increased 10 lbs., and when the the scale tips at 310 pounds the temperature is noted.

The number of heat units given to the water, in the barrel, by the steam and water from the boiler, is found by multiplying the 300 lbs. of water by the rise in its temperature.

The portion which was dry steam gives up its internal heat of evaporation in condensing, and the external work done by the air upon the fluid in compressing it from steam to water, together make the latent heat of evaporation; and the whole fluid then falls in temperature from that due to the pressure in the boiler to the final temperature of the barrel.

Deducting from the heat gained by the water in the barrel, ten times the difference between the boiler temperature and the final temperature in the barrel, and dividing the remainder by ten times the latent heat at the boiler pressure, the quotient will be the fraction of the whole which is dry steam.

It is easily seen that with any other weight the process would be the same; but in place of the ten we should use the number of pounds run in between the noting of the temperatures.

The preliminary 2 lbs. is to provide for any water which might have collected in the hose or connections while standing, and to render the operation uniform.

Sometimes a coil of pipe as a surface condenser is used, and the steam which is condensed therein is kept separate from the condensing water; but great care has to be used to get all the water condensed out of the coil. The accuracy of this method is dependent upon the delicacy of weighing and the reading of the thermometer; in unskillful hands the results are sometimes astonishing.

The second method is to put into the feed water a quantity of sulphate of soda, and to draw from the boiler, at intervals, from the lower gauge cock a small amount of water, keeping this water by itself; also to draw from the steam, condensing either by a coil of pipe in water, or a small pipe in air, taking care to draw only water without steam, at the same intervals, keeping the one separate from the other. A chemical analysis defines the proportion of sulphate of soda in each portion, and a division of the proportion of sulphate of soda in the portion from the steam by the proportion in that from the water gives the proportion of water entrained,—the basis of the method being the fact that steam does not carry the sulphate of soda, this being only carried by the hot water entrained. This method was used by Professor Stahlschmidt at the Dusseldörf Exhibition Boiler Trials.

A third method has been suggested: To enclose a portion of steam in a vessel placed inside the steam pipe, then closing it and removing it from the steam pipe, obtain the weight of the enclosed fluid, which, being in a known volume, the proportion of water can be found from the volume and density at the known pressure. There appear to be many practical difficulties in this method, and we are not aware that it has been used to any extent.

A fourth method is to have a small cylinder with piston enclosed in the steam, and to put a known volume of the cylinder in connection with the steam; then closing the communication, pull out the piston (which, of course, passes through proper stuffing boxes into the air) until the pressure in the cylinder begins to lower,—the water contained evaporating at the pressure, until, after it has been evaporated the pressure begins to fall with increase of volume. The increase of volume at constant pressure divided by the final volume is the proportion of water carried. This method promises well, but we have no knowledge of its use.

Steam formed in the presence of water is always saturated, that is, it is at the same temperature as the water, and cannot be raised above that temperature until the water is all evaporated; but after this has been done, or if the steam be heated in a separate vessel, the temperature rises nearly $2°$ F. for each unit of heat added to a pound in weight, while the steam increases in volume at first not very closely, but afterwards very nearly as a perfect gas, or by $\frac{1}{493}$ part of itself for each degree F. The amount of heat required to raise 1 ℔. weight of dry steam $1°$ F., is stated as 0.47 of a unit, and 0.5 by different authorities, the first including Rankine, and the second Hirn. Steam thus raised in temperature is said to be superheated, but our knowledge of this condition is still very limited and confined to the results of a few experiments.

CHAPTER II.

As steam can only do useful work by changing the volume of the vessel enclosing it, we find that to employ it in moving a piston in a cylinder is the most practical method of using it. There is, however, a certain class of pumping engines, in which steam in direct contact with a fluid, without intervening mechanism, is used for pumping water.

The motion of the piston to and fro in the cylinder is communicated to the outside of the cylinder by a rod passing through a steam-tight opening, where it is then, in some way, connected to the resistance which is to be overcome, either directly as to a pump rod, or indirectly by a connecting rod and crank to a rotating shaft, which is to be revolved against the resistance.

The steam has to be let in and out of one or both ends of the closed cylinder, and for this purpose there are used one, two, three, or four valves, which open and close two or four passage ways, or ports.

These valves are moved by mechanism of more or less complex form by the engine itself, and are either slides, lifting valves, or rotative valves.

The use of the slide valve and eccentric requires little illustration until we examine them more closely.

The piston of the engine is connected to the piston rod, which passes out of the cylinder, and is fastened to the cross-head, and this can only move in a straight line. The connecting rod is attached, at one end, to the cross-head by a pin and suitable box, and at the other end to the crank pin; thus, one end of the connecting rod can only move in a straight line while the other end moves in a circle.

The action of the slide valve by the eccentric is in a similar manner— one end of the eccentric rod moving in, or nearly in, a straight line, while the other end moves in a circle; for, it must not be forgotten that the eccentric may be, and sometimes is, defined as a crank with a small crank arm and large crank pin.

It is well known that the motion of the two ends of the connecting rod is not regular; that is to say, that for equal movements of the piston equal ones are not moved over by the crank, and further, that for equal distances moved by the piston from the end of the stroke, the angles moved over by the crank from the dead points are not alike; and, also, for equal arcs moved by the crank, the cross-head and piston move unequal distances. This is shown in Fig. 2, where the arcs 0-1 is equal to 6-7, 1-2 equal to 5-6, and 2-3 equal to 4-5, but the distances on the straight line between points with the same numbers are evidently not equal.

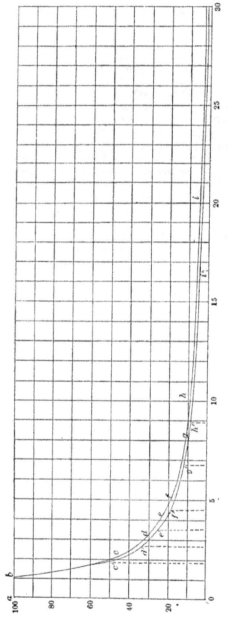

Upper curve shows volume and pressure of saturated steam.
Lower curve shows expansion in a non-conducting cylinder.

FIGURE 1.

An examination of this irregularity shows us that it increases as the lengths of the connecting rod and crank are more nearly equal, and decreases the more unequal they are. Now for any engine, the lengths of the connecting rod and crank are more nearly equal than the eccentric

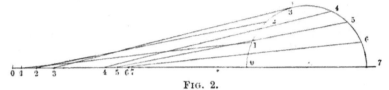

FIG. 2.

rod and eccentric radius for the same engine, and if the latter are 50 inches and 2 inches long, respectively; the greatest error introduced by them is less than 0.005 inch. We should be justified in neglecting this entirely, but we must remember that we can not do so for the irregularity due the connecting rod and crank; and it becomes convenient for us to refer the position of the slide to that of the crank arm instead of referring it to the piston, as is more usually done. While it is more natural to think of the position of the valve with the piston at half stroke, for example, yet when we reflect that this piston at half stroke gives two positions for the valve instead of one, it becomes evident that to define the position of the valve as that due a certain crank angle, 90° in the case taken, or crank position given by drawing or otherwise, is more exact. For we so easily find, by drawing, the place of the piston or cross-head when the crank position is given, or the reverse, that no difficulty will be met with in our study if we confine ourselves to the connection between crank and valve position, in place of the more usual statement, the connection between piston and valve positions. The methods used are, therefore, those of drawing, and little computation is needed.

The position of the valve with regard to its eccentric is readily found as follows: In Fig. 3, $A B$ is the throw of the eccentric, $F C$ the crank, and $C D$ the eccentric radius; D being the centre of the eccentric while C

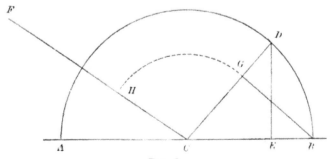

FIG. 3.

is the centre of the shaft. To find the position of the valve, draw $D E$ from E perpendicular to $A B$. Then will $C E$ be the distance the valve has moved from its middle position, and $E B$ and $E A$ the distances of the valve from the end of its travel in either direction. By combining this with $C F$, the position of the crank arm, we see that we have the angle between the crank and eccentric. A convenient method of examining the whole motion at once, is found to be by laying out on $C D$ or $C F$ the distance $C E = C G = C H$, and moving the point G or H as the shaft is turned.

We will take a position of Fig. 3 on a larger scale in Fig. 4, and make the construction for different positions by laying upon the eccentric arm the amount the valve has moved from the centre for that position of the eccentric. In doing this we see at once that if there be drawn from the point A, or end of the travel, a perpendicular upon the eccentric arm, $A F$, the distance $C E = C F$, which is the required distance from the middle position. Make $C F'$ on the crank arm $= C F$ on the eccentric arm. By

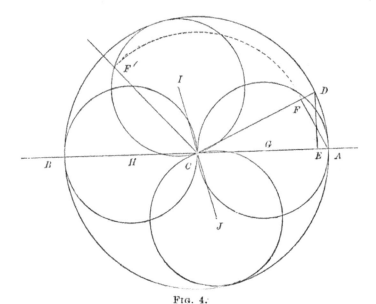

FIG. 4.

drawing these for different positions it will be found that the point F always falls upon one of two circles whose centres are at G and H, one half of $C A$ and $C B$ from C. This may be verified by trial, or by considering that $A F C$ is always a right angle and therefore inscribed in a semi-circle, since $C A$ is common to all.

The point F' will always lie on one of two circles having the same radii as before, but with centres I and J, which lie upon a line $I\,J$ making an angle with $A\,B$ at the point C, where it intersects it, said angle $I\,C\,A = D\,C\,F''$, the angle between crank and eccentric; for when the crank is at $I\,C$, the eccentric is at $C\,A$, and the valve is therefore farthest from the middle. We shall call the circles just found the distance circles, for by drawing any position $C\,F''$ of the crank, we find that the valve is distant $C\,F''$ from its middle position.

We are now in a condition to state and solve our first problem:

Given, the angle between the crank and eccentric arms and the travel of the valve; to find the position of the valve for any position of the crank.

FIG. 5.

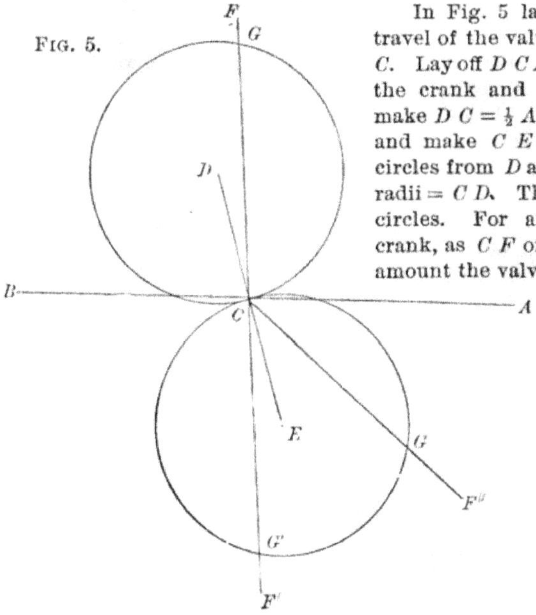

In Fig. 5 lay off $A\,B$, the full travel of the valve, and bisect $A\,B$ in C. Lay off $D\,C\,A$, the angle between the crank and eccentric arms, and make $D\,C = \frac{1}{2}\,A\,C$, also produce $D\,C$ and make $C\,E = D\,C$. Draw two circles from D and E as centres with radii $= C\,D$. These are the distance circles. For any position of the crank, as $C\,F$ or $C\,F''$, or $C\,F'''$, the amount the valve has moved from its middle position is given by the distance from C to G, G', or G''. If the crank arm cut the circle D the valve is to the right of the centre, if it cut the circle E, the valve is to the left of the centre.

If a rock shaft is used between the eccentric rod and valve rod, as usual with American locomotives, the same diagram can be used, but the crank arm must always be considered as if it were on the other side of the shaft from that which it actually is.

Now this construction is not any better than the one given before in Fig. 3, as far as finding any *one* relation, or the position of valve from one given crank position; but it is more comprehensive and we can easily follow the backward and forward movement of the valve as we have the rotating motion of the crank, the valve always moving to and fro on its seat, while its distance from the centre of its movement is seen always to be the amount cut off on the crank arm by the distance circle. Figure 6 shows a longitudinal section of the slide valve as usually constructed. When placed in its middle position it completely covers the cylinder ports

and projects beyond them on both sides. The name given to the external projection is lap, or steam lap, and to the internal projection, exhaust

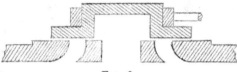

lap. These names are
used to denote the linear
amount of these projec-
tions as well as the pro-
jections themselves.

It is evident from the
diagram that the cylin-
der port at one end can

FIG. 6.

not be opened to the steam until the valve shall have moved away from that
end a distance equal to the steam lap; nor can the same port be opened
to the exhaust until the valve is moved from the centre towards the port
a distance at least equal to the exhaust lap; and if we lay one of these laps
on the crank arm it will describe with them two circles upon the centre
C. Introducing this element into our diagram we are ready to answer our
next problem:

*During what portion of the revolution is the cylinder open to the steam
and to the exhaust, the angle between the crank and eccentric arms, the
travel, and the laps being given?*

Lay off in Fig. 7 the full travel *A B* bisecting in *C*, and draw the line
D C E through *C*, making the angle *D C A* equal to the angle between

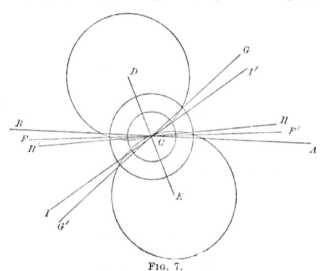

FIG. 7.

the crank and eccentric arms. On *D* and *E*, as centres, draw the two distance circles with *D C* and *E C* as radii. With the given steam and exhaust laps as radii, draw circles, or portions of circles, on *C* as a centre,

cutting the distance circles in eight points. Through these eight points draw radii from *C*. When the valve distance is greater than the lap circle, one side is open to the steam; and when the valve distance is greater than the exhaust lap, one side is open to the exhaust. When the valve distance is less than the steam lap, the steam is closed at one end and the exhaust at the other end is open, or closed, as the valve distance is greater, or less, than the exhaust lap.

From *F* to *G* the steam is open at the left end, and from *F″* to *G′* at the right end. From *H* to *I* the left end exhaust is opened, and from *H′* to *I′* the right end. For an engine without a rock shaft the cylinder is supposed to be at the right of the diagram, and for an engine with a rock shaft the cylinder is supposed to be at the left. The rotation is from *D* to *A* through *G*.

When the valve has moved to the right the right exhaust and left steam ports are open. When the valve moves to the left the left end opens to the exhaust and the right end opens to the steam. The valve moves to the right, if there be no rock shaft, when the crank cuts the circle *D*, and to the left when it cuts the circle *E*. With a rock shaft we may consider the crank arm to be moved 180° on the shaft without other change in the diagram. In this problem there are various points involved. First, the angle between the crank and eccentric arms; second, the travel of the valve; third, the position of the crank when the steam opens; fourth, the steam lap; fifth, the position of the crank when the exhaust opens; sixth, the exhaust lap; and we can, of course, with all these data, solve other important questions, one or two of which we shall introduce and construct.

Given, the travel and position of crank for opening and closing to the steam; to find the angle between the crank and eccentric arms:

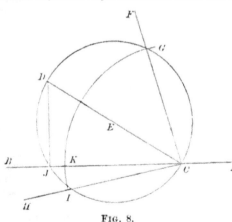

FIG. 8.

In Fig. 8 set off the trave *A B* bisecting at *C*, and through *C* draw the two positions of the crank when the ports are to open and close to the steam, *C H* and *C F* respectively. Bisect the angle *H C F* by the line *C D*. Then will *D C A* be the required angle between the crank and eccentric arms.

Given, the travel of the valve, angle between crank and eccentric and point of closing to steam; to find the lap.

In Fig. 8 set off *A B* equal to the full travel, bisecting in *C*; lay off *A C D* equal to the angle between the crank and eccentric arms; draw the distance circle from E as a centre through C with radius C E equal to ¼ A B, and draw C F, the required position of crank at point of cut off. C G is the steam lap, for where C F cuts the distance circle the valve is closing the steam port. Drawing the arc G I from C as centre, with C G radius, we find the steam opens at C I a little before the crank gets to the dead point. The distance J K is the amount the valve is open at the end of the stroke, and the opening, and amount of opening, are known as steam lead. If this opening be thought too great the eccentric must be moved on the shaft and the lap found again as before. As D C always bisects H C F, this presents no difficulty. And it is to be remembered that D J is always at right angles to A B.

Given, the travel, lap and lead; to find the cut off:

Set off in Fig. 8 the full travel A B bisecting at C. From C lay off C K equal to the lap, and make K J equal to the lead. Draw J D at right angles to A B, and make C D equal to A C, equal to C B, by taking C as a centre and striking an arc with A C as radius cutting the perpendicular J D in D. Bisect C D in E and draw the distance circle through D J and C, using E C as radius. Draw also the arc I K G with the lap C K as radius, and draw C F through G. C F is the position of the crank at cutting off steam.

A little practice with this method, first upon actual valves, and then by combining the foregoing problems, introducing also the exhaust, will soon give a feeling of confidence not easily obtained with the usual methods.

There is yet one case with a common slide valve which it is desirable to examine. In the foregoing examples we have supposed the eccentric rod to be nearly parallel to the line joining the centre of the shaft and the crosshead, either by placing the steam chest on the side of the cylinder, or, if it be on the top of the cylinder, by the use of rock shafts. Now the latter are always ugly, and, although much used, the former arrangement is to be preferred when possible. There are, however, cases in which it is convenient to lead the eccentric rod in an angle to the line from the shaft centre to the crosshead, the steam chest being on top of the cylinder and the valve rod jointed and guided; or else the steam chest is at one side of the cylinder, but is above or below the centre.

The action of an oblique connecting rod is seldom explained, or more rarely fully understood, and we shall therefore devote some attention to it. Looking at the general case in Fig. 9, we see that the further end of the connecting rod can come no nearer the shaft than the difference in length between the rod and crank, and can go no further from the centre of the shaft than the sum of the lengths of the rod and crank, and that these are absolutely the only limits imposed by the crank. Thus, in Fig 9, by taking C B as the length of the connecting rod, and C A as the length of the crank, by drawing from C as a centre two arcs with radii equal to A C + C B and C B − A C, the only limit to the stroke is that its ends shall lie on these lines and that it should take place between them.

The path of the outer end may be straight or curved. For slide valves worked in this manner it is usually straight, the end moving in guides; or nearly straight with attachment by a comparatively long link, so that the arc it moves in is flat and close to a straight line. Suppose it is straight, then it can be seen that the length of the stroke produced by a given crank may be varied considerably, as, for example, at $D\ E$ and $F\ G$, the latter being plainly the greater. Another feature is also introduced: that is, that for a uniform revolution of the crank, the times of forward and backward strokes, which are the same for $D\ E$, are not equal for $F\ G$, because the

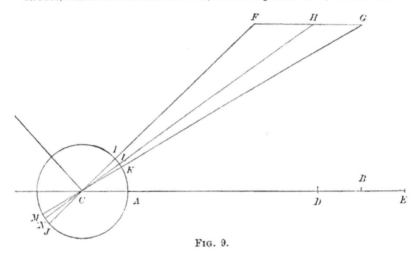

FIG. 9.

dead points, which always occur when the crank and rod are in the same line with each other, when the motion changes, are, for the stroke $F\ G$, at the points J and K. These are not on the same diameter, and it will take longer to pass from J to K and F to G than K to J and G to F, the revolution being right-handed. This is taken advantage of as a "quick return motion" in some slotting machines. If, now, the middle of the stroke $F\ G$ at H be found, and the straight line $H\ L\ N\ C$ be drawn, the dead points K and J will not lie on this line but near it, and the longer the rod is compared with the crank, and the smaller the angle $E\ C\ H$, the closer will be the agreement; and when the crank is on this line the other end of the connecting rod will be close to the points F or G, as the case may be. If the motion were studied on the line $A\ E$ only, being a parallel to $F\ G$ passing through C, it would take place as if moved by a crank arm $C\ A$ instead of $C\ L$, which is at the angle $A\ C\ L$ from the other, and, in fact, we may call $C\ A$ an equivalent crank for $C\ L$, for it will cause the stroke $D\ E$ to be made at the same time as $C\ L$ moves $F\ G$, the rod coming to D in one case when the other comes to F, and to E when the other arrives at G.

In applying the valve diagram to an engine of this kind, the only change we have to make is, that instead of using the actual angle between the crank and eccentric arms, we must use in its place the angle between the crank and the equivalent eccentric arm; that is, it must be changed by the angle between $C\,A$ and $C\,L$, or $A\,C\,L$, in other words, by the angle at the centre of the crank shaft between the lines there from one to the centre of the travel, and the one to the place where we have assumed our investigation to be made. These lines may also be said to pass from the centre of the shaft through the average dead points and the other through the equivalent dead point. This change will be an increase or decrease in the angle between the crank and eccentric arms, or rather, the travel line and the line joining the centres of the distance circles, according as the rotation is right or left-handed, there being no rock shaft used.

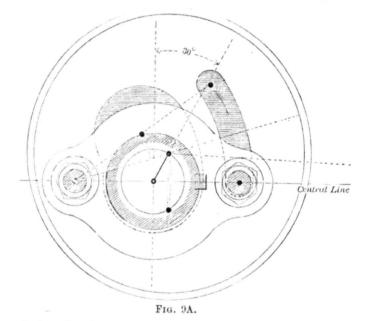

FIG. 9A.

Such engines are not very common, but the only objection lies in the necessity of guiding the end of the valve rod.

In the preceding paragraphs we have discussed the case of an eccentric fixed on the shaft, and moving a single slide valve, in such a manner that no change is made in the relation or movement of parts while the engine is in motion,—all adjustments being made during rest. This also may be taken to apply to the old-fashioned "D" slide, to "B" valve, and to piston valve engines, and these types are in most general use. The advantages of simplicity, durability and universal acquaintance are

found to outweigh many points, even the waste of steam. The desire to
change the points of cut-off, either with the engine stopped or in motion,
and the necessity of reversing the direction of rotation in many engines,
have led to the use of two eccentrics working one or two slide valves, and
in some cases to three eccentrics working two slides. The necessity of
reversing was the cause of the adoption of two eccentrics before any change
in the expansion was considered. The first reversing gear used with the
slide valve was probably some form of hook attachment to a rock shaft
carrying pins on both sides of the centre. If a valve be made without lap
or lead the steam follows the piston full stroke, and the position of an
eccentric is 90° in advance of the crank,—to reverse the position of the
eccentric it must be changed 180°.

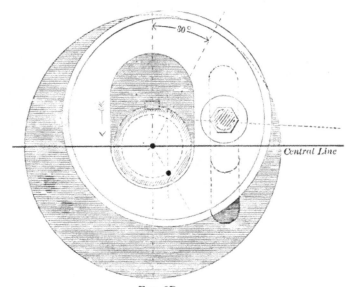

FIG. 9B.

When, however, there is lap, it is evident that there can not be an equal
opening for forward and for back gear with eccentric arms 180° apart; but,
as we have already stated, the eccentric arm is more than 90° in advance of
the crank, and all that is required is to use the same angle between the crank
and eccentric arms for each motion. Figs. 9 A and 9 B show two arrangements for accomplishing this with a single eccentric. The eccentric is not
keyed to the shaft, but is bolted to the face of a disc of smaller diameter,
rigidly fastened to the shaft. In one of the arrangements shown, the
eccentric can move freely about one of the bolts as a centre, while the
other projects through a curved slot. This second bolt can either be
tightened, holding the eccentric to the disc in any position between the

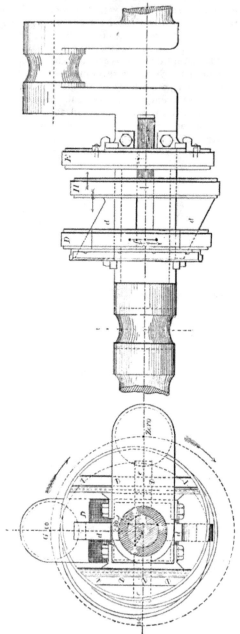

FIG. 9C.

ADJUSTABLE ECCENTRIC.

This originated, according to Auchincloss, see "Link and Valve Motions," in 1839. This eccentric reverses the engine and varies point of cut-off by being made to slide across the shaft. Wedges shown at *d d* and *e e* are attached to a disc *H*, which can be moved along the shaft between the eccentrics *D* and *E*. When it is next to *E* the eccentric *D* is in upper position, and when next to *D*, eccentric *D* is in lower position. Eccentric *E* is also moved by the wedges *e e*.

two extreme ones, thus allowing a change in the eccentric arm when the engine is still; or, the engine being moved till the eccentric comes to rest, with the end of the slot against the bolt, of course the eccentric will follow the motion of the shaft, and the crank and slot being properly arranged, the valve will keep the engine running in the direction in which it was started. If, on stopping, the engine be moved by hand so as to run in the other direction, the shaft and disc will move until the eccentric is caught up with, and the engine will drag it properly to continue the motion. It is therefore a simple reversing gear for engines small enough to be easily turned by hand. Sometimes a small fly-wheel has been mounted with the eccentric and a quick closing valve placed on the steam pipe. By closing the steam valve quickly the fly-wheel will carry the eccentric round so that the engine would start in the other direction; while on the other hand, if the steam valve be closed slowly the eccentric will remain in contact with the disc and the engine will start in the direction it had been moving—an arrangement hardly promising to remain long in working order. In larger engines the same curved slot, or the straight slot shown in the other figure, 9 *B*, is used, and the eccentric is traversed by a sleeve and key; the latter is spiral and is so arranged that by moving the sleeve along the shaft the eccentric is shifted across the shaft. The movement of the sleeve is effected by a yoked lever.

The construction of the valve diagram for different positions of these eccentrics, and the change in the cut-off produced thereby, is a very desirable study for the student. Where two eccentrics are used for moving a slide valve they are usually fastened to the shaft, and the rods are attached to the eccentric by straps or yokes; the other ends of the rods are connected by pins to a piece called the link. There are three varieties of the motion which goes under the name of link motion, but of late years one or both of the eccentrics have been omitted and the link moved from some other portion of the moving mechanism. The three kinds noted have been long in use, and are known as the shifting link, being the invention of Howe, a foreman in Stephenson's Locomotive Works, or the Stephenson Link, the Gooch, or Fixed Link, produced about the same time in the locomotive shops of Mr. Daniel Gooch, and the straight link of Alexander Allan, a combination of the other two.

Fig. 10 shows clearly the arrangement for the shifting link in its most simple form. The link joining the ends of the two eccentric rods is slotted out and the valve rod is pinned to a rectangular block, sliding in the slot, but which in this simple form can be clamped to the link. When loose, the link can be moved by the handle at its end until it occupies any given or desired position. It will be seen that if the link be placed with one end of the slot against the slider, the valve will move by the eccentric connected to that end of the link almost entirely, and we shall have to examine the motion when the slider is clamped at some intermediate point between the ends. In order that the centre of the valve may remain unchanged for all positions of the link, a curvature must be produced in the slot; otherwise, as the link is moved, say from its end to the centre, the valve is pulled over toward the shaft. The valve still has the same motion as a whole, its travel is simply displaced, thereby producing unequal distribution of the steam to each end of the cylinder. By curv-

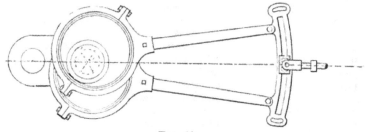

Fig. 10.

ing the link to an arc with a radius equal to the distance from the centre of the shaft to the centre of the slider when the valve is placed in its central position on its seat, this action is removed.

In Figure 11, for the sake of clearness, consider the link as a straight bar, the extremities of which are hung in such a manner that the ends L and L' can only move in lines nearly parallel to the line $A\ C\ B$; this may be the case exactly for either, or nearly, for one or both of the points $L\ L'$. Inasmuch as $C\ L$ and $C\ L'$ both make angles with $C\ A$, both ends

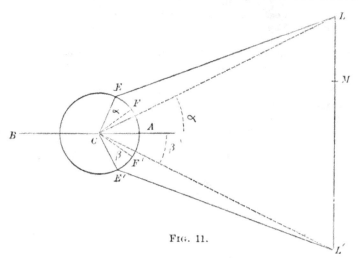

Fig. 11.

of the link may come under the case of oblique eccentric rods. But this presents no great difficulty. If the link were moved till L came to the slider M, the motion received by the valve would be that due to the eccentric E; but for the given position, the point L receives motion parallel to $A\,C$ as if it were driven by a *virtual* eccentric at F, with angle between crank and virtual eccentric arm, $A\,C\,F$ equal to $L\,C\,E$, while the point L' receives motion from F', as if moved by a virtual eccentric at F', with the angle $A\,C\,F'$ equal to the angle $L'\,C\,E'$. In general

$$A\,C\,F + A\,C\,F' = L\,C\,E + L'\,C\,E'.$$

$$E\,C\,E' - (A\,C\,F + A\,C\,F') = E\,C\,E' - (L\,C\,E + L'\,C\,E');$$

or, $E\,C\,F + E'\,C\,F' = A\,C\,L + A\,C\,L' = L\,C\,L' = $ the link angle.

Hence, also, the angle, $F\,C\,F'$, between the virtual eccentric centres is constant, and it swings around its vertex C as the link moves. If the link be divided in any proportion, the link angle should be divided in the same proportion; and an angle may be set proportionately to the number in which $L\,M$ divides $L\,L'$. L and L' then move exactly as if they were on the line $C\,A$ driven by the virtual eccentrics, F and F'; for E comes to its dead points when F comes to $C\,A$, and E', when F' comes to $C\,A$, the dead points for E and F being on, or very near the lines $C\,L$ and $C\,L'$ respectively.

We have now to examine the motion of a point on a bar, when the bar is moved at two points, as if connected with a crank or eccentric at each of such points. We have established for the points of connection L and L', the virtual eccentrics from which they receive motion, as far as the line $A\,C$ is concerned, and we come to the motion of the point M, as follows:

The motion of M may be found by considering that, if L' were fixed while L moves, the motion of M would be definite; and, also, if L were fixed while L' moves, the motion of M would again be definite; while if L and L' both move, the point M would have a motion equal to the

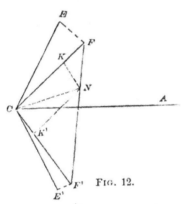

FIG. 12.

resultant of these two motions. Now, enlarging a part of our Fig. 11, we see in Figs. 11 and 12, using the virtual eccentrics F and F', as it has been shown we must do, that if L' be fixed, $E'\,L'$ disconnected, and $C\,K$ be made the same part of $C\,F$ that $L'\,M$ is of $L\,L'$, the point M will move as if driven by an eccentric with centre at K and a rod at $M\,K$; and also that if L be fixed while $E\,L$ is disconnected, and $C\,K'$ be made the same part of $C\,F'$ that $L\,M$ is of $L\,L'$, the motion of M will be as if derived from a single eccentric, centre at K', by a rod $K'\,M$. To combine these two motions at once, draw $K\,N$ equal and parallel to $C\,K'$; then does the point N revolve about K as K' does about C. And also draw $K'\,N$ equal and parallel to $C\,K$; then does the point N revolve about K' as K does about C. Either way we look at it N revolves about K while K revolves about C; or N revolves about K' while K' revolves auout C, and hence the point M moves as if directly connected with the point N by a rod $M N$ of fixed length. The point N may therefore be called the virtual eccentric centre, and $C N$ the virtual eccentric arm, for the point M. It is also seen that the point N is on the line $F F'$, which it divides in the proportion that M divides $L L'$; for the triangles $F K N$, $N K' F'$ and $F C F'$, are all similar, and the line $F F'$ may be drawn and the point N found at once by making $F' N$ the same part of $F F'$ that $M L$ is of $L L'$. This is a more convenient construction for the point N than the other, which was, however, only intended for demonstration. It may be necessary again to caution the reader that the components of motions are all understood to be parallel to $A C$.

If the link was, as a whole, fixed, or was not to be changed, we could find once for all the virtual eccentric for the end points L and L', and draw $F F'$ at once. But, as in the shifting link motion, we use all portions of the link which is moved about $C A$, we have F coinciding with E when L coincides with M, and then N falls on E. As the link is moved the triangle $F C F'$ is swung about C, and the point N travels along $F F'$ till the other end, L', of the link is brought to M when the point N reaches F' which coincides with E'. The line which includes all positions of the point N is a kind of spiral, but is approximated by Rankine to a circle, and by Zeuner, to whom the whole method is due, to a parabola. We will content ourselves with drawing this curve as the arc of a circle, and with finding a third point thereon by which it may be constructed. We have already found F and F' on this curve coinciding with E and E' respectively; then if, as is usually the case, $C F = C E$, the middle point of the curve between F and F' is easily found. Set off in Fig. 13 the angles $E C F$, $E' C F'$, each equal to one-half the link angle, $L C L'$, then the point found by the intersection of $F F'$ with $A C$ is, for this case, the middle point of the arc $E N E'$ desired, and a circle is passed through

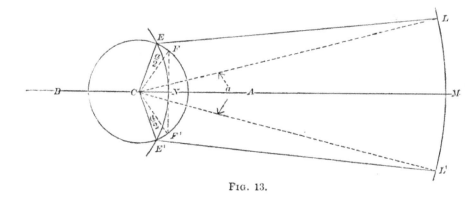

Fig. 13.

these three points. If the link be drawn in mid-gear and we take the intersection of the rods $L E$, $L' E'$, combining this with our valve diagram, we find a complete mastery over the link motion, and we will try to solve some of the cases which are of frequent occurrence.

Given, the full travel, the laps and the lead in full gear and the link angle; to find the mid gear travel and lead, and also the travel and lead with points of admission, cut off, compression and release for any given position of the link.

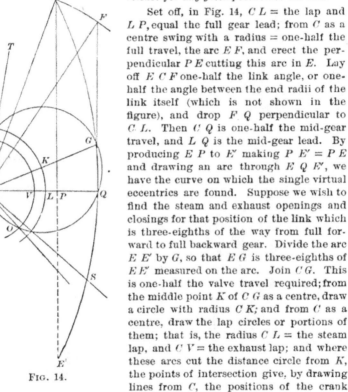

FIG. 14.

Set off, in Fig. 14, $C L =$ the lap and $L P$, equal the full gear lead; from C as a centre swing with a radius $=$ one-half the full travel, the arc $E F$, and erect the perpendicular $P E$ cutting this arc in E. Lay off $E C F$ one-half the link angle, or one-half the angle between the end radii of the link itself (which is not shown in the figure), and drop $F Q$ perpendicular to $C L$. Then $C Q$ is one-half the mid-gear travel, and $L Q$ is the mid-gear lead. By producing $E P$ to E' making $P E' = P E$ and drawing an arc through $E Q E'$, we have the curve on which the single virtual eccentrics are found. Suppose we wish to find the steam and exhaust openings and closings for that position of the link which is three-eighths of the way from full forward to full backward gear. Divide the arc $E E'$ by G, so that $E G$ is three-eighths of $E E'$ measured on the arc. Join $C G$. This is one-half the valve travel required; from the middle point K of $C G$ as a centre, draw a circle with radius $C K$; and from C as a centre, draw the lap circles or portions of them; that is, the radius $C L =$ the steam lap, and $C V =$ the exhaust lap; and where these arcs cut the distance circle from K, the points of intersection give, by drawing lines from C, the positions of the crank $C S$ for steam admission, $C T$ for cut-off, $O C$ produced for release, and $V C$ produced for compression.

It sometimes happens that the forward eccentric is the lower one when we make our examination, and in such a case we must lay $\frac{a}{2}$ on the other side of $C E$ and $C E'$ to find the virtual eccentric centres F and F'; making the necessary construction we have the middle point of the line $F F'$, or N, as the single virtual eccentric which drives the block in mid-link, and we may pass our curve through E, E' and this point as we did before; but

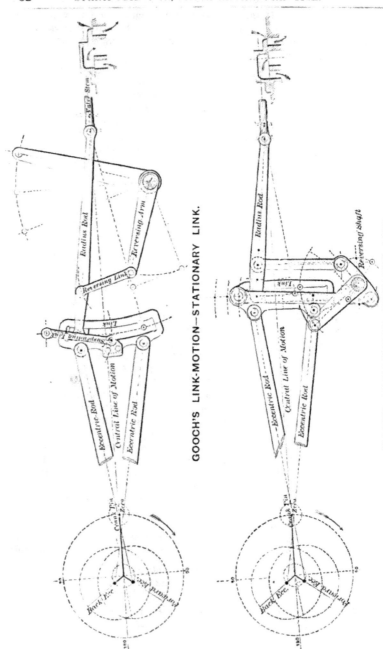

GOOCH'S LINK-MOTION—STATIONARY LINK.

ALLAN'S LINK-MOTION—STRAIGHT LINK.

we find it curved in the other direction, and the mid-gear lead is less than the full gear lead, while in the first case it was greater.

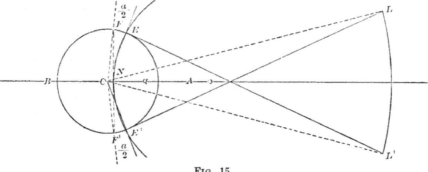

FIG. 15.

The fixed link, or Gooch's link-motion, is shown on page 32. A swinging rod called radius rod is attached to the valve stem and carries the slider at its free end. This rod is controlled from the foot board in the same way as the link in Stephenson's motion, and the actual eccentric centres are the virtual eccentrics. As the eccentric rods do not change their mean angle with the motion line the single virtual eccentric is found on the straight line $E E'$, Figs. 13 and 15, joining the *real* eccentric centres, and the lead does not change for any position of slider. This gear is a favorite in England, but is rarely seen in the United States.

In Fig. 16 the lap and valve circles are drawn for different gears and will be readily understood.

The difficulty experienced in fitting the curved links for the shifting and fixed link-motions, and the fact that the curvature in the link, required to keep the valve at the same place in mid-travel, was in different directions, led Mr. Alexander

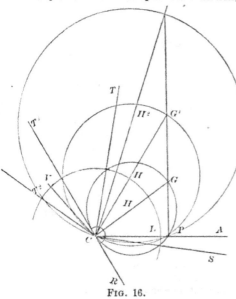

FIG. 16.

Allan, then employed at the Crewe shops, to design a link, shown on page 32, in which the radius rod was retained, although the link was also shifted;

and by proper proportions of the rocker arms, attached to link, and of radius rod, a straight link was secured. Of course these straight links were easier to fit than the curved ones. They are in quite general use in England and on the Continent, while in the United States they have been rarely, if at all, used.

In studying this link-motion we call the angle from the centre of shaft through which the link is shifted a, and set off one-half of it from the actual eccentric centres to find the position of the virtual forward and backward eccentric centres for mid-gear; and we then find the curve on which all our single virtual eccentric centres lie as in the case of the Stephenson link. The curve in this case is flatter, and the change from full to mid-gear lead is less than for the Stephenson link. The mid-gear lead may be greater or less than full gear lead according as the upper or lower eccentric is used for forward gear.

No drawing is required. The change of cut-off for different positions of the slider is shown by the distance and lap circles as already explained for the Stephenson and the Gooch links.

The rock shaft arms have to be proportioned to the segments into which the line from centre of shaft to centre about which radius rod vibrates is divided by the vertical through the centre of rock shaft.

All three of the gears described as having two eccentrics are used for reversing gears as well as for changing point of cut-off; and, in fact, were used only for the former purpose years before their value for the latter was appreciated. For many years these three were the only forms employed. Of late years, however, a variety of gears for varying point of cut-off and for reversing the motion of the engine have come into use, which we will discuss in order of complexity rather than of age.

One of the most widely extended modifications of the link-motion with two eccentrics is met with in the valve gear of Walschaert, or the Heusinger von Waldegg link-motion, shown on page 35.

In the ordinary form of link-motion we have two eccentrics attached to two points on the link, and we get more or less of the motion of one eccentric by connecting the valve rod to different points upon the link. Suppose, however, that while one eccentric attached to the combination arm remains constant as to length of its arm and the angle it makes with crank arm, we have the means of varying the length of the other eccentric arm, which is attached to a second point on the combination arm as shown in illustration. If, now, the valve stem be connected with a third point on the combination arm the movement of the valve can be controlled by giving more or less travel to the variable arm, and can be reversed by reversing the motion of this arm.

In the Walschaert gear, the link, or combination arm, is moved by an attachment rod from the cross-head, and its lowest point moves with the piston or main crank. This combination arm is attached at the upper end to the valve stem, and just below this attachment it is pivoted to a centre. If this centre were fixed the valve would receive only the motion due to a virtual eccentric in line with the crank, and with an arm which

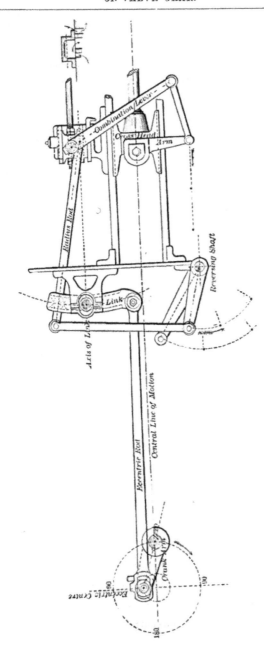

THE WALSCHAERT, OR THE HEUSINGER VON WALDEGG LINK-MOTION.

bears to the crank length the fraction that the short distance from valve stem to pivot is of the length from pivot to pin at cross-head connection. The other element of the motion is obtained by connecting the pivot of this lever to a vibrating slotted link, pivotted at its centre, by means of a rod attaching to a slider in the link. The vibration of this link is given by a small eccentric set at right angles to the crank, or by a return crank from the main crank pin. The effect of moving this slider in the vibrating link is to change the travel of the pivot in magnitude, or to reverse its motion; the pivot always reaches the end of the stroke and its centre at the same part of the revolution: *i. e.*, its period of vibration, or motion with respect to the motion of crank remains unchanged, however much the radius rod may be changed; but the amount of movement received by the valve stem is greater than that received by the pivot in the ratio of the whole length of the combination arm to the portion between the pivot and cross-head connection pin.

To illustrate: Suppose the stroke of the piston is 24 inches, while the combination arm is 26 inches, with the pivot 2 inches from the valve

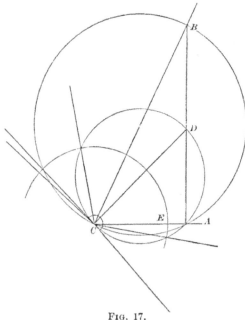

stem connection. The amount which the valve moves due to the piston movement only, is

$$\frac{24\,(26-24)}{24} = 2 \text{ inches}$$

nearly, not exactly, a slight error being introduced by the connecting bar from the cross-head to the link, which, in changing its inclination, reduces the travel near the ends where inclined to the stroke.

If the radius of the eccentric or return crank be 2 inches, and the extreme length of the vibrating link be 6 inches, 3 above and 3 below the centre, and the attachment of the vibrating link to eccentric is at 2 inches from the centre of the vibrating link, we can easily

FIG. 17.

draw valve diagram. In Fig. 17, set off horizontally 1 inch, which equals lap + lead, from the centre C on line $A\ C$, and then vertically a distance $= \dfrac{26}{24}$ the distance the slider is from the centre of the vibrating link $= 2\frac{1}{4}$ inches;

joining this point with C we use this line as the diameter of the valve circle, and by drawing the lap circles we have all the points as before for the opening and closing of the steam ports. This gear has been used in Europe, and was introduced into this country by the late William Mason, who placed it on many of the light engines used for passenger travel at Coney Island beach and about New York.

In designing the preceding forms of valve gear, many little points arise with regard to equalizing quantity of steam used at each end of the cylinder, and for so arranging the details that the wear shall be a mini-

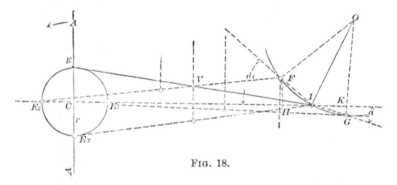

FIG. 18.

mum. A detailed study must be made in each case, while for many practical points the works on "Link and Valve Motions" by Zeuner, and also by Auchincloss, will be found of great service.

If in Fig. 18 we compel the end of the eccentric rod to move in the path $H K$ we know that the end of the rod will always reach the centre and ends

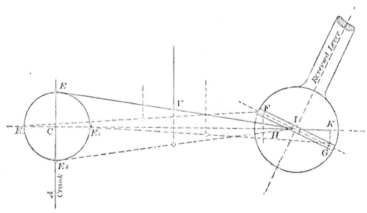

FIG. 18 A.

of the travel in defined time, while with regard to a motion at right angles thereto in this case the end will have none. Now, if the path is from F to G, it can be seen that the end of the rod has a very respectable component vertically, but that it reaches the end and centre of the travel at the same time as before, or nearly so, and the horizontal travel is $H\,K$ nearly, and the vertical is $F\,H + K\,G$. By changing the angle of the path we find the magnitude of the path may be changed and even the motion reversed, as F passes $C\,K$, and at the same time the vertical motion of the rod at the end may be increased or diminished. We have then all the elements for a link in the eccentric rod itself. One end moves up and down with the motion of the eccentric, and the other end moves up and down with the in and out motion and the eccentric rod becomes the link.

We can, of course, connect the valve stem to a slider, leaving the path

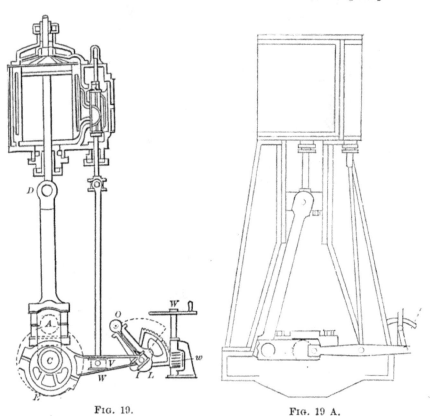

FIG. 19.   FIG. 19 A.

MARSHALL'S GEAR FOR MARINE ENGINES.

at the outer end fixed, or we can connect the valve stem to any point on
the link, as *V*, and change the angle of the path at the end, thus causing
the travel to vary; the time, however, of the outer end up and down
motion being the same as that of the in and out motion. The valve stem,
of course, in this figure moves vertically.

This form has been adopted by Mr. F. Marshall for moving the valves
of vertical marine engines. The arrangement is shown in Figs. 19, 19 A,
and 19 B. In Fig. 19, the form of path adopted for the outer end is the
arc of a circle, the end of the eccentric rod being connected by a radius

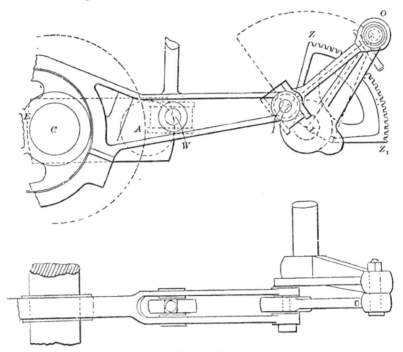

FIG. 19 B.

MARSHALL'S VALVE MOTION ENLARGED.

rod swung from the point *O*. The form may be either a slot or the arc of
a circle. Fig. 18 A shows a straight slot in the face of a disc attached to
the end of shaft connected with a reverse lever.

In Fig. 19, *C* is centre of shaft; *A*, crank pin; *A D*, connecting rod; *E*,
centre of eccentric; *E I*, link; *V*, valve stem connection; *O L*, arm fixed to
axis of geared arc *Z Z₁* at *L;* *W*, handwheel which moves the geared arc
by means of worm *w*, *O I*, radius rod which controls movement of end of
link, or eccentric rod.

Mr. Charles Brown, of Winterthur, Switzerland, introduced many varieties of this form, see Fig. 20. In most of them the eccentric was dispensed with, and the link attached to the connecting rod in such a manner that while the movement in the direction of the inclination is reduced, as in the Walschaert gear, the other component, that due the transverse vibration of the rod, is the one which is governed by the path used.

Mr. Brown usually employed some form of parallel motion at the outer end in place of the slotted guide. Most of his work was applied to engines with rods quite long in comparison with the movements taken from them, and both Marshall and Brown attached the valve stem either between the eccentric and guide, or outside of it as desired.

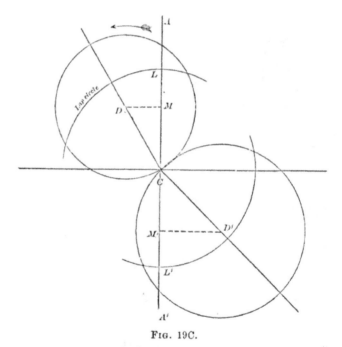

FIG. 19C.

DIAGRAM FOR MARSHALL'S VALVE GEAR.

Mr. David Joy has introduced, quite extensively, a form of gear similar to Brown's in some respects, but more carefully worked out in others; Figs. 21 and 21 A. Mr. Joy attaches to a point near the centre of the connecting rod a bar *H I;* Fig. 21 A. This bar is carried by a hanger from *J,* a fixed point in the frame of the engine. Now, as the

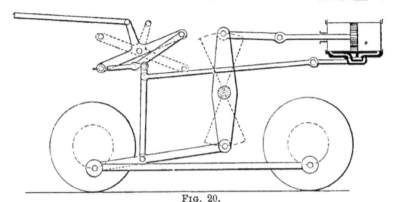

FIG. 20.

BROWN'S VALVE GEAR.

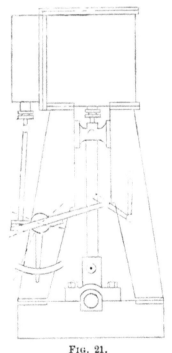

FIG. 21.

JOY'S VALVE GEAR ON A
MARINE ENGINE.

cross-head moves from D to E the point I moves in the arc of a circle, but because the length $H I$ is short it gets an extra pull in when the cross-head nears the end of the stroke. Mr. Joy therefore carries his link from K, a point on $H I$, to the guides L, and attaches the valve stem $M N$ to a point in $K L$, in this case produced, at M. The results have been very good, and in most cases pin joints are used for eccentric straps. In many cases Mr. Joy replaces the guide L, which he makes curved to radius depending on $N M$, by a swinging link having the same centre as the guide; this centre is mounted on an arm of a rock shaft, and the rock shaft centre coincides with that of the guide. Two more pin-joints are required but the wear on the guide is removed.

Mr. Kirk has patented a form of valve gear. In a marine engine he places a vibrating link on the air pump side levers in such a a manner that the centre of the link is moved thereby from the piston rod. The link is caused to vibrate by the transverse motion of the connecting rod and a compensation due the obliquity is introduced. In this case the levers adopted are in the form of a Watt parallel motion.

The motion used for a link in the Allen engine for driving a slide valve, and in the Porter-Allen for moving the steam valves, is exceedingly elegant and clearly set forth in Fig. 22. The link is part of the eccentric strap, and the centre of the link, of which only one-half is constructed for non-reversing engines, is guided, in an approximately straight line, by a swinging rod attached to the frame; so that the small versed sine of half the arc of swing is bisected by the centre line of engine and the chord of the arc is parallel to it. The eccentric is forged on the shaft and corresponds in Fig. 23 to the virtual arm *A B*. As we proceed up the link we find it also acting as a bell crank, and we see that by coming up the vertical *B* to *C* and making *B C* proportional to distance of slider above centre line, we have the virtual eccentric and distance circle for any point on the link.

To draw the valve diagram for any point on the link, lay off first the real eccentric radius on the motion line, and then from that point lay off at right angles to the motion line a distance equal to the real eccentric radius multiplied by the ratio of the distance of the slider above centre line to the distance from

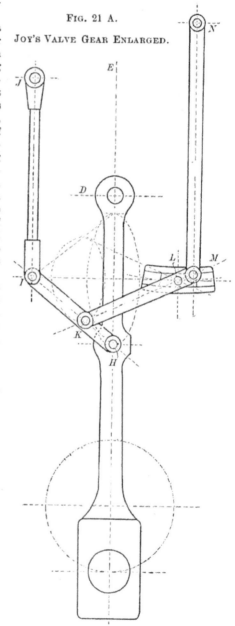

Fig. 21 A.

Joy's Valve Gear Enlarged.

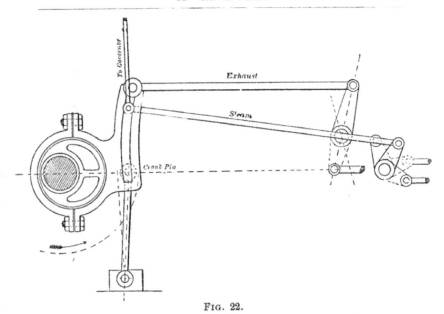

FIG. 22.

centre of eccentric to the point of attachment of rocker arm. The point thus found is the virtual eccentric centre moving the valve. The link is of course curved to the radius of length equal the radius rod. For a reversing gear the link is continued beyond the centre or pin from which it is hung.

Another form of gear was used in Germany by Herr Kaiser, of Berlin, and is very simple. Two lugs project from the eccentric strap at right angles. To one of them the valve stem is attached, and the other is guided in a slot which can be placed at different inclinations with line of motion. When the slot is in the line of the motion, the valve is moved as if by a single eccentric found in the diagram as follows:

Set off on the line of the motion the real eccentric radius, and at right angles to the motion, a distance equal to the real eccentric radius multiplied by the ratio of the distance from the centre of the eccentric to the centre of pin in the valve stem, to the distance from the centre of the eccentric to centre of pin in slider.

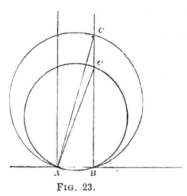

FIG. 23.

When the slide is inclined, the amount of vertical movement of the slide block caused thereby must be added to the eccentric radius before multiplying length of the lugs by the above ratio: as the sum of these two movements is used it is apparent that this motion is not well suited for a reversing gear.

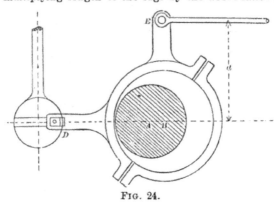

FIG. 24.

Instead of a slide a swinging link is often used, and by moving the point of suspension in an arc with a centre at the middle point of the motion a very good distribution is obtained.

In all the foregoing motions, or valve gears, we have considered the valve as the ordinary slide. By examining the valve diagrams already given, we find that when an early cut-off is given by the use of lap the eccentric has to be set forward, and that either release occurs very early, or if this be prevented by giving lap on the exhaust side the exhaust closes early and cushion begins. Now just where it is best to stop in either direction has not been decided, but the greater the clearance and number of revolutions the earlier the cut-off can be used with advantage. With 8 per cent. clearance and less than 100 revolutions it is not desirable to cut off before half stroke, but if the speed be increased to over 300 revolutions a cut-off at one-fourth stroke may be employed. If the travel of the valves on a locomotive for full gear be 4½ to 5 inches, for a lead of $\frac{1}{18}$ inch at full gear, and $\frac{5}{16}$ inch at mid gear, a steam lap of ¾ inch and no exhaust lap will

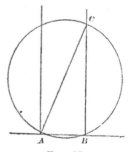

FIG. 25.

secure excellent results; but if the engine was never to run at a speed of over 20 miles an hour, an exhaust lap of ¼ inch could be used to advantage. Most builders of stationary engines give so much exhaust lap that a considerable back pressure is caused, and the engines can not be run at high speed, and for two reasons: 1st, that the steam does not get out of the cylinder fast enough, and, 2nd, there is not enough cushion to take up the fling of the connections at high speed. An early release and strong cushion are required for high speeds.

At moderate speed an early release and strong cushion deadens the motion of the engine over the centres, and the use of two slide valves, one on top of the other, was suggested by Meyer. A false valve seat was suggested by Rankine, with the object of obtaining a quicker cut-off, the seat being moved by one eccentric while the valve was moved by another. In this way the effect of an eccentric with greater throw was obtained.

The first change consisted in making the steam chest in two chambers. In the one next the cylinder the ordinary slide was employed while the steam came in through openings from the other chamber, these openings were covered by a simple slide moved by an eccentric. Thus the inlet and exhaust were regulated by the ordinary slide, but the second one cut off the supply of steam. As the principal objection to this was the large clearance space left in the main steam chest and the consequent waste of steam, the Meyer gear became the favorite.

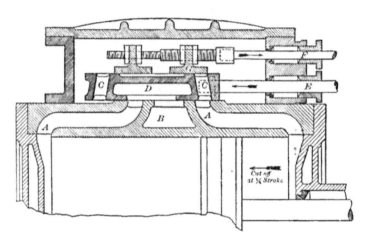

FIG. 26.   THE MEYER VALVE.

The use of an expansion valve on the back of the main valve allows the main valve to govern the admission, release, and cushion, but the cut-off is effected by the expansion slide closing the steam ports of the main valve. This combination enables the cut-off to take place more quickly with the sum of the motions of the two valves.

In Fig. 26, *A A* are the steam ports and *B* the exhaust port in the cylinder metal; *C C* are the steam ports and *D* the exhaust port in the main slide. The main slide is moved by rod *E*, the plates *G G*, on the top of the main slide, by rod *F*. Steam is usually admitted by the outer edges of the cut-off plates.

The eccentric of the expansion valve is usually placed in line with the crank, either on the same or opposite side of the shaft. This, however, is not essential, for there are four ways in which the cut-off may be varied by means of an expansion valve:

1. By changing the lap of the expansion valve, usually by means of a right and left thread on the valve stem.

2. By changing the travel of the expansion valve, usually by means of a radius rod joined to the valve stem, and a rocker link moved by the eccentric.

3. By moving the eccentric round the shaft, of which, perhaps, the "Buckeye Engine" is the best example.

4. By the use of a link motion for the expansion valve.

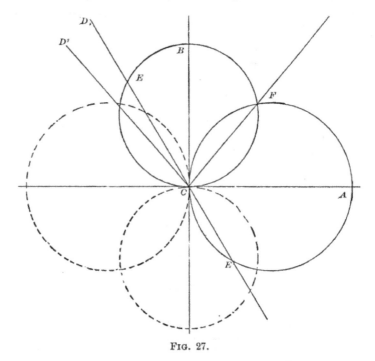

Fig. 27.

We shall examine hereafter these methods more fully; but to begin with will take up the case in which the expansion valve is without lap, and is moved by an eccentric placed opposite the crank, the main valve being without lap or lead, or, "line and line," having, of course, its eccentric set at right angles to the crank. The valve diagram may be drawn from the known position of the eccentrics, each valve being represented by its own distance circle.

In Fig. 27, let *C B* be the diameter of the distance circle for the main valve and *C A* the diameter of the distance circle of the expansion valve.

Then, it being remembered that with the piston at the right end of the cylinder, the position of the crank arm is *C A*, the expansion valve is farthest from its mid position and the main valve is at its mid position. As the crank moves on towards the position *C F*, the main valve rapidly opens the port while the expansion valve moves inward, at first slowly, but with increasing speed. At *C F* it is evident that the main valve and expansion valve are at the same distance from mid position. If, therefore, there be no lap on the expansion slide, it will at this point cover and

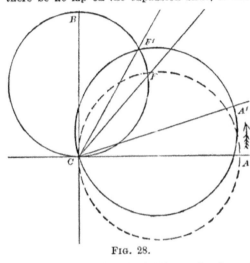

FIG. 28.

close the opening in the main valve, and *C F* is therefore the position of the crank at cut-off. The release of steam to the exhaust, being under the main valve, can in no way be dependent upon the upper, or expansion valve; but there is one thing to be carefully guarded against, which with this arrangement might happen: the main valve moves on outward and the expansion valve inward, until at *C B* the port in the main valve is wide open, while the expansion valve is at mid position. The continuation of the motion draws the main valve back, gradually closing the port while the expansion valve is now moving beyond mid position and would of itself cover the cylinder port if placed thereon. At *C D*, for instance, the main valve has not yet returned to the centre by the amount *C E*, while the expansion valve is past the centre by the amount *C E′*. We see that in this case there is no risk of opening the steam before the end of the stroke is reached, which was the danger to be shunned. Of course, at the end of the stroke steam is admitted to the other end of the cylinder by the main valve, its port at that end having been uncovered by the expansion valve when the crank was in the position *C D′*.

If with the given eccentrics we should desire to have the cut-off take place before the crank reach *C F*, we must add lap to the expansion valve so that its edge shall meet and cover the port in the main valve before the expansion valve becomes central thereto. On the other hand, if the cut-off is to come after *C F*, a strip must be taken from the edge of the expansion valve which must meet the port of the main valve after the slide has become central thereto, or the lap must be negative. We will consider this case more fully hereafter. With the simple figure we readily see the effect of changing the angular position of the eccentrics on the shaft, for the main valve is rarely set without lead cushion or a more prompt release.

If the expansion eccentric be brought nearer the main eccentric, or moved backwards on the shaft, we see in Fig. 28 that the intersection of the two circles takes place later, and that it may range to the end of the stroke, or more strictly speaking, to the cut-off given by the main valve due to its lap.

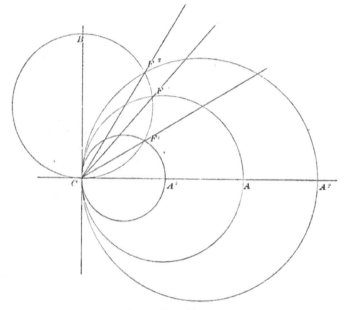

FIG. 29.

It may also be seen, that in the use of an expansion valve without lap the effect of a change of travel, see Fig. 29, in the expansion valve, the position of its eccentric remaining the same, will also vary the cut-off through a considerable range, but in this case we must expect inconvenience to arise from the greater length of steam chest required to accommodate the increased travel.

The effect of changing the lap on the expansion valve is best examined by combining the distance circles of the two valves as follows, see Fig. 30:

Take as before, *C B* and *C A*, the distance circles of the main valve and expansion valve, respectively. Join *A B* and draw *C G* parallel to *A B*, and *B G* parallel to *A C*. Upon *C G* as a diameter draw a circle. Then, for any position, as *C D*, of the crank, it may be easily shown that the distance of the centre of the main valve from the centre of the expansion

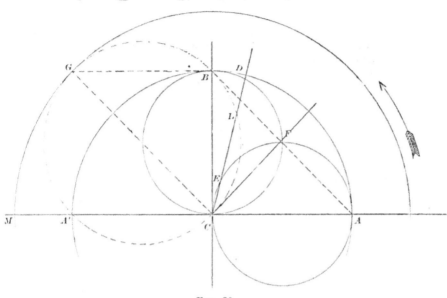

FIG. 30.

valve, $C D - C E = E D$, is equal to the chord, $C L$, of the arc of this last circle intercepted by the crank arm. Therefore, the circle $C G$ may be regarded as a resultant distance circle giving the position of the expansion valve upon the back of the main valve, without regard to the motion of the latter. If there be no lap on the expansion valve, we find it central with the main valve at $C F$, which is at right angles to $A B$; and we have already seen that with positive lap the cut-off takes place before $C F$, while with negative lap it takes place after $C F$ has been passed. Thus we see that by cutting from the edge of the expansion valve, or by increasing the negative lap, we can delay the cut-off till $C G$ is reached, at which point the expansion valve just closes the port in main valve for an instant only, and the steam continues to pass into cylinder until main valve closes. In order that the expansion valve may not open again before the main valve closes, it must close the port in the main valve at $C B$, or at half stroke in the case before us; that is, the distance of the edge of the expansion valve from the *far* edge of the port in main valve, *when both are in mid position*, must not exceed $C B = C A'$. This distance evidently depends for its value upon the lap of the expansion valve.

If the cut-off is variable, its maximum limit should not be beyond the point of cut-off of the main valve; if it is coincident with that of the main valve, it is evident that the diameter, $C G$, coincides with the position of crank arm when the main valve closes, and equals the distance of the edge of expansion valve from far edge of port as before stated. We have thus a limit which we did not meet with in our former case. The remedy is to increase the throw of the expansion eccentric, thereby rendering the angle *C A B* more acute, or else, of course, to move the expansion eccentric nearer the main eccentric.

By proper use of the distance circles and resultant circle all problems on the Meyer valve gear may be readily solved.

NOTE.—Figures 31, 32 and 33 work from the left instead of right, as heretofore.

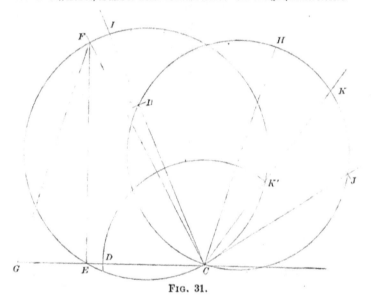

FIG. 31.

We will illustrate by a few examples:

Given, the lap and lead of the main valve, and the travel of both valves; to find lap of the expansion valve for a given cut-off.

First, in Fig. 31, from *C* set off horizontally *C D* the lap and *D E* the lead of the main valve, and with *C F* the half travel and *E F* a vertical line, construct the right angle triangle *C E F*. On *C F* as a diameter draw the main valve distance circle, and the lap arc *D K'* defines the crank position *C K* when the main valve closes. Set off *C G* the half travel of the expansion valve with the eccentric opposite the crank, and join *G F*. On *C H*, equal and parallel to *G F*, draw the resultant distance circle; and where it meets *C I*, the position given for the crank at cut-off, gives *C D*, the negative lap of the expansion valve, which we carry round to *J* in order to see that by the time the expansion valve again uncovers the port of the main valve at *C J*, the main valve has already closed the cylinder port at *C K*.

Given, the lap, lead and travel of the main valve, and the travel of an expansion valve having no lap; to find position of expansion eccentric to produce a given cut-off.

Find in Fig. 32 the distance circle and closure of the main valve, as before, and let *C I* be the crank for given cut-off. With *I*, where this intersects the distance circle, as a centre, and with *C* as the centre, swing radii *C A* and *I A*, each equal to ¼ the travel of the expansion valve, defining by

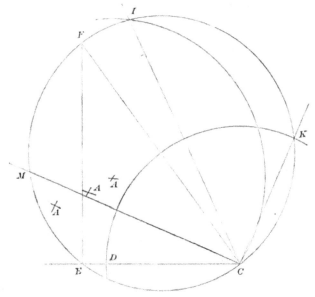

Fɪɢ. 32.

their intersection at *A*, the centre of the distance circle for the expansion valve passing through *I* and *C*. The position of the expansion eccentric is 180°—angle *E C A* ahead of the crank, or distant from the main eccentric by the angle *F C A*. If the point *A* falls above *C M* drawn at right angles to *C K*, the slide will not open the port until after the main valve has closed. But if *A* falls to the left of *C M*, a new eccentric must be taken.

Given, the same data, viz.: lap, lead and travel of main valve, and lap and travel of expansion valve; to find position for expansion eccentric to produce a given cut-off.

In Fig. 33, draw *C F* and *C K* as before, and on *C I*, the given position of crank at cut-off, set off *C A*, the negative lap of the expansion valve. From *A* draw *A J* at right angles to *C A*, and, with the half travel of the expansion valve, define from *E* on *A J* the point *L*. *C M*, equal and parallel to *L F*, is the position sought for the expansion eccentric arm.

Other problems will readily be solved if there be sufficient data, but we think we have given the most important, and enough to show the flexibility and power of the method.

When such valves as described are used, the engine is said to have an expansion valve. When the cut-off can be changed while running or when still, the engine is said to have variable expansion. When the cut-off is changed by the action of the engine itself, owing to change of speed, it is called automatic expansion.

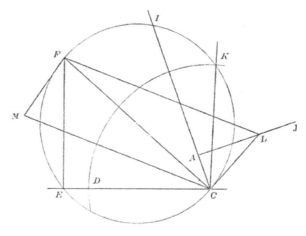

FIG. 33.

When the cylinder is so long that a single slide becomes inconvenient, two exhaust ports are used, and the valve is divided into two portions, one for each end of the cylinder. Care must here be taken that the exhaust port is not open to the steam by the valve having too much travel.

Sometimes a piston valve is used, which consists of two pistons on the valve stem, either arranged to give steam space between the pistons and the exhaust connections at the end spaces, or through the hollow piston; or with the exhaust port between the pistons and the steam space at the ends. Examples of these arrangements are given on page 55. The graphical method heretofore used will answer for all these varieties.

In large engines and in many paddle-wheel steamers four valves are used, generally "Equilibrium poppets," or the older "Cornish equilibrium:" these were introduced at a very early period in the history of the steam engine. The single unbalanced poppet is still used in small engines on the Mississippi, and a very common arrangement is a "relief valve," or a small poppet on the top of a large one, the small one being lifted first and its continued movement raising the large one. By the use of moveable seats and poppets set on the valve stem the "balance" may be carried to

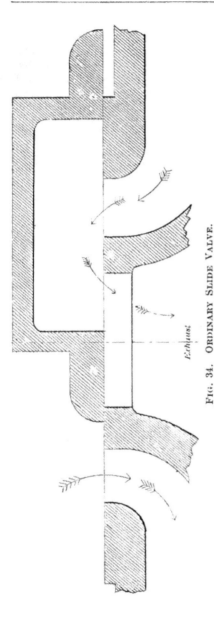

FIG. 34. ORDINARY SLIDE VALVE.

Exhaust

any desired extent. The ordinary forms, as also the Cornish, require one end of the valve to pass through the seat for the other end, thus limiting the degree of closeness of the agreement of areas or the "balancing."

The stems of these poppets are usually moved by levers, worked by cams on one or more auxilliary rock shafts placed near the cylinder. The valves are always moved vertically. The movement of the rock shafts is usually effected by an eccentric on the main shaft. On the Mississippi river, instead of an eccentric, a cam is used. One cam is used for full stroke in either direction, and the reversing is done by hooking to either one of a pair of arms on a rock shaft; a second cam is used for cutting off for the steam valves when running ahead only, the exhaust being moved by the full stroke cam. The forms of the cams are such as to give very rapid movements of opening and closing, as will be seen from the indicator diagrams taken from the steamer Phil. Chappel, shown in Chapter IV. The shape of cams and arrangement of valve gear is shown in the drawings of the engines of the steamer "Montana," as applied to the Mississippi boats, and also their application to Engine No. 1, High Service, St. Louis Waterworks, which is an example of the application usual near New York, and on the North River class of boats.

When poppet valves are

used with a drop cut-off, there is a shock which causes rapid wear on the valve and seat unless a dash pot is used to prevent it. At a speed of more than 30 revolutions per minute, poppet valves do not appear to give entire satisfaction, but with a small number of revolutions they work well. We have seen them used up to 70 revolutions, but have generally found upon enquiry that very frequent grinding was required.

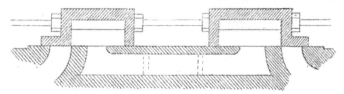

FIG. 35.   DOUBLE VALVE.

From the variations in steam pressure and work on stationary engines there necessarily resulted variations in speed, which for many reasons is exceedingly undesirable, and we find that Watt very soon produced his centrifugal governor, applied to the throttle valve in the well known manner. Under various forms this arrangement is still the most common one, and for small variations of speed it is perhaps as good as anything yet devised.

For large variations in speed it was found that with light loads the engine was so throttled that the initial pressure in the cylinder was much below the boiler pressure, and a manifest waste of steam resulted, the steam not yielding the amount of work which might be obtained there-

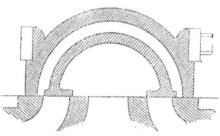

FIG. 36.   TRICK'S VALVE.

from, and a class of engines with four valves and a "drop cut-off," regulated by the governor, was introduced by Mr. Geo. H. Corliss.

The engine introduced by Mr. Corliss was in many respects a very great improvement. The valves were placed close to the cylinder and were rotary instead of sliding. The clearance space was very much reduced and the engines became very successful. The drop cut-off regulated by the governor kept the initial pressure of steam in the cylinder well up to the boiler pressure, and changes of speed were followed so closely by changes of cut-off, that in engines well proportioned to the work an economy never before attained was reached.

In the United States the term Corliss is applied only to engines with the rotative Corliss valve, but in Europe it has been used for any engine with cut-off regulated by the governor, as this was first successfully

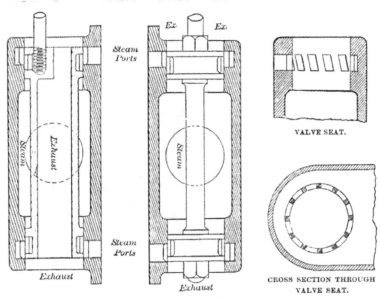

FIG. 37. PISTON VALVES.

applied by Mr. Corliss. A host of imitators soon followed, each with a
variation in the "let-off" gear, and with slide and poppet valves moved
by one or two eccentrics. Since the expiration of the Corliss patents a
crop of designs has come forward, all distinguished by the appendix
"Corliss." Of these we shall illustrate one built by Messrs. E. P. Allis &
Co., of Milwaukee, Wis., from the designs of their manager, Mr. Edwin F.
Reynolds, and placed in the St. Louis Cotton Mill.

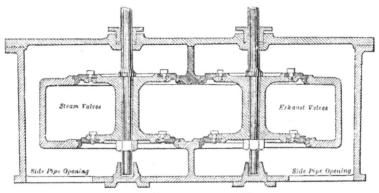

FIG. 38. DOUBLE POPPET VALVE.

A modification of the Corliss engine is manufactured by Mr. Jerome Wheelock, of Worcester, Mass., in which, with only two ports and two main valves, the steam admission is closed by two other valves adjacent to the main valves and worked from them by clutch links; all four valves are of the Corliss type. As built, the only objection to these engines is the difficulty of arranging the cushion to the varied requirements of practice.

The production of an engine with cut-off regulated by the governor, but without the let-off, or drop gear, which, by the way, is not adapted to higher speeds than 120 revolutions, has been secured in the Buckeye and the Porter-Allen engines. In the former, two ports, a balanced slide valve and an expansion slide are used, the cut-off being changed by the governor, and that by turning the expansion eccentric round the shaft by the centrifugal force of two weights held back by springs in a manner easily understood from the drawings. In the Porter-Allen engine there are four ports and the steam valves are balanced slides moved by an expansion link, already explained, and the exhaust is moved from the end of the same link. We shall give illustrations of these in Chapter IV which will more fully explain their principles.

In large engines using slide valves the ports are often made double, the valves having passages cast in them connecting the steam and exhaust ports. This in no way affects the valve diagram constructions already given.

When the cylinders are over 12 inches in diameter it is well to connect the metal across the ports by bridges, so that the heads shall not be rendered weak, or the pull on the bolts concentrated on those next the ends of the ports.

In some excellent examples of engines with four ports, gridiron slides are used, working transversely to the cylinders. These slides are moved usually by cams on a "lay shaft," and the cut-off is changed by shifting the cams along the shaft, bringing different portions of the cam face with different angular forces into action. A good example of this is found in the "Howard" engine. By this means a very sharp opening and closing can be given the valves, but in small engines a larger clearance is required than is desirable. Each valve can be adjusted by itself, which is a desirable feature.

Valve gear of this class has been employed with great success by Mr. E. D. Leavitt, Jr., in his celebrated pumping engines.

CHAPTER III.

Although we have no such engines as that which was described in the preceding chapter, it is desirable to assume, for the purposes of computation, and in order to obtain a view of complex operations in detail, that we use the steam in a non-conducting vessel whose volume can be varied: in other words, in a cylinder constructed of material which cannot conduct heat. But we must be very careful to remember that no such engine at present exists, and that we shall have to adapt the deductions made from such a case to real engines. Serious disappointment and useless expense have resulted from ignoring this fact in designing engines, and much discussion on the subject has arisen.

In the case of engines using steam non-expansively, or without "cutting-off," we should have very little trouble in computing the work done by a pound weight of steam, or the number of pounds of steam used to obtain a horse-power of work in the cylinder, as we shall very easily see.

We know that the equivalent of a unit of heat is 772 foot-pounds of work, and that 33,000 foot-pounds of work per minute is the standard horse-power:

$$\text{Hence, } \frac{33,000}{772} = 42\frac{75}{100} =$$

the number of heat units per minute which have to be expended to obtain a horse-power, provided, we had any means of transforming heat into work without waste. And

$42\frac{75}{100} \times 60 = 2,565$ heat units, the equivalent of a horse-power per hour.

In a full stroke engine with non-conducting cylinder, and without other losses, we should only have to divide 2,565 by the number of heat-units given in the Table of the "Properties of Saturated Steam," Chapter I, as heat expended in doing external work, or external heat, for one pound weight of steam at the boiler pressure, to obtain the number of pounds of water which must be boiled per hour to furnish, or to exert, one horse-power per hour for the work of the steam in the cylinder.

There are many reasons why the amount of steam used per hour, and per horse-power, should vary from this:

1. The steam passages may be too small to maintain the steam supply at the boiler pressure.

2. The boiler may be so small in steam room that the pressure in both boiler and cylinder may fall during the stroke.

3. The clearance, or waste space, in the cylinder will be filled with steam at boiler pressure before the piston starts, which will be discharged at exhaust without having performed any work.

4. The fact that the cylinder and piston receive heat when the steam comes in and give it out while the steam goes out. More will be said on this point later.

The power exerted by the steam in the cylinder is subjected to the following further losses before it can be utilized:

1. The vapor, or steam, on the exhaust side of the piston has to be pushed out of the cylinder by the advancing piston against the back pressure.

2. Mechanical work is absorbed in friction by the piston slides and connections of non-rotative engines, and by the main bearings of rotative engines.

These several points give rise to the measurement of horse-power in three ways:

1. The number of horse-power really exerted by the steam—called in English the total, and in French the absolute, horse-power.

2. The number of horse-power exerted by the steam after deducting that expended in sweeping out the exhaust. This is given by the ordinary indicator measurement, and is called the Indicated Horse Power: it is what is usually understood by the phrase Horse-power, without qualification, in the United States.

3. The power which may be taken from the shaft by a dynamometer, or by a belt, which represents the power of the engine to do useful work outside of itself. This is called the Net, or Effective Horse Power.

As these three quantities are for any given measurement produced by the same amount of water boiled, we find that, dividing the quantity of water used per hour by the number of horse-power, we have also three quotients, viz.: The number of pounds used per hour for Total, for Indicated, and for Net Horse Power. These may be considered as the "student's," the "ordinary," and the "commercial" standards of measurement. Engineers are obliged to retain all three of these quantities, for: In any given engine with given speed and circumstances, the work expended on the exhaust and friction is nearly constant, and hence, the greater the power of the steam used the less is the percentage of that uselessly expended.

In illustration of the process, referred to, we give the following examples:

Example I. What is the minimum steam consumption per hour for an engine using steam at full stroke, at 25 lbs. pressure above the atmosphere, with a vacuum of 12 pounds, and indicating 200 horse-power for a non-conducting cylinder? Clearance 8 per cent.

Steam pressure = 25 + 15 = 40 lbs. above zero.

Back pressure = 15 − 12 = 3 lbs above zero.

Pressure expended in obtaining the indicated horse-power is:

$$40 - 3 = 25 + 12 = 37 \text{ lbs.}$$

From the Table of "Properties of Steam" we find that the external work of 1 pound weight of steam at 25 lbs. pressure is equal to 77 heat units, and we should have to use to obtain a Total Horse-power, 2,565, the equivalent of heat units for a horse-power per hour, divided by 77 as above, which would give the number of pounds of water per hour,—neglecting clearance.

To obtain the indicated horse-power: we have $\frac{2565}{77} \times \frac{40}{37} =$ pounds per hour.

If the friction of the engine absorbs as usual 2 lbs. pressure, we shall have $\frac{2565}{77} \times \frac{40}{35} =$ lbs. of water per net horse-power per hour.

The number of Total Horse-power is $200 \times \frac{40}{37}$.

The number of Net Horse-power is $200 \times \frac{37}{35}$.

The water used per hour neglecting clearance is:

$$\frac{2565}{77} \times \frac{40}{37} \times 200;$$

and including clearance

$$\frac{2565}{77} \times \frac{40}{37} \times 200 \times 1.08.$$

Working out these figures, we shall have:
Water per Total Horse-power per hour = 33.3.
Water per Indicated Horse-power per hour = 36.0.
Water per Net Horse-power per hour = 38.0.
Water per hour = $200 \times 1.08 \times 36 = 7,720$ pounds.
When the cylinder is not non-conducting a much larger quantity of water will be consumed.

Example II. The following figures illustrate about as bad a case in actual practice, as ever came within the author's experience:
Steam pressure 60 lbs. above atmosphere.
Back   "   45 "   "   "
Steam pressure 75 lbs. above zero.
Back   "   60 "   "   "
Acting pressure on piston 75 — 60 = 15 lbs.
External heat for 60 lbs. = 79 heat units.

Water per Total Horse-power $\frac{2565}{79} = 32.4$ lbs.

Water per Indicated Horse-power $\frac{2565}{79} \times \frac{75}{15} = 162$ lbs.

Example III.—

Steam pressure 205 lbs. above atmosphere.

Back	"	2 "	"	"
Steam	"	220 "	above zero.
Back	"	17 "	"	"
Acting	"	183 "	on piston.

External work for 205 lbs. = 85 heat units.

Water per hour for　Total Horse-power　$\dfrac{2565}{85} = 30.2.$

" 　　" 　　" 　for Indicated　　" 　　$\dfrac{2565}{85} \times \dfrac{220}{203} = 32.3.$

" 　　" 　　" 　for Net 　　　　" 　　$\dfrac{2565}{85} \times \dfrac{220}{200} = 33.2.$

We see from examples I and III that, although in the intrinsic work of the steam there is not much gained by the use of high pressure steam in full stroke engines,

$$\frac{33.3 - 30.2}{33.3} = 9\frac{3}{10} \text{ per cent.,}$$

yet that high pressure non-condensing engines may be practically more economical than low pressure condensing ones; for supposing, as we did, that 3 pounds moved the engine only, we have:

$$\frac{38.0 - 33.2}{38.0} = 12\frac{6}{10} \text{ per cent.,}$$

as the practical gain in the cost of a Net horse-power: and there are the further advantages that the loss by the use of a conducting cylinder is less, and the machinery is far less bulky and complex.

This is a very fair comparison of the early steamboat engines when working full stroke, as used on the Atlantic ocean and the Mississippi river. The use of steam at a very high pressure, not only requiring cheaper machinery and of less weight, but actually using less steam to do the work, when worked at or near full stroke.

The process of computing the amount of steam used by expanding engines with non-conducting cylinders is much less easy to explain, although the work of computation is but little more difficult.

In order to study the action of expanding gases it is convenient to represent the volume and pressure for any given state and quantity by distances set off at right angles to each other, on convenient scales. Thus, by the distance of a point above a line we measure the pressure, and by the distance of a point to the right of a line, we measure the volume. For a different state of volume and pressure we have a different point; for states of volume and pressure, differing little, we have points near together, and for changing states of volume and pressure we have a moving point, which may be considered to trace a line. When a series of changes brings the gas back to its original state, the line traced will return into itself.

The product of a force into a distance through which it moves is known as energy exerted, and it is equal to the product of the resistance by the distance through which it is moved; or, what is known as the work done; and, as in an engine cylinder, the moving force on the piston is the pressure times the area of the piston, and, as for a small movement the pressure remains nearly the same, the energy expended is the product of the mean pressure, by the piston area, by the distance moved; or the pressure times the change in volume as the product of the piston area by the distance moved by the piston is the change in volume occupied. The number of cylinders in which such changes of volume take place is immaterial, as the total energy expended must be the sum of the energies expended in all such cylinders; hence, the statement, that the energy expended is the product of the mean pressure by the change in volume. Hence, also, the diagram, just explained, furnishes the data for finding the energy expended, as the latter must be represented by the area between the horizontal line of "no pressure," the two verticals at the end of the change of volume, and the line traced by the moving point.

In any series of changes in which the original state of volume and pressure is again reached, the energy effectively exerted is, of course, the difference between that expended on the piston and that exerted by the piston; or, that which is represented by the enclosed figure.

The first thing to be determined is the curve of expansion, or the curve which would be drawn by an indicator attached to such an expanding engine with a non-conducting cylinder; but as no such cylinders exist, we have to approximate the curve from the table of the "Properties of Steam."

If we set out with the volume of one pound weight of steam at a given pressure, and then assume it to expand by any defined law until its pressure has been lowered to a given amount, we can compute the external work done in changing the volume; then taking this heat from the total internal heat contained in the steam, if we find that the change in internal heat is less than that required to do the external work, as by assumption we find it in a non-conducting cylinder, some of the heat must be supplied by the condensation of the steam itself, and that, therefore, the volume must be reduced, and with it the external work, and, of course, also the heat required to do this external work. By a little care in approximating, we shall arrive at such a condensation that the change in internal heat added to the heat given by condensation will just balance the heat absorbed by the external work of expansion. Thus, a point on the expansion curve for the indicator diagram of steam expanding in a non-conducting cylinder is obtained.

The assumed law of expansion may be anything, but perhaps the best for the purpose is that given by the volumes and pressures of saturated steam, or, what is known as the "steam line." A common assumption is that, the product of the pressures and volumes is constant, though there is no basis for such an assumption.

The computation of the work done by the expansion can be performed in various ways, but for our purposes we shall plot the steam line and

compare the area of the diagrams by any of the methods or instruments
used for measuring indicator cards.

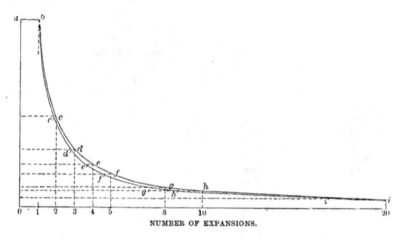

NUMBER OF EXPANSIONS.

FIG. 39.

Such a steam line or expansion curve for dry steam having been drawn,
see Fig. 39, and the areas measured: first, of the rectangle o a b 1 and next,
for the area under the curve, we find the quotient of the area under the
curve divided by the rectangle area for different expansions to be as follows:

	Area under curve.	Area under curve. Rectangle.
1		0
2	1 b c 2	0.68
3	1 b d 3	1.12
4	1 b e 4	1.33
5	1 b f 5	1.53
8	1 b g 8	1.97
0	1 b h 10	2.14
0	1 b i 20	2.73

Now, assuming 85 pounds as an average steam pressure, or, 15 + 85 =
100 pounds above zero, we have for the external work of evaporation, 81
units, and for the total internal work 1,100 units. Now, taking the rectangle o a b 1 in the figure as representing the work of 81 units, it is clear
that the work of expansion, in units of heat, will be obtained by multiply-

ing the 81 units by the number given in the quotients above, which will give values as follows:

r	Heat units in work of expansion.
1.....	0
2...	55
3...	91
4...	108
5...	124
8...	160
10...	173
20...	221

The terminal pressures are found by division and subtraction:

$$\frac{85 + 15}{r} - 15.$$

The corresponding internal heats for dry steam are given in the following table:

r	Terminal pressure.	Internal heat.	Heat units in work of expansion.	Heat units left after deducting work of expansion from 1,100 units.
1...................	85	1,100	0	1,100
2...................	33	1,090	55	1,045
3...................	16	1,083	91	1,009
4...................	8	1,079	108	992
5...................	3	1,079	124	976
8...................	4	1,071	160	940
10...................	6	1,069	173	927
20...................	11	1,060	221	879

Now the internal heat at the end of expansion is less than that given for dry steam at the same pressure; therefore, a part of the heat for expansion must have been furnished by the condensation of a portion of the steam. But such condensation reduces the work of expansion itself and hence the condensation supplies heat again and so on. The correct values for the curve in a non-conducting cylinder are approximated as follows:

r	Heat in dry steam.	Heat at end of expansion.	Excess required from condensation.	Change in Units.	Change in Excess.
1	1,100	1,100	0	0	....
2	1,089	1,045	44	2	42
3	1,084	1,009	75	7	72
4	1,080	992	88	9	79
5	1,079	976	103	12	91
8	1,071	940	131	20	111
10	1,069	927	142	23	119
20	1,060	879	181	38	143

But these values are now in error, for the one is assumed on the basis of more external work than has been done, and the other on less. The true value lies between them, and the assumption that the true value divides the difference in the proportion of the values found gives us a close approximation.

r	Per cent. of change.	Change in units.	Excess required from condensation.		Work of expansion.
			In units.	Per cent.	Gain.
1					
2	95	2	44	4	0.67
3	91	6	78	7	1.11
4	90	8	87	8	1.31
5	88	11	102	9	1.50
8	85	17	127	12	1.90
10	84	19	139	12	2.05
20	79	30	182	17	2.55

From the curve already drawn for Dry steam, we draw the new curve by changing the points for volume, reducing it by deducting the percentage for condensation. The points so found are marked on Fig. 39, with the same letter accentuated. A comparison of the areas under the new curve, between the same volumes, will give the last column of figures.

A similar curve drawn for steam at 25 pounds pressure, does not differ in the second place of decimals, and for steam at 185 pounds it only differs by 1 in the second decimals for ten expansions. The approximation made is within one heat unit and we may therefore use these results hereafter with confidence, remembering that we must obtain the last column for corresponding values of r for volumes not pressures.

The curve of expansion of steam in a non conducting cylinder has been called by Prof. Rankine, an "Adiabatic" curve, and by Prof. Clausius an "Isentropic" curve, and these terms may be met with in all works on steam, frequently adding to the difficulties of the student. They will, therefore, not be used, nor referred to, again in this work.

The amount of steam required to do the work in a non-conducting cylinder is found by dividing the amount per total horse power per hour for a non-expanding cylinder by 1, plus the ratio given in the last column of the preceding table, or, the ratio of the total work done compared with that done at boiler pressure.

From a large diagram constructed by the process described we have tabulated the following values:

PROPERTIES OF THE CURVE OF EXPANSION IN A NON-CONDUCTING CYLINDER.

No. of Expansions.	Ratio of Total Area to Area of Rectangle.	Ratio of Mean Total to Initial Total Pressure.	Ratio of Total Terminal to Initial Pressure.
1.1	1.090	0.991	0.90
1.2	1.180	.983	.82
1.3	1.261	.970	.75
1.4	1.333	.952	.69
1.5	1.396	.931	.64
1.6	1.459	.912	.59
1.8	1.576	.866	.52
2.0	1.666	.833	.46
2.5	1.873	.749	.36
3.0	2.035	.678	.30
4.0	2.278	.568	.21
5.0	2.476	.495	.17
6.0	2.629	.436	.14
7.0	2.746	.393	.12
8.0	2.854	.357	.10
9.0	2.953	.328	.087
10.0	3.034	.303	.077
11.0	3.106	.282	.070
12.0	3.169	.264	.063
13.0	3.232	.248	.058
14.0	3.286	.235	.053
16.0	3.385	.211	.046
20.0	3.547	.177	.036
25.0	3.709	.148	.028
30.0	3.835	.128	.023

From the preceding table, and the table of external work of steam, the following table is computed. The first line, or steam used for one expansion, or full stroke, is obtained, as already explained, by dividing 2,565, the number of units of heat for a horse-power per hour, by the number of units of heat for external work; and the other quantities by dividing these numbers by the gain by expansion, or ratio of total area of figure to area of rectangle. This has also been explained. From the ratio of total mean pressure to initial pressure, the three next tables are computed, by assuming that a back pressure of 4 pounds per square inch exists in the condensing. and 16 pounds, or 1.3 pounds above the atmosphere, in the non-condensing engine. In each case the mean total pressure is found and the back pressure deducted. The quantity of water per total horse-power is then multiplied by the ratio of the mean total to the mean indicated pressure, or the pressure left to act on the piston after deducting the back pressure, 4 or 16 pounds respectively, to obtain the consumption of water per indicated horse-power per hour in a nonconducting cylinder.

COST PER HOUR PER TOTAL HORSE-POWER, IN POUNDS, IN DRY STEAM IF WORKED IN NON-CONDUCTING CYLINDERS.

No. of Expansions.	BOILER PRESSURE IN POUNDS PER SQUARE INCH.									
	Atmos. 0	20	40	60	80	100	120	140	180	220
1	35.7	33.7	32.9	32.5	32.1	31.7	31.3	30.9	30.5	30.2
1.1	32.7	31.0	30.9	29.8	29.4	29.0	28.7	28.3	28.0	27.7
1.2	30.2	28.6	27.9	27.5	27.2	26.8	26.5	26.2	25.9	25.5
1.3	27.6	26.2	25.5	25.2	24.8	24.5	24.2	23.9	23.7	23.4
1.4	26.1	24.7	24.1	23.8	23.5	23.2	22.9	22.6	22.4	22.1
1.5	24.9	23.6	23.0	22.7	22.4	22.2	21.9	21.6	21.4	21.1
1.6	24.4	23.1	22.5	22.2	22.0	21.6	21.4	21.2	20.9	20.7
1.8	22.9	21.7	22.1	20.8	20.6	20.3	20.1	19.8	19.6	19.4
2.0	21.4	20.3	19.7	19.5	19.2	19.0	18.8	18.5	18.3	18.1
2.5	19.0	18.0	17.6	17.3	17.0	16.9	16.7	16.5	16.3	16.1
3.0	17.5	16.6	16.2	16.0	15.8	15.6	15.4	15.2	15.0	14.8
4.0	15.7	14.9	14.5	14.3	14.1	13.9	13.8	13.6	13.4	13.3
5.0	14.4	13.6	13.3	13.1	13.0	12.8	12.6	12.5	12.3	12.2
6.0	13.6	12.9	12.6	12.4	12 2	12.1	11.9	11.8	11.6	11.5
7.0	13.0	12.3	11.9	11.8	11.7	11.5	11.4	11.2	11.1	11.0
8.0	12.5	11.8	11.5	11.4	11.2	11.1	11.0	10.8	10.7	10.6
9.0	12.0	11.4	11.1	11.0	10.8	10.7	10.6	10.4	10.3	10.2
10.0	11.7	11.1	10.8	10.7	10.6	10.4	10.3	10.2	10.1	10.0
11.0	11.5	10.9	10.6	10.4	10.3	10.2	10.1	10.0	9.8	9.7
12.0	11.3	10.7	10.4	10.3	10.1	10.0	9.9	9.8	9.6	9.5
13.0	11.1	10.5	10.2	10.1	9.9	9.8	9.7	9 6	9.5	9.4
14.0	10.8	10.3	10.0	9.9	9.8	9.6	9.5	9.4	9.3	9.2
16.0	10.5	10.0	9.7	9.6	9.5	9.4	9.3	9.1	9.0	8.9
20.0	10.0	9.5	9.3	9.2	9.0	8.9	8.8	8.7	8.6	8.5
25.0	9.6	9.1	8.9	8.7	8.6	8.5	8.4	8.3	8.2	8.1
30.0	9.1	8.8	8.6	8.5	8.4	8.3	8.2	8.1	8.0	7.9

MEAN TOTAL PRESSURE IN POUNDS PER SQUARE INCH IN NON-CONDUCTING CYLINDERS.

No. of Expansions.	INITIAL PRESSURE ABOVE ATMOSPHERE.									
	0	20	40	60	80	100	120	140	180	220
1.1	14.9	34.7	54.5	74.3	94.1	114	134	154	193	233
1.2	14.7	34.4	54.1	73.7	93.4	113	133	152	192	231
1.3	14.5	33.9	53.4	72.8	92.1	112	131	150	189	228
1.4	14.2	33.3	52.4	71.6	90.5	109	129	148	186	224
1.5	14.0	32.6	51.2	69.7	88.4	107	126	144	181	219
1.6	13.7	31.9	50.2	68.4	86.6	105	123	141	178	214
1.8	13.0	30.3	47.6	94.9	82.2	99.5	117	134	169	203
2.0	12.5	29.2	45.8	63.9	79.1	95.8	112	126	162	196
2.5	11.2	26.2	41.2	56.2	71.2	86.2	101	116	146	176
3.0	10.2	23.7	37.3	50.9	64.4	78.0	91.6	105	132	159
4.0	8.5	19.9	31.2	42.6	54.0	65.3	76.7	88.0	111	133
5.0	7.4	17.3	27.2	37.1	47.0	56.9	66.8	76.7	96.5	116
6.0	6.6	15.3	24.0	32.7	41.5	50.2	58.9	67.7	85.1	103
7.0	5.9	13.7	21.6	30.1	37.3	46.2	52.9	60.8	76.5	92.2
8.0	5.3	12.5	19.6	26.7	33.9	41.0	48.1	55.3	69.5	83 8
9.0	4.9	11.5	18.0	24.6	31.2	37.7	44.3	50.9	64.0	77.1
10.0	4.6	10.6	16.7	22.8	28.8	34.9	41.0	47.0	59.2	71.3
11.0	4.2	10.1	15.5	21.2	26.8	32.5	38.1	43.8	55.0	66.4
12.0	4.0	9.2	14.5	19.8	25.0	30.3	35.6	41.8	51.0	62.0
13.0	3.7	8.7	13.6	18.6	23.7	29.2	33.5	38.4	48.4	58.3
14.0	3.5	8.2	12.9	17.6	22.3	27.0	31.7	36.4	45.8	55.2
16.0	3.2	7.4	11.6	15.9	20.1	24.3	28.6	32.8	41.2	49.7
20.0	2.7	6.2	9.8	13.3	16.8	20.4	23.9	27.5	34.5	41.7
25.0	2.2	5.2	8 2	11.1	14.1	17.1	20.0	23.0	28.9	34.9
30.0	1.9	4.5	7.0	9.6	12.1	14.7	17.3	19.8	24.9	30.0

MEAN EFFECTIVE PRESSURE IN CONDENSING ENGINES, NON-CONDUCTING CYLINDERS.

No. of Expansions.	INITIAL PRESSURE ABOVE ATMOSPHERE, IN POUNDS PER SQUARE INCH.									
	0	20	40	60	80	100	120	140	180	220
1.1	10.9	30.7	50.5	70.3	90.1	110	130	150	189	229
1.2	10.7	30.4	50.1	69.7	89.4	109	129	148	188	227
1.3	10.5	29.9	49.4	68.8	88.1	108	127	146	185	224
1.4	10.2	29.3	48.4	67.6	86.5	105	125	144	182	220
1.5	10.0	28.6	47.2	65.7	84.4	103	122	140	177	215
1.6	9.7	27.9	46.2	64.4	82.6	101	119	137	174	210
1.8	9.0	26.3	43.6	60.9	78.2	95.5	113	130	165	199
2.0	8.5	25.2	41.8	59.9	75.1	91.8	108	122	158	192
2.5	7.2	22.2	37.2	52.2	67.2	82.2	97	112	142	172
3.0	6.2	19.7	33.3	46.9	60.4	74.0	87.6	101	128	155
4.0	4.5	15.9	27.2	38.6	50.0	61.3	72.7	84.0	107	129
5.0	3.4	13.3	23.2	33.1	43.0	52.9	62.8	72.7	92.5	112
6.0	2.6	11.3	20.0	28.7	37.5	46.2	54.9	63.7	81.1	99
7.0	1.9	9.7	17.6	26.1	33.3	42.2	48.9	56.8	72.5	88.2
8.0	1.3	8.5	15.6	22.7	29.9	37.0	44.1	51.3	65.5	79.8
9.0	0.9	7.5	14.0	20.6	27.2	33.7	40.3	46.9	64.0	73.1
10.0	0.6	6.6	12.7	18.8	24.8	30.9	37.0	43.0	55.2	67.3
11.0	0.2	6.1	11.5	17.2	22.8	28.5	34.1	39.8	51.0	62.4
12.0	0	5.2	10.5	15.8	21.0	26.3	31.6	37.8	47.0	58.0
13.0	....	4.7	9.6	14.6	19.7	25.2	29.5	34.4	44.4	54.3
14.0	....	4.2	8.9	13.6	18.3	23.0	27.7	32.4	41.8	51.2
16.0	....	3.4	7.6	11.9	16.1	20.3	24.6	28.8	37.2	45.7
20.0	....	2.2	5.8	9.3	12.8	16.4	19.9	23.5	30.5	37.7
25.0	....	1.2	4.2	7.1	10.1	13.1	16.0	19.0	24.9	30.9
30.0	....	0.5	3.0	5.6	8.1	10.7	13.3	15.8	20.9	26.0

MEAN EFFECTIVE PRESSURE, IN POUNDS PER SQUARE INCH, IN NON-CONDENSING ENGINES, NON-CONDUCTING CYLINDERS.

No. of Expansions.	INITIAL PRESSURE ABOVE ATMOSPHERE IN POUNDS PER SQUARE INCH.									
	0	20	40	60	80	100	120	140	180	220
1.1	....	16.7	36.5	56.3	76.1	96	116	136	175	215
1.2	....	16.4	36.1	55.7	75.4	95	115	134	174	213
1.3	....	15.9	35.4	54.8	74.1	94	113	132	171	210
1.4	....	15.3	34.4	53.6	72.5	91	111	130	168	206
1.5	....	14.6	33.2	51.7	70.4	89	108	126	163	201
1.6	....	13.9	32.2	50.4	68.6	87	105	123	160	196
1.8	....	12.3	29.6	46.9	64.6	81.5	99	116	151	185
2.0	....	11.2	27.8	45.9	61.1	77.8	94	108	144	178
2.5	....	8.2	23.2	38.2	53.2	68.2	93	98	128	158
3.0	....	5.7	19.3	32.9	46.4	60.0	73.6	87	114	141
4.0	....	1.9	13.2	24.6	36.0	47.3	58.7	70.0	93	115
5.0	....	....	9.2	19.1	29.0	38.9	48.8	58.7	78.5	98
6.0	....	....	6.0	14.7	23.5	32.2	40.9	49.7	67.1	85
7.0	....	....	3.6	12.1	19.3	28.2	34.9	42.8	58.5	74.2
8.0	....	....	1.6	8.7	15.9	23.0	30.1	37.3	51.5	65.8
9.0	....	....	....	6.6	13.2	19.7	26.3	32.9	46.0	59.1
10.0	....	....	....	4.8	10.8	16.9	23.0	19.0	41.2	53.3
11.0	....	....	....	3.2	8.8	14.5	20.1	25.8	27.0	48.4
12.0	....	....	....	1.8	7.0	12.3	17.6	23.8	33.0	44.0
13.0	....	....	....	0.6	5.7	11.2	15.5	20.4	30.4	40.3
14.0	....	....	....	....	4.3	9.0	13.7	18.4	27.8	37.2
16.0	....	....	....	....	2.1	6.3	10.6	14.8	23.2	31.7
20.0	....	....	....	....	....	2.4	5.9	9.5	16.5	23.7
25.0	....	....	....	....	....	....	2.0	5.0	10.9	16.9
30.0	....	....	....	....	....	....	....	1.8	6.9	12.0

DATA FURNISHED BY EXPERIMENT.

In comparing the accompanying tables with the performance of actual
engines the back pressure may be found to vary from the 4 or 16 pounds
per square inch mentioned, so that the consumption of water is only
tabulated per total horse-power at present, and the comparisons made on
this basis are not affected by the back pressure.

In comparing experiments made upon the performance of actual engines, the fact must not be forgotten that the value of the results depend
on the data which have been used and the skill of the experimenters;
hence, it will differ. The most valuable data are those in which both the
heat received and the heat rejected by the engine have been measured.
These require measurements, preferably by weight, of the feed water furnished to the boiler, the pressure and temperature of evaporation, and
the dryness of the steam near the engine; the work done in the cylinder,
the quantity of injection water and its rise in temperature; the difference
between the heat delivered added to the work done by the engine; while
the heat received furnishes an important check. To appreciate the value
of this check one should examine some of the first experiments in which
this measurement was attempted, and which may be found in the Bulletin
de Societé Industrielle de Mulhouse for 1857; and the record of Hirn's experiments show the difficulties he overcame.

First, reliable experimental data can only be obtained from Stationary
Condensing Engines, on account of the impossibility of measuring condensing water: the difficulty of measuring the feed water precludes the
use of marine engines for such a purpose.

Next in point of value are experiments where the heat received and
delivered are carefully ascertained, either by measurements of the feed and
priming, or the water of condensation, and its rise in temperature. The
latter is the easiest measurement to be taken, but, for the most reliable
data is restricted to stationary condensing engines. Measurements of feed
water and priming can be made in all classes of engines, with the exception of large marine engines at sea, where the difficulty of getting at the
quantity of feed water has not yet been overcome, though it perhaps might
be by the use of a water meter.

Third in point of value are long-continued experiments made on engines in which the feed water only is noted, but in which the boilers are so
large that the priming may be neglected. Such are most of the experiments made by the United States Naval authorities.

Next to the latter in point of scientific value, but first in practical interest, are the records of the performances of the large ocean steamships
as to fuel used and power developed in long voyages; and again, the records
of the duty of pumping engines. In such records it is impossible to separate the performances of engine and boiler, but the results are comprehensive and of great value.

Last in point of value are short experiments in which the fuel or the
feed-water is measured, in some indirect manner, and the engine "indicated" only, as, of course it must be.

We give, in the following table, some engine trials made by various authorities, classing them under the three first summaries of value given above, as A, B and C. This table might be greatly extended, but only by the admission of experiments which are either isolated, improbable, or deficient in the required data.

A very casual examination of the table shows us that economy of steam is promoted by high pressure and high speed, while the cost in steam of a total horse-power is lessened by large expansion, and the cost of a net horse-power is least with moderate expansion.

Another fact brought prominently to the front is that the actual use of steam is very far in excess of that given by our tables for a non-conducting cylinder. This excess is due to several causes:

1. To the use of wet steam.
2. To the loss by clearance space.
3. To external radiation and loss of heat.
4. To internal radiation and the transfer of heat between the iron of the cylinder and its contained steam.

For our purpose we shall not individually consider these four causes of loss, but we may take up our table of experimental data and compute from the tables already given the amount of steam that would be used by a non-conducting cylinder, working with steam of the same initial pressure and expansion. Deducting this quantity from the quantity actually used we will examine the excess to ascertain what law, if any, can be found to account for it.

ENGINE TRIALS.—Single Cylinder Engines.

No. for Reference	Authority	Diameter of Cylinder (Inches)	Stroke (Inches)	Revolutions Per Minute	No. Indicated Horse-Power	Initial Steam Pressure, Absolute	Ratio of Expansion	Water Per Hour			Remarks	Class	Location
								Per Indicated Horse-Power	Per Total Horse-Power	Per Net Horse-Power			
1	Hallauer	24	78	30.41	106	56	7	19.38	17.24	21.9	Unjacketed.	Class A	Alsace.
2	"	"	"	30.65	144	52	4	20.92	18.61	22.8	Saturated steam.	"	"
3	"	"	"	29.98	112	56	7	16.24	14.67	18.0	Superheated steam, 196° C.	"	"
4	"	"	48	30.17	152	55	4	16.82	15.43	18.1	231° C.	"	"
5	"	"	"	30.31	124	55	2	19.07	17.35	21.0	273° C.	"	"
6	"	"	"	50.41	104	68	11	17.59	15.84	20.0	Jacketed Corliss.	"	"
7	"	"	"	51.12	135	66	8	17.50	15.95	19.2	"	"	"
8	"	"	"	49.34	156	68	6	17.53	16.10	19.0	"	"	"
9	J. W. Hill.	18	48	75	163	97	6.67	19.5	17.1		3 Unjacketed Corliss.	"	Cincinnati.
10	"Engineering."	27½	59	39.3	396	75	12	19.0	16.3	21.2	Double-jacketed Sulzer.	Class B	Augsburg.
11	"	32	48	82.8	540	70	4.1	20.5			"	"	"
12	Mass. Inst. Tech.	8	24	60	7.65	50	4	48.2	27.7		Condensing no vacuum.	"	Boston.
13	"	"	"	"	12.29		2.2	42.2	29.1		"	"	"
14	"	"	"	"	15.68		1.4	45.3	33.5		"	"	"
15	"	"	"	"	6.83		4	35.2	19.4		Superheated, 175°	"	"
16	"	"	"	"	12.37		2.2	31.7	21.7		139°	"	"
17	"	"	"	"	15.63		1.4	35.8	26.5		103°	"	"
18	B. F. Isherwood.	96	96	20.6	301	32.2	1.16	39.9	35.0	43.0	Unjacketed.	Class C	U.S.S. Michigan.
19	"	"	"	15.6	211	31.4	1.53	34.8	30.9	37.7	"	"	"
20	"	"	"	17.3	204	33.0	2.17	33.1	29.4	36.2	"	"	"
21	"	"	"	13.7	134	33.4	3.17	35.2	30.6	34.4	"	"	"
22	"	"	"	13.9	118	33.3	3.68	34.5	29.8	39.2	"	"	"
23	"	"	"	11.2	75	33.2	5.15	37.0	30.7	43.8	"	"	"
24	"	"	"	14.1	61	33.0	8.33	46.1	32.0	66.5	"	"	"

Class C U.S.R.S. Dexter

U.S. R. S. Dains.

U. S. R. S. Gallatin.

C. E. Emery.

	Description									
25	Unjacketed.	26.1	21.7	23.9	4.45	80.4	186	56.5	36	26
26	"	26.2	21.9	24.1	3.67	79.3	228	64.3		
27	"	26.0	21.8	23.9	3.50	79.2	219	61.0		
28	"	25.2	21.6	24.3	2.72	77.0	292	72.8		
29	"	32.6	25.6	28.8	3.34	52.3	124	59.8		
30	Single unjacketed cylinder.	32.1	25.9	28.9	2.42	51.4	162	55.2	30	36
31	"	34.9	28.2	31.8	2.08	54.6	196	60.7		
32	"	30.8	23.0	26.7	5.1	46.9	138	48.7		
33	"	29.5	13.3	27.0	3.4	47.9	187	56.9		
34	"	30.1	23.1	26.9	3.1	46.6	221	61.5		
35	"	32.1	24.8	28.9	2.9	45.9	243	64.5		
36	"	34.6	26.5	31.0	2.3	39.4	235	63.5		34.1
37	"	33.1	19.2	30.0	4.37	83.7	170	46.7		
38	"	32.1	19.4	29.3	3.48	79.1	205	51.7		
39	{ Condensing without vacuum. Jacket off.	28.4	16.9	25.9	4.07	82.6	190	49.5		
40	{ Condensing without vacuum. Jacket on.	29.9	18.1	27.3	3.52	78.8	212	53.2		
41	Cut-off and jacket off.	27.2	21.2	25.2	2.47	66.9	298	62.0		
42	" on.	24.9	19.9	23.0	3.45	70.2	238	58.6		
43	"	26.1	20.6	24.2	2.37	63.6	284	60.9		
44	Jacket off, steam chest drained.	23.4	19.8	21.7	4.90	82.4	289	60.2		
45	"	24.7	20.5	22.9	4.00	73.2	287	69.0		
46	Jacket on from boiler.	25.5	20.7	23.5	4.87	82.0	255	58.5		
47	"	27.4	22.3	25.3	3.83	78.0	282	61.6		
48	Jacket off.	26.4	21.5	24.3	4.46	76.1	269	60.5		
49	"	27.7	21.3	25.0	7.78	83.4	185	32.3		
50	"	29.9	20.6	21.8	5.03	80.8	231	56.0		
51	"	23.6	19.6	21.9	4.93	81.7	280	59.9		
52	"	25.8	21.5	24.0	4.25	74.0	243	59.5		
53	Jacket on.	23.8	19.7	24.3	4.50	77.8	282	61.6		
54	"	22.5	18.2	20.5	7.31	85.0	197	51.1		
55	"	22.3	18.3	20.6	5.68	85.3	270	58.6		
56	"	22.2	18.6	20.7	4.98	83.5	306	61.2		
57	"	23.0	19.2	21.4	4.46	81.7	296	61.3		
58	"	23.0	19.2	21.5	4.19	80.7	348	68.7		
59	"	47.9	32.8	40.4	2.01	25.3	87	40.0		
60	"	52.3	35.7	44.2	1.61	23.7	90	40.9		
61	"	39.1	27.4	33.3	2.00	26.3	95	41.3		
62	"	43.9	30.2	37.4	1.59	24.1	98	42.4		
63	"	40.4	28.6	34.0	1.80	23.9	90	41.1		
64	"	40.6	29.1	34.9	1.54	2471	103	42.3		
65	Jacket off.	29.6	22.4	26.0	5.92	56.2	123	43.0		
66	"	30.3	23.0	26.7	5.21	52.7	127	44.2		
67	"	26.5	21.3	24.0	3.73	55.8	182	50.8		

ENGINE TRIALS.—SINGLE CYLINDER ENGINES.
Continued.

No. for Reference.	AUTHORITY.	Diameter of Cylinder.	Stroke	Revolutions per Minute.	No. Indicated Horse-Power.	Initial Steam Pressure, Absolute.	Ratio of Expansion.	WATER PER HOUR. Per Indicated Horse-Power.	Per Total Horse-Power.	Per Net Horse-Power.	REMARKS.	CLASS.	LOCATION.
		Inches.	Inches.										
68	C. E. Emery.	34.1	30	50.1	182	51.8	3.16	26.3	22.5	29.0	Jacket off.	Class C	U. S. R. S. Gallatin.
69	"	"	"	56.0	237	52.3	2.72	24.5	21.8	26.6	"	"	"
70	"	"	"	55.7	237	50.3	2.23	28.0	23.4	30.6	Jacket on.	"	"
71	"	"	"	52.7	219	44.7	1.41	26.9	26.9	32.2	"	"	"
72	"	"	"	44.3	121	58.0	6.07	22.9	19.3	26.2	"	"	"
73	"	"	"	46.0	137	63.9	5.07	24.0	20.8	27.1	"	"	U. S. Eutaw.
74	"	"	"	45.9	136	54.6	4.82	22.4	19.3	25.3	"	"	"
75	"	"	"	50.3	163	54.7	4.49	24.8	21.4	27.8	"	"	"
76	"	"	"	49.2	166	54.7	3.71	23.2	20.1	25.8	"	"	"
77	"	"	"	51.	185	52.4	3.32	25.7	21.8	28.4	"	"	"
78	"	"	"	34.5	213	49.3	2.40	23.0	23.0	27.7	"	"	"
79	"	"	"	58.3	255	50.4	2.21	26.5	23.4	23.8	"	"	"
80	B. F. Isherwood.	38	105	5.49	154	25	3.37	39.6	36.4	42.8	Unjacketed cylinder.	"	"
81	"	"	"	6.58	229	25	2.70	30.6	29.2	32.6	"	"	"
82	"	"	"	8.60	373	25	1.86	32.7	32.7	34.3	"	"	"
83	"	"	"	7.51	282	22	1.86	36.6	32.1	38.8	"	"	"
84	"	"	"	9.19	415	23	1.64	31.4	30.5	32.9		"	"
85	"	"	"	6.50	218	26	2.70	29.2	26.5	32.6	Superheated, 97°	"	"
86	"	"	"	9.00	391	27	1.86	27.8	26.2	29.2	88°	"	"
87	"	"	"	6.50	207	26	2.92	30.1	28.8	32.2	125°	"	"
88	"	"	"	9.15	407	26	1.86	25.1	24.4	26.3	124°	"	"
89	"	"	"	9.46	453	26	1.64	27.1	26.5	28.4	122°	"	"
90	C. A. Smith.	85	120	12.4	765	40	3.5	24.5	19.6	......	Without jacket	"	St. Louis Water Works, No. 1

DOUBLE CYLINDER ENGINES.

No.	Name	Cylinders										Description	Remarks
91	C. E. Emery.	24 and 38	27	70.8	266	82	6.2	18.4	16.1	20.5		Jacketed.	Class C U. S. R. S. Rush.
92			"	55.5	167	50	4.0	22.1	18.8	25.7		"	"
93	M. Longridge.	27 and 45	72	42	493	84	10	16.7	12.7	.....			Oak Mill, Farnsworth.
94	"	"	"	42	486	84	11	16.8	13.1	.....			"
95	"	"	"	42	493	63	6.25	18.1	14.4	.....			"
96	"	"	"	42	487	63	7.1			.....			"
97	"	"	"	42	490			18.1	14.4	.....			Mean of 2 preceding.
98	"	20 and 34	60	48	313	96.4	8.27	16.7	14.5	.....			Class A Blackburn.
99	"	"	"	48	314	96.7	8.78	17.4	14.9			Unjacketed.	"
100	"	"	"	48	319	97.1	8.71	17.1	15.0			Low pressure jacketed.	"
101	"	"	"	48	314	98.8	9.82	16.8	14.5			Receiver	"
102	"	"	"	48	313	96.5	8.58	16.1	14.0			All	"
103	"	"	"	48	314	95.2	8.29	16.2	14.7			High pressure	"
104	"	"	"	48	338	94.7	8.49	17.0	14.7			None / All	"
105	Hallauer.	21.7 / 39.3	56.3	25.25	342	72	9	19.0	15.7	21.7			Munster.
106	"	"	78.7	25.20	263	60	7	19.3	15.3	22.8		Beam engine.	"
107	"	"	"	25.4	182	50	5	21.4	15.3	27.3		"	Malmerapach.
108	"	"	"	24.18	199	67	6	19.5	16.3	22.7		"	"
109	"	"	"	25.47	212	70	13	18.0	15.1	20.9		"	"
110	"	"	"	24.83	217	70	13	18.1	15.4	21.0		Horizontal engine.	"
111	"	"	"	26.20	141	67	28	18.2	17.0	22.0		"	"
112	"	"	"	25.93	147	67	25	18.2	15.0	21.8		"	"
113	"	"	"	39.37	128	53	6	20.1	16.1	23.3		"	"
114	"	15.1 × 34.3	51.7	39.67	180	54	6	19.6	16.1	22.0		"	"
115	B. F. Isherwood.	9 and 16	18	221.5	150	134.8	7.1	16.3	12.0	17.6		Superheated, 62°	Class B S. S. Leila.
116	"	"	"	215.9	145	130.7	7.1	16.0	12.2	17.2		69°	"
117	"	"	"	192.2	100	109.0	7.9	16.7	12.7	18.4		37°	"
118	"	"	"	181.1	86	97.6	8.2	17.4	13.0	19.4		34°	"
119	"	"	"	166.5	64	83.7	8.2	18.7	13.9	21.4		30°	"
120	"	"	"	145.4	43	64.6	7.9	20.9	15.1	25.0		18°	"
121	"	"	"	111.5	21	42.5	7.8	24.9	16.5	33.6		2°	"
122	"	"	"	94.7	13	32.3	7.7	32.7	18.3	50.7		0°	"
123	"	"	"	188.1	94	114.1	8.3	18.5	14.8	20.4		43°	"
124	"	"	"	167.3	60	87.3	8.4	20.1	15.4	23.2		36°	"
125	"	"	"	145.9	39	66.7	8.0	23.9	17.2	29.0		32°	"
126	"	"	"	197.9	108	77.5	3.2	21.0	15.0	23.0		52°	"
127	"	"	"	129.6	33	33.1	3.2	28.6	19.8	34.7		43°	"
128	"	"	"	189.5	84	70.6	3.2	28.1	21.3	31.5		49°	"
129	"	"	"	191.6	99	54.5	2.6	25.4	21.0	27.4		52°	"
130	"	"	"	147.6	42	30.9	2.4	31.9	24.8	36.6		42°	Large cyl. only.

ENGINE TRIALS.—DOUBLE CYLINDER ENGINES.

Continued.

No. for Reference.	AUTHORITY.	Diameter of Cylinder.	Stroke.	Revolutions per Min'te.	No. I.H.P.	Int'l Steam Pressure. Absolute.	Ratio of Expansion.	WATER PER HOUR. Per I.H.P.	Per T.H.P.	Per N.H.P.	REMARKS.	CLASS.	LOCATION.
131	B. F. Isherwood.	Inches. 10½ & 18	Inches. 18	146.5	66.7	.....	12.9	17.9	13.5	20.7			Class B S. S. Siesta.
132	"	"	"	169.4	85.0	.....	9.5	18.9	13.7	21.6			"
133	"	"	"	170.3	88.1	.....	9.6	17.9	14.0	20.2			"
134	"	"	"	190.2	131.2	.....	5.9	16.7	12.1	18.4			"
135	"	"	"	177.9	100.9	.....	6.2	18.5	13.1	29.8			"
136	"	"	"	178.5	105.3	.....	6.4	18.0	14.0	20.1			"
137	"	"	"	174.3	92.9	.....	6.3	20.6	16.5	23.0			"
138	"	"	"	177.1	96.9	.....	6.0	20.6	16.5	23.2			"
139	"	"	"	176.7	106.9	.....	5.8	19.2	16.1	21.4			"
140	"	"	"	193.2	141.0	.....	3.2	21.0	14.8	21.9			Large cyl. only.
141	"	"	"	185.3	113.1	.....	3.3	24.8	19.5	27.6			"
142	"	"	"	184.4	119.3	.....	3.3	23.8	19.3	26.3			"

J. G. MAIR'S EXPERIMENTS.

No. for Reference.	Authority.	Diam. of Cyl. and Stroke.	Revolut'ns per	No. I. H. P.	Ratio of Expans'n.	Steam Pressure. Absolute.	DRY STEAM Per I. H. P.	Per T. H.P.	Class.	Remarks.
143	J. G. Mair.	Inches. 45×66	14.62	101.78	6.5	48	22.06	19.52	Class B	Jackets on.
144	"	22×43	17.84	75.9	9.3	58	26.62	23.13	Class A	" off.
145	"	34×66	19.62	75.2	15.76	62	17.34	15.32	"	" " on.
146	"	24½×41	38.73	267.86	9.64	85	17.73	16.7	Class B	" " "
147	"	38×66	34.22	267.95	9.56	88	17.39	16.49	"	" " off.
148	"	15¾ & 28½ × 56	34.52	267.92	7.77	89	19.24	17.85	"	None.
149	"		80.45	120.30	11.48	85	21.65	17.66	Class A	
150	"		81.51	149.75	11.64	85	20.88	17.64	"	
151	"	21 and 36 × 60	23.98	127.4	13.61	76	14.84	13.67	"	On and interheater
152	"	68¾×96	12.84	.....			24.15	19.21	"	Cornish.

SINGLE UNJACKETED CYLINDERS.

To continue our investigation, we may set forth our results, obtained from the foregoing table, as follows:

U. S. S. S. "MICHIGAN."

	Steam used per to-tal horse-power per hour.	Steam used in Non-conducting Cylin-der per tot'l horse-power per hour.	Excess per total horse-power per hour.	Excess per hour used.
1	35	29	6	2,065
2	30.9	23.3	7.6	1,709
3	29.4	20.0	9.4	2,160
4	30.6	16.3	14.3	2,200
5	29.8	15.4	14.4	2,071
6	30.7	13.5	17.2	1,552
7	32.0	11.7	20.3	1,782
		13,539 ÷ 7 = 1,934 pounds, mean.		13,539

The excess found clearly follows no law connected with the expansion, and we shall hereafter be justified in taking the mean value as that to be followed.

U. S. R. S. "DALLAS."

	Steam used per to-tal horse-power per hour.	Steam used in Non-conducting Cylin-der per tot'l horse-power per hour.	Excess per total horse-power per hour.	Excess per hour used.
8	23.0	13.2	9.8	1,562
9	23.3	16.0	7.3	1,584
10	23.1	16.2	6.9	1,778
11	24.8	16.3	8.5	2,400
12	26.5	19.5	7.0	1,935
		9,259 ÷ 5 = 1,852 pounds, mean.		9,259

U. S. R. S. "DEXTER."

13	21.7	13.6	8.1	1,660
14	21.9	14.7	7.2	1,810
15	21.8	15.0	6.8	1,420
16	21.6	16.4	5.2	1,710
		6,600 ÷ 4 = 1,650 pounds, mean.		6,600
17	25.6	15.9	9.7	1,360
18	25.9	18.0	7.9	1,430
19	28.2	19.7	8.5	1,870
		4,660 ÷ 3 = 1,553 pounds, mean.		4,660

SINGLE UNJACKETED CYLINDERS.—*Continued.*

U. S. R. S. "GALLATIN."

	Steam used per total horse-power per hour.	Steam used in Non-conducting Cylinder per tot'l horse-power per hour.	Excess per total horse-power per hour.	Excess per hour used.
20	19.2	13.8	5.4	1,430
21	19.4	15.1	4.3	1,330
22	21.2	17.2	4.0	1,420
		4,180 ÷ 3 = 1,393 pounds, mean.		4,180
23	19.8	13.1	6.7	2,120
24	20.5	14.3	6.2	1,990
25	21.5	13.6	7.9	2,410
26	21.3	11.3	10.0	2,170
27	20.6	12.4	8.2	2,200
28	19.6	13.1	6.5	2,030
29	21.5	14.0	7.5	2,360
		15,280 ÷ 7 = 2,183 pounds, mean.		15,280
30	22.4	12.5	9.9	1,450
31	23.0	13.2	9.8	1,440
32	21.3	14.9	6.4	1,310
33	21.8	16.9	4.9	1,310
34	23.4	18.7	4.7	1,340
		6,850 ÷ 5 = 1,370 pounds, mean.		6,850

MILLERS' EXHIBITION AT CINCINNATI.

35 36 37	17.1	11.5	5.6	1,058

HIRN'S ENGINE.

38	17.24	11.8	5.4	650
39	18.61	14.4	4.2	660

1,310 ÷ 2 = 655 pounds, mean.   1,310
This will be increased on account of the French units used, and will equal 733 pounds, mean.

U. S. S. "EUTAW."

40	36.4	15.4	21.0	3,520
41	29.2	17.5	11.7	2,810
42	31.1	21.5	9.6	3,760
43	32.1	21.6	10.5	3,370
44	30.3	23.0	7.5	3,210
		16,670 ÷ 5 = 3,337 pounds, mean.		16,670

HIGH SERVICE PUMPING ENGINE, NO. 1, ST. LOUIS WATER WORKS.

	1	15.3	4.3	4,120

MASSACHUSETTS INSTITUTE OF TECHNOLOGY.

46	27.7	14.4	13.3	173
47	29.0	19.6	9.5	175
48	33.5	24.0	9.5	197
		545 ÷ 3 = 182 pounds, mean.		545

It will be observed that we have summed up the experiments, made at the Millers' Exhibition, at Cincinnati, on three different competing engines. These showed so little difference that the results of our investigation on one may be taken to represent the three.

We have also summed up the following data from the table:

U. S. STEAMER "MICHIGAN."—Seven experiments: Cylinder 36″ × 96″. Initial steam pressure, 20 lbs. above atmosphere. Back pressure, say 5 lbs., equal to 10 lbs. below atmosphere. Mean excess of water per hour over that required in a non-conducting cylinder.. 1,934 lbs.

U. S. REVENUE STEAMER "DALLAS."—Six experiments: Cylinder 36″ × 30″. Initial steam pressure, say 30 lbs. above atmosphere. Mean back pressure, say 5 lbs. above zero. Mean excess of water per hour above that required by a non-conducting cylinder.................................... 1,852 lbs.

U. S. REVENUE STEAMER "DEXTER."—Four experiments: Cylinder 26″ × 30″. Mean back pressure, say, 5 lbs. above zero. Initial steam pressure above atmosphere, 68 lbs. Excess of water per hour above that required by a non conducting cylinder... 1,650 lbs.

Three experiments: Cylinder 26″ × 30″ Mean back pressure, say, 5 lbs. above zero. Initial steam pressure above atmosphere, 40 lbs. Excess of water per hour above that required by a non-conducting cylinder.............................. 1,553 lbs.

U. S. REVENUE STEAMER "GALLATIN."—Mean of seven experiments: Cylinder 34.1″ × 30″. Mean back pressure, say, 5 lbs. above zero. Initial steam pressure 70 lbs. above atmosphere. Excess of water per hour above that required by a non-conducting cylinder.............................. 2,183 lbs.

Mean of five experiments: Cylinder 34.1″ × 30″. Mean back pressure, say, 5 lbs. above zero. Initial steam pressure 40 lbs. above atmosphere. Excess of water per hour above that required by a non-conducting cylinder................ 1,370 lbs.

Mean of three experiments: Cylinder 34.1″ × 30″. Mean back pressure, 2 lbs. above atmosphere. Initial steam pressure, 70 lbs. above atmosphere. Excess of water per hour above that required by a non-conducting cylinder................ 1,393 lbs.

MILLER'S EXHIBITION AT CINCINNATI.—Mean of three engines: Cylinder 18″ × 48″. Initial steam pressure, above atmosphere, 82 lbs. Mean back pressure, say 4 lbs. Excess of water per hour above that required by a non-conducting cylinder.... .. .. 1,058 lbs.

HIRN'S ENGINE.—Mean of two experiments: Cylinder 24″ ×
  78″. Initial steam pressure above atmosphere 54 lbs. Mean
  back pressure, 2 lbs. Excess of water, per hour, above that
  required by a non-conducting cylinder...................... 733 lbs.

U. S. STEAMER "EUTAW."—Mean of five experiments: Cylinder
  58″ × 105″. Initial steam pressure, 25 lbs. above atmosphere. Mean back pressure, 4 lbs. Excess of water, per
  hour, above that required by a non-conducting cylinder... 3,337 lbs.

MASSACHUSETTS INSTITUTE OF TECHNOLOGY.—Mean of three
  experiments with Corliss engine: Cylinder 8″ × 24″. Initial
  steam pressure, 50 lbs. above atmosphere. Excess of water
  per hour above that required by a non-conducting cylinder. 182 lbs.

HIGH SERVICE PUMPING ENGINE, No. 1, ST. LOUIS WATER
  WORKS.—One experiment: Cylinder 85″ × 120″. Initial
  steam pressure, 40 lbs. above atmosphere. Excess of water
  per hour above that required by a non-conducting cylinder... 4,120 lbs.

Of the four causes of excess in steam used over that required by a
non-conducting cylinder, which we have already mentioned, the first or
that of steam entering with water caused by foaming or priming, we shall
neglect here, as, in some of our experiments, to-wit, the last two, this has
been eliminated, and in others can scarcely be very large. The third, or
that of external radiation, is usually very small and can not exceed that of
a steam-heating coil of the same area as the external surface of the cylinder. The second is a loss which may, in determining the cost of a total
horse-power, be considered to vary with the volume of clearance space,
but which ranges from less than 1 to 15 per cent. of the piston displacement, and is, on an average, about 8 per cent. thereof. This, in a cylinder
full of steam at the terminal pressure, is not a great loss in itself, but
there is a loss during the expansion also. In any case it is not large comparatively, is nearly proportional to the volume, and, consequently, varies
with the piston area and a percentage of the stroke.

The fourth source of loss is by far the largest, and is due to an action
first mentioned by D. K. Clark in his "Railway Machinery," in 1851, and
afterwards elaborated by M. G. A. Hirn, in 1854 and again in 1857, in the
Bulletins de la Societé Industrielle de Mulhouse, and therein repeated at
frequent intervals up to the present date. This action was subsequently
noted by Isherwood in the second volume of his "Experimental Researches
in Steam Engineering," and it was rediscovered by Mr. G. B. Dixwell, of
Boston, and communicated by him to the Society of Arts of that city.

The internal radiation, or the action of the internal surfaces of the cylinder upon the within contained steam, may be explained as follows:
Steam enters the cylinder from the boiler at a temperature corresponding

to the pressure, and leaves the cylinder at a lower temperature corresponding to the lower pressure. The metal of the cylinder being a very good conductor of heat, receives heat from the incoming and delivers heat to the outgoing steam at every revolution. In detail the action is thus: When the steam-valve opens there is admitted from the boiler hot steam which first fills the clearance space, coming in contact with the cool surfaces which have just been open to the exhaust surfaces, and which are from 100° to 200° Fahr. lower in temperature than the incoming steam. The amount in weight of the steam is small and the amount in surface of the enclosing metal being large, the result is naturally that the steam condenses until heat enough has been given to the metal to raise its surface to the temperature of the steam. The piston moves and the condensation continues up to the cut-off. During the expansion, as the pressure falls, the warmed surface begins to give out heat to the steam as the pressure and temperature of the steam fall, while, as the piston moves, the metal which has been exposed to the exhaust is opened to the steam and the action is the reverse of that going on at other portions of the surface, while during exhaust the action continues to transfer heat from the metal to the steam which is swept out of the cylinder.

There is experimental reason to believe that the temperature of what may be called the skin of the metal scarcely varies from that of the steam, while the depth to which the influence extends, or what may be called the thickness of this skin, depends upon the intensity and rapidity of the changes of temperature to which it is subjected.

The experimental evidence is as follows: A metallic pyrometer must be so made that a thin sheet of metal can be exposed to the steam in the cylinder, or connected to the indicator fittings, having a needle so adjusted and arranged as to show changes of length in the sheet of metal. The instrument must be rated by exposure to steam free from air at atmospheric pressure and to water of a known temperature. On exposing such an instrument to the action of the steam in the cylinder, a change of temperature will be noted at each stroke.

If the shell be made of iron 0.03 inch thick, and the piston have a speed due to 60 revolutions of the crank per minute, nearly the whole change of temperature due to the change in pressure, and the needle, will remain stationary during nine-tenths of the exhaust stroke.

If the instrument be filled with mercury so that heat may be transmitted to the interior through the skin, while the freedom of movement of the skin, by which alone the change of temperature can be observed, is not interfered with, at a piston speed due to 85 revolutions per minute, the same change has been observed in the action of the instrument as before the introduction of the mercury.

If the number of revolutions per minute be increased beyond, say 100, the indications of the instrument decrease, and are, approximately, inversely proportional to the number of revolutions.

The problem of the transfer of heat to and from the steam, in an engine cylinder, although complex, is probably within the compass of pure mathematics, but we shall not attempt to analyse it here, for it would be foreign to the spirit of this work.

The fourth loss might be considered to be proportional to: 1. The whole internal surface of the cylinder: 2. To the area of the cylinder and piston heads and a fraction of the barrel: 3. To the area of the piston: and, 4. To the diameter of piston. It may also be considered to vary with the difference of temperature between initial pressure and that of the condenser or exhaust pipe.

A careful examination of the table of experiments shows: that neglecting priming and external radiation the whole excess of water used per hour over that required in a non-conducting cylinder is rudely proportional to the difference of temperature between the incoming and outgoing steam, and to the diameter of the piston; and that such excess is nearly constant for the great range of piston speed and revolutions therein found, and moreover is entirely independent of the expansion.

We give some of the figures connected with the experiments in reference to the above points:

U. S. STEAMER "MICHIGAN."

Seven experiments. Diameter of piston, 3 feet. Excess of water in pounds per hour over that required by a non-conducting cylinder = 1,934.

Temperature of steam............................ 259°
Temperature of condenser........................ 104°

$259° — 104° = 155° =$ change of temperature:

$155° \times 3 =$ diameter of piston $= 465 =$ product of change of temperature $\times$ diameter of piston. $1,934 \div 465 = 4.16 =$ pounds of water in excess per hour, per foot diameter of piston, per degree Fahr. of change in temperature.

U. S. STEAMER "DALLAS."

Diameter of piston, 3 feet. Excess of water in pounds per hour over that required by a non-conducting cylinder = 1,852.

Temperature of steam............................ 274°
Temperature of condenser........................ 104°

$274 — 104 = 170° =$ change of temperature:

$170 \times 3 = 510 =$ product of change of temperature $\times$ diameter of piston. $1,852 \div 510 = 3.63 =$ pounds of water in excess per hour, per foot diameter of piston, per degree Fahr. of change of temperature.

U. S. STEAMER "DEXTER."

Diameter of piston 2.17 feet. Excess of water in pounds per hour over that required by a non-conducting cylinder = 1,650.

Temperature of steam............................ 315°
Temperature of condenser........................ 104°

$315 — 104 = 211° =$ change of temperature:

$211 \times 2.17 =$ say $458 =$ product of change of temperature $\times$ diameter of piston. $1,650 \div 458 = 3.60 =$ pounds of water in excess per hour, per foot of piston diameter, per degree Fahr. of change of temperature.

Excess of water in pounds per hour over that required by a non-conducting cylinder = 1,553.

Temperature of steam................................ 287°
Temperature of condenser........................... 104°

$$287 - 104 = 183° = \text{change of temperature:}$$

$183 \times 2.17 = 397 = $ product of change of temperature × diameter of piston. $1,553 \div 397 = 3.91 = $ pounds of water in excess per hour, per foot diameter of piston, per degree Fahr. of change of temperature.

U. S. REVENUE STEAMER "GALLATIN."

Mean of seven experiments: Diameter of piston 2.84 feet. Excess of water in pounds per hour over that required by a non-conducting cylinder = 2,183.

Temperature of steam................................ 316°
Temperature of condenser........................... 104°

$$316 - 104 = 212° = \text{change of temperature:}$$

$212 \times 2.84 = $ say $602 = $ product of change of temperature × diameter of piston. $2,183 \div 602 = 3.62 = $ pounds of water in excess per hour, per foot diameter of piston, per degree Fahr. of change of temperature.

Mean of five experiments: Excess of water in pounds per hour over that required by a non-conducting cylinder = 1,427.

Temperature of steam................................ 287°
Temperature of condenser........................... 104°

$$287 - 104 = 183° = \text{change of temperature:}$$

$183 \times 2.84 = $ say $520 = $ product of change of temperature × diameter of piston. $1,370 \div 520 = 2.63 = $ pounds of water in excess per hour, per foot diameter of piston, per degree Fahr. of change of temperature.

Mean of three experiments: Excess of water in pounds per hour over that required by a non-conducting cylinder = 1,380.

Temperature of steam................................ 316°
Temperature of condenser........................... 212°

$$316 - 212 = 104° = \text{change of temperature:}$$

$104 \times 2.84 = 295 = $ product of change of temperature × diameter of piston. $1,393 \div 295 = 4.72 = $ pounds of water in excess per hour, per foot diometer of piston, per degree Fahr. of change of temperature.

MILLER'S EXHIBITION AT CINCINNATI.

Mean of three engines: Diameter of piston 1.5 feet. Excess of water in pounds per hour over that required by a non-conducting cylinder = 1,058.

Temperature of steam......... .... 326°
Temperature of condenser................. .... 104°

$$326 - 104 = 222° = \text{change of temperature:}$$

$222 \times 1.5 = 333 = $ product of change of temperature × diameter of piston. $1,058 \div 333 = 3.17 = $ pounds of water in excess per hour, per foot diameter of piston, per degree Fahr. of change of temperature.

HIRN'S ENGINE.

Diameter of piston 2 feet. Excess of water in pounds per hour over that required by a non-conducting cylinder = 733.

Temperature of steam............. .... 302°
Temperature of condenser......................... 104°

302 — 104 = 198° = change of temperature:

198 × 2 = 396 = product of change of temperature × diameter of piston. 733 ÷ 396 = 1.85 = pounds of water in excess per hour, per foot diameter of piston, per degree Fahr. of change of temperature.

U. S. STEAMER "EUTAW."

Diameter of piston = 4.83 feet. Excess of water in pounds per hour over that required by a non-conducting cylinder = 3,334.

Temperature of steam............................ 267°
Temperature of condenser......................... 104°

267 — 104 = 163° = change of temperature:

163 × 4.83 = 787 = product of change of temperature × diameter of piston. 3,337 ÷ 787 = 4.24 = pounds of water in excess per hour, per foot diameter of piston, per degree Fahr. of change of temperature.

MASSACHUSETTS INSTITUTE OF TECHNOLOGY.

Diameter of piston = 0.67 foot. Excess of water in pounds per hour over that required by a non-conducting cylinder = 182.

Temperature of steam............................ 298°
Temperature of condenser......................... 212°

298 — 212 = 86° = change of temperature:

86 × 0.67 = 58 = product of change of temperature × diameter of piston. 182 ÷ 58 = 3.14 = pounds of water in excess per hour, per foot diameter of piston, per degree Fahr. of change of temperature.

HIGH SERVICE PUMPING ENGINE, NO. 1, ST. LOUIS WATER WORKS.

Diameter of piston = 7.08 feet. Excess of water in pounds per hour over that required by a non-conducting cylinder = 4,120.

Temperature of steam............................ 287°
Temperature of condenser......................... 120°

287 — 120 = 167° = change of temperature.

167 × 7.08 = 1,182 = product of change of temperature × diameter of piston. 4,120 ÷ 1.182 = 3.48 = pounds of water in excess per hour, per foot diameter of piston, per degree Fahr. of change of temperature.

SUMMARY.

Pressure of steam in pounds above atmosphere.	Diameter of cylinder in inches.	Number of experiments.	LOCATION.	Mean excess of water in pounds per hour as per previous figures.	Mean × number of experiments.
20	36	7	U. S. Steamer "Michigan"............	4.16	29.12
30	36	6	U. S. Steamer "Dallas".........	3.63	21.78
70	26	4	U. S. Steamer "Dexter".............	3.60	14.40
40	....	3	" " "	3.91	11.73
70	34	7	U. S. Steamer "Gallatin"............	3.62	25.34
40	....	5	" " "	2.63	13.15
70	no vacuum	3	" " "	4.72	14.16
25	58	5	U. S. Steamer "Eutaw"	4.24	21.20
80	18	3	Miller's Exhibition...............	3.17	9.51
40	85	1	St. Louis Water Works, No. 1 H. S..	3.48	3.48
54	24	2	Hirn..............................	1.85	3.70
50	8	3	Mass. Institute Technology........	3.14	9.42
		49			176.99

176.99 ÷ 49 = say 3.6 = mean pounds of water in excess per hour, per foot of piston diameter, per degree Fahr. difference of temperature.

In the 49 experiments, above recorded, we find a certain variation in the resulting excess per foot of piston diameter per degree of change of temperature, but in connection with this we must remember that we have not taken into account the difference of clearance between the different engines. For instance, the lowest value given above is that for Hirn's engine, and this has the least clearance, while the condition of the steam and the amount of cushion are in all the cases neglected. Furthermore, while the results are widely different, yet the error in per cent. of the whole steam used is a much smaller one, and we shall find that adding to the steam used in a non-conducting cylinder the excess found above, we shall arrive at a close approximation to the steam actually used.

When we examine the cases of single-jacketed cylinders, we find, as a whole, a less excess in the use of steam above that used in a non-conducting cylinder, but the gain so made does not appear to be reduced to any such simple law as that found for unjacketed engines, and, in fact, the use of larger expansion, and consequent loss by back pressure work, very often neutralizes the gain achieved.

The compound engines, in our table, give very little better results than the simple engines, with the same steam pressures and expansions, in the cost of steam per total horse power; while per net horse power the larger amount of back pressure work, and the actual friction of two pistons, with their rods and set-off connections, go very far to neutralize any very great gain in such types.

We find that the data are not sufficient to give an empirical formula for the excess of water over that used in a non-conducting cylinder; but we see that it is not very far from that of a single-jacketed cylinder of the same size as the large one. We are obliged, therefore, to await further experiments.

We do not claim, even, for the single unjacketed cylinder that our method of investigation is either final, exhaustive, or rational, but that the results are all that our present knowledge of the subject will give us, will, we think, be admitted. What is required is a great number of experiments under the conditions of class A, upon all kinds and sizes of engines; we can then hope to frame a much more accurate and rational theory than the crude one we have given.

We add a few tables, the application of which will be readily seen.

NUMBER OF POUNDS OF WATER USED PER SQUARE FOOT OF PISTON PER HOUR, FOR A PISTON SPEED OF ONE FOOT PER MINUTE IN A NON-CONDUCTING CYLINDER.

No. of Expansions.	INITIAL PRESSURE IN POUNDS PER SQUARE INCH ABOVE ATMOSPHERE.									
	0	20	40	60	80	100	120	140	180	220
1.1	2.12	4.69	7.35	9.66	12.1	14.4	16.8	19.0	23.6	28.2
1.2	1.92	4.30	6.64	8.86	11.1	13.2	15.4	17.4	21.6	32.5
1.3	1.75	3.88	5.93	7.99	9.99	11.9	13.9	15.7	19.5	23.3
1.4	1.63	3.60	5.51	7.42	9.28	11.1	12.9	14.6	18.1	21.6
1.5	1.52	3.36	5.14	6.91	8.66	10.4	12.0	13.6	16.9	20.2
1.6	1.46	3.22	4.93	6.64	8.31	9.91	11.5	13.1	16.2	19.3
1.8	1.30	2.86	4.38	5.90	7.38	8.83	10.2	11.6	14.4	17.2
2.0	1.17	2.58	3.95	5.44	6.65	7.95	9.21	10.5	13.3	15.5
2.5	0.933	2.06	3.16	4.25	5.29	6.36	7.37	8.36	10 4	12.4
3.0	0.777	1.72	2.63	3.54	4.43	5.30	6.14	6.97	8.66	10.3
4.0	0.583	1.26	1.97	2.66	3.32	3.97	4.58	5.23	6.49	7.74
5.0	0.466	1.03	1.58	2.17	2.66	3.19	3.69	4.18	4.96	6 19
6.0	0.389	0.859	1.32	1.77	2.07	2.65	3.07	3.48	4.32	5.16
7.0	0.333	0.736	1.12	1.55	1.90	2.32	2.63	2.99	3.71	4.42
8.0	0.292	0.644	0.987	1.33	1.66	1.98	2.30	2.61	3.25	3.87
9.0	0.258	0.571	0.875	1.18	1.47	1.76	2.04	2.32	2.88	3.43
10.0	0.233	0.516	0.789	1.06	1.33	1.59	1.84	2.09	2.60	3.09
11.0	0.212	0.235	0.717	0.966	1.21	1.44	1.68	1.90	2.36	2.81
12.0	0.194	0.430	0.658	0.886	1.11	1.32	1.54	1.76	2.16	2.58
13.0	0.180	0.397	0.593	0.818	1.03	1.25	1.39	1.61	2.00	2.38
14.0	0.167	0.369	0.564	0.759	0.949	1.14	1.32	1.49	1.85	2.21
16.0	0.146	0.322	0.494	0.664	0.831	0.993	1.15	1.31	1.62	1.93
20.0	0.117	0.258	0.395	0.531	0.665	0.775	0.921	1.04	1.30	1.54
25.0	0.0933	0.206	0.316	0.425	0.532	0.636	0.737	0.836	1.04	1.21
30.0	0.0777	0.172	0.263	0.354	0.443	0.526	0.587	0.697	0.866	1.03

NUMBER OF TOTAL HORSE-POWER FOR EACH CUBIC FOOT OF SPACE SWEPT BY PISTON PER MINUTE.

No. of Expansions.	INITIAL PRESSURE IN POUNDS PER SQUARE INCH ABOVE ATMOSPHERE.									
	0	20	40	60	80	100	120	140	180	220
1.1	0.0649	0.151	0.238	0.324	0.410	0.497	0.584	0.670	0.843	1.020
1.2	0.0644	0.150	0.236	0.322	0.408	0.494	0.579	0.665	0.837	1.010
1.3	0.0635	0.148	0.233	0.317	0.402	0.487	0.572	0.656	0.825	0.995
1.4	0.0624	0.145	0.229	0.312	0.395	0.478	0.561	0.644	0.810	0.977
1.5	0.0609	0.142	0.224	0.304	0.386	0.467	0.548	0.629	0.792	0.955
1.6	0.0597	0.139	0.219	0.299	0.378	0.458	0.537	0.617	0.776	0.935
1.8	0.0567	0.132	0.208	0.283	0.359	0.435	0.510	0.585	0.737	0.888
2.0	0.0545	0.127	0.200	0.279	0.345	0.418	0.491	0.563	0.725	0.854
2 5	0.0490	0.114	0.180	0.245	0.311	0.376	0.441	0.507	0.638	0.768
3.0	0 0444	0.103	0.163	0.222	0.281	0.340	0.400	0.459	0.577	0.696
4.0	0.0372	0.0868	0.136	0.186	0.235	0.285	0.335	0.384	0.483	0.583
5.0	0.0324	0.0756	0.119	0.162	0.205	0.248	0.292	0.335	0.421	0.508
6.0	0.0286	0.0667	0.105	0.143	0.181	0.219	0.257	0.295	0.371	0.448
7.0	0.0257	0.0599	0.0942	0.131	0.163	0.201	0.231	0.265	0.334	9.402
8.0	0.0233	0.0545	0.0856	0.117	0.148	0.179	0.210	0.241	0.303	0.366
9.0	0.0215	0.0501	0.0788	0.107	0.137	0.165	0.193	0.222	0.279	0.337
10.0	0.0199	0.0463	0.0728	C.0994	0.126	0.152	0.179	0.205	0.258	0.311
11.0	0.0185	0.0441	0.0678	0.0924	0.117	0.142	0.166	0.191	0.240	0.290
12.0	0.0173	0.0403	0.0633	0.0864	0.109	0.132	0.155	0.183	0.224	0.271
13.0	0.0162	0.0379	0.0595	0.0811	0.103	0.127	0.146	0.168	0.212	0.254
14.0	0.0154	0.0359	0.0563	0.0768	0.0973	0.118	0.138	0.159	0.200	0.241
16.0	0.0138	0.0323	0.0507	0.0692	0.0877	0 106	0.125	0.143	0.180	0.217
20 0	0.0116	0.0271	0.0426	0.0580	0 0735	0.089	0.104	0.120	0.151	0.182
25.0	0.0097	0.0227	0.0356	0.0486	0.0615	0.0745	0.0874	0.101	0.126	0.152
30.0	0 0084	0.0195	0.0307	0.0418	0.0530	0.0638	0.0753	0.0865	0.109	0.131

NUMBER OF INDICATED HORSE-POWER FOR EACH CUBIC FOOT SWEPT BY PISTON PER MINUTE FOR CONDENSING ENGINES.

No. of Expansions.	INITIAL PRESSURE IN POUNDS PER SQUARE INCH ABOVE ATMOSPHERE.									
	0	20	40	60	80	100	120	140	180	220
1.1	.0475	0.134	0.221	0.307	0.393	0 480	0.567	0.653	0.826	1.003
1.2	.0470	.133	.219	.305	.391	.477	.562	.648	.820	0.993
1.3	.0461	.131	.216	.300	.385	.470	.555	.639	.808	.978
1.4	.0450	.128	.212	.295	.378	.461	.544	.627	.793	.960
1.5	.0435	.125	.207	.287	.369	.450	.531	.612	.775	.938
1.6	.0423	.122	.202	.282	.361	.441	.520	.600	.759	.918
1.8	.0393	.115	.191	.266	.342	.418	.493	.568	.720	.861
2.0	.0371	.110	.183	.262	.328	.411	.474	.546	.708	.837
2.5	.0316	.097	.163	.228	.294	.359	.424	.490	.621	.751
3.0	.0270	.086	.146	.205	.264	.323	.383	.442	.560	.679
4.0	.0198	.0694	.119	.169	.218	.268	.318	.367	.466	.566
5.0	.0150	.0582	.102	.145	.188	.231	.275	.318	.404	.491
6.0	.0112	.0493	.088	.126	.164	.212	.240	.278	.354	.431
7.0	.0083	.0425	.0768	.114	.146	.184	.214	.248	.317	.385
8.0	.0059	.0371	.0682	.100	.131	.162	.193	.224	.286	.349
9.0	.0041	.0327	.0614	.090	.120	.148	.176	.205	.262	.320
10.0	.0025	.0289	.0554	.0820	.109	.135	.162	.188	.241	.294
11.0	.0011	.0264	.0504	.0747	.100	.125	.149	.124	.223	.273
12.0	....	.0229	.0459	.0690	.092	.115	.138	.166	.207	.254
13.0	....	.0205	.0421	.0637	.086	.110	.129	.151	.195	.237
14.0	....	.0185	.0389	.0594	.0799	.101	.121	.142	.183	.224
16.0	....	.0149	.0323	.0518	.0703	.089	.108	.126	.163	.200
20.0	....	.0097	.0252	.0406	.0561	.0716	.087	.103	.134	.165
25.0	....	.0063	.0193	.0312	.0441	.0571	.0700	.084	.109	.135
30.0	....	.0021	.0133	.0244	.0356	.0464	.0579	.0691	.092	.114

NUMBER OF INDICATED HORSE-POWER FOR EACH CUBIC FOOT SWEPT BY PISTON PER MINUTE IN NON-CONDENSING ENGINES.

No. of Expansions.	INITIAL PRESSURE IN POUNDS PER SQUARE INCH ABOVE ATMOSPHERE.									
	0	20	40	60	80	100	120	140	160	220
1.1	....	0.073	0.160	0.246	0.332	0.419	0.506	0.592	0.765	0.942
1.2	....	0.072	0.158	0.244	0.330	0.416	0.501	0.587	0.759	0.932
1.3	....	0.070	0.155	0.239	0.324	0.409	0.494	0.578	0.747	0.917
1.4	....	0.067	0.151	0.234	0.317	0.400	0.483	0.566	0.732	0.899
1.5	....	0.064	0.146	0.226	0.308	0.389	0.470	0.551	0.714	0.877
1.6	....	0.061	0.141	0.221	0.300	0.380	0.459	0.539	0.698	0.857
1.8	....	0.054	0.130	0.205	0.281	0.357	0.432	0.507	0.659	0.810
2.0	....	0.049	0.122	0.201	0.267	0.340	0.413	0.485	0.647	0.776
2.5	....	0.036	0.102	0.167	0.233	0.298	0.363	0.439	0.560	0.690
3.0	....	0.025	0.085	0.144	0.203	0.262	0.322	0.381	0.499	0.618
4.0	....	0.009	0.058	0.108	0.157	0.207	0.257	0.306	0.405	0.505
5.0			0.041	0.084	0.127	0.170	0.214	0.257	0.343	0.430
6.0			0.027	0.065	0.103	0.141	0.179	0.217	0.293	0.370
7 0			0.016	0.053	0.085	0.123	0.153	0.187	0.256	0.324
8.0			0.009	0.039	0.070	0.101	0.132	0.163	0.225	0.288
9.0				0.029	0.059	0.087	0.115	0.144	0.201	0.259
10.0				0.021	0.048	0.074	0.101	0.127	0.180	0.233
11.0				0.014	0.039	0.064	0.088	0.113	0.162	0.212
12.0				0.009	0.031	0.054	0.077	0.105	0.146	0.193
13.0					0.025	0.049	0.068	0.090	0.134	0.176
14.0					0.019	0.040	0.060	0.081	0.122	0.163
16.0					0.010	0.028	0.047	0.065	0.102	0.139
20.0						0.011	0.086		0.073	0.104
25.0							0.009		0.048	0.074
30.0									0.031	0.053

CHAPTER IV.

ON THE INDICATOR, THE INDICATOR DIAGRAM, AND THE DIFFERENT CLASSES OF ENGINES.

James Watt constructed an instrument for observing the volume and pressure of the steam in the engine cylinder to which he gave the name of "Indicator." It consisted of two parts: One, a rectangular frame moving in guides backward and forward and actuated by the engine, to the beam of which it was connected by a cord, with a weight or spring attached to keep the cord stretched. In this way the frame moved with the piston, stopping when that member stopped, and corresponding with it completely. The other part carried a small cylinder with piston, piston rod, and a spring in connection therewith. Steam being admitted to this cylinder from the engine cylinder, the pressure would vary and the piston would consequently rise and fall within the cylinder against the spring.

By attaching a pencil to the top of the piston rod, and with a piece of paper secured to the frame, a diagram is obtained in which the position of a point, vertically, in relation to a line traced when the steam is shut off from the instrument, is governed by the steam pressure; while its position horizontally is proportioned to the movement of the piston of the engine, or the volume occupied by the steam. The diagram thus produced is proportioned to the pressure in height and to the volume occupied in length, and the area is therefore proportional to the work done in the engine cylinder per stroke. The mean pressure in pounds per square inch is found, either, by measuring at ten equi-distant places, or by measuring the area of the figure and dividing by the length, of course taking into account the stiffness, or scale, of the spring. The mean pressure times the piston area in square inches multiplied by the stroke in feet gives the number of foot pounds per stroke of engine.

By using the piston speed in feet per minute, in place of the stroke, and dividing this by 33,000, the number of horse-power exerted is determined.

By using a mean pressure of two pounds less, the number of net horse-power may be estimated. By setting off the line of no pressure, 14.7 pounds below the atmospheric line, and drawing verticals to the ends of the diagram, and by using this as the diagram of an engine without back pressure, we can find the mean total pressure and the number of total horse-power.

In such an instrument, however, there are many imperfections. The moving springs are subjected to sudden changes of pressure, or tension, and vibrations in the springs are set up by the inertia of the moving parts. This is true for both the pencil and paper movements. The motion of the paper from the engine motion is subject to errors both geometric and mechanical: the former can only be reduced at the expense of the latter.

The remedy for vibrations of spring is to reduce the weight of the moving parts, to decrease the amount of motion therein, and to increase the stiffness of the spring itself.

The mechanical errors of connection are: the variations in length of cords, and vibrations, and the slack in the bars used for reducing the motions. There is also a loss in pressure caused by the leakage of the indicator piston, and for engines with small cylinders an error is introduced by cylinder condensation in the indicator.

In large, slow moving engines these errors are all small and may be neglected, but they increase in importance with the number of revolutions, and, inversely, with the size of the engine.

The indicator was first improved by McNaught, with Richards, Thompson, Crosby, Tabor and Professor Sweet, following, in their efforts to reduce the weight of the moving parts, all using, however, a separate instrument. We give an illustration of Thompson's Indicator as a good example.

THOMPSON'S STEAM ENGINE INDICATOR.

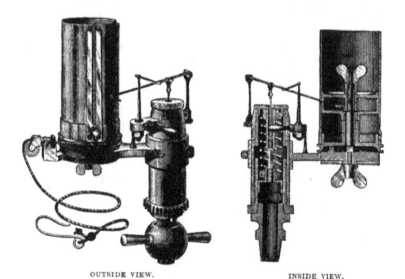

OUTSIDE VIEW.   INSIDE VIEW.

M. G. A. Hirn employed the beam of the engine, the deflection being properly multiplied, for the spring opposing the steam pressure; and Mr. William E. Worthen has proposed the use of the spring of the cylinder head of the engine for the same purpose. This would give very satisfactory results with proper means for multiplying the motion.

In France a device has been tried which can be applied to engines running with nearly constant load, but which is not well suited for engines with quick acting automatic cut-off gear. An adjustable yoke confines the movement of the pencil within narrow limits, and by changing this adjustment the card may be taken piecemeal. An elegant adaptation of this method was used on the South Eastern Railway of France, where the adjustment was made by compressed air, and the diagrams from the cylinders taken in the dynamometer car.

Engines may be classified as single acting and double acting, according as the working steam is used in one or both ends of the cylinder; and condensing and non-condensing, according as the steam from the cylinder is cooled by water and condensed, or is exhausted directly into the air.

There are two kinds of single-acting engines. The one, the older, is mainly employed in the pumping of water; and the other, the modern type, maintains a high speed of revolution on a shaft, with the connecting rods kept under stress of one kind, usually compression, so that the shock on the boxes, due to change of force from compression to tension, and the effects of wear, are avoided. These two kinds of engines are entirely different in design and construction.

The oldest form of engine was worked by admitting steam from a boiler to the cylinder, below the piston, which was connected with a beam and pump rod. The weight of the pump rod forced the water up from the pump and also carried the piston to the top of the cylinder. A jet of water was then thrown into the cylinder condensing the therein contained steam, which had been previously shut off from the boiler. The pressure of the atmosphere now drove the piston down, at the same time lifting the pump rod, when after it had reached the bottom the water was discharged from the cylinder and the process was repeated.

James Watt devised the separate condenser and covered the cylinder so as to introduce steam at its upper end, thereby lifting the pump rod. When the piston reached the bottom of the cylinder the steam was cut off from the boiler. An arrangement, called the equilibrium valve, opens communication between the two ends of the cylinder, and the steam now pressing equally above and below the piston, the weight of the pump rod carries the piston to the top of the cylinder, driving the steam which was above the piston to its lower end, and doing the pumping at the same time. The steam is now admitted above the piston as before, but the bottom of the cylinder is opened to the condenser and a vacuum is produced below the piston at the same time as the steam exerts its pressure above it.

These engines were introduced into the mines of Cornwall, and into deep shafts, and with ample boilers and high pressure steam they became famous as the "Cornish Pumping Engines." With the quick admission of high pressure steam a sudden pull was exerted on the pump rods, which, being constructed of wood and of long length, readily absorbed this jerk and began to rise. An early cut-off allowed the rapidly falling steam pressure in the cylinder to be helped out by the inertia of the weight lifted, which came slowly to rest, and then reacted upon the column of water, commencing gradually,—conditions very favorable for the pumping part of the work. The boilers used gave very high evaporation by reason of the very moderate manner in which they were worked, and the duty, or number of foot pounds of water raised per pound, or per bushel of coal, was also, usually very high. In these mines systematic record was kept and published monthly, and competition was thus induced among the men in charge of the engines. High pressure steam and high expansion here received its first practical confirmation.

When, however, these engines were applied to pumping water for water works, it was found that without the elasticity of the long and heavy pump rods used in the mines, the pump was apt to jump, if high pressure steam was used; that is, the plunger would rise without the pump filling and a very hard shock was the result. In consequence the use of high pressure steam, and high expansion, was abandoned in such engines built for waterworks purposes in the United States, and it is safe to say that for such purposes no more of this class of engine will ever be built in this country. In no case where used for water works has any such duty been reached as was obtained by these engines in the mines. The indicator diagrams for this class of engines are to be placed one above the other; any difference between the exhaust line of the steam end and the admission line of the exhaust end being so much lost pressure and work.

In the class of Cornish engines, introduced by Captain Bull, the beam was dispensed with and the cylinder placed directly over the pump, the steam being introduced at the lower and the exhaust taken from the upper end. A pair of such engines are used at the River Pumping Station of the St. Louis Water Works, but, as suggested above, with steam at a low pressure. The diagrams given herewith show the limited expansion possible.

The other class of single acting engines was introduced in order to attain a higher speed of rotation than had been found convenient in the ordinary double acting engines, where the inertia of the rods and the change from thrust to tension brings first one side of the box and then the other into bearing. Unless this change is a gradual one it is accompanied by a shock more or less disastrous to the machine. By keeping, say, a thrust continually on the rods the boxes are always in bearing on one side and no such shock occurs. The steam during admission and expansion causes a pressure in one direction on the piston which is not changed during exhaust and compression. The irregularity of action may be remedied by a heavy fly-wheel or by the use of one or more cylinders. As examples: for two cylinders engines we select the Westinghouse; for engines with

three cylinders, Brotherhood's, of London; and with six cylinders, the
Colt Disc Engine, from West's and Darkin's patents, manufactured by the
Colt's Fire Arms Company, of Hartford, Conn. These machines have, at
the time of writing, been used more particularly with electric apparatus,
and in small boats, but have attained much popularity in other directions.
The exhaust is taken into the chamber where it lubricates the main

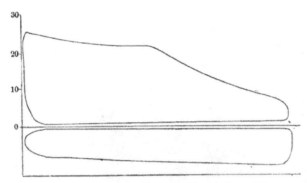

DIAGRAM FROM CORNISH ENGINE, No. 1, LOW SERVICE,
ST. LOUIS, MO., WATER WORKS.

56″ × 138″ × 9 double strokes per minute.

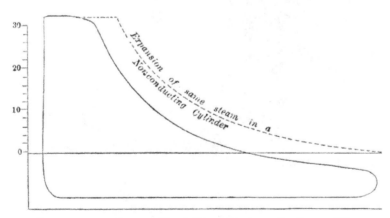

DIAGRAM FROM ENGINE No. 1, HIGH SERVICE, ST. LOUIS, MO.,
WATER WORKS.

85″ × 190″ × 11½ revolutions per minute. I. H. P. 705.

THE WESTINGHOUSE ENGINE.

FRONT VIEW.   160 H. P.

THE WESTINGHOUSE ENGINE.

REAR VIEW.　160 H. P.　(One fly-wheel removed.)

THE WESTINGHOUSE ENGINE.

Section Through Shaft.

A A, Cylinders. *B*, Valve Chamber. *C*, Bed, or Crank Case. *D D*, Pistons. *F F*, Connecting Rods. *G G*, Cranks. *H H*, Crank Shaft. *I*, Eccentric. *J*, Valve Guide. *K*, Centre Bearing. *M*, Steam Connection. *N*, Exhaust Connection. *R*, Oil Pipe. *V*, Valve. *W*, Wiper. *Y*, Fly-Wheel. *Z*, Pulley. *a a*, Cylinder Heads. *b b*, Steel Wrist Pin. *c*, Crank Case Head. *d d*, Crank Shaft bearings. *d'* Cover. *e*, Oil Passage. *f f*, Oil Cups. *g g*, Bolts. *h*, Bonnet. *j j*, Spider Heads. *k k*, Rings. *l*, Hollow Valve Bolt. *n*, Syphon Overflow. *o*, Hole in Funnel Head. *r*, Eccentric Rod. *t t*, Collar Washers. *v*, Lead Washer. *x x*, Bobs on Crank.

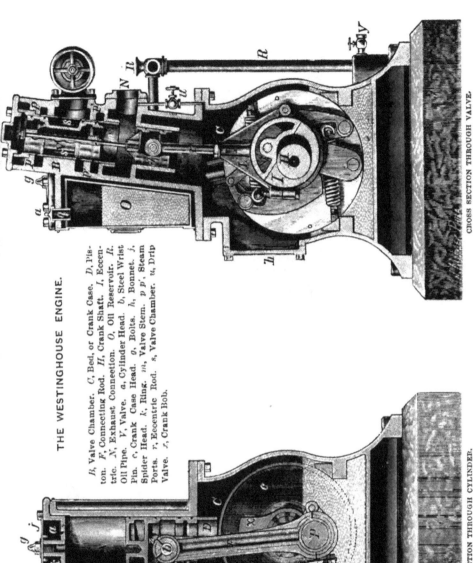

THE WESTINGHOUSE ENGINE.

B, Valve Chamber. C, Bed, or Crank Case. D, Piston. F, Connecting Rod. H, Crank Shaft. I, Eccentric. N, Exhaust Connection. O, Oil Reservoir. R, Oil Pipe. V, Valve. a, Cylinder Head. b, Steel Wrist Pin. c, Crank Case Head. g, Bolts. h, Bonnet. j, Spider Head. k, Ring. m, Valve Stem. p p', Steam Ports. r, Eccentric Rod. s, Valve Chamber. u, Drip Valve. z, Crank Bob.

CROSS SECTION THROUGH VALVE.

CROSS SECTION THROUGH CYLINDER.

THE WESTINGHOUSE ENGINE.

MARINE ENGINE.

B, Valve Chamber. J, Valve Guide. M, Steam Connection. N, Exhaust Connection. V, Valve. i, Neck of Valve. j, Spider Head. k k, Rings. m, Valve Stem. p p', Steam Ports. r, Eccentric Rod. s, Valve Chamber.

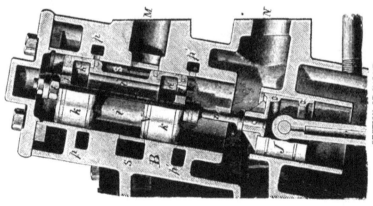

SECTION OF VALVE.

THE WESTINGHOUSE ENGINE—GOVERNOR.

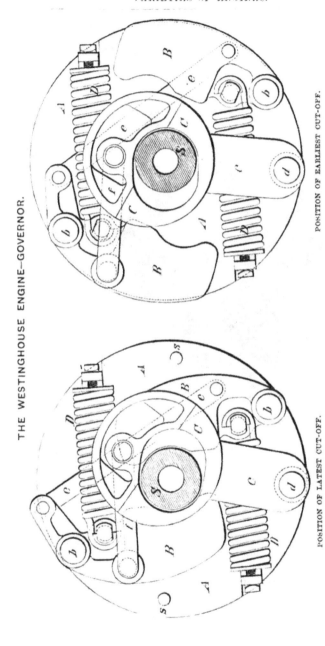

POSITION OF LATEST CUT-OFF.

POSITION OF EARLIEST CUT-OFF.

The Disc *A* is cast solid to one of the Cranks. The Loose Eccentric, *C*, is suspended by the arm, *c*, from the pin, *d*, around which it has a motion of adjustment; *B B* are the Governor Weights, pivoted on the pins *b b*; one of the weights is connected to the eccentric by the Link, *f*, and both weights are connected to operate in unison by the Link, *e*. Coil Springs, *D D*, furnish the centripetal or returning force. The Eccentric circles the Shaft *S*, the opening being elongated to admit of the proper motion. The Stops, *s s*, limit the motion of the weights.

THE BROTHERHOOD THREE-CYLINDER ENGINE.

PERSPECTIVE ELEVATION.

bearing with the wet steam and the oil introduced by the steam pipe. The Brotherhood engines are also used with compressed air for driving torpedoes, and we have seen one, driven by a Westinghouse Air Compressor used for drilling in a locomotive repair shop.

It appears to us that these engines are well adapted for constant work, but for intermittent use the temptation to run them without cleaning must be so great as to render them liable to a rapid deterioration.

When indicator diagrams from large, slow moving engines are examined, and the weight of steam present at any two points of the stroke, such as at cut-off, and release, is calculated by the aid of the table of the "Properties of Steam," and the volume, pressure, and density thereof, we shall rarely find any kind of agreement in the two results. And, if there has been also a careful measurement of the quantity of feed water consumed per stroke, the amount will be found to be much in excess of that given by

THE COLT DISC ENGINE.

West's and Darkin's Patents.

PERSPECTIVE ELEVATION.

computation. This difference, in an engine with a tight piston, is only to be accounted for by the action of the metal of the cylinder which transfers heat to and from the within contained steam. This has already been explained in Chapter III. We shall consider the effect of this action upon the indicator diagram, and the loss of work which occurs compared with that which should be done in a non-conducting cylinder; or, in other words, the consequent increase in the quantity of steam used for a given work shown.

Let us take for example the data of the experiment conducted by Mr. J. W. Hill at the Miller's Exhibition, held at Cincinnati. The experiment from which we obtain the following was made upon one of three Corliss engines, built by different makers, but all having the same general dimensions, viz:

THE COLT DISC ENGINE.

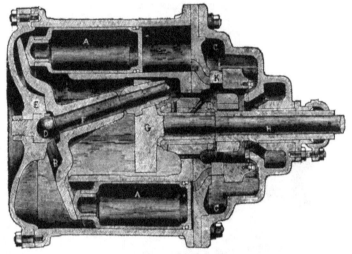

LONGITUDINAL SECTION.

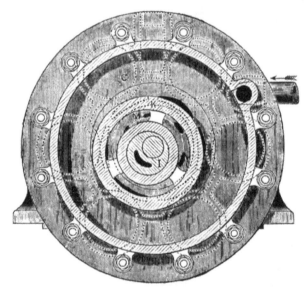

CROSS SECTION, SHOWING CIRCULAR VALVE, PORTS, ETC.

THE COLT DISC ENGINE.

CROSS SECTION, SHOWING INTERIOR OF ENGINE, STEAM PORTS AND
EXHAUST PASSAGES

The main body of the engine consists of one casting, containing six cylinders, arranged in a circle, and parallel with one another. The pistons A take the form of a hollow plunger, one end terminating in a blunt cone which bears continuously against the periphery of the disc B. They are single acting, being subject to steam pressure upon the flat end only. Steam is admitted successively to the six cylinders from the steam chest C, three pistons being constantly in action at different points of the stroke, thereby imparting a uniform rolling motion to the conical disc B, which is steadied at its center by the ball and socket joint D, and rolls upon the conical surface of the back plate E, which receives the full thrust of the pistons, and protects the ball and socket joint D from strain. The crank pin F is securely fixed in the centre of the conical disc B, the rolling motion of the disc causing the pin to describe a circle, and by means of the crank G, imparting a rotary motion to the shaft H. The shaft H passes through the centre of the steam chest and carries an eccentric giving motion to the circular valve K. The valve K is a flat circular ring which slides steam tight but perfectly freely between the port face and a balance plate. The steam is admitted to and fills the annular space C left in the steam chest outside the circumference of the valve ring K, the eccentric motion of which alternately opens and closes all the steam ports, successively admitting steam to the cylinders, from which it again escapes to the exhaust chamber M formed by the inside of the valve ring, and thence through openings into the body of the engine, and is finally discharged by the exhaust pipe N.

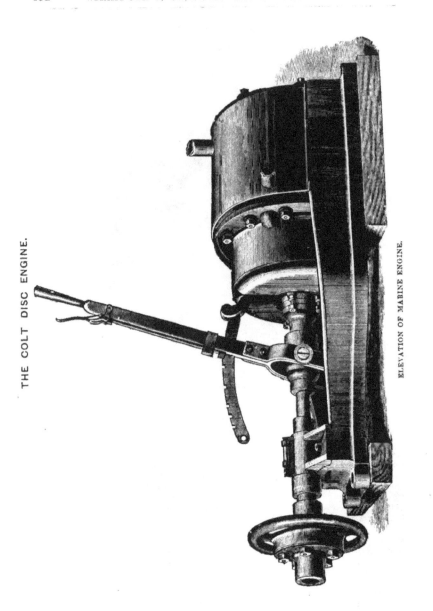

THE COLT DISC ENGINE.

ELEVATION OF MARINE ENGINE.

Cylinder, 18″ × 48″; number of revolutions, 75.4; steam at 80 pounds pressure, cutting off at 13 per cent. of the stroke for the Allis Engine: cut-off pressure, 84 pounds; piston area = 1.7 square feet; piston displacement = 6.8 cubic feet;

13 per cent. of 6.8 = 0.884 cubic feet.

Clearance volume = 0.2 cubic feet; volume occupied by steam at cut-off, 1.084 cubic feet; density of steam at 84 pounds = 0.231;

0.231 × 1.084 = weight of steam at cut-off = 0.250 pounds;

weight of feed water per hour = 3422.6 pounds; weight of feed water per stroke = 0.378 pounds:

0.378 − 0.250 = 0.128 pounds condensed at cut-off;

or, 34 per cent. of all the fluid present is water; or, the water present equals in weight 50 per cent. of the steam.

$$\text{Real expansion} = \frac{7.0}{1.084} = 6.4.$$

Now taking the length of the diagram to represent 6.8 cubic feet, and adding the clearance = 0.2 cubic feet, or, say 3 per cent. of the stroke, we set off at the cut-off pressure a volume 50 per cent. greater than the cut-off

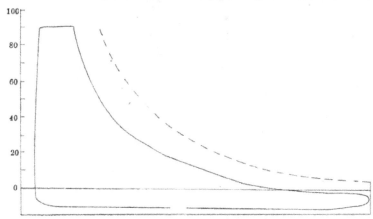

DIAGRAM FROM REYNOLD'S CORLISS ENGINE,

Cylinders 18″ × 48″ × 75 revolutions per minute, at Millers' Exhibition, Cincinnati, O.

volume; and if from this point we draw a curve of expansion for steam in a non-conducting cylinder till we reach the pressure of release, and thence draw a vertical line to the back pressure, we have the diagram which the water boiled should have given per stroke in a non-conducting cylinder; and the difference between the area of this diagram and the real diagram represents the loss which has taken place by the action of the sides of the cylinder. Measuring the area of the diagram by the planimeter we have 4.40 square inches, and for the area of the new diagram, 5.91 square inches, which makes the latter 0.34 per cent. larger. The indicated horse-power is 152.7, which in a non-conducting cylinder would be nearly 204, so that a loss of 50 indicated horse-power, or, say 25 per cent., is caused by the transfer of heat in the sides of the cylinder.

This experiment is a good one by which to examine other matters, so that we may see what can be obtained from an indicator card.

In the above experiment the quantity and rise of temperature of the injection water were measured, and the steam supplied was found to be dry by calorimeter tests. We abstract from the report of the trial the following:

Dry steam supplied per hour for ten hours.........3422.6   pounds.
Dry steam per stroke.................................0.3782 pounds.

The injection water = 30.88 times the feed and rose from 72° to 102° Fahr., which gives 0.3782 × 30.88 × 30 = 351 heat units rejected per stroke.

Mean indicated pressure...................... 34.26 pounds.
Mean total pressure........................... 40.5 pounds.
Area of piston...............................253   square inches.

$$\text{Total work per stroke} = \frac{253 \times 40.5 \times 4}{772} = 53 \text{ units.}$$

Heat per stroke, feed at 32° = 0.3782 × 1181.................446 units.	
Deduct for feed at 102 − 32 = 0.3782 × 70.................. 26 "	
Heat given to engine per stroke.. ....420 "	
Heat expended in work per stroke...................... 53 "	
Heat in external radiation, say................... .... 4 57 "	
	363 "
Heat found in rise in injection water................ ....351 "	
	12 "

$$\text{Error in measurement} = \frac{12}{446}, \text{ or, say 3 per cent.}$$

This error in the experiment probably arose in the measurement of the injection water, and perhaps, from not obtaining the average of the hot well accurately.

At cut-off we observed that of the amount of 0.378 pound of feed water evaporated per stroke, 0.25 pound was steam, while the balance, equal to 0.1282 pound, had condensed.

Units.
At this time the internal heat of the steam present = ...1100 × 0.25 = 275
  "   "   "   "   "   water   "   = ...298 × 0.1282 = 38
                        275 − 38 = 313, or,

Heat in fluid present.................................. 313
Heat received from boiler as given above................... 446
Heat absorbed by cylinder = 446 − 313 =............. 133

At the end of the stroke the volume occupied is 7 cubic feet, with a total pressure of 12 pounds; density = 0.031:

Weight of steam present, 7 × 0.031..........................0.217 pounds.
Weight of water present, 0.3782 — 0.217................ ..0.1612 pound.
Internal heat in steam present, 0.217 × 1072...... ....233 units.
Heat in water present, 0.1612 × 170........ ....27 "
—
Heat in fluid present...260 "
Heat used in expansion... 36 "
—
Heat accounted for...296 "
Heat in fluid at cut-off...................................... ....313 "
Heat added to iron during expansion, 313 — 296................. 17 "
Heat in iron at end of stroke, 133 + 17.........................150 "

And this latter amount is necessarily thrown away during the exhaust, from the iron of the cylinder into the condenser, and is the cooling effect of the latter upon the former.

The computation at the end of the stroke is never so satisfactory as at cut-off, because the changes of volume are much greater for small changes of pressure with low pressure steam than with high. Suppose for instance the terminal pressure be taken as 2 pounds below the atmosphere instead of 3. The density will equal 0.034, and the weight of steam 0.238 pounds, while its internal heat will equal 0.238 × 1072 = 255 units.

The water will equal 0.1402 pounds and its heat $= \dfrac{24}{279}$

This will make 19 units more accounted for in the fluid present, and will give 131 units in the iron at the end of the stroke, instead of 150, by reason of the cooling effect of the condenser. If the agreement between the heat rejected and that given from the boiler had been closer, we should have found a check upon this cooling effect of the condenser, as follows:

Heat found in condenser...................................351 units.
Heat given by back pressure work............. 7

Fluid heat at end of stroke, 260 or 279 units, according to the terminal pressure taken. But this is too large, as the temperature of the water in the condenser is 102° and not 32°, and we have 0.3782 × 70 = 26 units to deduct as before, which leaves 234 or 253 units received into the condenser from the fluid; or from the fluid and work of exhaust 241 or 260 units. Deducting these amounts from 351 units, we have 110 or 91 units as the heat received from the iron; but if we had found 13 units more in the condenser the values would be 123 and 104 units, thus rendering the lower value of terminal pressure the more probable. A very slight amount of water in the steam supplied would account for much of the inconsistency of these results. We shall give in Chapter V examples of such computations by M. O. Hallauer, showing more consistent results.

With the use of high pressure steam, and high expansion, as employed by Trevithick, in Cornwall, the shock and change of pressure in the cyl-

inder between the beginning and end of the stroke, of course, became
considerable, and it was suggested by Hornblower, in England, and long
afterwards by Woolf, in Germany, that the steam should be first introduced
into a small cylinder, whereby the strain, produced on the connections by
the sudden influx of high pressure steam, might be reduced, and that after
acting for more or less of the stroke at boiler pressure, the steam should
be put in communication with a larger cylinder in which the expansion
should be completed. But while pushing the large piston forward there
is a tendency to retard the motion of the small one. The following diagram, Fig. 40, will explain the indicated work and the total work:

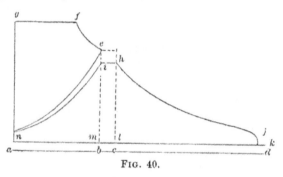

FIG. 40.

Let *a b* represent the volume of the small cylinder, *b c* the clearance
between the small and large cylinder and *a b + c d* the volume of the
large cylinder.

The area *a g f e b* is the total work done in the small cylinder and the
area *a n i h j k d* is the total work done in the large cylinder. The indicated work of the small cylinder is *n g f e* and the back pressure work is *a
n e b*. The indicated work of the large cylinder is *n i h j k n*, while the
back pressure work is *a n k d*. We see that the work *a n m b* has been

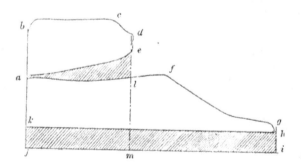

FIG. 41.

counted twice, which is once too many; and we also see that there are two ways of representing the portion $n\, m\, i$, which may be considered as part of the back work of the small cylinder while it is forward work for the large cylinder. Or we take it as part of the forward work of the small cylinder, giving $a\, g\, f\, e\, b$ as the forward work, while $a\, n\, m\, b$ is the back pressure work in that cylinder, leaving $n\, g\, f\, e\, m$ as the indicated work; while, for the large cylinder we have $c\, h\, j\, d$ for the total, $l\, h\, j\, k$ for the indicated and $c\, l\, k\, d$ for the back pressure work.

If the receiver between the cylinders be small, the pressure at the beginning of the stroke of the large cylinder is nearly equal to that at the end of the stroke of the small cylinder. With a large receiver the pressure is apt to be much less, while it can be raised by a cut-off on the large cylinder.

The amount of clearance volume between the cylinders affects the form of the curves $e\, n\, h\, j$ and $i\, n$; and when very large, regarding $c\, d$, the work done in each cylinder is measured by itself without any deductions and the diagrams are placed one under the other, as in figure 41, where: $a\, b\, c\, d\, e\, a$ is the high pressure diagram, and $a\, f\, g\, h\, k$ the low pressure diagram. The enclosed areas are the indicated work; the area $j\, k\, h\, i$ the back pressure work on the large piston, and $a\, e\, m\, j$ that of the small piston.

When the question of indicated power only is under discussion the measurement of the diagram by the ordinates or by the planimeter is sufficient. Each piston by itself is taken and the work done on it found and added. Much misconception of this subject appears to have prevailed, and one modern writer claimed, in 1883, a generalization and geometrical construction which is given in Rankine's Steam Engine, in the first edition.

Many forms of compound engines are to be met with, some of which may be briefly described as follows:

1. Engine with two cylinders of equal stroke acting on one crank pin, the steam from one end of the small cylinder passing to the farther end of the large one. The cylinders are usually in line, or "tandem."

2. Engine with two unequal cylinders attached to the same end of a beam, the steam passing from one end of the small cylinder to the further end of the large one. This form was the original one introduced by Woolf.

3. Engine with two cylinders of the same diameter, set side by side, with two cranks at 180°, the steam from the small cylinder passing across to the near end of the large one.

4. Engine with two cylinders attached to opposite ends of a beam, the steam from the top of the small cylinder passing to the top of the large. This form has been largely used by McNaught and lately with horizontal cylinders.

5. Engine with two cylinders attached to two cranks at an angle of 90° with each other and a more or less intermediate receiver. With vertical cylinders they have been more used than any other form for marine engines.

6. Engines with three cylinders attached to cranks at 120° with each other, one of them being used for high pressure and the two others, of the same, or greater diameter, for low pressure. This class has been successfully used on the very largest marine engines. Those of the steamships Arizona, Alaska, Servia, Aurania and Oregon may be instanced.

7. Engine with four equal cylinders attached to cranks at 45°, using one as high pressure and the other three as low pressure.

8. Two pairs of tandem engines driving two cranks at 90°.

9. Three pairs of tandem engines driving three cranks at 120°.

10. Three unequal cylinders driving three cranks at 120°, the steam passing through all three cylinders.

11. Two pairs of tandem engines driving two cranks at 90°, the steam passing through all four cylinders and two interheaters.

The use of receivers of comparatively large volume between two cylinders was first suggested by Ernest Woolf, and the great progress made in marine engines by its use, under the name of compound engines, has been mainly due to its adoption by the engineers of Glasgow.

For marine service the compound engine with high pressure steam has developed the best practical results. The most usual type adopted is that with two cylinders, the smaller, or high pressure, and the larger or low pressure, being coupled by cranks at 90°. The most usual type of screw engine being vertical, we find the small cylinder occasionally placed on top of, and in line with, the large cylinder, both pistons working on the same rod. Two or three such engines are used with cranks at 90° with two cylinders, and at 120° when three cylinders are employed.

When the use of two cylinders would require the low pressure cylinder to be excessively large, two low pressure cylinders are used in connection with one high pressure cylinder, coupled to cranks, generally at 120°.

The use of three cylinders of different sizes has been tried with steam at 125 and 140 pounds pressure, the higher pressure was adopted on the Steamer Propontis. Although the boilers in this instance had to be abandoned, the results were very good while the high pressure could be maintained.

The following table prepared with great care by Mr. Marshall gives the results of the progress in marine engine practice. While the economy in the use of high pressure steam and the compound engine, taken together, is evident, it must be confessed that it is not easy to separate the effects of the two causes; and while the mechanical advantages of compounding for marine engines of large size, for which it is especially useful, are well known, yet it may be stated that with steam of moderate pressure no advantage in economy has been found when the compound engine is compared with single cylinder engines of good design and construction, and working steam at the same pressure.

It is also readily conceded that higher rates of expansion may be used with the compound engine than with single cylinder engines, using steam at the same pressure; but it may be doubted whether any practical economy has resulted therefrom, as may be seen from an examination of the table of engine trials and the paper by Hallauer in Chapter V.

THE AVERAGE CONSUMPTION OF COAL PER I. H. P. PER HOUR,

By Steamships using Compound Engines in long sea voyages. A table reduced from one accompanying a paper read before the Institution of Mechanical Engineers, London, in 1881, by F. C. Marshall.

No. of Reference.	Cylinders. Receivers at 90°.	Piston Speed.	Condenser Area.	Diam. of Screw.	Working Pres're Above Atmos.	No. of Boilers.	Total Heating Surface.	Grate Area.	Indicated Horse-Power.	Coal in Pounds per I. H. P. per hour.	English Tons in 24 hours.
		Ft.	sq. ft.	ft. in.			sq. ft.	sq ft.			
1	34&61×45	450	2466	15 3	70	2	4216	140	900	1.5	14.00
2	42&80×48	552	......	......	72.5	2	6000	......	1881	1.8	32.25
3	35&70×48	400	2400	17 0	90	2	4440	160	1200	1.63	21
4	46&87×57	484	5000	19 0	80	3	7803	250	2200	1.66	40
5	22&44×30	360	705	11 0	100	1	1402	49.5	920	1.67	7.5
6	50&86×54	540	4865	17 6	72	4	7722	273	2673	1.67	48
7	35&70×48	424	2000	17 0	90	2	4774	150	1200	1.69	21.5
8	54&94×60	530	7420	18 3½	75	6	10839	313	2207	1.70	40.3
9	54&94×60	486	7422	18 0	82.5	6	11340	324	1801	1 70	32.8
10	30&58×39	400	1513	14 2	80	2	2608	69.7	650	1.72	12
11	29&56×33	350	1250	13 3	70	2	2379	66	500	1.76	9.5
12	34&66×42	406	1700	15 6	80	2	3474	107.2	875	1.76	16.5
13	36&68×42	434	1821	16 3	77	2	3714	110	854	1.76	16.75
14	54&97×60	480	7427	18 10½	70	6	11045	329	2000	1.80	38.6
15	51&88×60	590	5000	17 6	75	4	9248	332.5	2745	1.83	54.
16	28&53×38	380	1560	14 0	75	2	2433	78	560	1.84	11
17	50&86×54	540	5500	17 6	70	4	7525	273	2422	1.85	48
18	39&70×48	416	2600	17 9	80	..	4864	65	1160	1.85	23
19	35&70×48	408	2005	17 0	90	2	4826	150	1099	1.87	22
20	35&70×48	440	2000	20 9	90	2	4396	136	1135	1.89	23
21	34½&64×42	560	1647	15 4	80	2	2950	106	880	1.90	18
22	48&84×60	550	4468	19 0	70	3	8200	340	2300	1.90	47
23	50&86×54	510	4842	17 9	70	6	9839	310	2213	1.90	43.5
24	54&94×60	441	7420	17 9	70	6	11750	312	2400	1.90	48.9
25	56&97×54	504	5000	18 6	70	6	8215	292	2500	1.93	51.9
26	30&60×36	372	1600	13 0	90	2	2753	115	600	1.94	12.5
27	30&70×45	560	2900	13 0	75	2	4622	166	1600	2.00	32
28	36&64×36	450	2059	13 0	70	2	2854	106	1020	2.12	22
29	36&68×42	530	2500	13 0	70	2	3462	130	1250	2.25	29
30	36&67×42	530	2400	13 0	70	2	3451	129	1230	2.25	28
		mean 467			mean 77.4					mean 1.828	
	Tandem--										
31	48&83×60 d'ble.	523	9000	23 6	70	8	19104	624	4900	1.77	93
32	26&58×45 sin.	444	1700	15 0	80	2	3160	99	820	1.90	16.75
33	27&56×52 "	395	1730	15 9	80	1	3244	102	730	1.92	15.1
34	27&56×52 "	412	1650	15 9	75	1	3570	102	771	1.93	16
35	28&60×54 d'ble.	504	4100	20 0	90	3	7400	300	1900	1.96	40
36	28&60×54 "	522	4100	20 0	80	3	7413	302	1850	2.01	40
37	16&34×30 "	360	768	12 6	68	1	1350	47.2	270	2.25	7
38	26&52×42 "	336	2400	17 3	70	2	3650	132	900	2.47	24
		mean 437			mean 76.7					mean 2.026	
39	60&{ 90 / 90 }×66	605	......	21 0	90	7	19500	780	6300	1.63	110

While Mr. Marshall's table is of great value, it must not be forgotten that the gain and rapid advance is due to the increase of pressure and the higher expansion used; and must not be confounded with the great gain which resulted from the introduction of the compound engine following the surface condenser. Of this a portion was a mechanical one, due to smoother action, and the remainder, the saving of the heat lost by constant blowing off when salt water was fed to the boilers.

Mr. Marshall compares with a paper read by Mr., now, Sir F. J. Bramwell, in 1872, in which Mr. Bramwell gave particulars of twenty-eight steamships.

The average consumption of coal per indicated horse-power per hour, from nineteen of these vessels, was 2.11 pounds, the steam pressure ranging from 45 to 65 pounds above the atmosphere. The steam averaged, say, 52.5 pounds, and the piston speed was 376 feet per minute.

We see that the average steam pressure, was, in 1881, 77.4 pounds, the average piston speed 467 feet, while the coal consumed per indicated horse-power per hour, was 1.83 pounds, or 13.4 per cent. less; and the boiler surface is also less per horse-power. This gain is shown to be that theoretically due to the higher initial pressure, the same terminal and back pressure being assumed. the number of expansions being in the one case 5.15, and in the other 7.05.

Now with steam of 60 pounds total working pressure, and with 4.57 expansions, the theoretical steam is 21.93 pounds per indicated horse-power per hour; for 6 expansions 19.09 pounds, and for 8 expansions 18.8 pounds. The difference between 21.9 and 18.8 = 3.1, which shows the gain by increasing from 4.57 to 8 expansions.

The gain from 6 to 8 expansions, or from 19.1 to 18.8 pounds, of steam is only 0.3, or, for 7 expansions say 18.9 pounds; so that we find that most of the gain must come from the increase in pressure and very little from the increase in expansion.

The value of jacketting and compounding is still on open question. For slow moving engines, both appear to add to the economy; but for high speed engines little gain is observed. In Chapter V, in the Alsatian experiments, we shall find a very strong argument in favor of the single cylinder unjacketed engine using superheated steam. In comparing the economy of the engines of the "Leila," using compound unjacketed cylinders, with those of the "Siesta," we find for the cases of maximum power that little was added by the superheating but the smaller engine was driven the harder. Looking at the Miller's Exhibition engine we find that with the cylinder of the same size it used but little more steam per net horse-power,—steam of the same pressure.

We present here two diagrams from Porter-Allen engines. One taken at a trial using superheated steam, made at the American Institute Fair in New York several years ago, and interesting mainly as showing an expansion curve similar to that of steam in a non-conducting cylinder. The other is from a compound engine, jacketed, and with interheater. The diagrams then taken are given, and also the combined diagram; the latter shows two curves of expansion for a non-conducting cylinder, the inner one for the steam passing through the engine and the outer one for all the steam used. A comparison of the enclosed areas with that of the outer curve shows the loss. We also give illustrations, and detailed drawings of some of the principal features of the Porter-Allen engine which re-

DIAGRAMS FROM PORTER-ALLEN ENGINE.

16″ × 30″, 125 revolutions per minute.

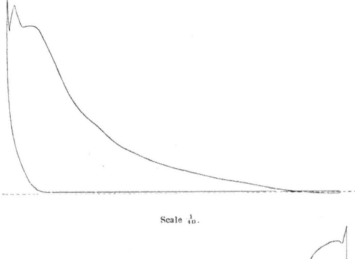

Scale $\frac{1}{40}$.

Record, 1 horse-power per 25.8 lbs. of water per hour

quire no explanation, see pages 167 to 187. They are given as an example of the most skillful design which has been attended with the best workmanship ever used in engine building.

We also give illustrations and many details of the Reynolds Corliss

Scale $\frac{1}{50}$.

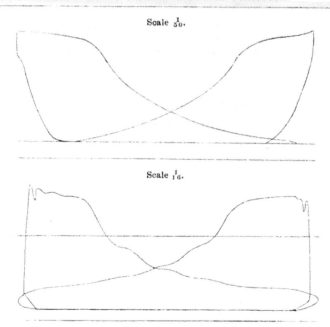

Scale $\frac{1}{16}$.

DIAGRAM FROM PORTER-ALLEN COMPOUND ENGINE.
12″ and 21″ × 24″, at 180 revolutions per minute.

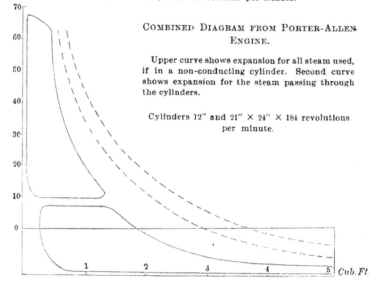

COMBINED DIAGRAM FROM PORTER-ALLEN ENGINE.

Upper curve shows expansion for all steam used, if in a non-conducting cylinder. Second curve shows expansion for the steam passing through the cylinders.

Cylinders 12″ and 21″ × 24″ × 184 revolutions per minute.

engine built by Messrs. E. P. Allis & Co., of Milwaukee, Wis., which were kindly furnished by Mr. Edwin Reynolds, and these require no further explanation, see pages 153 to 162.

On pages 163 to 166 we also give some illustrations of details of the Lambertville, N. J., Iron Works, Automatic Cut-off Engine.

The class of engines with poppet valves we illustrate by some details of the engines of the Mississippi River Steamboat, "Montana," pages 119 to 121, and an elevation of the High Service Engine, No. 1, of the St. Louis Water works, page 114.

We illustrate herewith the action of river engines by diagrams taken from the Steamboat "Phil. E. Chappel" and the "James Howard." A dia-

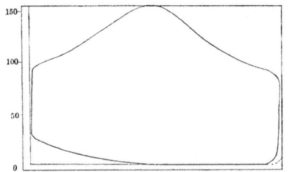

DIAGRAM FROM LARGE CYLINDER OF ENGINES OF RIVER STEAMER "PHIL. E. CHAPPEL."

22 revolutions per minute.

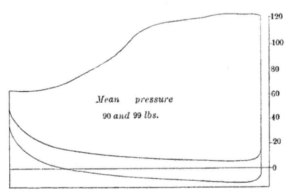

Mean pressure

90 and 99 lbs.

DIAGRAM FROM ENGINES OF RIVER STEAMER "JAS. HOWARD."

34⅛" × 120" × 11¼" with condenser, 12¼" without condenser.
1247 I. H. P., both engines with condenser.
1268 I. H. P., both engines without condenser.

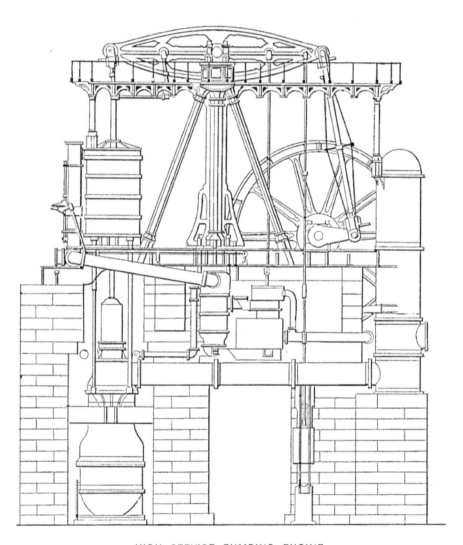

HIGH SERVICE PUMPING ENGINE,

No. I, St. Louis, Mo., Water Works.

Steam cylinder 85″ × 120″.

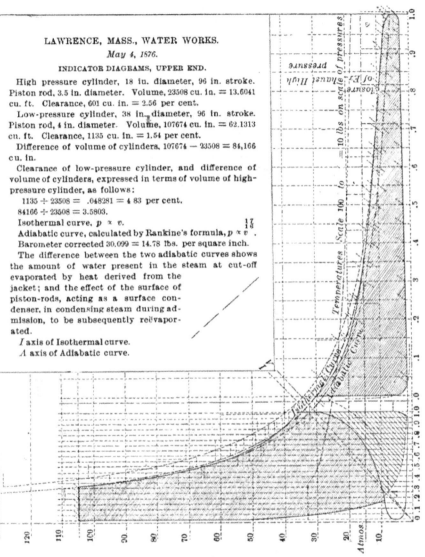

LAWRENCE, MASS., WATER WORKS.

May 4, 1876.

INDICATOR DIAGRAMS, UPPER END.

High pressure cylinder, 18 in. diameter, 96 in. stroke. Piston rod, 3.5 in. diameter. Volume, 23508 cu. in. = 13.6041 cu. ft. Clearance, 601 cu. in. = 2.56 per cent.

Low-pressure cylinder, 38 in. diameter, 96 in. stroke. Piston rod, 4 in. diameter. Volume, 107674 cu. in. = 62.1313 cu. ft. Clearance, 1135 cu. in. = 1.54 per cent.

Difference of volume of cylinders, 107674 − 23508 = 84,166 cu. in.

Clearance of low-pressure cylinder, and difference of volume of cylinders, expressed in terms of volume of high-pressure cylinder, as follows:

1135 ÷ 23508 = .048281 = 4 83 per cent.

84166 ÷ 23508 = 3.5803.

Isothermal curve, $p \propto v$.

Adiabatic curve, calculated by Rankine's formula, $p \propto v^{\frac{17}{16}}$.

Barometer corrected 30.099 = 14.78 lbs. per square inch.

The difference between the two adiabatic curves shows the amount of water present in the steam at cut-off evaporated by heat derived from the jacket; and the effect of the surface of piston-rods, acting as a surface condenser, in condensing steam during admission, to be subsequently reëvaporated.

I axis of Isothermal curve.

A axis of Adiabatic curve.

The indicated work done in smaller cylinder may be taken as including the portion only fine shaded, in which case the work indicated in large cylinder includes from the point *A*, the clearance being curved on the indicated work in small cylinder is to be taken as including the portion with coarse shade, the clearance loss being vertical and the work indicated in long cylinder is that fine shaded only.

NOTE.—The Rankine formula for an adiabatic curve is $p\,v^{\frac{10}{9}}$ = const., and not $p\,v^{\frac{11}{16}}$ = const., as given above.

DIAGRAMS FROM ENGINES OF S. S. "ARIZONA."

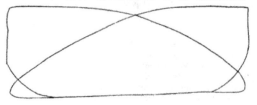

HIGH PRESSURE.

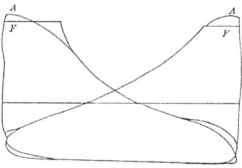

LOW PRESSURE.

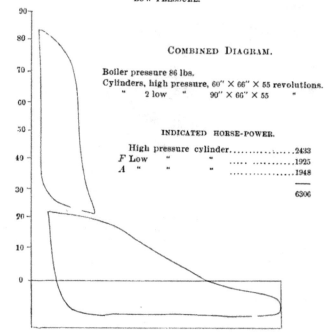

COMBINED DIAGRAM.

Boiler pressure 86 lbs.
Cylinders, high pressure, 60″ × 66″ × 55 revolutions.
    "   2 low   "   90″ × 66″ × 55   "

INDICATED HORSE-POWER.

High pressure cylinder..................2433
F Low   "   " 1925
A "   "   " 1948
                                      ‾‾‾
                                     6306

DIAGRAMS FROM ENGINES OF THE S. S. "ABERDEEN."

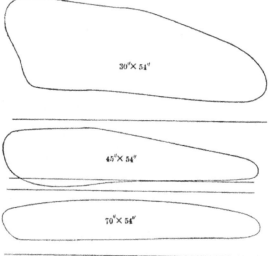

$30'' \times 54''$

$45'' \times 54''$

$70'' \times 54''$

SINGLE DIAGRAMS.

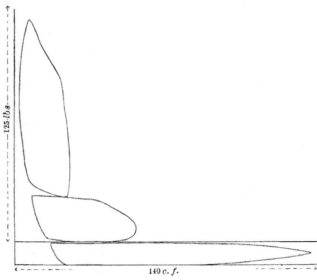

125 *lbs*

140 *c. f.*

COMBINED DIAGRAM.

gram is also given on page 91, from the St. Louis Water Works engine, and there is drawn thereon an expansion curve for the same quantity of steam in a non-conducting cylinder.

As illustrating the action of a non-receiver compound engine we give, page 115, a combined diagram from the trial of the Lawrence Pumping Engine, and have noted the matter of indicated work thereon,—the point being that is more than the sum of the finely shaded areas.

Single and combined diagrams are given for the engines of the S. S. "Arizona," the two low pressure diagrams combining as one under the high pressure diagram; and we also give single and combined diagrams from the triple expansion engines of the S. S. "Aberdeen," see pages 116, 117.

As examples of the exteriors of modern marine engines we have reproduced illustrations of the engines of the steamships "Grecian," the "Parisian" and the "Aberdeen," see pages 125 to 129, which with the above diagrams from the "Arizona" and "Aberdeen" are taken from "*Engineering*," of London.

We also give illustrations of a compound engine of the non-receiver type, for the U. S. Lighthouse Steamer "Manzanita," pages 122 to 124, designed and built by Mr. H. A. Ramsay, of the Vulcan Iron Works, Baltimore, Md. The "throws" of the two cranks are placed immediately opposite each other or 180° apart, and the steam after doing its work in the high pressure cylinder, is released, and passes at once into the large cylinder when the piston is found at the commencement of its stroke ready for the steam to exert its force upon it. Hence the interposition of a receiver, which is required when the cranks are placed at right angles to each other, is not necessary. The only objection to the arrangement is the supposed greater difficulty in handling the engine as both cranks are on their dead centres at one time, but this is easily obviated by care on the part of the engineer. The cylinders are 22 inches and 36 inches diameter, and the stroke of pistons is 34 inches. In order to work the valves with one pair of eccentrics the valve faces are placed at right angles to each other. This arrangement simplifies the number of parts and renders them easily accessible for adjustment. There are no expansion or cut-off valves on either cylinder but both which are of the ordinary locomotive type, are provided with sufficient lap to enable them to suppress the steam at three-fourths of the stroke of the pistons. By the proper arrangement of passages and valves, the engines are arranged to work as simple condensing engines, compound and high pressure or non-condensing, as may be desired. The surface condenser which is of the usual rectangular cast-iron box shape forms the frame for supporting the cylinders on one side, while the other side is supported on wrought-iron columns. The air pump has a trunk plunger and bucket actuated by wrought-iron levers connected to the cross-head of the low-pressure cylinder.

The condenser is arranged to pass the condensing water, furnished by an independent steam pump, making three turns through the condenser. The circulating pump has a cylinder of 12 inches diameter and 15 inches stroke.

MISSISSIPPI RIVER STEAMER "MONTANA."
Cylinder and Valves.

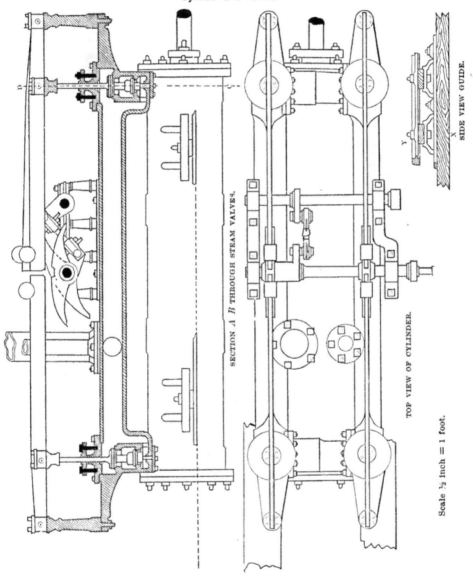

SECTION *A B* THROUGH STEAM VALVES.

TOP VIEW OF CYLINDER.

SIDE VIEW GUIDE.

Scale ½ inch = 1 foot.

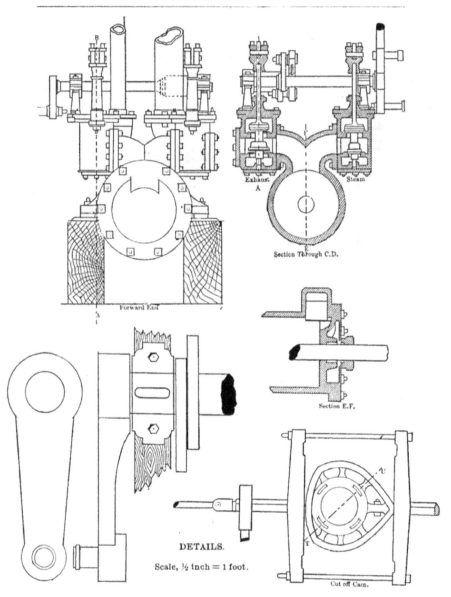

Exhaust
A

Steam

Section Through C.D.

Forward End

Section E.F.

DETAILS.

Scale, ½ inch = 1 foot.

Cut off Cam.

MISSISSIPPI RIVER STEAMER "MONTANA."

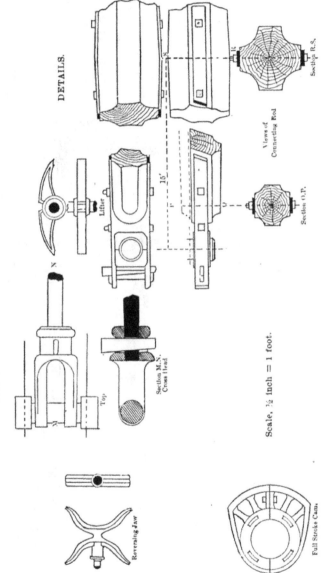

DETAILS.

MISSISSIPPI RIVER STEAMER "MONTANA."

Section R.S.

Views of Connecting Rod

Section O.P.

Lifter

Section M.N. Cross Head

Top

Reversing Jaw

Full Stroke Cam.

Scale, ½ inch = 1 foot.

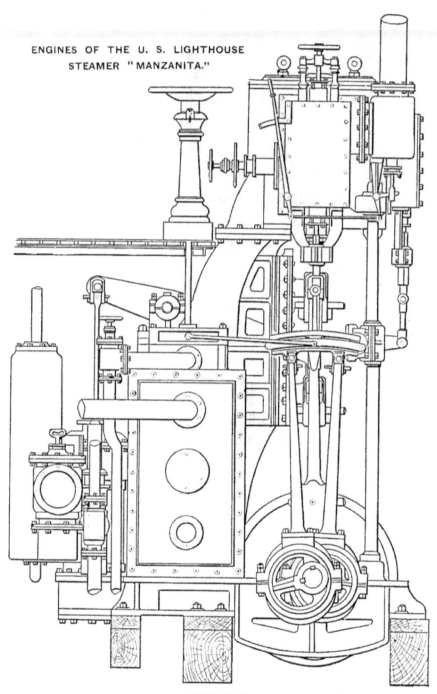

ENGINES OF THE U. S. LIGHTHOUSE
STEAMER "MANZANITA."

ELEVATION.

ENGINES OF U. S. LIGHTHOUSE STEAMER "MANZANITA."

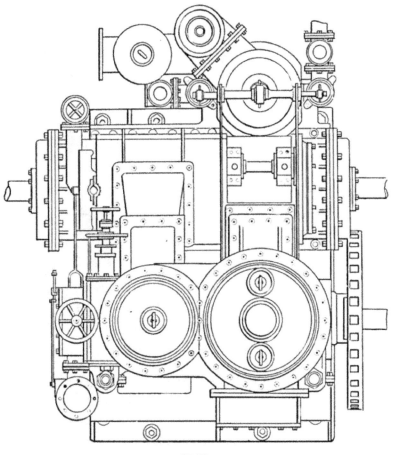

PLAN.

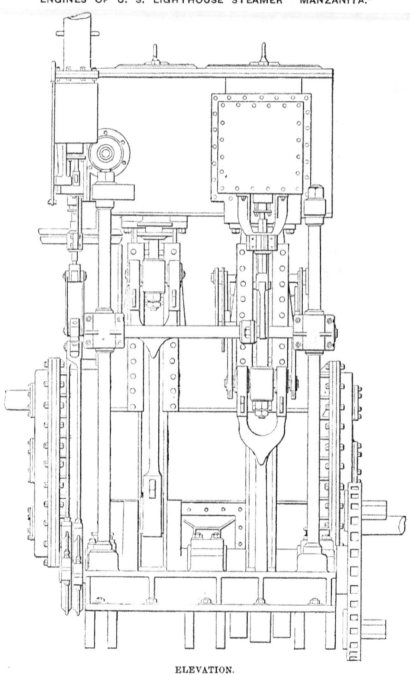

ELEVATION.

TRIPLE-EXPANSION ENGINES OF S. S. "ABERDEEN."

PERSPECTIVE VIEW.

Cylinders 90", 45" and 70" × 54" stroke.

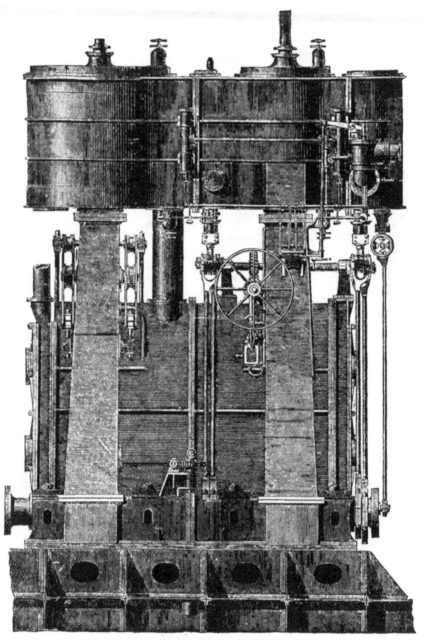

SIDE ELEVATION.

Cylinders 48" and 84" × 54" stroke.   2000 horse power.

COMPOUND ENGINES OF S. S. "GRECIAN."

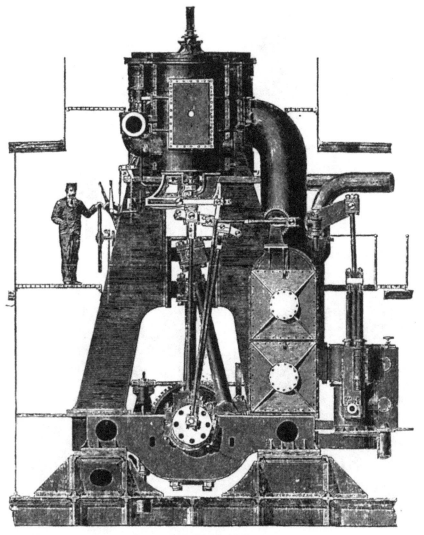

END ELEVATION.

THREE-CYLINDER COMPOUND ENGINE OF S. S. "PARISIAN."

Cylinders 60″, 85″ and 85″ × 60″ stroke.

THREE-CYLINDER COMPOUND ENGINES OF S. S. "PARISIAN."

On pages 138 and 139 will be found illustrations of the engines of the steam yacht "Leila," built by the Herreshoff Manufacturing Company, Providence, R. I.

The Buckeye engine we illustrate in detail, see pages 141 to 152. It appears at first sight to have only an expansion valve on the back of the main slide, with the change in the cut-off given by the rotating weights on the shaft turning the expansion eccentric round the shaft. But the connection between the expansion eccentric and its slide is through a rocking lever with equal arms, carried at its centre at the middle of a rocking lever pivotted at the lower end. The effect of this, while throwing the expansion slide to the other side of the main slide, is also to render the movement of the expansion slide on the back of the main slide entirely independent of the position of the latter; for the expansion slide is in its central position on the main slide when the two working levers are in line, which only requires the expansion eccentric to be in a given place. The arrangement is therefore as if the expansion slide worked on a fixed seat, dividing the steam chest, with the advantage of a very small clearance.

In drawing the valve diagram we find from the distance circle for the main valve, the points of admission, release and cushion; but we draw either on the same, or a separate diagram, the distance circle for any position of the expansion eccentric, and remembering the lap is negative, we draw the lines for the opening and closing of the ports in the slide by the expansion slide.

By turning these round from the place where the cut-off is made by the main slide to any early limit desired, the range and throw, or range and lap, may be determined. This presents no difficulty, and is simpler than the case of the common engine in which the expansion eccentric is also turned round the shaft.

On page 136 we give an illustration and description of the Steam Engine Governor used by the Cummer Engine Company, of Cleveland, O.

Four port engines are the oldest type of vertical engines with poppet valves, and the lifting is usually performed by cams. The first attempt at expansion was made by Stevens. The rock shaft holding the cams was moved by a rod from the eccentric; the end of the rock shaft carried an arm with a pin thereon and the rod from the eccentrics, passing on this pin, was slotted. By using a large eccentric, set much in advance, this rod acquired considerable motion in either direction before the rock shaft was put in motion, and the opening of the valves was made much more rapidly. As the cams could move down without any effect after the valve had seated, the closure was made earlier and also more promptly. A drop cut off was afterwards devised by Sickles, and the steam valve stems were lifted by clutches and released at any point desired. This gear could be altered by hand while running. Pumping engine, No. 1, High Service, St. Louis Water Works, has been given as a good example of this kind of machine.

The credit of the Automatic cut-off, or expansion varied by the governor, must be accorded to Geo. H. Corliss, of Providence, Rhode Island. He introduced a four port engine with twisting valves, adding various devices in the way of connections and adjustments, until he secured a very rapid opening of the steam valve, and rapid opening and closing of the exhaust valves. The latter were permanently attached to, and moved by, the eccentric, and only by moving the eccentric of the shaft and by changing the length of the rods can any change be produced in their movement. The steam valves were lifted by clutches, which met with a releasing piece at some point of the opening determined by the governor, the earlier the faster; the mean effective pressure in the cylinder is thereby reduced, the speed lowers and is again increased. By a delicate governor these variations may be made almost imperceptible.

The undoubted gain made by these engines in the use of steam, is due to the fact that the initial pressure up to the cut off is kept nearly that of the boiler, and that with the large ports and quick opening valves the back pressure is reduced to the least possible amount. The piston speed, number of revolutions, and steam pressure are all increased while the clearance is very greatly reduced. And, in fact the gain is due to a general fitness and skillful combination of things, all of which were good in themselves, and which in no way disturbed each other, when combined.

The closing of the steam valves after being tripped has been caused by weights, by springs, by compressed air, by air of reduced pressure, and by steam, as well as by combinations of these forces. The best results have been given in this country by weight and vacuum tending to close the valve, with an air dash pot to take up the shock.

At the expiration of the patents covering Mr. Corliss' improvements, a number of builders commenced making engines of almost exactly the same pattern. Of these imitations which contain very many improvements, perhaps those built by Mr. Wm. A. Harris, of Providence, are best known in the East, while those of Messrs. E. P. Allis and Co., of Milwaukee, working from the designs and under the supervision of Mr. Edwin A. Reynolds, have suited the requirements of the Western practice.

To take an example of a four-port engine with poppet valves we select the western river Steamer "Montana," given on pages 119 to 121. The four valves are moved by four cams from two rock shafts, driven by rods from triangular cams on the shaft. The engines can be worked by hand or not, at full stroke, backward or forward, and at a fixed cut-off never earlier than one-half stroke while running forward.

A single cam on the shaft connected to the steam rock shaft is used for the cut-off, while the exhaust side rockshaft is driven by the other cam. To use full stroke this is disconnected and the two rockshafts hooked to work together from the exhaust; while to reverse, the full stroke cam is hooked to the rock arm driving the exhaust on the other side. The rapid movements of the valves in opening and closing are seen from the diagrams taken from the steamer "Phil. E. Chappel." Two cards are given

THE WHEELOCK ENGINE.

Sections of Cylinders Showing Valves, Ports, etc.

from the "James Howard" shown with and without the use of the condenser. The condenser was opened to the cylinder after the bulk of the steam had been exhausted into the air, say when the piston had moved one-tenth of the stroke backwards, the increase of pressure found was about ten pounds or 10 per cent., and the great size of condenser and air pump were reduced because little of the steam was left. It was found practically that the increase of the range of temperature between the incoming and outgoing steam was enough to so increase the internal waste that no economy but a positive loss was attendant upon its use.

Following the Corliss type of engine closely is that of Mr. Jerome Wheelock, of Worcester, Mass., which is however, only two-ported. The valves are of the Corliss pattern and two are used for opening to steam and for opening and closing the exhaust. The closing of the steam is governed by two other valves of the same kind placed upon the steam passage leading to the main valves, and moved from the main valves by clutch links which are tripped by the governor. This engine has a future, but as built, it leaves a separate eccentric for the steam and exhaust valves, and a general increase in strength, to be desired. The use of two eccentrics, one for the steam, and one for the exhaust, valves, has been followed in this country by the Atlas Engine Works, of Indianapolis, and is generally desirable. One of the best frames made with the Corliss engine has been a modification of that used by Wm. Wright, in his four-port slide valve engines and has been adopted by Messrs. Smith, Beggs & Rankin, of St. Louis.

The Porter-Allen engine is a four-port slide valve engine with steam slides balanced and worked from a link, the position in the link of the radius rod attached to the valve stem being controlled by the governor; the balanced exhaust valves are worked from some fixed part of the link. The engine is intended to run at high speed both in revolutions and piston travel, and on this engine was first studied and developed the actual effect of the weight of the reciprocating parts of the engine, the piston, rod, cross-head and connecting rod. These pieces evidently have to be started on the stroke before any pressure from the steam can reach the crank pin and main journal, and if they are heavy and the speed high, almost all the pressure of the steam upon the piston may be absorbed in starting this dead weight. In any case the full force of the steam acting upon the piston is reduced before it reaches the crank pin. After the engine has passed mid stroke where this weight is now moving at its greatest speed we find that the steam pressure has very much fallen if the cutoff be early, and that the inertia of the moving parts is now pressing with the steam pressure against the crank. Thus the weight of the moving pieces tends in connection with the varying cylinder pressures to equalize the pressure, wear, and rotation.

In some cases we have examined we found that the load on the engine was so light and the boiler pressure so low, the cut-off taking place early. Under these conditions the crank pin was started entirely by the fly wheel and the crank pin actually dragged from one end the weight which

the steam was pushing at the other. At mid stroke the steam pressure
had fallen considerably and the inertia of the weight now moving fast did
all the work from there to the end of the stroke.   This of course is not desirable, but it may be considered that to have half the initial pressure
transmitted to the pin, while half is taken up in moving the weight to be
given out again at the end of the stroke, is the best adjustment possible.

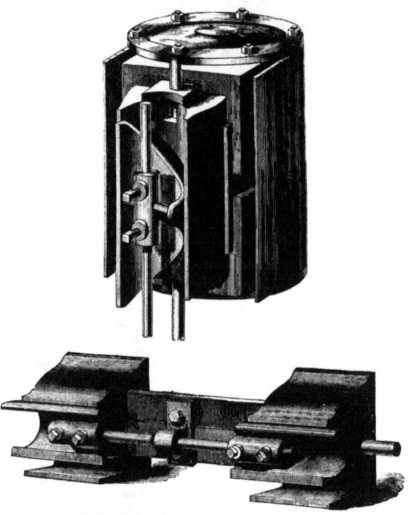

THE RIDER AUTOMATIC EXPANSION GEAR.

This, of course, can only be done for one speed and steam pressure by properly designing the weight, and average results only can be reached. This action combined with the high rotation speed on the fly wheel causes these engines to run with what appears to be a simply marvelous smoothness, and the quick acting governor maintains the speed, changing in height under variations of revolution which are too small to be otherwise noticed. Illustrations of this engine are given on pages 167 to 187.

Among stationary engines in England, by far the most common type is that of a slide valve with an expansion slide on the back, and it is the most common type in Europe. The arrangement is very often used with small engines, as small as those with 8 inch cylinders, without means of varying the expansion, and with the speed regulated by a throttle and govenor as usual. In the United States, on the other hand, this form (non-adjustable) is rarely to be met with. While the use of an expansion slide varied by hand is by no means common, a very neat type is made at Erie, Pa., of the class in which the negative lap is varied by a right and left hand screw and handwheel projecting from the end of the steam chest. By this wheel the expansion can be changed while the engine is running.

One of the neatest automatic, or governor, expansion gears, is that of Rider, of the Delamater Iron Works, New York City. The back of the main slide is hollowed into a part of a cylinder whose axis is the centre of the expansion slide. The lap edges of the expansion slide and steam edges of main slide are tapered in such a manner that by rotation of the expansion slide the lap is changed as in the ordinary manner. This rotation is accomplished by a spindle attached to the govenor, gearing into a sector on the valve stem.

When an expansion slide is used in connection with a link motion for the main valve, in many cases the expansion slide is driven by its eccentric set opposite the crank, and change of cut-off is given by change of lap and a right and left hand thread and handwheel. In such cases the link is usually worked full-gear only, and the cut-off applied after the engine is in motion. The lap is negative.

A more common form with large engines, where the weight becomes harder to handle, is to cut into two parts the expansion valve rod and to connect one of them to a link, making the other a radius rod pinned to the valve stem, and working with slides in the link. The position of the slider in the link is determined by a screw and handwheel. Thus a change of travel is effected in the expansion valve. The diagram is readily constructed, and the results are good, but the steam chest has to be made longer than would be otherwise required.

A more complex arrangement is found in some cases with the link motion, a third eccentric and second link being added. The second link is attached to the expansion eccentric at one end and the main valve stem at the other. The expansion slide is moved by its valve stem, and either by a radius rod and link curved to fit the radius

THE CUMMER ENGINE GOVERNOR.

DESCRIPTION.

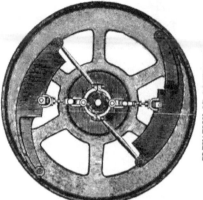

The main eccentric is cast solid with the governor. The cut-off eccentric, with its sleeve, fits loosely on the governor shaft, and is connected with the flying ends of the governor weights by means of rods or links, shown in the elevation of governor, in such a manner that the cut-off eccentric, with its sleeve, is moved around the governor shaft, either forward or backward, as the flying weights change their position; by this means, the steam is cut off correspondingly earlier or later in the stroke as the governor or flying weights adjust themselves to the load. The governor shaft is driven from the main shaft by a train of gears, one of which appears in the vertical section. The governor case, to which is attached the flying weights, is keyed to the governor shaft, and revolves with it. It will be noticed the governor shaft is hollow, and has a thrust rod passing through it. One end of this thrust rod is attached to a cross bar, which, passing through a slot in the governor

ELEVATION OF GOVERNOR.

shaft, is thereby made to revolve with it. The cross bar is connected with the governor by suitable connections and bell cranks. The other end of the thrust rod fits into a step which is jointed to the vertical arm of the large bell crank. Any movement of the weights in the governor case will cause the thrust rod to move correspondingly out or in, and thus operate or change the relative position of the large bell crank and cause the weight located under the engine and attached to the end of the horizontal arm of the bell crank to be raised or lowered in an amount corresponding to the outer or inner position of the governor weights. It will be seen that the cut-off eccentric is attached to a long sleeve, the flying ends of the governor weights are connected by means of two rods and a clamp collar, with the sleeve of the cut-off eccentric, so that, as the governor weights change their position, the eccentric, with its sleeve, moves around the shaft either forward or backward.

When the cut-off eccentric is rotated forward the steam is cut off earlier in the stroke; when the eccentric is rotated backward, the steam is cut off later in the stroke. The dead weights suspended from the horizontal arm of the large bell crank, can be varied or adjusted in amount and they thus regulate the speed of the engine without stopping it.

rod, or by a double curved link. This combination of links can be sketched as follows:

A is the crank, and *C* the shaft centers. *B*, *D*, and *E* are the virtual centers of the three given eccentrics, while *F* is the virtual eccentric for a

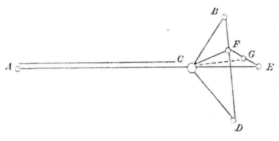

given position of the main link, and *G*, on *E F*, dividing it as the expansion slider divides the second link, is the virtual eccentric driving the expansion slide.

The diagram for the cut-off is then readily constructed from these two virtual eccentrics by the ordinary methods.

The use of this class has been confined as far as we are aware to the beautiful marine engine of Messrs. Herreshoff, of Bristol, R. I.

An automatic engine built under patents of Messrs. Armington & Simms is a good example of neat and careful design. The engine is worked by a piston valve, and the governor is like that of the Buckeye and many other engines, a pair of weights attached to the main shaft. But in the Buckeye the governor acts only on the expansion valve eccentric, pulling it ahead on the shaft if the speed is increased. In the Armington & Simms engine the pair of weights flying out pull on what may be called a compound eccentric. This compound eccentric is the peculiar feature of the engine; the ordinary eccentric, loose on the shaft, carries instead of the usual strap, a second eccentric with about one third the arm of the first. The weight is a heavy casting, pivoted at one end to the governor disc; at the free end it is connected to the lugs on the inner eccentrics, and at its middle to the outer eccentric, but on the other side of the shaft, the result being that the eccentrics are pulled around the shaft in opposite directions. The effect is that the outer eccentric centre changes both in angle and in arm, very much as it is varied in a more simple manner in the Westinghouse automatic engine, already illustrated. The rest of the engine requires no comment.

With large cylinders the valves become large, but while the steam port edge which regulates admission increases with the diameter, the volume to be filled varies with the square of the diameter. And in order to give length enough, the only way it can be increased, the edges are often doubled, or the body of the value cored with passages to the exhaust, while steam is admitted from the sides of the value to the additional ports. When the cylinders are large these valves become very complicated, and are matters of special study.

Locomotive and portable engines assume special forms but the only real difference is that boiler and engines have to be so attached as to move

ENGINES OF THE STEAM YACHT "LEILA."

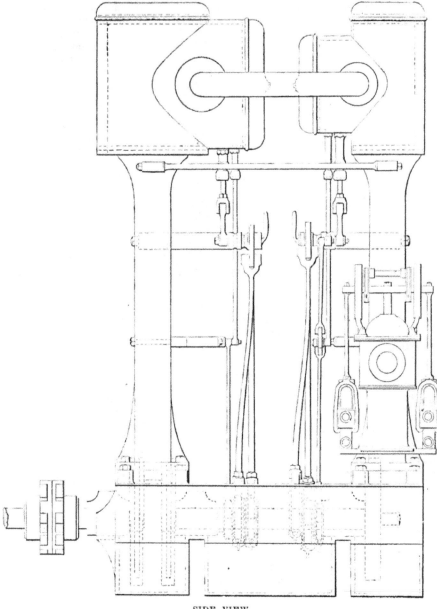

SIDE VIEW.

Cylinders 9" and 16" × 18".

ENGINES OF THE STEAM YACHT "LEILA."

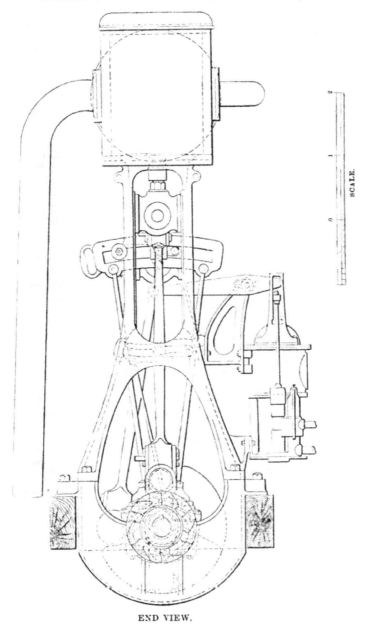

END VIEW.

together. The locomotive has always two cylinders,* operating upon cranks at right angles, and carried on from four to twelve wheels, of which from two to twelve have the same diameter and are coupled together thus acting as driving-wheels. The remaining wheels are smaller and act only as bearing wheels. The wheels are set with bearings in a frame to which the cylinders are firmly connected. Upon this frame is set the boiler and its appurtenances. The water and fuel are carried in some forms upon this frame, but more usually upon a separate frame and wheels called the "tender."

The engine proper is the pair of cylinders with their connections to the wheels and the valve gear back from the wheels to the steam. The valve is almost always the three ported slides driven by a link motion, and there is no difference whatever in the use of steam in the engine itself from any other engine of the same type. The number of revolutions is at times high, and the piston speed great, but the engine is rarely kept at hard work for more than an hour at a time.

Cylinders are used up to 24 inches in diameter while the stroke is rarely over 26 inches. A few engines for the Central Pacific Railway have a 30-inch stroke, and have an expansion slide on the back of the main slide, but such engines have been tried before and the only gain is likely to be that due clearance, for at slow speeds and late cut-off the expansion valve adds nothing; while at high speed and early cut-off the cushion produced by the link motion and single slide is found to be essential in reducing shock and increasing durability. And it may be safe to say that no other than the single slide in some of its forms, driven by the link or kindred motion, is likely to be used; for in spite of many attempts to improve it, George Stephenson left the locomotive as it still remains in all essential points, and that the only improvement worth noting is the addition of the automatic air brake which may be called the most important adjunct to railway train service after the locomotive.

The varieties of engines and cut-off gear are almost endless, but we have endeavored to restrict ourselves to the ordinary and well-defined successful constructions. New patterns are being used every day, and we have omitted a number of beautiful and apparently successful forms, manufactured by well-known builders, wholly because they have only been in operation for a comparatively short time.

---

*The London and Northwestern Railway, England, have built a number with three cylinders which have been very successful, and the Boston and Albany is building one with four cylinders, both of these cases being compound engines. Mr. Fairlie and others have built locomotives with four cylinders, which were, however, properly speaking, duplex locomotives.

THE BUCKEYE AUTOMATIC CUT-OFF ENGINE.

FRONT VIEW—NEW TANGYE PATTERN.

THE BUCKEYE AUTOMATIC CUT-OFF ENGINE.

BACK VIEW—NEW TANGYE PATTERN.

THE BUCKEYE AUTOMATIC CUT-OFF ENGINE.

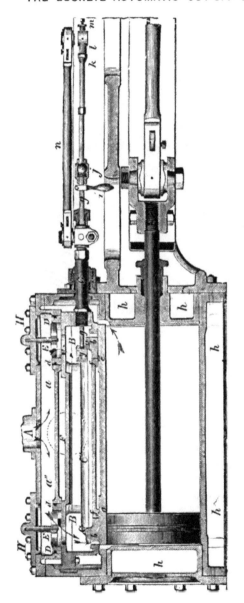

SECTION OF CYLINDER AND VALVES.

A, Steam Supply. *a a''*, Steam Passages. *D D*, Open Pistons. *B B*, Box Slide Valve. *b b*, Ports in Cylinder. *C c*, Cut-off Valves. *C'*, Rods Connecting Cut-off Valve. *g*, Cut-off Valve Stem. *G*, Hollow Stem of Main Valve. *e e*, Recesses in Valve Seats, as "relief chambers." *f f*, Holes in face of Valve, admitting steam to relief chambers.

THE BUCKEYE AUTOMATIC CUT-OFF ENGINE.

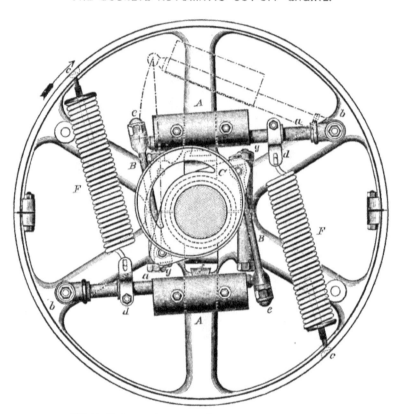

THE BUCKEYE ENGINE COMPANY'S ISOCHRONAL REGULATOR.

EXPLANATION.

Two levers, *a a*, are pivoted to the arms of the containing case at one of their ends
as at *b*, while the movable ends are connected by links *B B*, to ears, or flanges, on the
sleeve of the loose eccentric, *C*, so that their outward movement, in obedience to centrifugal force, as indicated by dotted lines, advances the eccentric forward in the direction of revolution. Springs, *F F*, of tempered steel wire, furnish the centripetal force.
The tension of the springs is adjusted by a screw at *c*. The proper speed is obtained by
adding more or less weight at *A*, or within certain limits by shifting the weights along
the levers. The case, which is made in halves, is clamped to the shaft by pinch bolts, *g*.
The spring clips, *d*, are adjustable along the levers. The parts are shown in their
proper position for motion in the direction of the arrow; for motion in the opposite
direction, the levers are pivoted to the other arms of the case and the springs are
reversed.

GENERAL DETAILS.

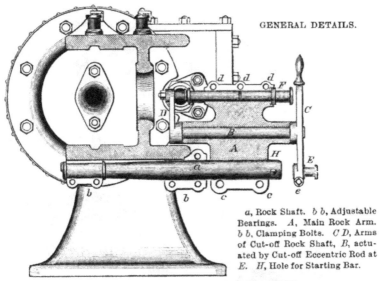

a, Rock Shaft. *b b*, Adjustable Bearings. *A*, Main Rock Arm. *b b*, Clamping Bolts. *C D*, Arms of Cut-off Rock Shaft, *B*, actuated by Cut-off Eccentric Rod at *E*. *H*, Hole for Starting Bar.

CROSS SECTION OF BED AND COMPOUND ROCK ARM.

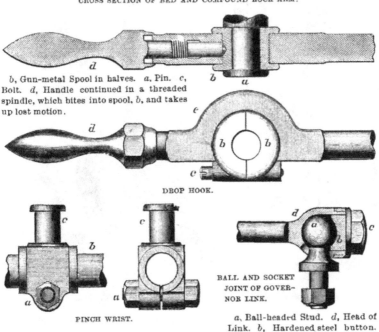

b, Gun-metal Spool in halves. *a*, Pin. *c*, Bolt. *d*, Handle continued in a threaded spindle, which bites into spool, *b*, and takes up lost motion.

DROP HOOK.

PINCH WRIST.

c, Wrist clamped to stem, *b*, by bolt, *a*.

BALL AND SOCKET JOINT OF GOVERNOR LINK.

a, Ball-headed Stud. *d*, Head of Link. *b*, Hardened steel button. *c*, Cap, to screw down solid.

SECTION OF ECCENTRIC.

BALL AND SOCKET JOINT IN CUT-OFF
VALVE STEM.

b, Sleeve Nut screwing over head of stem
d, jammed by Sleeve Nut *c*. *e*, Clamp Handle set at about 45°.

CROSS HEAD FOR GIRDER BED TYPE.

Cross-head is in halves, pinched on the
thread of piston rod, *a*, by bolts, *ff*. *b*, Pin.
c c, Tongue Gibs. *d*, Wedges. *e e*, Screws.

DEVICE FOR OILING CRANK PIN.

c, Hole in Crank Pin. *b*, Tube communicating
with *c*. *a*, Ball to receive oil; *a*, being stationary,
the oil is fed into tube by the centrifugal force.

AUTOMATIC WASTE COCK.

THE BUCKEYE AUTOMATIC CUT-OFF ENGINE.

Some Details of a 20″ × 40″ Engine.

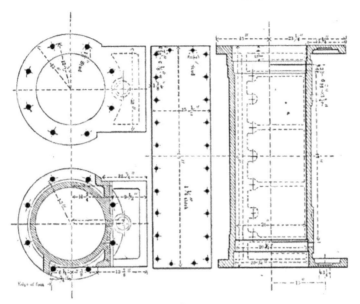

CYLINDER.

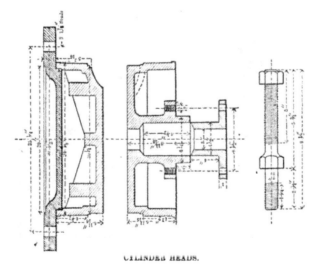

CYLINDER HEADS.

THE BUCKEYE AUTOMATIC CUT-OFF ENGINE.

SOME DETAILS OF A 20″ × 40″ ENGINE.

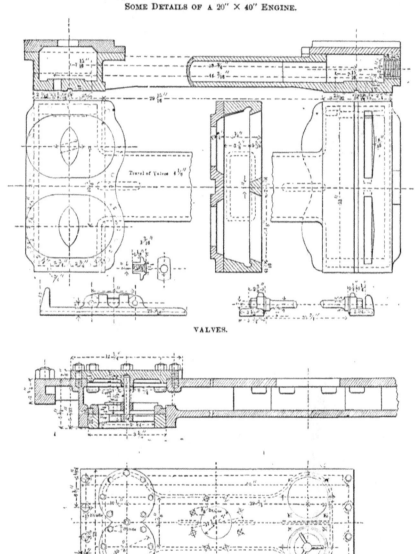

VALVES.

VALVE CHEST COVER, ETC.

THE BUCKEYE AUTOMATIC CUT-OFF ENGINE.

SOME DETAILS OF A 20″ × 40″ ENGINE.

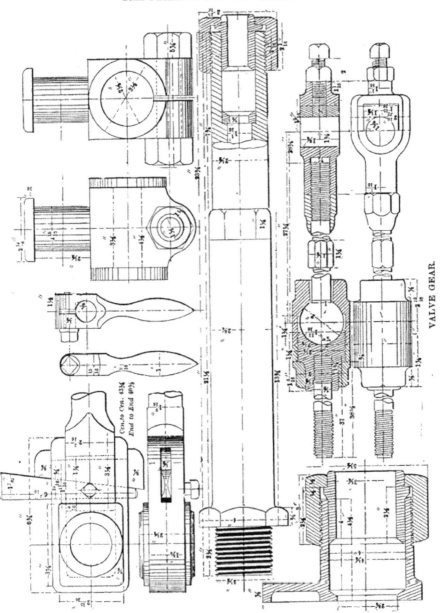

VALVE GEAR.

THE BUCKEYE AUTOMATIC CUT-OFF ENGINE.

SOME DETAILS OF A 20″ × 40″ ENGINE.

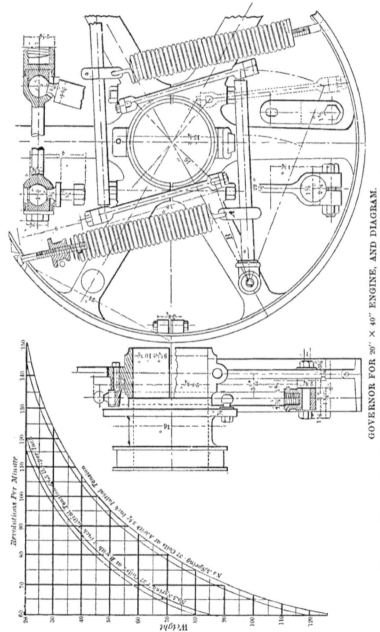

GOVERNOR FOR 20″ × 40″ ENGINE, AND DIAGRAM.

The Initial Tension Should not be less than ⅔ of the distance between the centre C and point of attachment.

THE BUCKEYE AUTOMATIC CUT-OFF ENGINE.

SOME DETAILS OF A 20″ × 40″ ENGINE.

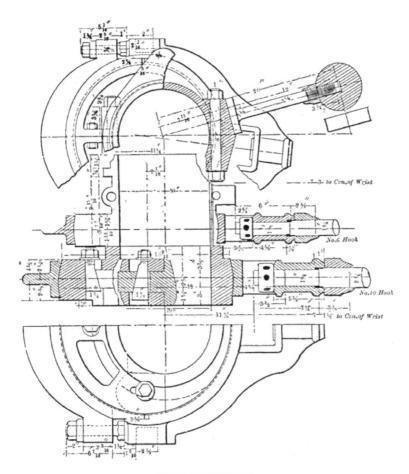

SPLIT ECCENTRICS.

THE BUCKEYE AUTOMATIC CUT-OFF ENGINE.

SOME DETAILS OF A 20″ × 40″ ENGINE.

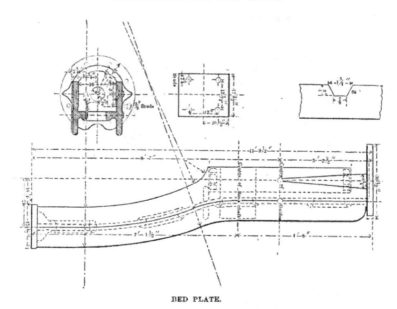

BED PLATE.

CONNECTING ROD.

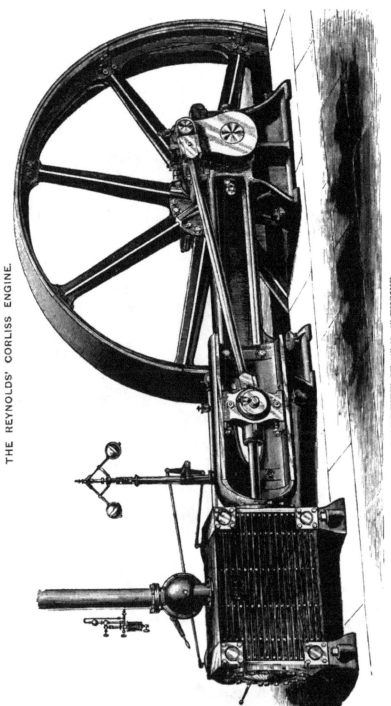

THE REYNOLDS' CORLISS ENGINE.

FRONT VIEW OF 26″ × 48″ ENGINE.

THE REYNOLDS' CORLISS ENGINE.

BACK VIEW OF 26" × 48" ENGINE.

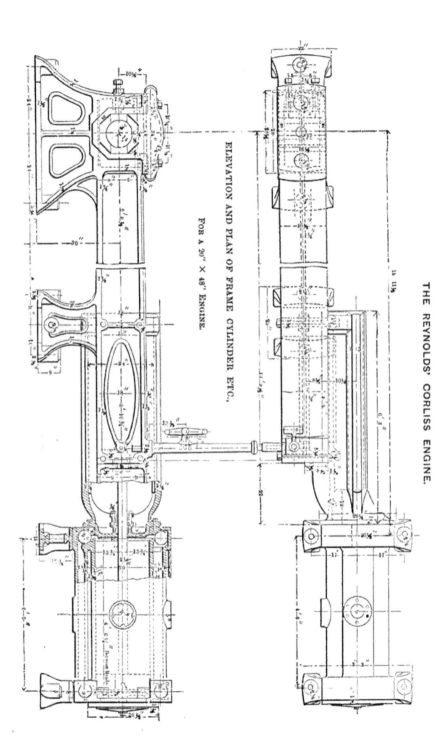

ELEVATION AND PLAN OF FRAME CYLINDER ETC.

FOR A 20″ × 48″ ENGINE.

THE REYNOLDS' CORLISS ENGINE.

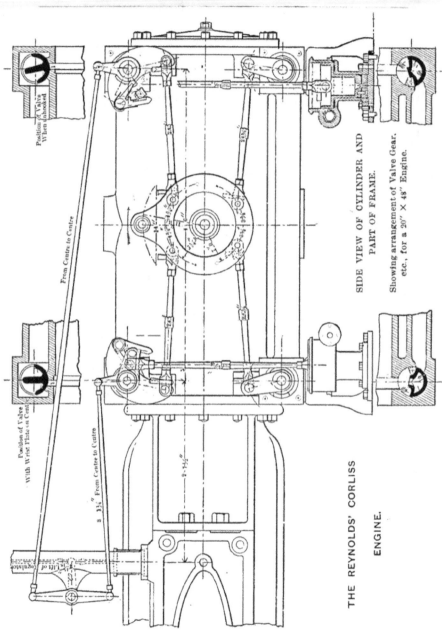

SIDE VIEW OF CYLINDER AND PART OF FRAME.

Showing arrangement of Valve Gear, etc., for a 20″ × 48″ Engine.

THE REYNOLDS' CORLISS ENGINE.

THE REYNOLDS' CORLISS ENGINE.

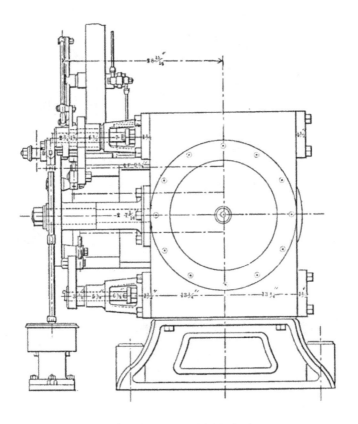

END VIEW OF CYLINDER, ETC.

Showing arrangement of Valve Gear for 20″ × 48″ Engine.

THE REYNOLDS' CORLISS ENGINE.

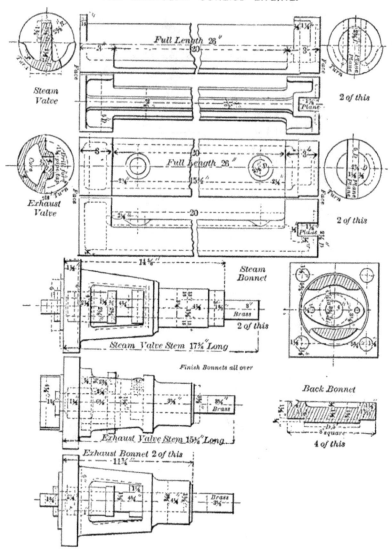

VALVES, ETC., FOR A 20″ × 48″ ENGINE.

THE REYNOLDS' CORLISS ENGINE.

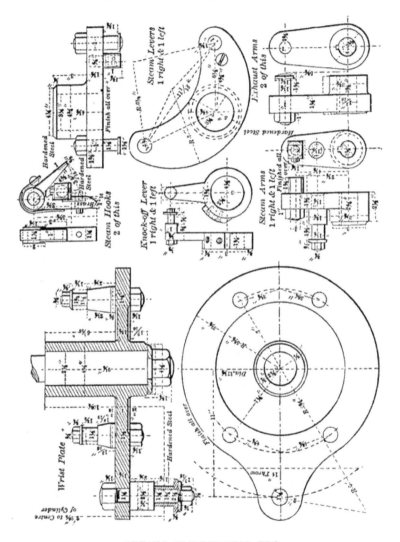

DETAILS OF VALVE GEAR, ETC.

FOR A 20″ × 48″ ENGINE.

THE REYNOLDS' CORLISS ENGINE.

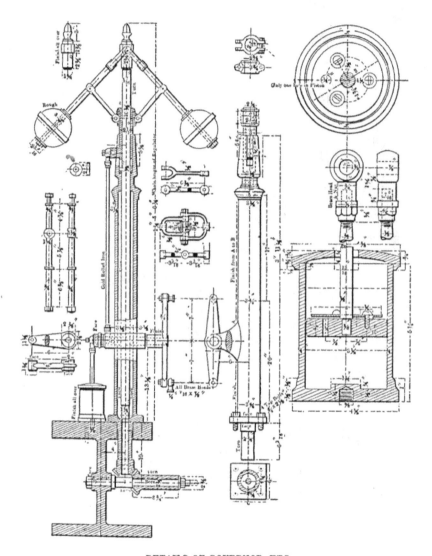

DETAILS OF GOVERNOR, ETC.

For a 20″ × 48″ Engine.

THE REYNOLDS' CORLISS ENGINE.

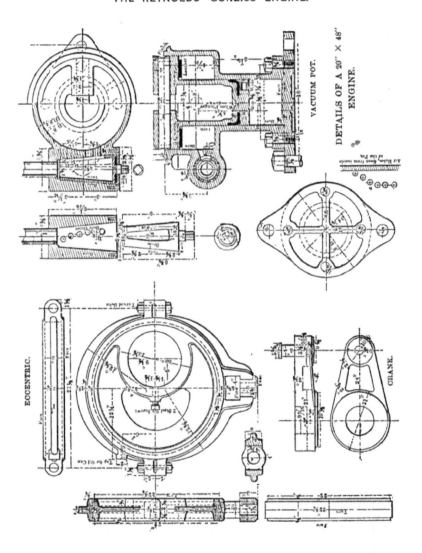

THE REYNOLDS' CORLISS ENGINE.

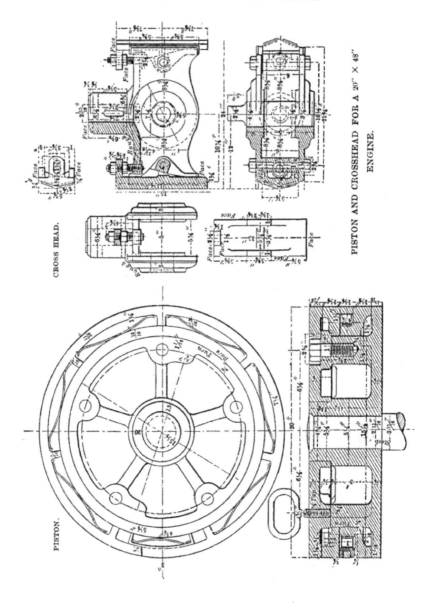

CROSS HEAD.

PISTON.

PISTON AND CROSSHEAD FOR A 20″ × 48″ ENGINE.

THE LAMBERTVILLE, N. J., IRON WORKS PATENT AUTOMATIC CUT-OFF ENGINE.

SECTIONAL VIEW OF CYLINDER AND VALVES.

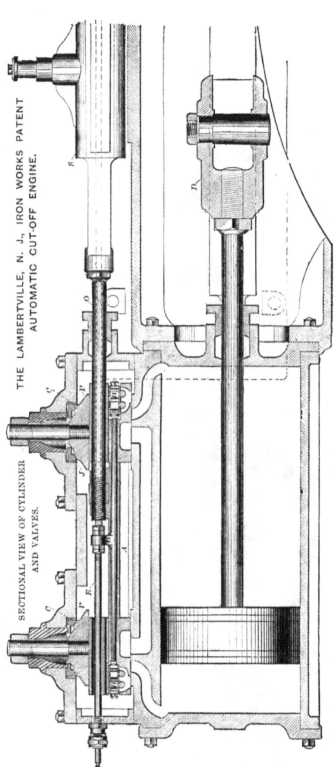

The main valve, A, is of the long D slide valve type, with multiple ports at the ends, through which the steam enters the cylinder. It is operated from an eccentric on the crank shaft, in the usual manner, giving a positive lead and exhaust, without regard to the point of cut-off. The cut-off valve, B, is also operated from the motion of an eccentric upon the crank shaft. The rod or stem, E, of the cut-off valve passes through the main valve rod, O, and slide, S. Upon its outer end are tappets which engage with corresponding tappets attached to the cut-off eccentric rod. The latter is pivoted to and supported centrally between the tappets by the rock arm, see pages 164 and 165, the opposite end of the rock arm having motion upon a pin or bearing in the governor slide, which is adjusted to position, up or down, by the action of a cam, operated by the governor balls. The slide, S, is of cylindrical form, and encloses a spring and dash pots with discs attached to the cut-off valve rod, by means of which the valve is closed. The motion from the two eccentrics for operating the valves is relatively in the same direction, but of different throw; the stroke of the cut-off eccentric being greater by an amount necessary to open the multiple ports, and having also sufficient angular advance to cause the ports to be well open for the admission of steam when the engine is on its centre, so that no loss is occasioned by wire drawing of the steam, even at the shortest point of cut-off. As the cut-off valve is opened by the tappets, the spring will be compressed to an amount equal to the difference in the strokes of the eccentrics, and so long as the governor balls are in their lowest position the tappets will be in contact, and no release or tripping will take place, the engine working precisely as a plain slide valve engine. As the speed of the engine increases the centrifugal force of the governor balls will lift the tappets apart until a release occurs, when the valve will be instantly closed by the reaction of the spring, and the two valves will then travel together as one valve for the balance of the stroke. This operation may take place at any part of the stroke indicated by the governor.

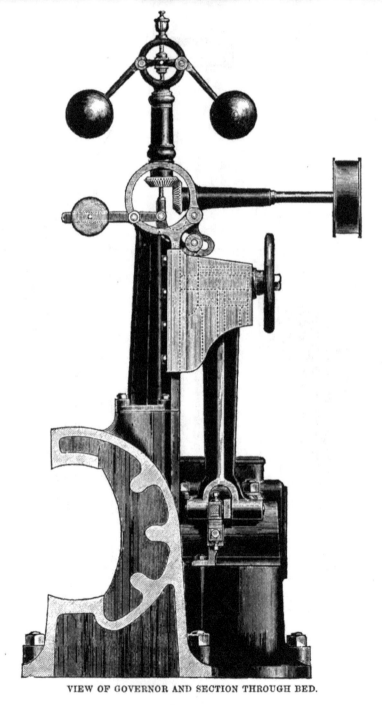

VIEW OF GOVERNOR AND SECTION THROUGH BED.

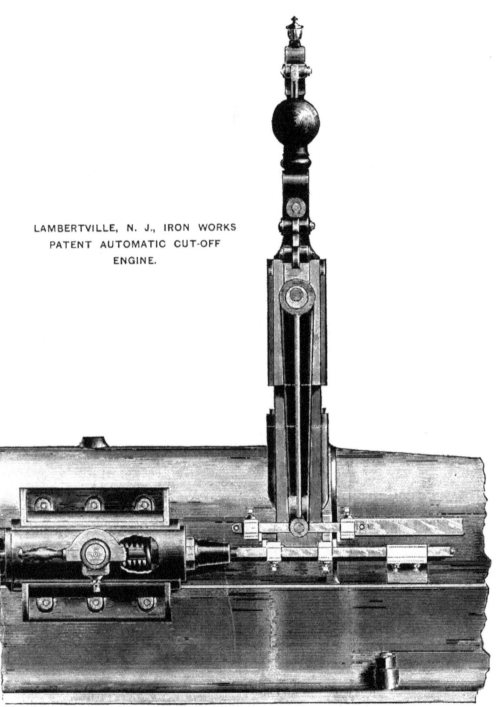

LAMBERTVILLE, N. J., IRON WORKS
PATENT AUTOMATIC CUT-OFF
ENGINE.

GOVERNOR—SIDE VIEW.

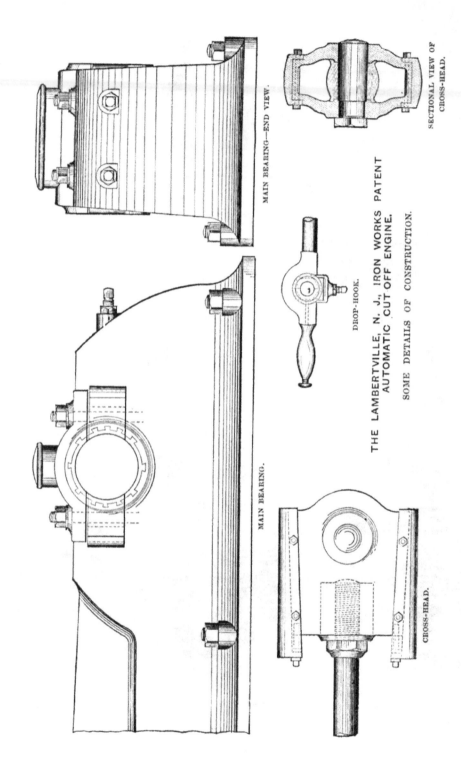

MAIN BEARING—END VIEW.

SECTIONAL VIEW OF
CROSS-HEAD.

MAIN BEARING.

DROP-HOOK.

CROSS-HEAD.

THE LAMBERTVILLE, N. J., IRON WORKS PATENT
AUTOMATIC CUT OFF ENGINE.

SOME DETAILS OF CONSTRUCTION.

THE PORTER-ALLEN ENGINE.

PERSPECTIVE VIEW OF A PAIR OF 11¼" × 16" ENGINES.

THE PORTER-ALLEN ENGINE.

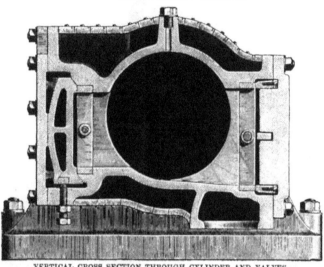

VERTICAL CROSS SECTION THROUGH CYLINDER AND VALVES.

SECTIONAL PLAN OF CYLINDER THROUGH STEAM AND EXHAUST VALVES.

THE PORTER-ALLEN ENGINE.

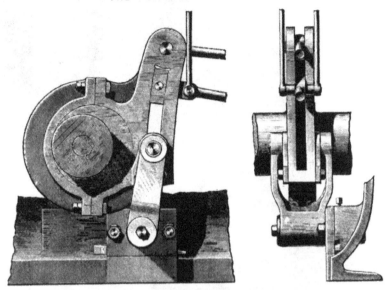

SIDE AND FRONT ELEVATION OF ECCENTRIC AND LINK.

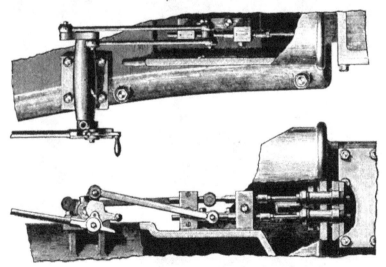

ELEVATION AND PLAN OF VALVE CONNECTIONS.

PLAN AND ELEVATION OF MAIN SHAFT BEARING.

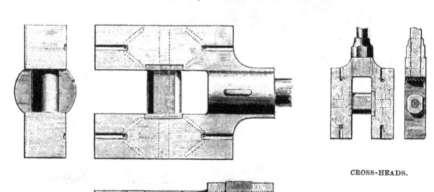

CROSS-HEADS.

THE PORTER-ALLEN ENGINE.

CRANK PIN OILER.

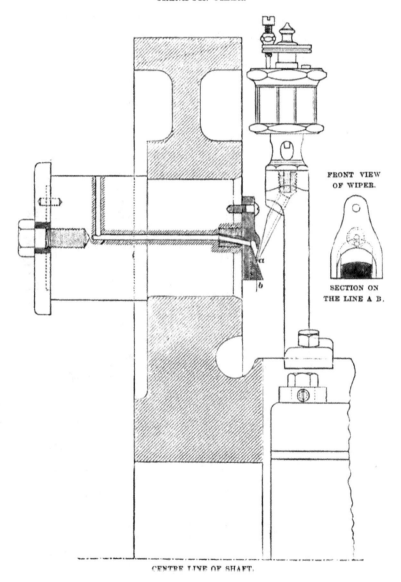

FRONT VIEW
OF WIPER.

SECTION ON
THE LINE A B.

CENTRE LINE OF SHAFT.

THE PORTER-ALLEN ENGINE.

FRONT ELEVATION.

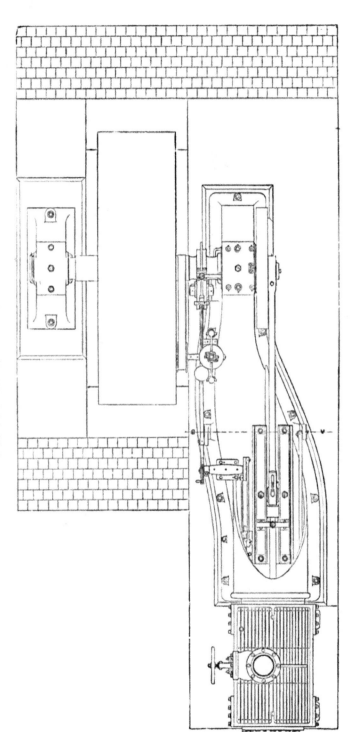

PLAN.

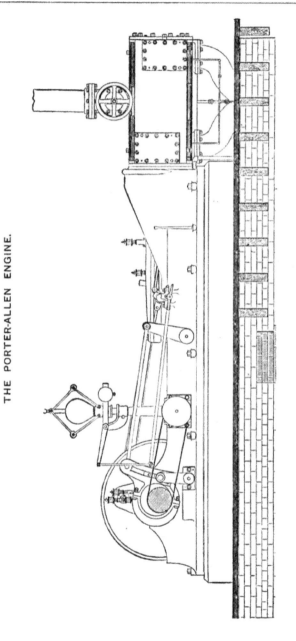

THE PORTER-ALLEN ENGINE.

REAR ELEVATION.

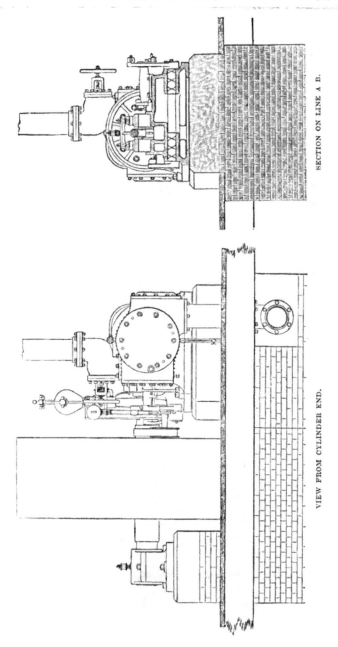

THE PORTER-ALLEN ENGINE.

SECTION ON LINE A B.

VIEW FROM CYLINDER END.

THE PORTER-ALLEN ENGINE.

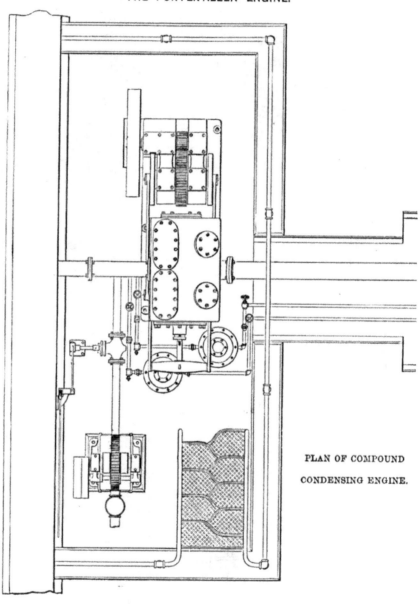

PLAN OF COMPOUND

CONDENSING ENGINE.

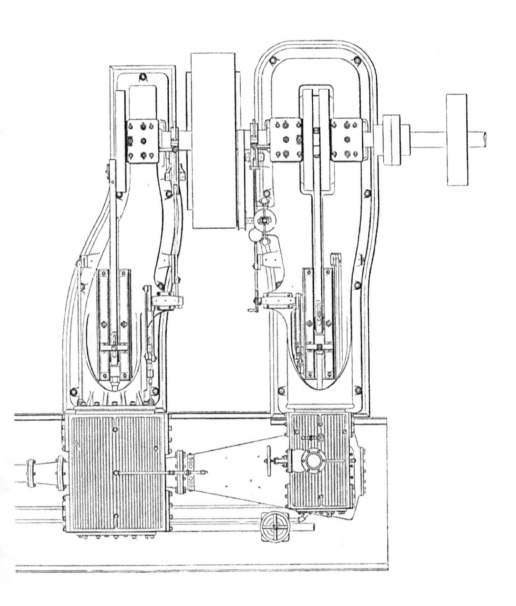

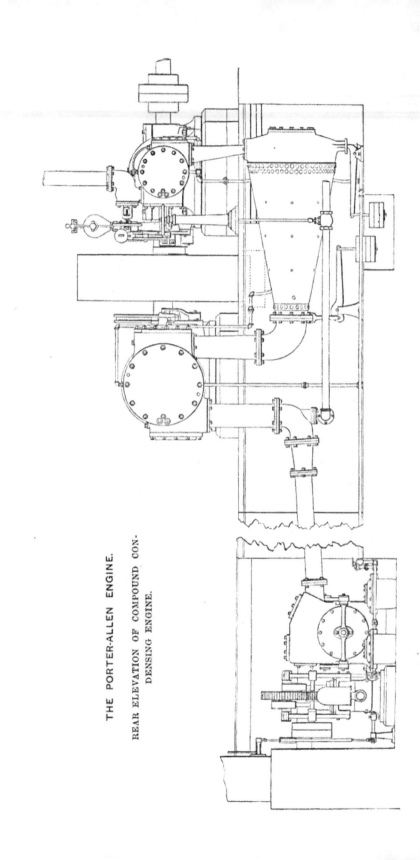

THE PORTER-ALLEN ENGINE.

REAR ELEVATION OF COMPOUND CON-
DENSING ENGINE.

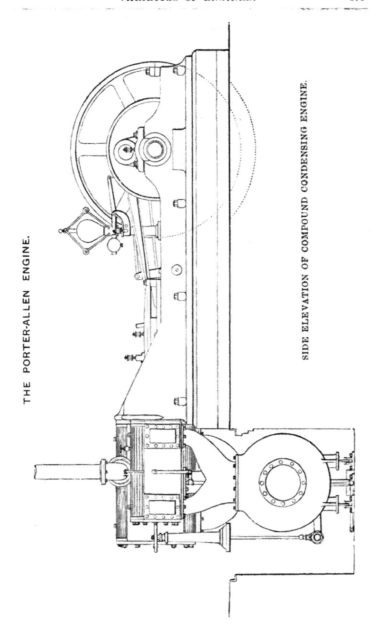

THE PORTER-ALLEN ENGINE.

SIDE ELEVATION OF COMPOUND CONDENSING ENGINE.

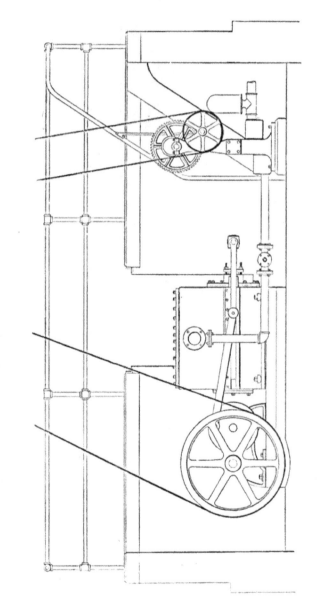

THE PORTER-ALLEN ENGINE.

SIDE ELEVATION OF PUMPS OF COMPOUND CONDENSING ENGINE.

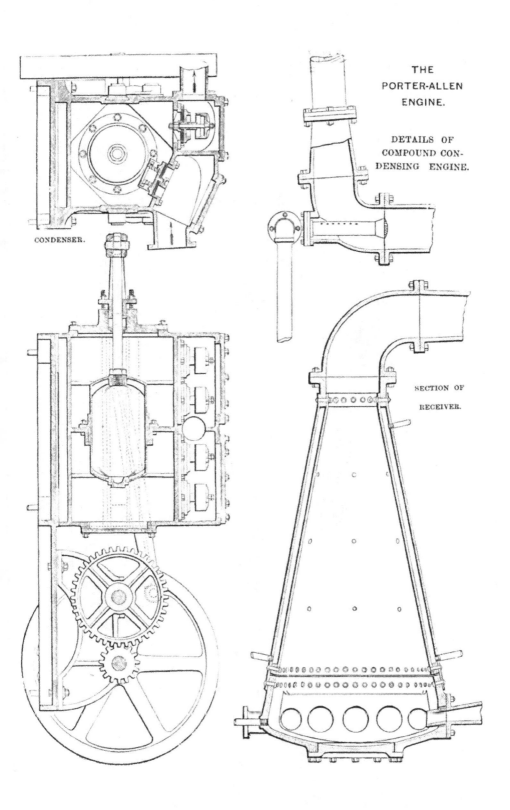

THE
PORTER-ALLEN
ENGINE.

DETAILS OF
COMPOUND CON-
DENSING ENGINE.

CONDENSER.

SECTION OF
RECEIVER.

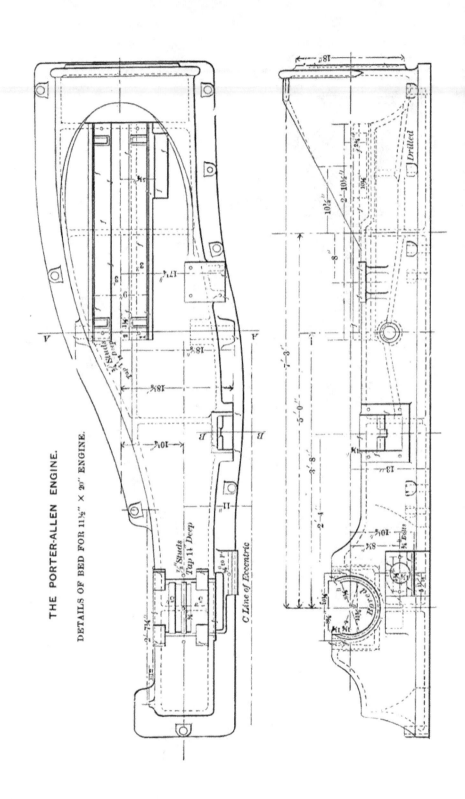

THE PORTER-ALLEN ENGINE.

DETAILS OF BED FOR 11½" × 20" ENGINE.

C *Line of Cylinder*

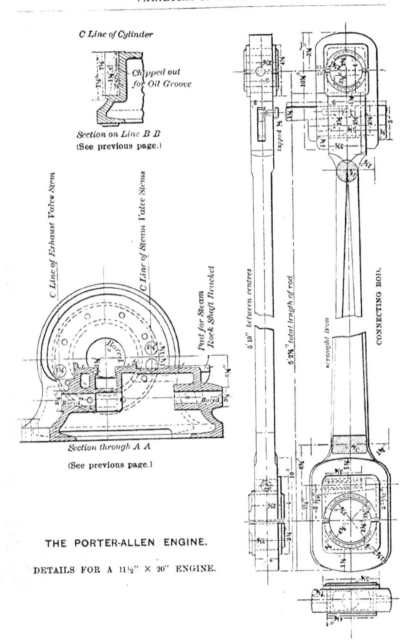

Ch[i]pped out
for Oil Groove

Section on Line B B
(See previous page.)

C *Line of Exhaust Valve Stem*

C *Line of Steam Valve Stems*

*Pad for Steam
Rock Shaft Bracket*

Bored

Bored

Bored

Bored

Section through A A

(See previous page.)

5' 10" *between centres*

5' 9¾" *total length of rod*

wrought iron

CONNECTING ROD.

THE PORTER-ALLEN ENGINE.

DETAILS FOR A 11½" × 20" ENGINE.

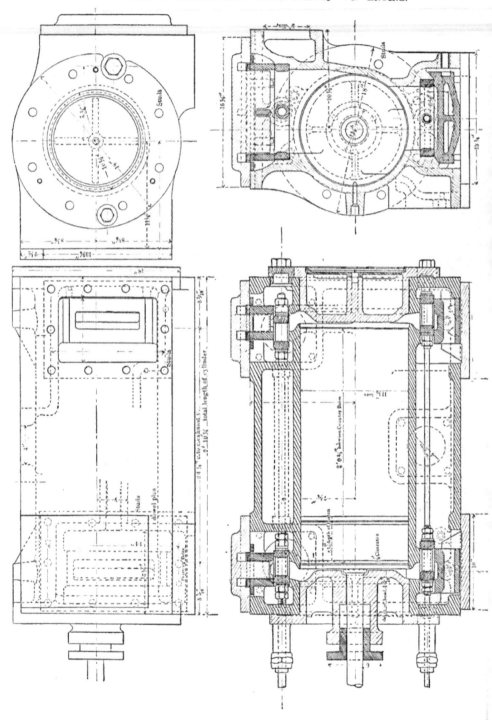

THE PORTER-ALLEN ENGINE.

VALVE GEAR FOR 11½″ × 20″ ENGINE.

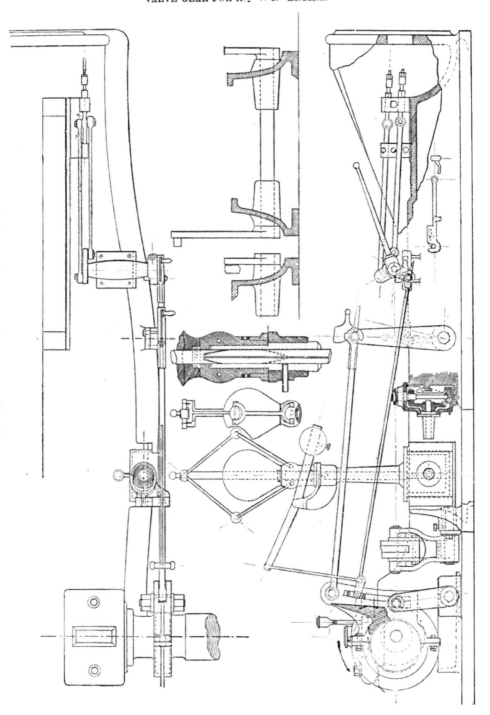

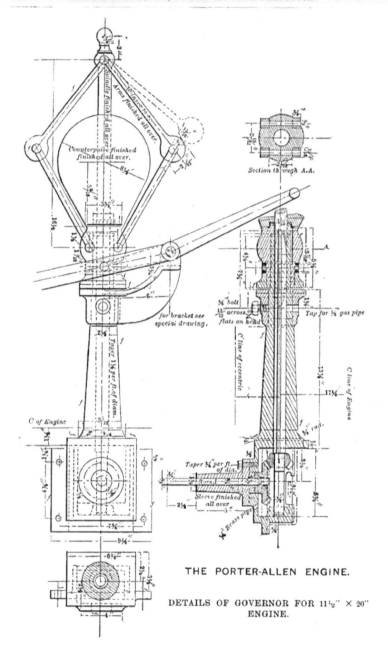

Section through A.A.

for bracket see
special drawing.

THE PORTER-ALLEN ENGINE.

DETAILS OF GOVERNOR FOR $11\frac{1}{2}'' \times 20''$
ENGINE.

THE PORTER-ALLEN ENGINE.

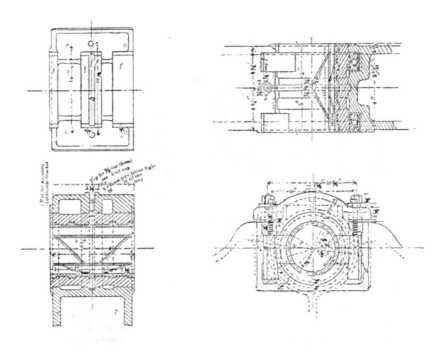

DETAILS OF MAIN BEARINGS FOR A 11½″ × 20″ ENGINE.

CHAPTER V.*

THE ALSATIAN EXPERIMENTS—THE WORK OF MESSRS. HIRN AND HALLAUER.

REPORT ON A MEMOIR PRESENTED BY M. O. HALLAUER, UPON "STEAM ENGINES." BY M. KELLER.

The work of M. Hallauer is, as its title suggests, a study of the economic influence of the degree of expansion (point of cut-off) in various types of steam engines. It tends also to support by analyses, more and more numerous, the conclusions of the last paper of the author—the equality in the matter of industrial consumption of simple and compound engines, the advantage being rather on the side of the former.

It is divided into three parts: the first comprises researches relative to double cylinder engines; the second concerns single cylinder engines, and the third sums up and compares the results obtained. We will follow M. Hallauer successively in the order adopted by him in the study which occupies us, viz., first, the compound, then the simple engines, and, summing up for each type, we will conclude upon the whole work.

FIRST PART.—DOUBLE CYLINDER ENGINES, KNOWN AS "WOOLF," OR COMPOUND.

M. Hallauer states, first, all that has been said concerning the advantages of this system, and after discussion arrives at the conclusion that the only really serious consideration, "a priori," which cannot be gainsaid, and which stands in its favor, is this:

That the difference of force at the commencement and at the end of the stroke is smaller than for other types of engines, and that, in consequence of this better distribution the running of the machine is much smoother. In regard to the useful effect of the compound engine, the brake experiments, executed under the auspices of your mechanical committee, have shown that the "Woolf" engines absorb more force in themselves than single cylinder engines, a result easily foreseen.

Passing then to the study of the influence of the cut-off in the small cylinder, M. Hallauer commences by verifying the results obtained:

First. In a series of experiments executed by himself in 1877 with a "Woolf" beam engine, at Münster, which was made at the shops of the Alsatian Society for the Construction of Machines.

Second. In the experiments executed in 1876, under the auspices of

---

*This chapter comprises translations of some valuable papers contained in the "Bulletin de la Société de Mulhouse," a journal not commonly seen in the United States. The author has endeavored to preserve the form of original thought as nearly as possible.

your Mechanical Committee upon a horizontal "Woolf" engine of the same make, which appeared in the bulletin for July-August, 1877.

Third. In those executed in February, 1877, by the Alsatian Association of Steam Owners upon an engine at Malmerspach built by the same company, but provided with a variable expansion in the small cylinder, controlled by the governor, and provided by the machine company of Bitschwiller-Thann.

Fourth. In the experiments executed at St. Remy by M. Quém, and at Rouen by the Normandy Association of Steam Owners, upon two "Woolf" beam engines, from the shops of Messrs. Thomas & Powell, of Rouen.

Having discarded the experiments of which the verification is not exact enough, M. Hallauer determined the consumption of dry saturated steam per hour, and for each absolute horse-power, per indicated horse-power per hour, and per effective horse-power per hour, based upon the sum of the calories* brought into the cylinder by the steam and water leaving the boiler; in other words, substituting for the entrained water the quantity of steam which could furnish to the cylinder the same number of calories which had been brought by that water, and taking account of the calories left in the jacket by the steam which was condensed therein. He passes then to the analysis of each experiment, and determines the quantity of steam and water contained at the end of admission and at the end of stroke; the variations of the internal heat, and finally of the cooling in the condenser *Rc*.† This cooling is verified by two different methods, already explained many times by Mr. Hallauer in your bulletins.

I should stop a moment to say some words upon the verification of the experiments.

M. Hallauer's very elegant manner of operating has already been given in his last work. However, I believe it is not useless to again speak of it here in order to clearly comprehend its importance.

When it is desired to render an account of the quantity of steam expended during a given time by an engine, the water fed to the boiler is measured. This quantity of water, augmented or diminished by a weight easily calculated, according as the level in the boiler is higher or lower at the end of the experiment than it was at the beginning, gives the quantity of steam used. A method given by M. G. A. Hirn, and many times described in your bulletins, permits the determination of the proportion of water entrained with this vapor. This constitutes the direct gauging, which is verified by the following method:

Knowing the weight of water and of steam leaving the boiler and the pressure of steam therein, it is easy to determine the number of calories brought to the engine per stroke. This number of calories, diminished by the external cooling and the heat absorbed by the work done, should be equal to the number of calories absorbed by the water of condensation,

---

*A calorie is $\frac{9}{5} \times 2.204 = 3.9672$ British heat units.
†I understand by *Rc* the cooling effect of the condenser upon the steam in cylinders.—C. A. S.

a quantity obtained by gauging the water leaving the condenser, and measuring the initial and final temperature. The manner of operation has been many times described. The difference between the number of calories brought to the engine diminished by the work done and by external radiation, and that of the calories found in the condenser divided by the total number of calories, gives the per cent. of error which has been committed.

A word also concerning the term "absolute horse-power" which has not always been easily understood.

The fine work of M. Hirn has shown the enormous influence of the sides of the cylinder upon the action of the steam therein contained. When two engines of different types and dimensions are compared, or the work of the same engine under varying conditions, it is the influence of the internal surfaces which should be determined to render an account of the manner in which the steam is utilized in each experiment. But whatever system of condenser is used, the influence of the internal surfaces can only vary little; but on the other hand, the vacuum may vary within wide limits, and consequently the indicated work. The variable vacuum, being a point to be considered if one compares engines by their indicated horse-power, can falsify the comparison. We are then forced to suppose that engines, presented for comparison, are furnished with an ideal condenser keeping a perfect vacuum behind the piston, and to compare between the engines an account of the work furnished with this perfect vacuum. That is the work which constitutes the absolute work of the engine, and it is the consumption for this absolute work which permits the comparison between different engines or of different conditions of working.*

It is well understood, for the rest, that from the practical and industrial point of view the better the condenser the better the results; this is the affair of the builders, but can have little influence upon the manner in which the steam comports itself in the interior of the cylinder.

The absolute work is then the term to be employed for comparison of two engines of different types, or working under different conditions, but the effective work will be always the term of comparison to be employed from the industrial point of view.

This stated, I sum up in the following table the results of the verifications and analyses of M. Hallauer, and with him I arrive at the deductions shown.

The experiments executed upon the engine at Münster, in which the variation of work is obtained by throttling, give as the difference of consumption per absolute horse-power per hour for the extremes of work 3 per cent., and this represents the effect of throttling.

In passing to the effective horse-power per hour, the economy is much more considerable, and reaches 20 per cent., which shows the influence of

---

*In English it is usually called the total, or forward work.—C. A. S.

COMPOUND ENGINES—FRENCH UNITS.

	ENGINE AT MUNSTER			ENGINE AT MALMERSPACH					VERTICAL WOOLF		THOMAS & POWELL	
	Expt. I.	Expt. II.	Expt. III.	Expt. B.	Expt. C.	Expt. D.	Expt. E.	Expt. F.	Weak Load.	Full Load.	Expt. Nor. Ass.	Expt. Quem.
Degree of expansion	1·9	1·7	1·7	1·6	1·13	1·13	1·28	1·26	1·6	1·6	1·22	1·19
Indicated horse-power	347	267	185	201·6	215	219·92	143·11	149·53	130	181	……	137
Per cent. error committed, found by verification	1.25	0.23	1.2	2.8	4.9	2.9	3.2	2.5	1.13	0·6	9	3.5
Steam per absol. H. P. p. h. indic.	7.112	6.945	7.384	7.402	6.878	6.943	6.731	6.821	7.290	7.328	……	6.840
" " indic.	8.614	8.739	9.780	8.847	8.149	8.210	8.273	8.260	9.120	8.878	……	7.591
" " effec.	9.864	10.357	12.411	10.301	9.465	9.517	10.011	9.898	10.563	9.975	……	9.702
Proportion condensed in jacket	8.6	9	10.4	5.1	7.7	……	8.5	……	10	10.8	……	……
Per cent. water in steam at end of admission	16.17	14.21	21.17	12.8	23.7	……	40	……	11.2	10.8	……	……
Per cent. at end of stroke in the small cylinder	19.1	……	……	……	13.1	……	19.1	……	……	……	……	……
Per cent. at end of stroke in the large cylinder	6.6	5.39	7.39	11.5	17.9	14.9	17.6	17.5	5.34	4.5	……	……
Per cent. back pressure work to forward work	17.43	20.52	24.1	16.4	15.6	……	18.6	……	20.06	17.3	……	9.9
%c. rejected in per cent. of that received	21.89	6.65	13.48	8.44	31.44	……	19.34	……	1.95	1.16	……	……
	3.38	1.32	3.5	2.1	8.3	……	7.8	……	1.19	6.5	……	……

BRITISH UNITS.

	Expt. I.	Expt. II.	Expt. III.	Expt. B.	Expt. C.	Expt. D.	Expt. E.	Expt. F.	Weak Load.	Full Load.	Expt. Nor. Ass.	Expt. Quem.
English I. H. P.	342	263.3	192.4	198.8	212	217	141	147.4	128	180	……	135
Pounds water per hour forward H. P.	15.67	15.31	16.27	16.31	15.16	15.39	17.04	15.03	16.07	16.15	……	15.07
Lbs. water per hour I. H. P.	18.98	19.26	21.45	19.60	17.96	18.10	18.23	18.20	20.10	19.57	……	16.73
" " E. H. P.	21.74	22.83	27.354	22.70	20.86	20 98	22.04	21.81	23.28	21.98	……	21.38
Rc in heat units	68	26	54	33.6	125.6	……	77.2	……	7.6	4.4	……	……

Rc is heat radiated to the condenser by the cylinder.

the back pressure measured with the work done, and the coefficient of friction which augments in the same circumstances.

M. Hallauer has then reached the conclusion in his preceding work that the most simple process of regulation is an expansion valve regulated by hand and the governor throttle, the control by hand being used for the larger variations and the throttle for maintaining the speed uniform in spite of the minor variations of work which may occur every instant.

The author also explains by simple considerations, based always upon the action of the internal surfaces, some apparent anomalies which seem to occur in the experiments. I will not enter into these details, which would compel us to present the entire work, they all prove that the practical theory pointed out by M. Hirn and applied here by M. Hallauer, permits the explanation of all the phenomena which take place in the interior of cylinders. After having studied the condensation and evaporation in the interior of the small and large cylinders, and noting the marked differences which occur from an expansion more or less prolonged in the small cylinder, M. Hallauer reaches the important conclusions which follow, and which I sum up under a slightly different form from that which he has adopted.

1. Given a boiler working at 5.5 k.* of pressure, for instance, and a "Woolf" engine which can furnish a maximum work of A horse-power, there is a possibility of obtaining, industrially at least, 10 per cent. economy by cut-off in the small cylinder, instead of throttling down the steam at the times when, because of circumstances, the engine has to supply only the half of A horse-power; this economy will be diminished by the measure in which the work approaches to A horse-power.

2. The engine working nearly to its maximum capacity, there can be produced by throttling a variation of force of 10 per cent. without any marked change in the economic regime.

We see at once the importance of these conclusions, and in reality, there are few "Woolf" engines working at full power; furthermore, some builders of our district, when they furnish an engine, declare it at less than one-half the power that it really is.

Thus, an engine sold at 100-horse power can ordinarily furnish 200-horse power without reaching its maximum. This mode of operation has practical advantages, but it is none the less true that when the engine only gives 100-horse power, thanks to the throttling, it consumes 10 per cent. more than it would have consumed if the work of 100-horse power had been obtained by admitting full pressure and cutting off in the small cylinder.

I do not agree with M. Hallauer when he recommends a cut-off variable by hand. I believe that from the practical point of view a governor cut-off works better, for it disposes of the neglect of the engineer, who may not be able very well to give the desired cut-off the moment that it should be applied. We have nearly always observed that an automatic expansion procures a more regular speed than a governor throttle.

*14.223 pounds per square inch = 1 k. per square centimetre.

SECOND PART.—INFLUENCE OF CUT-OFF IN SINGLE CYLINDER ENGINES.

M. Hallauer proceeds for these engines as he did for the compound engine. He first verifies the experiments upon which he rests; then he analyzes them.

The documents which have served for this study resulted from the following experiments:

First. Those executed under the auspices of your mechanical committee in April and May, 1878, upon a Corliss engine, constructed by Messrs. Berger, André & Co., of Thann.

Second. Those undertaken in 1873 and 1875 by Messrs. Hallauer, Gros·seteste and Dwelshauvers-Dery, under the inspiration of M. G. A. Hirn, and executed upon an engine deprived of its jacket, and working with superheated and with saturated steam. We group the results of the verifications and analyses in the table which follows.

The examinations of these results show:

First. That for the Corliss engine, with steam jacket, there is a theoretical economy per absolute horse-power of 1_{10}^{6} per cent. when the cutoff is changed from $\frac{1}{6}$ to $\frac{1}{11}$, but that industrially, this economy disappears and changes sign, and there is a practical gain per effective horse-power of $4\frac{1}{2}$ per cent. by working at $\frac{1}{6}$ cut-off in place of $\frac{1}{11}$.

Second. That for the engine, without jacket and without superheating, the economy furnished by the cut-off is much more considerable than the Hirn engine working with saturated steam, and that there is a theoretic gain of 7.4 per cent. by changes to cut-off $\frac{1}{2}$ from $\frac{1}{4}$, and that, industrially, this economy remains at 4 cent.

Third. In taking account of the difference of superheating, the experiments I. and II. (106° C. and 231° C.), establish the fact that the influence of the cut-off in the unjacketed engine, with superheated steam, remains as it did with saturated steam.

Experiment III., with superheated steam, shows still more the great economy of the cut-off in these circumstances, where one passes certain limits, for between admissions of $\frac{1}{2}$ and $\frac{1}{4}$ there is 15 per cent. economy, which would have been more considerable if, in experiment I., we had worked with the same superheating as in experiment III.

Fourth. In the Hirn engine the experiments with saturated steam give at the end of the stroke the same weight of water, 0.0940 k.* and 0.0927 k., and the refrigeration is also the same, 37.53° C. and 37.02° C., while without any jacket the same weights of water gave the same values of *Rc.* For the Corliss engine, on the contrary, the weights of water differ at the end of the stroke, 0.0298 k. and 0.0398 k., and the same refrigeration, 11.21° C. and 11.15° C., results showing the steam jacket. For experiments II. and III., with superheating, the weights of water at the end of the stroke are 0.0367 k. and 0.0373 k., and the refrigerations 16.61° C. and 20.34° C., a difference which should be attributed to superheating, for in the same con-

---

*1 k. = 2.204 pounds.

SINGLE CYLINDER ENGINES—FRENCH UNITS.

24″ × 48″.

	CORLISS, WITH JACKET.			HIRN UNJACKETED.				
	Saturated Steam.			Saturated.		Superheated Steam.		
	I.	II.	III.	L.	II.	I. 196°.	II. 281°.	III. 273°.
Degree of expansion	1-11	1-8	1-6	1-7	1-4	1-7	1-4	1-2
Indicated horse-power	105	137	158	107	146	113	154	125
Per cent. error committed	3.1	2.3	2.4	0.1	0.7	0.6	0.8	0.6
Steam per actual horse-power per hour	7.188	7.236	7.307	7.822	8.449	6.655	7	7.874
" indicated horse-power per hour	7.983	7.939	7.955	8.837	9.367	7.370	7.633	8.655
" effective horse-power per hour	9.071	8.724	8.646	9.929	10.341	8.188	8.207	9.511
Per cent. condensed in jacket	6.5	6	5.3	......	......	......	......	superhe't'd
Per cent. water at end of admission	38.3	31.7	25.3	37.0	31.0	24.6	6.5	13.2
" " expansion	21.7	19.2	18.5	35.2	25.2	21.4	12	
Rc, heat radiated to the condenser by the cylinder	11.21	11.14	11.15	57.01	37.53	18.80	16.61	20.34
Rc in per cent. of heat received	12.3	9.8	8.0	21.6	15.4	12.5	7.8	10.5

BRITISH UNITS.

	CORLISS, WITH JACKET.			HIRN UNJACKETED.				
British I. H. P.	104	135	156	106	144	112	152	124
Pounds water per hour total H. P.	15.84	15.95	16.10	17.24	18.61	14.67	15.43	17.354
" " I. H. P.	17.59	17.50	17.53	19.48	20.32	16.24	16.82	19.075
" " E. H. P.	19.99	19.23	19.05	21.88	22.79	18.05	18.09	20.96
Rc, heat units	44	44	44	148	148	73	65	80

Revolutions, 50.4   51.2   49.3

ditions saturated steam rejects heat in the condenser according to the weight of water evaporated at the end of the stroke. This shows that superheating acts in a different manner from jacketing.

Analyzing the variations of internal heat in the various experiments before us, and the values of the refrigeration in the condenser which result from differences of cut-off, according as they work with or without a jacket, and with or without superheating, M. Hallauer comes to the same conclusion as to the different modes of action of the jacket and superheater. The jacket acts more energetically than the superheater, and similarly during the period of expansion, but becomes disadvantageous during that of condensation, for then it furnishes heat to the water which lines the internal surface of the cylinder, and augments that rejected into the condenser, which is not the case with superheating; this renders the latter more economical in most cases. Examining, then, the theoretic economy, and comparing the consumption per absolute horse-power per hour, the industrial economy and the amounts per effective horse-power per hour, the author agrees with M. Zeuner that large expansions are economical from a theoretical point of view, and with M. Hirn that the reverse is the case from an industrial standpoint.

Thus the conclusions of these two savants, which had the air of contradiction, are found to be in accord, taking account of the different considerations which guided them; the one, M. Zeuner, having made a general study of steam engines based upon conditions non-realizable (non-conducting internal surfaces of the cylinder); the other, M. Hirn, on the contrary, having studied them from the industrial basis, and taking account of the action of the internal surfaces and the work done in friction.

THIRD PART.—COMPARISON OF THE DIFFERENT TYPES OF ENGINES STUDIED.

The close of M. Hallauer's work includes the comparison of compound and simple engines; still taking the analysis of the experiments which served for the two first parts of the work, he restates what he understands by absolute, indicated, and effective horse-power.

The absolute work is the work which would have been given by the engine with an ideal condenser, making a perfect vacuum behind the piston,—the theoretical work.*

The indicated work is that furnished by the steam upon the pistons; it includes the influence of back pressure;—it is the work which the diagrams traced by the indicator enables us to calculate.

The effective work is then the work industrially disposable; it takes account of the back pressure and the friction of the various parts of the engine itself.

That stated, we have two of the verified experiments: one executed upon the Corliss engine, cutting off at $\frac{1}{5}$, the other at the Malmerspach

---

*The forward work.

engine, cutting off at $\frac{1}{3}$, in which the figures approach each other as closely as possible.

	Corliss.	Woolf.
	per cent.	per cent.
Water contained at the end of admission	$25\frac{3}{10}$	$23\frac{7}{10}$
" " " " expansion	$18\frac{5}{10}$	$17\frac{9}{10}$
Difference of initial and final heat	$1\frac{83}{100}$ C.	$1\frac{24}{100}$ C.
Rejected in condenser	$8\frac{3}{10}$ ° "	8° "

The comparison of these two experiments brings us to very interesting conclusions.

A phenomenon to be first noted for the "Woolf" engine destroys a false idea held hitherto: that for the double-cylinder engine a portion of the force is withdrawn from the cooling influence of the condenser.

In reality, in the small cylinder the expansion from half stroke gave place to an evaporation of 10.6 per cent. of the weight of water contained at the end of admission, and the internal heat increased much more rapidly than in the Corliss engine. Then the mixture of steam and water passed to the large cylinder with 13.1 per cent. of water, and in place of the evaporation continuing in this cylinder there was, on the contrary, condensation, in spite of the jacket, till at the end of the stroke 4.8 per cent. more water was deposited than at the end of the stroke in the small cylinder. This shows that the great condensation at the moment of entrance into the large cylinder is strong enough, in spite of the jacket; that all the steam condensed in the large cylinder, and that which has come from the small cylinder, cannot be evaporated.

In the Corliss engine, on the other hand, there is a continuous evaporation till the end of the expansion. We see that the influence of the large cylinder in the case of expansion, commenced in the small cylinder, does not always tend to lessen the rejected heat, but, on the contrary, may sometimes augment it, which is the reverse of that which has been hitherto admitted.

The consumption of dry saturated steam per absolute horse-power per hour gives the theoretic economy realized by the one or the other motor. If we compare the consumption of the Corliss with that which it would have had with an expansion of 13, which is that of the "Woolf" engine, for the experiment with which we compare, we find that the theoretic economy is 4 per cent. in favor of the "Woolf" engine; but the influence of the back pressure, and still more that of the friction, reduces this economy when we pass into the industrial domain. It then changes sign, and we find that the practical economy becomes 8.7 per cent. in favor of the Corliss.

Comparing, then, the horizontal "Woolf" engine with the Corliss, and taking account of the lack of compression in the former, M. Hallauer finds again a theoretic economy of 4 per cent. for the "Woolf" engine, but that economy also disappears in practice, and the Corliss becomes industrially superior by 9.05 per cent. to the horizontal compound. Meanwhile, considering the construction of this latter, the difference falls to 2 per cent., and then the horizontal "Woolf" engine consumes only 8.8 k. of dry saturated steam per effective horse-power per hour, which is the smallest consumption at which we can arrive by a careful construction of condenser, and a very strong compression. In closing, M. Hallauer sums up in a table the consumption of steam per hour per horse-power, absolute, indicated and effective, adding the consumption per effective horse-power per hour of coal, on the basis of an evaporation of 8.

The table shows that the various types of double cylinder engines consume from 9.1 to 9.5 k. of steam per effective horse-power per hour; the Corliss, with cut-off ¼, only uses 8.6 k., while the Hirn engine, with superheated steam, and ½ cut-off, only uses 8 k., or 17.6 pounds.

To sum up: The work of M. Hallauer, which is one of those laborious and conscientious studies to which he has so long accustomed our society, is above all very remarkable in its conclusions and tends once more to prove the impossibility of stating anything with precision concerning steam-engines, if one does not rest on verified experiments of existing engines.

We have been compelled in this summary to leave untouched many interesting things, aiming mainly to unite the divers conclusions of M. Hallauer; but all parties concerned in steam-engines will certainly find in his work exceedingly useful material to serve them in many circumstances. We are cognizant of owing many thanks to M. Hallauer for all these investigations which demand so much time, patience, and reflection, all of which he has not been sparing in this his last memoir; you know, for the rest, what he is accustomed to do, by the numerous works which he has already presented to our society, and of which this last gives the most interesting practical conclusions.

EXPERIMENTS WITH A STEAM ENGINE.—A MEMOIR, PRESENTED BY M. O. HALLAUER, RELATING TO THE EXPERIMENTS DIRECTED BY M. G. A. HIRN, EXECUTED BY M. M. DWELSHAUVERS-DERY, W. GROSSETESTE AND O. HALLAUER.

In his recent work on Thermodynamics M. Hirn describes the remarkable progress that the judicious employment of the principles of this new science has brought about in the study of heat engines, at the same time that it shows that various edifying theories were far from the reality; finally it proves with evidence the impossibility of general theories.

If we take up this question so fully treated by him; if we analyze one after the other the experiments made under his direction; it is to the single end, as he himself has well said, "of shunning the numerous blunders" of practical men who have wished to pursue such studies; and it will also be seen how we have obtained an experimental solution of many important problems not yet studied, so that we can encourage engineers on a track so fruitful of results, for we are certain that researches of this nature lead to one useful end, the reduction of fuel. But in order that this memoir may serve as a guide in new work, it is essential to give here the method of experiment so happily inaugurated by M. Hirn and so often described by him.

METHODS OF EXPERIMENTS.—BRIEF DESCRIPTION OF THE ENGINE.

The engine with which we worked was a beam engine, with vertical un-jacketed cylinder and four valves, two for admission and two for exhaust. A differential movement of the two cams which worked the admission permitted us to vary the angle at will, and, consequently, at various degrees following the needs of the experiments. The steam brought to the cylinder immediately on leaving the boiler passed through many tubes, of cast-iron, placed behind the boiler in a special chamber where the simple movement of two registers brought in the hot gas. The steam carried with it a degree of superheating which ranged from 195° C. to 231° C., while it could be brought to the engine in the state it left the boiler by changing the registers to give direct passage to the pipe. The consequence of this analysis will lead us to see that M. Hirn in constructing the most practical engine actually known, has also made a veritable instrument of precision for researches in experimental physics. The dispositions, as simple, as ingenious, which he adopted to assure the exactness of the operations have served in most cases.

Observations Taken.—These are grouped into three distinct series: the measurement of the water consumed and rejected from the condenser, those of temperatures and the work.

1. The quantity of steam that the engine consumed was obtained by direct measurement; the easiest made the water for the feed pump flow through a reservoir of constant known volume, alternately filled and emptied. If the water level in the boilers is noted evening and morning, and account taken of this difference of level, the only precaution necessary is to ascertain by hydraulic pressure that no leaks exist in the boiler, superheater and pipes. The total weight of feed water passing the gauge tank divided by the number of strokes, B, during the day, gives us the water consumed per stroke, M.

That rejected by the air pump is also gauged, but differently. At the outlet a pit of masonry is arranged; its capacity at different heights was determined by putting in known weights of water, and at the bottom of this plate a copper plate was placed, pierced with a circular orifice 0.06 m. diameter, out of which continually flows, under a head of from 0.6 m. to 0.8 m., the water brought from the condenser. The discharge of this orifice is found experimentally by closing it tightly by a stopper, filling to a known height and noting the time it takes to lower each 0.1 m.

Let S be the horizontal section of the pit, s the area of discharge, and

n an unknown coefficient of contraction, h the head above the centre of the orifice, and t the time. We then have:

$$- Sdh = nsdt \sqrt{2gh}$$
$$2 S' (\sqrt{H_0} - \sqrt{H_1}) = n s T \sqrt{2g}$$
$$ns \sqrt{2g} = \frac{2 S}{T} (\sqrt{H_0} - \sqrt{H_1})$$

This gives at once $ns \sqrt{2g}$ when the time T is noted, while the level falls from H_0 to H_1.

The volume of water, or the weight rather, running out under head H, is $II = (ns \sqrt{2g}) \sqrt{H}$.

During the days of experiments we noted every fifteen minutes the heads h_0, h_1, h_2. . . these varied little and

$$\sqrt{H_m} = \frac{\sqrt{h_0} + \sqrt{h_1} + \sqrt{h_2} + \cdot \cdot \cdot}{N} \; ; \; \text{or, more simply even}$$

$$\sqrt{H_m} = \sqrt{\frac{h_0 + h_1 + h_2 + \cdot \cdot \cdot}{N}},$$

$$\text{whence } II = (ns \sqrt{2g}) \sqrt{h_m} \pm \frac{S (h_1 - h_N)}{T}$$

h_1 and h_N are initial and final heads of an experiment whose duration was T. If in this time the engine made B strokes the weight of water rejected per stroke was $II_0 = \frac{II \, T}{B}$. The injection per stroke was $II - M$.

We give in tabular form the values obtained in eight experiments, each consuming an entire day:

TABLE I.

DATE.	Superheat'ng.	Expansion.	Weight of Steam Consumed.	Injection Water.
Nov. 18, 1873...............	231° C	4	0.3065	9.3500
Nov. 28, 1873...............	none "	4	0.3732	9.29175
Aug. 26, 1875...............	215° "	5	0.2651	8.7291
Aug. 27, "	223° "	2 throttled.	0.2822	8.5983
Sept. 7, "	195° "	7	0.2240	8.7384
Sept. 8, "	none "	7	0.2634	8.9132
Sept. 29, "	220° "	2 throttled.	0.2265	5.9810
Oct. 28, "	220° "	non-condens- ing.	0.2715	....

2. *Temperatures.*—Part of these are noted directly, but with different instruments. To arrive at the superheating a good thermometer is simply placed in mercury in a copper pocket open at one end and closed at the other and let into the steam pipe; this measurement is easy to obtain.

The rise of temperature of the injection water in the condenser necessitates a more careful measurement—a special thermometer known already to the readers of our *Bulletins*, the differential air thermometer

The practical arrangements that M. Hirn brought about this instrument permitted the obtaining to the fiftieth of a degree the increase in temperature. We will only indicate the method of procedure with its use without entering upon any detailed account of the construction of the instrument.

Two thermal reservoirs filled with perfectly dry air, connected to indicating tubes by capillary copper tubes, are both plunged into the cold injection water and put, by opening three-way valves with which they are fitted, into communication with the external air. The temperature of the cold water is also noted with a good mercurial thermometer reading to the tenth of a degree, also the divisions where the indicating liquid in the pressure tubes stops; finally, the height of the barometer. A turn of the three-way valve closes the connection to the external air, while it leaves open that between the reservoirs and indicating tubes of the apparatus. Placing then one reservoir in the cold water brought to the injection, the other in the warm water rejected, we note every quarter of an hour the heights of the liquid. The averages for an entire experimental day are transformed to degree, centigrade, and give by their difference the rise in temperature of the water during that day. The formula for the air thermometer is as follows:

Let B=height of barometer at start.

i=temperature of cold water at start.

B'=mean height of barometer during the day.

t=temperature sought.

γ=Coefficient of dilatation of the reservoir, usually copper.

a=that of the air.

$\beta=$ " " " indicating liquid.

$a=$temperature " "

V=volume of reservoir.

$sh=$ " " liquid moved in tube.

Then:

$$13.596\, B' + \frac{h_0}{1 + \beta a} = 13.596\, B \left(\frac{V}{V + s h}\right)\left(\frac{1 + \lambda i}{1 + a i}\right)\left(\frac{1 + a t}{1 + \lambda t}\right)$$

By taking large reservoirs, $\dfrac{V}{V + s h} = 1$ nearly.

Practically, when we only have in view industrial results, the employ-ment of a good mercurial thermometer reading to tenths of a degree con-

TABLE II.

	Nov. 18.	Nov. 28.	Aug. 26.	Aug. 27.	Sept. 7.	Sept. 8.	Sept. 29.
Temperature of injection	31.3	33.65	33.09	35.26	30.42	32.25	37.81
Temperature of rejection...........	12.6	11.83	16.50	16.50	16.37	16.50	15.85
Difference.....	18.7	21.82	16.59	18.76	14.05	15.75	21.96

duces to results sufficiently close, but there are times when their use is far from being as convenient as that of the air thermometer.

The other temperatures corresponding to the steam pressures are taken from the tables of Regnault. They are thus obtained indirectly, and are experimental; for these, tables of pressure and temperature are deduced from observation.

The values which serve us were obtained by a generator and free-air manometer, and in the interior of the cylinder by measurement upon the diagrams of work, which gives, as all know, the curve of pressure for each point in the stroke of the piston.

TABLE III.

	Nov. 18.	Nov. 28.	Aug. 26.	Aug. 27.	Sept. 7.	Sept. 8.	Sept. 29.	Oct. 28.
Temperature in boiler.............. ...	150.15	148.20	151.00	150.00	150.77	150.77	151.20	146.20
Temperature at cut-off	144.96	140.78	148.74	124.00	142.00	141.30	115.80	137.49
Temperature at end stroke............	97.24	98.24	92.05	94.40	85.00	84.33	87.36	101.89
Temperature during exhaust..........	73.49	73.42	58.86	58.25	58.44	61.15	57.11	......

3. *Measurement of the Work.*—This requires the most minute care and was effected by the aid of two sets of apparatus, the one checking the other—the indicator of Watt and the pandynamometer of flexion of Hirn —this latter, above all, installed in very favorable conditions, has furnished us values most remarkable for their exactness. We have then, based upon the results which it gave, analyses in which the determination of the various works, with full pressure, with expansion, the total forward work, plays an important part; also the measurement of pressures at the points of the stroke where we wish to study the thermic conditions of the steam and the transformations to which it is submitted.

It is owing to the happy idea of utilizing as a spring the beam of the engine that M. Hirn arrived at the construction of the instrument which he has already described in our *Bulletins*. This apparatus draws at each instant the deflection of the beam, and gives a curve, of which the abscissas are proportioned to the stroke and the ordinates to the pressures.

The study of the diagrams drawn by these instruments is nearly the same. The indicator, then, is less exact for engines with a single cylinder, but it has been long used, not as an instrument of analysis, but as a means of measuring work, while we only insist on the curves traced by the pandynamometer.

With this latter the scale of abscissas is obtained by direct measurement upon the movable plate and for equal parts of the stroke; that of the ordinates by a direct comparison; the engine is brought to one of its dead points, the steam turned into the cylinder at a known pressure, the force exerted on the piston is transmitted to the beam which deflects an amount measured by the pencil of the apparatus. Then to check in the reverse direction, the crank is put on the other dead point and the operation repeated. M. Hirn has established, every twentieth of the stroke, the load, in kilogrammes, needed to bend the beam such an amount that the pencil of the dynamometer shall describe an arc of a circle of one metre in development; it is the unit of measure at each corresponding twentieth of the stroke.

All the curves drawn have been carefully measured; the mean ordinates transformed into kilogrammes upon the piston are set off on the corresponding lines, 10 millimetres for 1,000 kilogrammes. At the same time we trace below the axis, to the same scale, the values of the vacuum given by. the indicator alone, joining the extremities by a curve, drawn full for the pressure, and dotted for the vacuum. Between these curves we have the pressure carried at each moment by the piston. If the absolute vacuum could have been reached on one side, while the steam acted on the other, nothing is more easy than to establish the pressure per square metre; the load divided by the piston area gives it.

This known, the tables of Regnault, or the formula of Roche, fix the corresponding temperature, and we can calculate then:

γ the densities,

λ the total heat of evaporation,

U the internal heat, etc.,

of the steam at points of the stroke which interest us, without which values any analysis is impossible.

Finally, the planimeter, by a measure of the area, gives us the different kinds of work, the forward work at full pressure, the total forward work, the total indicated work, and the effective work, or the difference between the indicated work and that absorbed by the friction of the parts of the engine.

TABLE IV.

	Nov. 18.	Nov. 28.	Aug. 26.	Aug. 27.	Sept. 7.	Sept. 8.	Sept.29.	Oct. 28.
Revolutions per minute.	30.1736	30.5494	29.969	30.306	29.98	30.41	30.13	30.00
T. H. P. in. ch.d. v. of 75 kgms. in forward work..	144.36	136.46	135.77	125.17	113.08	107.81	99.53	78.30

Checking the Consumption.—Thanks to the data taken, we can establish an equality in the heat brought to the engine and that used in work and rejected from the condenser, so that we can make a first verification showing with what approximation we have noted the consumption of steam.

The first fundamental proposition of thermodynamics experimentally established is that, heat acting upon a body gives place to mechanical work and a quantity of heat proportioned to the work disappears; the relation between work produced and heat disappearing is constant and depends in no way upon the body by which it acts. We should then have between the heat brought to the engine and that found in the injection water a difference, a decrease proportioned to the external work done, or the forward work. The value of this decrease is no other than the quotient of the number of kilogrammetres furnished by the engine per stroke, divided by 425 kilogrammetres, the equivalent of a calorie transformed into work.

Take for example the experiment of August 26, 1875, with steam at 215° C. The mean consumption per stroke for this day is 0.2651 k. Taking the boiler pressure, 49,938 kgs. per sq. metre, a temperature of 151° C., it takes from the boiler 0.2651 k. $\times h = 0.2651$ k. $(606.5 + 0.305 \times 151)$; but before reaching the cylinder it traverses the superheater, which raises its temperature to 215° C., and furnishes to the fluid $0.5 \times 0.2651\,(215{-}151)$ more. The specific heat of steam being 0.5, finally, when this fluid leaves the condenser, it takes with it $0.2651\,f = 0.2651 \times 33.09$, which it is necessary to take away from the amount brought, and we have for the heat available in the cylinder.

$$Q_o = 0.2651 \text{ k. } (606.5 + .305 \times 151^\circ + 0.5\,(215^\circ - 151^\circ) - 33.09.) =$$
$$172.79 \text{ c.}$$

The cold water of injection, measured as above is, 8.7291 k.; it receives from the steam which it condenses $Q_1 = 8.7291$ k. $(f - i) = 8.7291$ k. $+ 16.59$ $= 144.82$ c.

There has disappeared in the interval:

$$172.79 - 144.82 = 27.97 \text{ c.}$$

But we have used externally 135.77 ch., say 10,193 kgms. per stroke, which has absorbed 23.99c. The external radiation of the cylinder has been 2.5c., total of 26.49c., a difference of 1.48c., say of 0.8 per cent. of 172.79c. brought to the cylinder. This is the error and check upon the consumption, as the distinction between the observations is clearly defined.

TABLE V.

	Nov. 18.	Nov. 28.	Aug. 26.	Aug. 27.	Sept. 7.	Sept. 8.	Sept. 29.	Oct. 28.
Heat brought.	202.72	228.80	172.79	184.41	144.34	161.51	147.05	Non-condensing.
Heat in work and radiated	27.82	26 15	26.49	24.36	22.47	21.27	19.99	
Difference..	174.90	202.65	146.30	160.05	121.87	140.24	127.06	
Heat rejected	174.84	202.75	144.82	161.30	122.77	140.38	131.34	
Error.........	+0.06	—0.10	+1.48	—1.25	—0.90	0.14	—4.28	

We see that all the errors but that of the 29th September are less than 1 per cent. The latter has an error, of which we cannot discover the cause, which does not exceed 3 per cent.

Verification of the Work.—To be more correct, we should describe the verification of the indicator, for the simple inspection of the curves drawn by the aid of the pandynamometer renders evident the superiority of this method of valuing the force. And we may add that many successive experiments always led M. Hirn to the same results and the same coefficients for the scales of pressures. On the other hand the sufficiently large curves permit us to obtain, with much exactness, not only the pressures but also the fractions of the stroke and consequently the volumes affected by the cut-off; also, by taking these curves and comparing them with the indicator diagrams taken under the same conditions, we form the following table:

TABLE VI.

	Aug. 26.	Aug. 27.	Sept. 7.	Sept. 8.	Sept. 29	Oct.28.
Pressure in metres of mercury:						
Pandynamometer	3.013	2.790	2.91	2.91	2.93	2.475
Indicator	3.007	2.806	2.80	2.91	2.94	2.475
Full pressure forward work, kgm.:						
Pandynamometer	4.175	6.285	3.365	3.235	4.880	4.800
Indicator	3.990	6.148	3.120	3.135	4.930	4.702
Difference per cent	+4.43	+2.17	+7.25	+3.09	—1.00	+2.08
Forward work of expansion:						
Pandynamometer	6.700	3.930	6.185	5.965	3.120	6.575
Indicator	6.621	3.875	5.885	5.985	3.192	6.697
Difference per cent	+1.19	+1.39	+4.85	—0.33	—2.30	—1.85
Total forward work:						
Pandynamometer	10.875	10.215	9.550	9.200	8.000	11.375
Indicator	10.611	10.023	9.006	9.120	8.122	11.399
Difference per cent	+2.42	+1.91	+5.69	+0.86	—1.52	—0.21
Indicated work:						
Pandynamometer	9.870	9.293	8.675	8.220	7.065	6.163
Indicator	9.606	9.101	8.131	8.140	7.187	6.187
Difference per cent	+2.67	+2.07	+6.27	+0.98	—1.72	—0.38

The Watt indicator should give us the pressure in the interior of the cylinder and should give greater values than the pandynamometer, as the friction of the packings should diminish the results obtained by the latter. This difference only exists on September 29 and October 28, clearly defined on September 29, but for all the other experiments is reversed. To what cause of error is this anomaly to be attributed? We can only see such as may be caused by the construction of the apparatus in the small dimensions, a little piston, strong springs and too high a speed of the engine giving results which have not the exactness wished.* M. Hirn has avoided the oscillations due to the motion of springs, and notwithstanding all our care with the indicator the pressures are too low. I insert the diagrams of boiler pressure taken on September 7, in which they are notably lower than given by the dynamometer. But the greatest error with these two pieces of apparatus does not exceed 2.4 per cent. of the work, and the indicator is valuable in practice to measure, rapidly and closely, the power of an engine in motion; in certain circumstances it can serve for an exact

*Probably leaky piston of indicator more than all others.—C. A. S.

analysis, as in the case of compound engines making 20 to 30 revolutions per minute. In this case the uniformity of the pressure is greater than in simple engines, which is favorable to the indicator, and the beam dynamometer is useless, as it would only give the resultant force on the beam without separating the effect of each cylinder. The indicator giving the action of each cylinder permits as a consequence the obtaining of the temperatures, density, internal heat, etc., of the working steam and to follow the transfers of heat.

THE INFLUENCE OF THE INTERNAL SURFACES—THE ERRORS WHICH MAY BE COMMITTED BY NEGLECTING THEIR ACTION.

We believe that it will be useful before commencing this study to recall briefly some preliminary notions, to enumerate some of the facts incontestable in themselves but of which the consequences have been violently discussed.

Each of us knows that the cause of the movement of engines, the force which acts through the medium of water reduced to steam, which sets in action the different pieces of the engine, is the force of heat. Heat is the direct cause of the movement. The first study naturally imposed upon us is, then, the phenomena which give birth to the action of this force upon an intermediate body. Actually completed this study has been made in the cabinet of the physicist beyond all practical applications, and holding no account of the circumstances in which the fluid is called to work.

Assuming that there is no interchange of heat between the surface of the cylinders and the fluid which they contain, considering them as simple geometrical receptacles impenetrable to heat, is evidently contrary to the truth; but for a long time it was considered that the errors of this theory in practice could be neglected, and to destroy this error, to prove how far it was from the reality, a series of precise experiments, so well verified, of which some are given in the work of M. Hirn, was needed, to which we shall add others which we will develop.

Without doubt it is possible in that which concerns the engine, that is to say, the weight of steam used per stroke, to directly measure it, for we have checked it by comparing with it the heat used and rejected by the condenser, directly measured also. If the consumption had been incorrect this error would have exceeded 1 per cent.

If we desire to calculate at cut-off and the end of the stroke the weight of dry saturated steam inclosed in the cylinder, it is a simple matter.

The volume swept by the piston and the densities of the steam are all that is needed. We recall the diagrams taken with the indicator, or the pandynamometer, where the abscissas are proportioned to the stroke, and seeing how clearly the intersection of the curves with full pressure and with expansion are defined when produced, this point fixes the cut-off and pressure thereat. To the volume generated by the piston we add the clearance volume which is occupied by steam. In the same way at the end of the stroke the last ordinate gives the pressure, and the clearance added to the volume generated gives the volume occupied; the same could, of course, be done for any other point of the expansion.

The densities are obtained by two relations, one established by Zeuner, a direct function of the pressure,

$$\gamma = 0.6061 \, P^{\,0.9393},$$

P being the pressure in atmospheres, the other a function of temperatures and therefore indirectly of the pressures, the corresponding temperatures being taken from the tables of Regnault or the formula of Roche, deduced from the same tables:

$$\gamma = \frac{1}{u+w} \text{ and } u = \frac{1}{A} \frac{1}{P} \; (31.1\,c + 0.096\,t - 0.00002\,t^2. - 0.000000\,t^3)$$

where w is the volume of the unit of water and $u + w = v$, that of the steam $\gamma = \dfrac{1}{v} =$ density. We will take as examples the calculations relative to the experiment of August 26, 1875, cut-off at one-fifth.

The volume swept during admission augmented by the clearance is, $v_0 = 0.1048$ mc., and the pressure is 41,415 kgms. per sq. metre, whence the density is $\gamma = 2.5175$ k. The weight of dry steam at the commencement of expansion is $m_0 = 0.1048$ mc. $\times$ 2.5175 k. $= 0.26383$ k., while the feed water per stroke was 0.2651 k., an error of $\dfrac{0.2651 - 0.26383}{0.2651} =$ less than one-half of one per cent. Passing to the end of the stroke, the final volume including clearance is 0.490 mc., the pressure 7,722 kgms. per sq. m., whence we have a density $\gamma_1 = 0.46096$ and a weight of steam of $m^1 = 0.490$ mc. $\times$ 0.46096 k. = 0.21859 k.; the difference is 17.5 per cent. What has become of this steam which has disappeared during the expansion? We hope that the examination of all our experiments will make this clear to all. We place them in the following tables with the differences:

TABLE VII.

	Nov. 18.	Nov. 28.	Aug. 26.	Aug. 27.	Sept. 7.	Sept. 8.	Sept. 20.	Oct. 28.
Weight of feed............	0.3065	0.3732	0.2651	0.2822	0.2240	0.2634	0.2265	0.2982
Weight at cut-off m_0......	0.28656	0.2571	0.26383	0.2866	0.1688	0.1656	0.2208	0.2625
Difference............	9.01994	0.1124	0.00217	0.0044	0.0552	0.0948	0.0057	0.0357
Per cent...................	+6.5	+30.4	+0.83	−1.5	+24.64	+36	+2.52	+12
Weight at end of stroke, m_1	0.2698	0.2792	0.21859	0.24496	0.1761	0.1707	0.1906	0.2982
Difference.................	0.0367	0.0940	0.04651	0.03724	0.0479	0.0927	0.0359	0
Per cent........	+12	+25.2	+17.5	+13.2	+21.38	+35.18	+15.85	0

We find their marked differences nearly always less between the calculated and measured weights. What are the causes? Let us review them.

For those who know how difficult it is to keep a metal-packed piston tight, nothing is more simple than to suppose leakage. To those who have not learned all the arrangements adopted, we explain that it is easy to make a tight piston. Suspending the piston and with two cast-iron rings sprung in make a tight piston. But in many cases a vertical cylinder cannot be used. We believe that the piston rod should be carried at both ends of the cylinder, to avoid leaks, and to use softer cast-iron for the rings than for the cylinder.

What is important for us is to see that the vertical engine on which we experimented possessed a tight piston, and that the natural hypothesis of leakage is inadmissible.

How could we believe that these losses could give an increase over that directly gained, for example on August 27, and how could the piston of the same engine, working with almost the same initial pressure, vary from 0.83 to 36 per cent. in a few days, August 26 to September 7 and 8; or from 25 to 36 per cent. from September 7 to September 8? There is no doubt that all conditions were the same, except the superheating, and we should suppose that the hotter steam would leak the easier; on the contrary the leakage is least then.

Finally, we will note some results which will support the views we shall advance, knowing that the piston was tight.

It will be remarked that in the table given there is for many of the experiments less steam accounted for at the end of the stroke than at the cut-off. On November 28 it decreases from 30.4 to 25.2 per cent., and on September 7 from 24.64 to 21.38 per cent., but in the non-condensing run of October 28 it changed from 12 to 0 per cent. at the end of the stroke.

Let us recall the progress of the steam in the engine, and see if this is not an impossibility with a leaky piston.

The consumption per stroke was measured with all the precautions stated above; it is then the weight of fluid which passes through the cylinder, leakage or no leakage. The computation based on the volume and density gives the actual quantity of steam present. Is the difference lost? If so, how explain the irregularity in amount, or the excess in some cases? Every one must see that this is absurd, and the hypothesis of leakage cannot be maintained. One of the most important propositions of applied physics gives us the key.

When steam is introduced into a reservoir of invariable dimensions, of which the surface has not everywhere the same temperature, the final pressure of the steam is that which corresponds to the lowest temperature.

It was upon the facts from which this proposition is deduced, that Watt based one of his best discoveries, the condenser; it will serve us to explain the apparent disappearance of the steam which we have stated.

The study of the phenomena to which the action of heat upon water gives birth has been made in the cabinet of the physicist, ignoring at the start perturbing influences. The results thus obtained are as exact as the laws from which they are derived, and if we have an error to note, at least it is not from applying erroneous principles. We will not repeat too much, transporting to the domain of practice the physical data relative to steam, without considering the circumstances in which the steam is called to work. Regarding engine cylinders as simple geometric receptacles impenetrable to heat, of stating that there is no exchange of heat between the steam and its surrounding metal, is from all evidence contrary to the truth and has never been sustained. But for a long time it has been implicitly considered that the various errors arising from this supposition were insignificant. We shall see if it is possible to neglect them.

Remarking, first, that when the steam is taken directly from the boiler, experiments, November 28, 1873, and September 8, 1875, as is usually the case, we have to do with a vapor in contact with its liquid, a so-called saturated vapor, that is to say, in such a state of equilibrium that it is impossible to take away the smallest quantity of heat without condensing a portion, that almost always the gas itself has entrained and mixed with itself a portion more or less great of the fluid from which it came. Neglected for the two experiments which occupy us it is sometimes 5 or 6 per cent. of the weight of steam introduced. In this condition it is impossible to add heat without evaporating a part of the fluid in suspension.

This state of saturation or unstable equilibrium of a vapor mixed with its liquid in more or less quantities is such that any addition or subtraction of heat, how small soever it may be, brings immediately and necessarily the evaporation or condensation of the liquid or vapor. In such a condition does the mixed fluid pass from the boiler to the cylinder.

At the end of the steam pipe it finds in the steam chest the valve open to the cylinder, the piston at or near the end of the stroke, and the steam then fills the clearance spaces between the valve and the piston. In the engine we are studying the clearance is 5 litres, very small relatively to the inclosing surfaces, the cylinder head and piston have 0.5699 sq. m., and are instantly filled; the steam is thus brought against an extended surface which has been cooled during the preceding strokes by the expansion and the exhaust to the condenser. The incoming fluid tends to impart its temperature to the surfaces, and a large portion condenses, yielding its heat of evaporation. By virtue of the proposition enunciated above, the pressure of the fluid would fall if the communication from the boiler was not open and did not permit a constant influx of steam coming to replace that liquified till the moment that the interior of the cylinder has acquired the temperature due the pressure.

All these phenomena are produced in the almost inappreciable interval of time the piston is at the end of the stroke, and afterward the piston uncovers fresh cooled surface which also condenses, but much less rapidly than than at the first instant, for whatever be the speed of the piston at midstroke the surface is much less in proportion to the inclosed volume than at the end of the stroke. Finally the valve, after opening, closes the steam port and the expansion commences without interrupting the action of the surfaces, but the supply of heat from the boiler being ended the reverse action begins, while at the same time steam is condensing on the cool surface uncovered by the piston it is forming from the heads which had been previously warmed.

Take the experiments of November 28 and September 8 made with saturated steam. When the expansion commences, we have shut up in the cylinder a mixture of 69.6 per cent. steam and 30¼ per cent. water in one case; 64 per cent. steam, and 33 per cent. water in the other.

This water, as we have shown before, came nearly all from direct con- densation on the metal; it is deposited on the surface lining it and pos- sessing its temperature and that of the steam in the cylinder. The piston advances, the work of expansion demands a certain quantity of heat, the fresh cool surface, uncovered, condenses more steam, the pressure falls, and the water lining the surfaces instead of increasing, grows less or re- mains the same in quantity, 25.2 per cent. instead of 30.4 per cent. and 35.19 per cent. instead of 36 per cent. This shows clearly that evaporation has been produced from the surfaces which first condensed and were then warmed by the steam.

During the expansion the pressure and temperature fall at each instant. The cylinder surface and water covering it, keep at each instant a temper- ature little higher than that of the steam, but at each instant this temper- ature tends to equality with that of the mass of steam, which can only occur through the medium of the deposited water evaporating at the expense of its own heat, or yielding its excess to the metal, or drawing from it. The steam and condensed liquid, evaporating or condensing, serve as the vehicle of heat so well that at the end of the stroke we have different proportions from those at the end of admission.

All this concerning the vapor of saturated steam is only the natural consequence of the laws of the transmission of heat, and it is matter of astonishment that it has been contested; not that the principle has been denied, but it has been called insignificant in its influence from the fact that gases are bad conductors of heat, and assuming the time of a stroke to be too short to permit any considerable exchange of heat by radiation, we have come to see that it is by direct contact and not by radiation that this action can condense up to 36 per cent. In this case the error would be in not taking account of the action of the surfaces: it is far from being one that may be neglected, as it has been.

Let us see what happens when the steam from the boiler by a special apparatus has its temperature raised about 100° C. above that of saturated steam when it is superheated. Brought in that state to the cylinder, one can believe that it will act as a gas, losing, without doubt, its heat, its superheat, but never falling below that of saturated steam. The experi- ment of September 7 shows us the contrary, that steam at 195° C. can con- dense on the surface, giving 24.64 per cent. of water, and the heat of evaporation of this water is given to the metal, besides the superheat, which it gives first. When the expansion commences there is then only saturated steam containing one-fourth water in the cylinder, most of the water being on the surfaces. We are in identical conditions with the experiment of November 28 and September 8. All the phenomena we have already described take place. Condensation and evaporation going on simultaneously in different parts of the cylinder, we find at the end of the stroke 21.38 per cent. water, showing that 3 per cent. has been re-evaporated.

Between this experiment and that of November 28, one with super-heated steam and the other with saturated steam, the analogy is striking. It is far from being so with the others, which appear almost in part as exceptions to the laws which we state.

On September 29, and August 26 and 27, the condensation at the begin-ning of expansions, 2.52 per cent. and 0.83 per cent., are very small, and on August 27 the steam remained superheated, since the weight of steam calculated is greater than that directly measured. To give an account of what passes let us recall what we said in our two experiments with satu-rated steam.

At the commencement of the stroke only the clearance space is open to the incoming steam. The condensation is then very energetic; we can perhaps say that nearly all the steam which comes first is liquified against the metallic surface, whether it be superheated to 223° C. or not, for what is the heat of superheating compared with the weight of surrounding metal to be warmed, and the steam first introduced into the clearance space is small in amount of heat compared with the quantity to be given up. The steam then introduced instantly loses its superheat and the piston begins to move. We have then saturated steam in contact with a large portion of water, which we unfortunately cannot directly determine, but of which we can affirm the existence, for our experiments proved that the proportion of water liquified was very considerable, though the time was very short, that is to say, with the surface increased inversely as the weight of steam introduced, we could bring it all to water. The piston then moves more and more swiftly, and steam flows in from the boiler through the super-heater at a temperature of 223° C.; it meets the saturated steam, with which it mixes, then the water covering the surfaces and yielding heat to it evapo-rates it so well that on August 27 the whole was superheated, since the cal-culated weight of steam at the end of admission was one per cent. greater than the gauged weight per stroke. At other times, since the weight com-puted is little greater than measured, the difference being with the errors of observation, we will therefore suppose the vapor saturated but dry. During the expansion we see that the liquifaction, in spite of an introduction of nearly half stroke, reaches 13 per cent. at the end of the stroke. A con-densation takes place because the surface originally warmed did not receive heat enough to prevent it. This is shown by the experiments of August 26 and September 29, and for November 18.

We then arrive at the last of our experiments, remarkable as we shall see, in analyzing that of October 28 at high pressure non-condensing. The steam heated to 220° C. is admitted for one-quarter of the stroke, expands to one atmosphere and is exhausted into the air.

The clearances of the engine we are studying are 5 litres, say 1 per cent. of the cylinder volume. We have in our preceding experiments neglected the weight of steam shut up at the closing of the exhaust. With low pressure and density the weight may be neglected, but such is not the case when the exhaust is at the atmospheric pressure. The compressed steam rises even above the pressure of admission, and its weight is 0 0268 k., say 10 per cent. of that consumed per stroke.

It is easy to obtain, as we know the closing of the exhaust valve, the pressure and volume. We then find the density a function of the pressure. As this steam at this point is dry and saturated, as we shall see, its weight represents the whole steam in the cylinder, a quantity put into the cylinder at the first revolution and in a manner remaining there till the engine is stopped; but if this weight is constant its temperature is not, for it participates along with the new steam in all the exchanges of heat of which the engine is the seat.

The first action is during the cushion and before the steam valve opens. The weight calculated at the closing of the exhaust was 0.0268 k. of steam that we know to be dry. If we value it again when it only fills five litres of the clearance volume we find only 0.0093 k.; the balance has been condensed upon the surfaces, having a lower temperature than the compressed vapor, of which the pressure is constantly increasing. Then the steam valve opens, and steam rushes in and mixes with that compressed, abandoning its superheat and at the end of admission containing 12 per cent. of water. The expansion commences, and at the end of the stroke the deposited water has evaporated, and we have dry steam.

Summing up, the examination of each of our experiments brings us to the conclusion that we can by no means neglect the action of the surfaces. To a certain depth the metal of the cylinder is penetrable by heat; it plays the *role* of a reservoir, which receives heat during admission and gives it out during expansion, or continues to receive but gives it out again during exhaust. This action is shown clearly by the figures in Table VII. There we find the proportion of water, which sometimes could be neglected, following the conditions under which the experiments have been made. Thus with steam superheated, cut-off, $\frac{1}{4}$, $\frac{1}{2}$ and throttle, the condensations are 1 per cent., 2 per cent., and even superheated; while with saturated steam, cut-off $\frac{1}{4}$, we find water 25 per cent., 30 per cent. and 36 per cent.

Above all, this series of eight experiments removes all doubts, and it no longer can be denied that these exchanges of heat actually take place, variable in intensity and intimately connected with the conditions of temperature and expansion in which the engine is worked.

Cooling due to the Condenser.—We can enumerate the various changes to which the steam submits during its passage through the cylinder, following the exchanges of heat upon the surfaces or in the fluid inclosed by them; this is not the only question, but only the first step in the road to which our analysis has led us, for we can find not only the manner of the distribution of heat, but the exact values by obtaining that which is consumed on the one side by work done, and on the other the various losses produced during expansion and exhaust. This study requires us to refresh our memory with some of the facts established by thermodynamics, among others what is meant by the internal heat U of a mixture of steam m and water $M - m$, this value U is the total heat of the mixture less that of the external $A\,Pu$; it is expressed

$$U = \lambda - A\,Pu = M \int_0^t cdt + m\,p$$

$$U = M\,(t + 0.00002\,t^2 + 0.0000003\,t^3) + m\,(575 - 0.791\,t).$$

From the elementary principles of thermodynamics the value of U can only vary: 1. If the total mass M does external work, positive or negative, augmenting or diminishing in volume under an external pressure, and then the variation of U is proportioned to the work done. 2. If the mass, without doing work, receives or loses heat by contact with any other body. 3. If these two phenomena take place together; in this case the change in U may be zero. We know the heat consumed by the work of expansion, since this is given by the diagrams, and it suffices to divide the number of kilogrammetres by 425 to have this quantity in heat units. Putting then the internal heat U and the work of expansion AF^u we have:

TABLE VIII.

	Nov. 18.	Nov. 28.	Aug. 26.	Aug. 27.	Sept. 7.	Sept. 8	Sept. 29.	Oct. 28.
Internal heat at cut-off U_0 c.........	176.81	173.92	160.42	169.94	110.22	114.19	133.10	163.73
Internal heat at end of stroke, U_1..............	164.44	175.79	134.37	149.42	108.26	109.07	116.28	177.91
Difference..............	+12.37	—1.87	+26.05	+20.52	+1.566	+5.12	+16.82	—14.24
Heat given to iron........	23.26	57.73	9.84	11.56	33.95	48.10	14.80	29.40
Work of Exp. $A\,F^u$.......	16.52	15.835	15.79	9.24	14.31	13.70	7.22	14.50

In this table we also give the heat which the fraction $M - m$ gives to the metal during admission, by condensing upon the surfaces increased by the superheat lost by the mass M, we shall call it the heat stored by the surfaces.

The internal heat U sometimes increases, or diminishes, or remains nearly stationary. Let us examine each case.

1. On October 28 it is 14.24 c. more at the end than the beginning of the expansion, and there has also been done 14.5 c. of external work which should have been at the expense of the internal heat U and this should have decreased instead of increased. This must have had heat from outside, and as the boiler is cut-off it must have come from the cylinder metal, and as there is no jacket the metal must have taken it from the incoming steam as previously explained. The metallic surface has condensed a portion of the steam brought from the boiler, the temperature is raised and the heat penetrates the metal to a depth more or less, but which matters little; it in a manner stores up heat which we can value directly from the superheating, $M \times 0.5\,(\theta - t) = 0.2717\,k. \times 0.5\,(220^\circ - 137.49^\circ) = 11.20$ c.; where $M =$ the mass, $0.5 =$ specific heat of steam, $\theta =$ temperature of steam, $t =$ temperature of saturated steam at same pressure. To

this value is added the heat obtained from condensing 0.0357 k. liquified during admission.

$$0.0357 \text{ k. } \times r = 0.0357 \times 509.78 \text{ c. } = 18.29 \text{ c.}$$

$$11.20 \times 18.20 = 29.40 \text{ c.}$$

The work of expansion was...14.50 c
The external radiation was......... .... 2.50 c
The increase in internal heat was........... ....14.24 c

Total.. ....31.24 c

being with 1.84 c. of the other, an error of less than 1 per cent. of the 186.72 c. brought to the cylinder.

2. When the variations of internal heat are very small, November 28 and September 7, for example, we may consider it as remaining nearly stationary during the expansion, and the external work done during expansion must have been furnished by the metal and not by the internal heat; the metal must have received it during admission, but this is only a portion of their action, for if we compare the amount the surface has received 33.95 c. on September 7, when the work of expansion is 14.31, the external radiations 2.50, leaving 18.80 c. to be accounted for per stroke—what has become of them? Given to the surface per stroke it is impossible to have them remain there, for the temperature would rise to such a point as to melt the iron under an increase of heat of 18.80 c. per stroke; they must have gone to the condenser during exhaust unless the piston leaked, and we showed above that it was tight. The difference we call Rc, refrigeration by the condenser. It is the form first known of the action of the internal surfaces, an influence long doubted and far from being admitted in our day. We refer to table VII., and find there, except for the non-condensing experiment, that there is from 12 to 35 per cent. of water at the end of the stroke whether it entered saturated, wet, or superheated, the result of all the exchanges of heat being the condensation of a greater or less portion of the steam which works. This action is due to the sides covered with a layer of water very thin and at the temperature of the metal.

When the exhaust valve opens the steam rushes out, its pressure falls rapidly, and its temperature still faster till it reaches that of the water in the condenser, this, in the cylinder in spite of the smallness of the connecting passages, and the temperature is lower than that at the end of the stroke; but the surfaces of the cylinder and the water which covers them are higher in temperature and the water upon them evaporates, and the heat is taken from the metal in which it had accumulated during admission.

We see here the reverse of the phenomena during admission, the surfaces cooled during exhaust are warmed by the incoming steam which they condense and evaporate during exhaust, and are again cooled. These two opposing actions are the result of the same physical cause, the permeability to heat of the surfaces and that which they inclose.

If even to-day, resting upon the poor heat-conducting power of gaseous fluids and the shortness of time, it is believed that the effect of the surfaces can be neglected, the following table will again prove that it is not small, that the cylinder loses during exhaust a certain number of calories which are far from being small, and which do no work whatever, and which even exceed those expended in the work done.

As we have seen, the values of Rc are deduced from the very simple relations of the internal heat, the work done and the heat given up to the metal during admission.

$$r(M - m) = U_1 - U_0 + A F_4 + 2.5 c. + Rc.$$

For September 7, $33.95 c. = -1.66 + 14.31 + 2.5 c. + Rc.$

$$Rc = 35.61 - 16.81 = 18.80 c.$$

But these values can be checked by a different computation, which we shall follow out, knowing that Rc is the heat taken from the iron during exhaust.

If this heat is retained in the metal up to the opening of exhaust, it will not be in the final internal heat at the end of the stroke U_1, but we shall find it increased by the work of expulsion, in the water rejected from the condenser, and the difference will give it to us. For September 7, $U_1 = 108.56$ c., less that remaining after condensing 6.81, added to the back pressure work 2.14 c. gives.............. ....103.89 c.
The heat found in condenser is...................................122.77 c.

Difference, Rc.. ...... 18.88 c.
The other method gave.. 18.80 c.

Error .... 0.08 c.

TABLE IX.

	Nov. 18.	Nov. 28.	Aug. 26.	Aug. 27.	Sept. 7.	Sept. 8.	Sept. 29.	Oct. 28.
Rc 1st method................	15.61	37.53	17.60	20.34	18.80	37.02	21 90	1.84
Rc 2d "	15.79	35.33	17.03	19.66	18.88	37.37	20.09	Non-condensing.
Error..........................	0.82	2.20	0.57	0.68	0.08	0.35	1.81	
Total heat per stroke............	212.31	241.36	181.56	194.36	151.15	170.00	154.10	
Rc per cent. of this............	7.80	15.60	9.70	10.50	12.43	21.76	14.21	

Here again it is not easy to construct any gratuitous hypothesis The explanation we have given of the observed phenomena is based upon precise figures. It is the expression of the truth. We state from direct observation that the surfaces inside the cylinder are covered with a water film, condensed from dry or even superheated steam. This water upon the surface at a temperature greater than the exhaust is evaporated and carries away from the iron a certain quantity of heat which is taken again from the boiler during the admission at the next stroke. The consequence is that during admission it condenses steam enough to do the work of expansion, and more yet the external radiation, and the internal radiation, to the condenser Rc, and we can also value this Rc in two ways, and the greatest error has been 1.84 or 1.17 per cent. of the heat used by the engine per stroke.

.If I insist upon this point, it is because this value Rc has been not only discussed but badly understood by some engineers who have found for Rc large negative values, and who have tried to give a reason for this anomaly which was simply due to an error of observation as the only negative value under exceptional circumstances, that we have in our table. In a word, any negative value of Rc is absurd.

3. The internal heat diminishing to the end of the stroke in this case, the loss of internal heat added to that stored by the surfaces goes into the work of expansion and into the external radiation, and any excess is lost by the cooling by the condenser, Rc, which is found as before.

The water present in the steam at the end of the stroke is the cause of the phenomena we are studying. Nothing is easier than to see that the figures of our table are closely connected with the final proportion of water varying with it. Even the $Rc = -1.84$ c., that is within 1 per cent. of nothing for the non-condensing experiment, for which the steam is dry at the end of the stroke; but this case is uncommon. If we admitted that Rc could be negative, it would only be saying that the condenser was sending heat to the cylinder in the place of cooling the steam contained in it. The second method, serving as a check, could only give Rc negative, by having too large a value of U_1 after accounting for the work of expulsion, but as this internal heat is all that the steam contains after having worked in the engine, we should at least find that in the water of condensation. If the observation gives us a quantity too small, some heat must have been lost between the cylinder and the point at which the measurement is made; this can only be produced by leakage, but one could easily detect that, for it could only be in the exhaust pipe, or by the loss of heat by conduction from a very moderately heated pipe 70° or 80° C. only.

Resuming, this loss Rc unexplained and neglected in the study which denies the action of the surfaces, which may reach 22 per cent. of the steam used, constitutes a useless expense which merits attention and for which we should seek a remedy.

At the point to which we have attained in our analysis there should no longer remain any doubt in the minds of our readers of the action of the internal surfaces of the cylinder; but it may be useful before quitting the subject to show how errors committed in the account of steam can extend in the account of work; to see if the steam condensed during admission really corresponds 1st, to the external work of expansion; 2d, to the external radiation, and 3d, to the internal radiation during exhaust.

Thermodynamics establishes the general equation

$$dQ = Mcdt + dmr - \frac{mr}{T} dt$$

which connects the quantity of heat dQ at each instant with the mass m of steam and $M - m$ of water inclosed in the cylinder, the heat of evaporation r, the absolute temperature T and the specific heat c of the liquid.

Since in whatever manner the heat Q has been added to or subtracted from the work of expansion, $A \, F_d = Q + (U_0 - U_1)$ the internal heat at the beginning and end of expansion is known from the temperatures and pressures. Proceeding thus, the expansion curve is verified from its two ends.

But for Q we find ourselves in the presence of two theories. The generic theory of the engine with non-conducting cylinder, and the other called the practical theory, which admits the action of the surfaces as a reservoir of heat. We shall see under another form which answers to the facts. Denying the action of the surfaces in stating that

$$dQ \text{ and } Q = O, \text{ or, } AF_d = U_0 - U_1:$$

Tabulating these values for all our experiments we have

	Nov. 18.	Nov. 28.	Aug. 26.	Aug. 27.	Sept. 7.	Sept. 8.	Sept. 29.	Oct. 28.
$U_0 - U_1$ c	+12.37	−1.870	+26.05	+20.52	+1.66	+5.12	+16.82	−14.24
AF_d c	16.52	15.835	15.79	9.24	14.31	13.17	7.22	14.50
Differences c	+4.15	+17.705	−10.26	−11.28	+12.65	+8.58	−9.60	+28.74

The figures of this table are, as we see, very eloquent; there is even the absurdity of negative work on November 28 and October 28, for instance, and the generic theory is untenable.

We have to return to the equation

$$dQ = Mcdt + dmr - \frac{mr}{T} dt,$$

and sum these quantities during the expansion to find a function which may be integrated. M. Hirn has arrived at it by a very natural idea which he developes as follows:

"After many fruitless researches I decided to return here in the track traced by the experimental method itself. As the action of the surface consisted not only in taking heat from or yielding it to a gaseous mass, but in partially condensing a mass of saturated vapor, or of evaporating partially a mass of water in contact with it, I thought that the hypothesis nearest truth would consider the active part of the surface as a portion of, and at the temperature of, the water covering it. Whatever, in reality, may be the temperature of the surface, the water covering and evaporating or condensing must be at the temperature of the saturated steam. The exactness of this view has been fully sanctioned by experience."

We can always represent, by a proper weight of water at temperature T, varying by dT, the position of the mass of the surface which is warmed during admission and cooled during expansion and exhaust. Let μ be this weight, changing by a quantity of heat, $\mu c dT$.

$$d Q = - \mu c d T = M c d T + d m r - \frac{m r}{T} d T.$$

$$- (M + \mu) c \frac{d T}{T} = \frac{d M r}{T} - \frac{m r d T}{T^2} = d \frac{m r}{T}.$$

Integrating both sides from T_0 to T_1

$$- (M + \mu) \int c \frac{d T}{T} = \frac{m r}{T} + \text{constant.}$$

$$- (M + \mu) \; C_= \; log. \; \frac{T_0}{T_1} = \frac{m_1 \, r_1}{T_1} - \frac{m_0 \, r_0}{T_0}.$$

Taking one of our experiments for example—that of September 7, for instance:

$$M = 0.2240 \text{ k.}, \; m_0 = 0.1688 \text{ k.}, \; m_1 = 0.1761 \text{ k.}$$
$$C_= = 1.006096, \; T_0 = 414.85°, \; T_1 = 357.85°.$$
$$r_0 = 506.55 \text{ c.}, \; r_1 = 547.10 \text{ c.}$$

$$- (0.2240 \text{ k.} + \mu) \; 1.006096 \; log. \; \frac{414.85}{357.85} = \frac{0.1761 \times 547.10}{357.85} - \frac{0.1688 \times 506.55}{414.85}$$

$0.2240 + \mu = 0.42445$, $\mu = 0.20045$, and the heat yielded by this equivalent weight of water is $\mu (q_0 - q_1) = 0.20045 \, (143.26 - 85.32) = 11.61$ c.

Finally, the work of expansion deduced from this heat yielded, and the difference between the internal heats at the beginning and end of expansion is $A F_4 = Q + U_0 - U_1 = 11.61 + 1.66 = 13.27$ c., while the value from the diagrams is 14.31, an error of only 1.04 c., while the generic hypothesis was an error of 12.65 c.

The following table gives the value of the work of expansion, calculated in this way, and also from the diagrams, with their difference. The greatest error is 1.51 c., while the others are mostly less than 1—an error of less than 1 per cent. of the total heat brought.

TABLE XI.

	Nov. 18.	Nov. 28.	Aug. 26.	Aug. 27.	Sept. 7.	Sept. 8.	Sept. 29.	Oct. 28.
Calculated $A F_4$	16.003	15.72	15.01	7.73	13.27	12.75	6.78	14.52
Direct	16.520	15.83	15.79	9.24	14.31	13.70	7.22	14.50
Difference	0.523	0.11	0.78	1.51	1.04	0.95	0.44	0.02

We have shown how the water deposited upon the surface at the end of the stroke is partly evaporated during exhaust, how it carried with it a certain quantity of heat Rc, which we have called the cooling by the condenser. The cylinder in these conditions works as a boiler, producing steam which goes to the condenser with a certain quantity of water entrained with it the amount of which is easily determined. The condenser here being a large edition of that used in determining priming, the method of calculation is identical; that for September 7, for example, is as follows:

Mean back pressure 1881 kgs. per square metre:

Temperature t corresponding 58.44°.

$q = 58.57$ c. $\lambda = 624.32$ c. $r = 565.75$ c.

The heat found in the condenser, as we have seen above, is 122.77 c., the weight of fluid per stroke is 0.2240 k., and the final temperature of the water is 30.42°, whence the weight of entrained water:

$$m c = \frac{0.2240\,(\lambda - 30.42°) - 122.77}{r}$$

$$= \frac{0.2250\,(624.32 - 30.42) - 122.77}{565.75}$$

$$= 0.01815 \text{ k.} \quad \frac{0.01815}{0.2240} = 8.1 \text{ per cent.}$$

The following table shows the weight of water and its proportion of the steam. It is easy to see that it depends solely on the proportion of water at the end of the stroke.

TABLE XII.

	Nov. 18.	Nov. 28.	Aug. 26.	Aug. 27.	Sept. 7.	Sept. 8.	Sept. 29.	Oct. 28.
Carried over wt. of water k.	0.0150	0.0349	0.0211	0.0087	0.01815	0.0280	0.0025	Non-condensing.
Per cent.....................	4.6	9.4	7.9	3.11	8.1	10.63	1.1	....

General Conclusions.—The statement of the method used in experimenting, the checks upon the results reached, which accumulate, shows us with what exactness the data have been obtained; they are indisputable, as well as the results derived from them, such as the temperatures, heats of evaporation, densities, etc., of the steam which proceeds from the pressures following certain physical laws, which are mostly expressed by empirical formulæ from experiments, and are contested by no one in our day.

We find ourselves with this group of exact data in the presence of two theories of the engine, that which till to-day has been universally received, the generic theory, which does not consider the properties of the bodies and fluid which are under the influence of heat; in a word that which considers the steam as working in a non-conducting cylinder. The other, the theory that M. Hirn has so judiciously called "*practical,*" holding account of the actions which take place between the steam and the surrounding masses of metal. This latter theory could only be established by experiments. It is the study of the working engine, and each condition imposed demands a new experiment and a new analysis.

One easily understands that it is convenient to construct from the laws of physics a theory of the steam engine without the long and tedious process of experimenting and computing which we have shown, and this is a great part of the reason that for so long we have had the generic theory only. We are far from contesting its utility, as it often points out the road to be followed in seeking for the truth; but we are obliged to discard its equations when we wish to get even approximate results.

To harmonize the data and derived results, for they are only the manifestations of a single cause, the action of heat on steam and the metallic masses surrounding it while doing external work, has naturally led us to condemn practically the generic theory of the steam engine.

Meanwhile it is very useful, serving as a guide in our researches, for we have been led by it to make this study of the densities and volumes of the steam. We have had to give up the hypothesis of leaks, the proportions were so variable; but it became evident that the generic theory led to errors of 36 per cent., for the weight of steam given by the product of the volume and density led us to the discrepancy and to seek its cause.

In a non-conducting cylinder the difference of internal heat at beginning and end of expansion, $U_0 - U_1$, should give as the work of expansion AF_1. Our researches showed us that heat furnished from outside from the metal which had stored it up by condensing steam during admission, but storing up more than was needed for the work of expansion, the external radiation and the change of internal heat, which led us directly to the discovery of the internal radiation or cooling due the condenser Rc, which we verified by the heat found in the condenser, another form of the action of the surfaces. Finally, when we wish, by the aid of the relation

$$d\,Q = M\,c\,d\,T + d\,m\,r - \frac{m\,r}{T}\,d\,t$$ to verify the work of expansion AF_1, by

supposing it in a non-conducting cylinder, we arrive at absurdities and impossibilities, and on the other hand the natural hypothesis of considering a part of the mass of metal as water, has led M. Hirn to a relation which verifies the work of expansion in a very remarkable manner. To sum up all of our analyses shows that it is only by the practical theory that we can render an exact account of the facts.

DIRECT PRACTICAL RESULTS OF THESE EXPERIMENTS.

In all that has preceded we have only had one aim, that of showing the very energetic action of the metallic surfaces inclosing the steam, showing that the errors found in the results of the ordinary theories of steam engines were due to neglecting their influence.

Each of our readers will have already perceived the importance of this group of experimants in designing engines. Without doubt practice has led to more than one happy idea, for example, the separate condenser and the steam jacket of Watt; but these improvements, to be valued in exact figures, demanded a complete analysis of the engine, such as we have given, for it is only then that the results cannot be gainsaid. For in ou day we find some engineers affirming that it is possible to work a high-pressure engine as economically as with condensation; and the utility of steam jackets is not yet put beyond doubt, as M. Hirn has well said in his "Analytical and Experimental Exposition of the Mechanical Theory of Heat:" "I have already said that the effect of the steam jacket has been alternately affirmed and denied without there being any real knowledge of the matter.   Some say the jacket has no useful effect, others, that it gives 40 per cent. more work with the same steam.   It is easy for us to perceive the origin of so diverse statements, knowing that under certain circumstances each of them has a foundation.   The essential action of the jacket consists in diminishing the quantity Rc of heat that the steam takes from the surface to the condenser, and in augmenting the work of expansion AF_4, but this action varies with the engine itself.   In the study of the single cylinder engine we found that in diminishing Rc and increasing AF_4 the jacket only gave little heat to steam during expansion, and that the greater part of the useful heat given by the surface came from the heat stored during admission.

"The study of the double cylinder 'Woolf' engine shows us on the contrary that it is the heat given by the jacket which increases $A F_4$. Before such striking differences, due to such apparently insignificant difference of details, we are brought to recognize that a single cylinder unjacketed engine may by reason of details better utilize the heat stored in the surface during admission than any other.   It is not impossible, but even probable, that the relation between $A F_4$ and Rc depends, for instance, upon the proportion between diameter and stroke, or the total volume to the volume at cut-off.   It is evident that the jacket will give results less marked upon the engine which works best without it, and better when $A F_4$ is small compared with Rc.   In a word, the results of a steam jacket may vary within 10 to 25 per cent."

The same method of analysis gives the economy which should be realized by compression.   This economy stated by Zeuner can be experimentally verified.   I have found 10 per cent. for a "Woolf" engine, but it was only by following all the transformations of steam in the cylinders, that it was possible for me to solve this problem and to bring a first experimental confirmation to the fine theorem of Zeuner.

We give, then, summing up in a last table, on opposite page, the results of our eight experiments, believing it easier to follow the problems with their experimental conclusions, for a glance will establish the relations.

The first anomaly that strikes us is that the consumption in experiments made in 1873 is different from those of 1875 under the same conditions.   The explanation is that the engine had a new cylinder with larger ports, and the exhaust was considerably earlier.   Thus a modification which in the limits made would seem unimportant, has produced an improvement of 9 per cent.   This proves that nothing should be neglected in designing an engine.

We shall be forgiven if we speak again upon the question of leakage, the practical importance of the subject is reason for returning to it, not for this engine, which we showed to be sufficiently tight, but as general conditions bearing upon the construction of engines.

TABLE XIII.

	Expansion.	Press're at cut-off.	Work in H P. of 75 kilogrammes.	Steam per I. H. P. per hour.	Per cent. water at end of stroke.	Per cent. of *Re.*
			k.			
Nov. 18, 1873, steam at 231° C	4	4.2449	144.36	7.688	12.00	7.8
Nov. 28, 1873, saturated	4	3.7773	136.46	10.026	25.20	15.6
Aug. 26, 1875, steam at 215° C	5	4.1415	135.77	7.002	17.05	9.7
Aug. 27, " " " 223° C. (throttled)	2	2.3070	125.17	8.199	13.20	10.5
Sept. 7, " " " 195° C	7	3.9128	113.08	7.126	21.38	12.43
" 8, " saturated	7	3.8339	107.81	8.915	35.19	21.76
" 29, " steam at 229° C. (throttled)	2	1.7458	99.53	8.227	15.85	14.21
Oct. 28, " steam at 229° C. (non-condensing)	4	3.4333	78.30	12.315	......	......

We have seen that it was impossible to attribute to leakage the steam condensed during admission, and we had to conclude that the engine piston was tight, the packing of the most simple kind—two cast iron rings turned larger than the cylinder, cut and sprung in, the two ends coming together. Some builders think this lacks elasticity; for cylinders of large diameter, over one metre, they prefer to have segments set out with springs. Whichever are used we can always have tight packings when well set up and working vertically.

It is easy to see that it is the vertical disposition which keeps the packing in order, for it places the segments in the most favorable conditions possible. Resting on the follower, they are in a manner equilibrated during motion in the same condition at all points of the stroke, with nothing to counteract the lateral pressure they exert on the cylinder. They can be set with little tension so as to keep them tight with the least possible friction. One should not hesitate for large power with room enough, almost always to be had with stationary engines, to give the preference to vertical engines.

But if the problem of tight pistons has been solved for vertical engines, the results with others is far from being satisfactory; they nearly always leak, if not at first, after a short time; and it could not be otherwise from the cylinder wearing oval from the weight, and the segments not being carried by the piston.

They have tried to remedy this defect, more or less happily in many cases, by a steam packing; but this is difficult to adjust and gives the greatest wear at the ends of the cylinder. Sometimes the leaks may be neglected, but we usually find the horizontal piston in default.

In the marine service they have obtained very good results with rings of "anti-friction" metal, but these are often changed, and watched with great care. In any case, it is indispensable to set the piston in such a manner that its weight shall not be carried by the ring; to give it a rod with rigidity enough to keep it from flexures and to carry it on guides at each end. Unfortunately this gives a double extent of cooling surface for the rod alternately exposed to steam and air.

We do not insist upon the economy of the use of superheated steam, for the experiments made in 1865 by the Committee of the Society have sufficiently proved that. And we only verify the results of that time. There is 23 per cent. for the experiments of November 18 and 28, and 20 per cent. for those of September 7 and 8.

But it may be useful to rapidly enumerate the evils which are said to be involved with its use; to examine its mode of action which Hirn has so well described in his new work on thermodynamics. After having analyzed the effect of the jacket, he shows that bringing into the interior of the cylinder a greater quantity of heat than comes with the saturated steam is more energetic than surrounding the cylinder by a jacket. For the heat brought by the jacket, steam condensing on the outside of the cylinder has to cross the metal before it can modify the condensation during admission, it can not do this rapidly enough, and we find condensations even in the small cylinder of compound "Woolf" engines, which are open to the boiler nearly full stroke; for the heat, and above all, the superheat, the steam brings directly into contact with the surface, which has been cooled, and we have seen in one of our experiments the expansion commences with superheated steam. Another precious advantage, it furnishes heat without condensing, giving dryer steam at the end of the stroke, diminishing by that the internal radiation to the condenser Rc. It does not, as the jacket does, furnish its heat at the wrong time when open to the exhaust. When this commences the surfaces of cylinders using superheated steam are at temperatures little higher than that corresponding to the terminal pressure, the heat lost when the steam escapes is then small, while the jacket steam at the boiler temperature accelerates the evaporation of the water which covers the surface, sending to the condenser the most heat when it should send the least to make Rc a minimum.

As for the objection, raised against superheating, we shall say with Hirn, that "Setting aside some excellent but purely theoretical works we stop before the critical judgment of those who to-day call themselves 'practical.' We discard all opinions resting upon anything but facts and the spirit of impartial investigation." We can only discuss those among them which appear to have a real basis. They always say that superheating burns the oil which should lubricate the piston and rod packings. Practice has shown that this is not true up to 230° C. (446° F.), and that it is not necessary to renew the oil more frequently than with common steam; that the surfaces of the cylinder are kept in as good condition without cutting, but we know that the steam in the cylinder is still saturated, only dryer. Even if brought in at 230° C., it is impossible to sustain that it will burn the oil and destroy the cylinder in which it is worked.

There are three questions of the highest interest long discussed in many theoretical works which can only be answered by experiments, and this solution is so natural that one is astonished to see it so long unemployed: 1. The limits of economic expansion. 2. The effects of throttling. 3. The use of the condenser.

Influence of Expansion.—The universal opinion to-day is that the greater the expansion the greater the economy of fuel, and one is brought naturally to continue it to the pressure of exhaust, and the dimensions given the cylinder are only limited thereby. But as M. Hirn has remarked in his book, if we push expansion too far we have less upon the piston than is required to move the engine and overcome friction—we then do no good. It is a lower limit which should never be passed, and if we wish to know how far we can reduce the initial volume compared with the final volume with a constant consumption our experiments give us the necessary figures for this comparison. For a long time the question has been treated differently in purely theoretical works, and we shall see to what errors the generic theory has led, such as calculating from inexact experimental data the law of expansion, for this law is only an empirical statement of the exchanges of heat during expansion, changes which vary with the conditions imposed upon the engine, and of which analyses such as we have given can alone define the value and employment.

We have operated with an introduction from $\frac{1}{2}$ to $\frac{1}{7}$ the limits of valve gear. The experiment with cut-off $\frac{1}{2}$, it is true, was made with engine throttled; but we will justify this later, treating of the question of throttling, and we have the results of a lower pressure than with the other experiments.

Taking the figures from the preceding table, with superheated steam we have 1 per cent. in favor of five expansions over seven expansions. Exact values: Introduction 0.1628, consumption 7.126 k.; introduction 0.2570, consumption, 7.002. If we correct by 9 per cent. the experiments of November 18 and 28, 1883, for the reasons given above, we see that the consumption of November 18, 6.996 k., is very close to those cited. This constancy of consumption holds also with saturated steam as well as with superheated, a more remarkable circumstance. Thus correcting, the experiment of November 28, 1873, 9.024 k., and for September 8, 1885, 8.915 k. per I. H. P., figures within 1.2 per cent. Such are the results of experience. Let us see, if possible without a full analysis, which is preferable.

Between the experiments of 7th September and 26th August, 1875, the work varied from 113 to 136 H. P.; the water at the commencement of expansion from 24.6 to 0.8 per cent. But it is objected, on the 7th September the superheating is 20° less. This is only 2.24 c. loss, or $\dfrac{2.24}{151.5} = 1.4$ per cent., almost exactly the difference in consumption.

$$\frac{7.126 - 7.002}{7.126} = 1.7 \text{ per cent.}$$

Thus, while using superheated steam, we have in the one case the steam dry, in the other with one-fourth water condensed on the surfaces. All the functions of the engines are completely changed in these two experiments. On August 26 the internal heat U of the steam diminishes during the expansion, doing the work thereof, and as the surfaces have only absorbed 9 c., during admission, a part also is radiated to the condenser in Rc. While on September 7 the internal heat U of the steam is nearly constant during expansion within 1.66 c., it is the surface which does the work of expansion, Rc having received 33.95 c. As we see a radical difference in the mode of transmitting heat, and in each experiment the same weight of steam has produced the same work, the final result being the same. In the presence of such facts, how can one say, from the diagram only, for example, how much expansion should be given? To establish this, the verified data are needed which we have already used.

We find that when we have carried the introduction to half stroke, but throttling also to give 125 H. P. for one and 99 H. P. for the other experiment, that for each case the consumption is not affected by the throttling, which was different in the two cases. This permits us to compare these experiments with those cutting off at $\frac{1}{4}$ and $\frac{1}{2}$ stroke, finding a saving by the latter of $\dfrac{8.199 - 7.002}{8.190} = 14.59$ per cent. by the greater expansion.

On the other hand, we see that as the work was diminished the proportion of water at the end of the stroke was increased, as also the dead loss Rc. By cutting off less than $\frac{1}{4}$ we should find a point where Rc would change the law and the consumption would increase, but, unfortunately, the valve gear would not admit of such a trial.

We have referred to the indicated work, but this is lessened by friction for the useful work, and the friction is not proportioned to the indicated work. This limits the cut off to between $\frac{1}{4}$ and $\frac{1}{6}$ for the best results for the single cylinder engine.

Effects of Throttling.—The question of restricting the area of the orifices of admission has been less often agitated than the cut off, and like that can only be resolved by direct experiments, fully analyzed. Before stating the results we have obtained, we will review the opinions put forward. Some engineers, basing on the proposition that dry steam falling in pressure without doing external work becomes superheated, have asserted that throttling was beneficial by evaporating the water entrained with the steam. But if they look at the second part of the proposition "without doing external work," they must admit that the amount of heat wrought per unit of weight is the same in either case.

Others, considering only the loss of work resulting, condemn entirely all methods of regulation based on the throttle as essentially defective, proscribing all governor throttles. They have generally attributed the *economy* that they *believed* to exist in the Corliss engines, or others of the class, to the rapid introduction of steam at nearly the boiler pressure.

We should attribute this radical difference of opinion to the conditions in the engines observed. We have seen that in certain limits of expansion the consumption is constant, or is increased. If we wish light work we may compare $\frac{1}{2}$ cut off with $\frac{1}{6}$ cut off, and should not be astonished at a difference of 14 per cent. between those of August 26 and September 7 with $\frac{1}{6}$ and $\frac{1}{2}$ cut-off, and those of August 27 and September 29 with $\frac{1}{2}$ throttle.

To compare, we should not take the basis of work done, but the cut-off, and the two experiments at half stroke, with the valve more or less closed.

The pressure, on August 27, of steam at 223° C. was brought to 2.307 k. at cut-off, and on September 29, with a temperature of 220° C., to 1.7458 k., a difference of 0.5612 k. more than half an atmosphere, and the consumption was altered $\dfrac{8.227 - 8.199}{8.227} = 0.3$ per cent. The increase is then due to the less expansion, as we have seen.

But here, contrary to what was found with different expansions, the percentage of water is almost the same—1.5, or slight superheating, and 2.52 per cent. at the beginning and 13.02 and 15.85 per cent. at the end of expansion, while the internal heat has decreased 20.52 c. and 16.82 c. In wide enough limits, as we see, the throttle has no influence upon the consumption.

Effect of the Condenser.—As we have said, resting upon facts from which the following proposition is derived, that a vapor introduced into a reservoir with constant volume, of which the surfaces are not everywhere of the same temperature, its final pressure depends upon the lowest temperature, that Watt deduced for his condenser.

The figures that we have show an economy of 43 per cent. by the condenser over exhaust to the air, a result needing little comment.

Let us see, however, as we have done, how this effects the changes of heat.

At the cut-off we have 12 per cent. condensed and 29.4 c. stored heat, the work of expansion requiring only 14.5 c., and Rc is zero, as also the proportion of final water. The excess from the surfaces has increased the internal heat from 163.72 to 177.97 c. We see that the loss Rc exists in a different form, the exhaust carrying off an excess of 14.24 c. to the air, as an increase in its internal heat, and we have lost work by the increase of back pressure.

It is not enough that Rc should be zero, as we have said, but the internal heat should not increase to put the engine in the best condition, and there should be no lost work, or the best vacuum should be obtained. This imposes the following condition—the surfaces should absorb only the work of expansion.

Although all our study has shown us how little freedom we have in imposing conditions upon the action of the surfaces, we believe, resting upon the experiment of August 26, cut off $\frac{1}{6}$, that by the use of super-heated steam and a jacket, the loss of internal heat would have been reduced from 26.05 c., and with dry steam at the end of the stroke diminished *Rc.*, but the jacket should be fed by a separate supply pipe, in order not to cool too much the working steam.

There only remains for us to examine what proportion of heat given has been utilized to finish these practical deductions.

When one measures the efficiency of an hydraulic motor, one divides the power utilized by that furnished, but for heat engines this is not the case.

Whatever be the body used, in a heat engine of maximum efficiency, the efficiency depends upon the difference of temperatures between which it works, divided by the absolute temperature of the source of heat. In these unrealizable conditions we should get 249 H. P. for 100 calories, as shown by Hirn. The best of our experiments give 135.77 H. P. for 172.79 c., or 75.8 H. P. for 100 calories; $\dfrac{78.5}{249} = 31.5$ per cent.

We see how far we are from the theoretic effect, and while stating that it never can be reached, we should hope for an improvement over what is practically 30 per cent.

To sum up, thanks to the numerous checks which the method employed permits, we have established the considerable influence of the action of the internal surfaces upon the action of steam in engine-cylinders, and have shown how, by employing superheated steam without prejudice to jackets, a considerable loss may be brought to a minimum, the cooling due the condenser *Rc.*, and within what limits it is judicious to confine expansion.

Such are the results of the series of experiments carried out under the direction of M. Hirn, and our readers can judge of their great importance.[*]

EXPERIMENTAL STUDY COMPARING THE INFLUENCE OF EXPANSION IN SIMPLE AND COMPOUND ENGINES.—A PAPER READ BEFORE THE INDUSTRIAL SOCIETY OF MULHOUSE, DECEMBER 30, 1878, BY M. O. HALLAUER.[†]

The comparison of the many experiments made upon "Woolf" engines, and the engine of M. Hirn, with superheated steam, led me to a principle which has been confirmed by the analysis of the compound engines in use in the French navy. I had stated the conclusion in a paper presented to the Society on the 30th January, 1878:

One can always construct a single cylinder vertical-beam engine, steam jacketed with four valves, which shall be at least as economical as the vertical " Woolf" beam engine, for expansions from 4 to 7, if the clearance does not exceed 1 per cent. of the cylinder volume.

This conclusion is based upon the total work of the engine, supposing

[*]These papers are given in the direct reverse of the order of their original publication, but perhaps not of their value.—C.A.S.
[†]M. Keller's summary of the following experiments was given in the opening section of this Chapter.—C. A. S.

a perfect vacuum—in a word, we consider the intrinsic work of the steam itself.

In this memoir I have had occasion to examine the various considerations which serve to establish the superiority of the "Woolf" system, outside of the experimental domain.

These same considerations I have again found developed under a form nearly identical but very marked in two works, concerning the "Woolf" engines, with expansion in the small cylinder. The authors there sum up what is generally admitted in favor of the "Woolf" system, which I will cite literally to allow the reader to appreciate the utility of my previous paper.

The first of these works was published at Rouen by MM. Thomas & Powell, engineers. It contains the experiments made in June, 1876, by M. H. Roland, Engineer of the Norman Association of Steam Users, and it opens thus:

"Double cylinder engines, in which the steam acts successively, produce motive force most economically when well constructed and managed. The advantage is because the small cylinder is only in communication with the condenser for a moment, the large cylinder only being more continually so, and the first action is to withdraw a portion of the force produced from the cooling action of the condenser and the internal condensation which is the immediate consequence.

"The steam arrives at the large cylinder partly expanded, and consequently at a lower temperature than that in the jacket, and is easier warmed and the condensation notably lessened.

"The employment of two cylinders permits us to carry the principle of expansion to its extreme limit with the best economic conditions, the force generated is divided, the efforts better carried and the differences of power between beginning and end of stroke are less than in a single cylinder engine; working with the same admissions there results a smoother operation. Because of the vertical cylinders and perfect equilibrium of the pieces attached to the beam the frictions are reduced and the useful effect is very high. It is to these qualities that the long life of these engines is to be attributed. We can cite some which have worked thirty years and which, after modifications with comparatively little cost, are in perfect order for work and consumption.

"The addition of a 'Correy Governor Expansion Gear,' assures to the engines which are furnished with it a perfect uniformity of speed and economic utilization under all loads."

The second work, published in 1878, in the Annual of the Society of Graduates of the Schools of Arts and Trades, under the title of "Notes Upon Double-Cylinder Engines," contains the results of experiments made by M. Quém, upon engines at St. Remy, constructed by MM. Powell.

"Among the different types of engines actually in use," says M. Quém, "the 'Woolf,' with two cylinders jacketed, in which the steam acts successively, is that which gives the best economy in production of motive force.

"In these engines the steam acts first with or without expansion in the small cylinder, then with expansion in the large cylinder. The latter only is in communication with the condenser. By this arrangement a portion of the force produced escapes the cooling action of the condenser and the internal cylinder condensation.

"Finally, because the jackets are connected with the boilers, the expanding steam in the large cylinder is at a temperature below that of the jacket, and is warmed thereby, and the cylinder condensation is notably lessened.

"The employment of two cylinders permits the best realization of expansion, which in these 'Woolf' engines can be carried to its limit.

"The difference of force between the beginning and end of the stroke is less in double than in single cylinder engines; there results smoother working.

"Because of the lesser difference of pressures there are less risks of breaking.

"Finally, leakage of steam by the admission valve is less prejudicial than in single cylinder engines.

"In 'Woolf' beam engines the balancing of weights reduces the friction, and the useful effect is consequently high.

"We have said that their principle assures to the 'Woolf' engines regularity of speed. That is true, but the regulators which have been applied for the purpose of rendering the speed uniform under variable loads have been far from perfect or from giving the desired results.

"The apparatus, long employed upon single-cylinder engines, is the conical governor and butterfly throttle.

"Not only is the governor throttle unsatisfactory in point of speed, but its operation is bad from the standpoint of economy.

"In effect it operates upon the steampipe, opening or closing a passage.

"There results a throttling which produces an expansion not only useless but prejudicial in the pipe and steam chest, consequently a lowering of initial pressure, which loss of force augments the consumption of fuel.

"It had been desirable to put on 'Woolf' beam engines a variable expansion gear which should be easily put on, which should give these engines great regularity of speed, avoid the evils of throttling, and obtain a greater expansion.

"Valves with lap which had been applied for some years to these engines were a great improvement, but the expansion was fixed and was not sufficient in most cases, and moreover the throttle was retained.

"Correy's variable gear permits us to add to the advantages of the 'Woolf' engines the removal of the throttle, retaining an economic use of steam under all loads."

Of all the foregoing considerations one only is not to be contested; it is as MM. Powell say, that the efforts are better distributed and the differences of force between the beginning and end of the stroke are less than in single-cylinder engines, and the movement smoother. But it should not be concluded from this long-known fact that the useful effect of double-cylinder engines is high and economical. The brake experiments made by the Mechanical Committee of the Industrial Society of Mulhouse have proved that the friction of the engines absorbs more power in 'Woolf' engines than in single-cylinder engines.

I have already shown in my paper of 1878 what economy can be realized by expansion in a separate cylinder. But the principle which I have stated has raised so many contradictions that our mechanical committee has deemed it prudent to hold itself in reserve when it states in these terms at the close of my work: "Many times already the committee has given its entire approbation to the fruitful experimental method followed by our colleague, and recommends to the attention of all engineers the results of the experiments contained in this work, results which appear to him unattackable. On the contrary, the committee believes it should be less positive in the conclusions of the author; it desires to see them confirmed by a great number of cases, and above all by varied experience in the widest field." I believed it useful to renew this question with new data, and more, I have added the study of an expansion, more or less, in the small cylinder of the 'Woolf' engine.

INFLUENCE OF EXPANSION IN "WOOLF" ENGINES.

Can there be a notable economy in cutting off in the small cylinder of a "Woolf" engine and expanding, for example, 28 times? Such is the first question which we shall attempt, for it is necessary to verify the consumption reported in each of the experiments which we shall cite, and this defines the degree of confidence which we shall give them.

It may be useful to recall to our readers, in the interest of the question which occupies us, the passage in my memoir of 1878, bearing upon this question of the influence of expansion.

The three engines where the expansion was effected in a separate cylinder are ranged in order of their consumption per total horse-power per hour.*

Vertical Woolf engine, 7.112 k. (15.4 lbs.); horizontal "Woolf" engine, 7.290 k. (15.9 lbs.); compound engine, 7,510 k. (16.4 lbs.). But this is also the order of expansion: Vertical "Woolf," 7 times; horizontal "Woolf," 6 times; compound, 5 times.

The fact that the consumption per total horse-power per hour was increased by changing the cut-off from ½ to ¼ was also found with the single cylinder engine using superheated steam. But we should observe that the reduction of the volume at cut-off causes a reduction of useful work by the engine, and at the same time a relative increase in the back pressure work. In the engine with superheating, and above all in the "Woolf" engines, this increase of back pressure work not only annuls the

---

*The French weights are for a Cheval de Vapeur, translated H. P. English equivalents are in parentheses.—C. A. S.

economy of a prolonged expansion, but even causes a greater expense. Also the back pressure work passing from 17 to 20 per cent. destroys the economy of the vertical "Woolf," when the regulating valve lowering the pressure reduces the work from 347 to 267 horse-power.

The documents which will serve us in the study of expansion are:

1. Experiments made in 1877 at Munster upon a "Woolf" beam engine, built by the firm of André Koechlin (really the Alsatian Society of Mechanical Constructions), and figuring in my memoir of 1878.

2. Brake Experiments by the Mechanical Committee of the Industrial Society in 1876 upon a horizontal *"Woolf" by the same builder, and given in the *Bulletins*, July, 1877.

3. Experiments made in 1877 by the Alsatian Association of Steam Users upon a vertical "Woolf" engine at Malmerspach having a variable cut-off in the small cylinder, by the same builder.

4. Experiments made upon "Woolf" beam engines with expansion in the small cylinder, built by MM. Thomas and T. Powell, of Rouen, and tried, one in 1877 at St. Remy upon Arne by M. Quèm, and the other, in 1876, by the Norman Association of Steam Users, this latter running the shops of MM. Fauquet-Lemaitre at Bolbec. The direct results of these experiments upon the Powell engines and that at Malmerspach have been given me by M. H. Walther-Meunier, Engineer of the Alsatian Association of Steam Users. I have checked and analyzed them. The analysis of the other experiments is given in my preceding paper, as I have already said: André Koechlin, "Woolf" Beam Engine working at Munster, variable power by throttle expansion, 7 times.

CHECK UPON CONSUMPTION, GAUGED DIRECTLY, TAKING AS A BASE THE HEAT GAINED BY THE COLD WATER INJECTED TO THE CONDENSER.[†]

I.—Forces des Chevauxs, translated horse-power, I. H. P., 347.16; revolutions per minute, 25.25; net H. P. on brake, 303.16; mechanical efficiency, 87.3 per cent.; proportion of back pressure work to total work, 17. 43 per cent.; back pressure on large piston, 0.293 k. (4.2 lbs. per sq. in.) (Boiler pressure, 67 lbs. above atmosphere.)

Per Single Stroke.

Heat brought by dry saturated steam........0.9123 k. × 654.03 c. = 597.19 c.
"   "   " water entrained.........0.0290 k. × 157.47 c. =   4.44 c.
"   "   " steam condensed in jackets 0.0884 k. × 496.56 c. =   43.89 c.

Total heat brought to engine.................................645.52 c.
Heat kept by the steam leaving condenser......0.9413 × 34.25 =   —32.24 c.

Q_0.. 613.28 c.

---

*In the table given, on page 191 this engine is headed as "Vertical Woolf." The error is in the original.—C. A. S.

[†]As these computations are checks, all the French units will be retained, and anything added from other sources will be put in ( ).

Heat given to water of condensation, Q_1........$29.1072 \times 18.05 = 525.38$ c.

$Q_0 - Q_1 = 613.28$ c. $- 525.38$ c..............................$= 87.90$ c.

The total work absorbed.................................72.79 c.

The external radiation.................................... 7. c.
———— 79.79 c.

Instead of 87.90; or an error of..............$\dfrac{87.90 - 79.79}{645.52} = 1.25$ per cent.

The heat found in the water of condensation should have been 613.28c. —79.79 c. = 533.49 calories; it was only 525.38 c. consequently too little. The total heat brought to the machine per stroke is 645.52 c. which to be more intelligible we will transform into a weight of dry saturated steam. In accounting for the work of the engine this weight will serve as a unit of comparison for other engines, and will be better comprehended under that form than the number of calories expended per horse-power which it stands in place of.

Consumption of dry steam per stroke, $\dfrac{645.52 \text{ c.}}{654.03 \text{ c.}} = 0.98698$ k.; weight of dry steam per total horse-power per hour, 7,112 k.; per indicated horse power, 8.614 k.; per net horse-power, 9.864 k.[*]

II.--I. H. P., 267.85; revolutions per min., 25.2.; net on brake, 226; mechanical efficiency, 84.3 per cent.

Proportion of back pressure to total work 20.52 per cent.

    "   " back pressure, 0.277 k. (3.9 lbs.).

(Boiler pressure, 60 lbs. above atmosphere.)

Per Single Stroke.

Heat brought by dry saturated steam......0.7124 k. $\times$ 652.93 c. = 465.14 c.

   "   "   " entrained water .... 0.0238 k. $\times$ 153.74 c. =   3.66 c.

   "   "   " steam to jackets ....0.0794 k. $\times$ 499.19 c. = 36.63 c.

   "   "   to engine... 505.43 c.

   " kept by steam leaving condenser.....0.7362 k. $\times$ 29.10 c. = -21.42 c

Q_0... 484.01 c.

Heat given to injection water ....29.3406 k. $\times$ 14.3 c. = Q_1 = 419.57 c.

Difference... 64.44 c.

The total work ....56.27 c.

" external radiation .... 7. c.
———— 63.27 c.

Error, $\dfrac{64.44 - 63.27}{505.43} = 0.23$ per cent.

The heat found in condenser is too small, it should have been 484.01— 63.27 = 420.74 c.

---

[*]These weights are from feed water at Q_0 c. I should suggest as divisor the term Q_0.—C. A. S.

The heat brought per stroke is 505.43 c.; it represents a consumption of dry saturated steam of

$$\frac{505.43}{652.93} = 0.77409 \text{ k.}$$

Weight dry saturated steam per hour per total horse power....... 6.945 k.
"   "   "   "   "   "   " indicated horse power .. 8.739 k.
"   "   "   ..   "   "   " net   "   "   ..10.357 k.

III.—I. H. P. 185.75; revolutions per minute, 25.4; net on brake, 145.52; mechanical efficiency, 78.3 per cent.

Proportion of back pressure work to total work, 24.1 per cent.; back pressure on large piston, 0.234 k. (3.3 lbs.).

(Boiler pressure 50 lbs. above atmosphere.)

Per Single Stroke.

Heat brought by dry steam.............. 0.5401 k. × 650.69 c. = 351.43 c.
"   "   " entrained water .... 0.0145 k. × 146.22 c. =   2.12 c.
"   "   steam condensed in jacket . 0.0640 k. × 504.47 c. = 32.28 c.

Total.. .... 385.83 c.
Heat kept by steam leaving condenser.... 0.5546 k. ×   23.46 c. = —12.65 c.

Q_0.. 373.18 c.
" found in injection water....,. 30.5688 k. × 10.56 c. = Q_1 = 322.80 c.

$Q_0 — Q_1$..........................,.................................. 50.38 c.
The total work .... 38.71 c.
External radiation .... 7. c.
                                                    ————
                                                    45.71 c.

Error. $\frac{50.38 — 45.71}{385.83} = 1.2$ per cent.

The heat found in the condenser is too little, it should have been 373.18 — 45.71 = 327.47 c.

The heat brought per stroke, 385.83 c.; it represents a consumption of $\frac{385.83}{650.69} = 0.59295$ k.

Weight of dry saturated steam per hour per total H. P.......... 7.384 k.
"   " "   "   "   " "   " ind. H. P.......... 9.730 k.
"   " "   "   "   " "   " net H. P.... ..... 12.411 k.

Uniting in one table the results of these three experiments, we find little difference per total horse-power, only 3.7 per cent. for a change from 183 to 347 horse-power.

TABLE I.

	I.	II.	III.
Force indicated..	347	267	185
Steam per hour per total H. P.. kilos.....................	7.112	6.945	7.384
Back pressure work in per cent. of total work	17.43	20.52	24.10
Steam per hour per indicated H. P..	8.614	8.739	9.730
Net work in per cent. indicated work	87.30	84.30	78.30
Steam per hour per net H. P.............................	9.864	10.357	12.411

We note that the cost of a total H. P. is 6 per cent. less for 267 than for 185 horse-power. This economy disappears for the indicated H. P., which is best for 347 H. P.

If these two sorts of consumption follow a distinct law we owe it to the back pressure work, which changes to 17 per cent. from 24 per cent. An analagous cause produces greater differences in the cost of a net H. P. The efficiency changes between 87 and 78 per cent. because of the friction, and we are not astonished to see the cost of a net H. P. differ by 20.5 per cent. It is the practical loss to which we put an engine working at 185 H. P. which can give 347, and is due to the back pressure and friction. But we should not conclude, as is often done, that this loss is due to throttling.

The difference of 3.7 per cent. that we find in the cost of a total H. P. is that due this evil influence, and is very little; or adding the slight increase over Experiment II.

I then legitimately concluded in my last work "that we are led to adopt the most simple regulator, an expansion variable by hand and a governor throttle." When the variations of work are large we can, by hand, without stopping the engine, change the introduction for the small intermediate differences the governor acts upon the valve. It is well understood that we do not here speak of engines where the force varies nearly instantly, for example, to double. This disposition permits us, as we have seen, to obtain all the benefits of a prolonged expansion, admitting that it gives a notable economy, of which the results of the following experiments will permit us to judge.

"WOOLF" BEAM ENGINE BY ANDRE KOECHLIN, AT MALMERSPACH.

Expansion in the small cylinder. Checks on the gauged consumption from the heat gained by the injection water.

E.—I. H. P., 143.11; revolutions per minute, 26.2; net horse-power, 118.38; efficiency, 82.7 per cent.; back pressure work in per cent. of total work, 18.6; back pressure on large piston, 0.181 k. (2.5 ℔s.); expansion, 28 times. (Boiler pressure, 67 ℔s. above atmosphere.)

Heat brought by dry steam . . . . 0.3479 k. × 654.03 c. = 227.53 c.
  "   "   entrained water . . . . 0.0200 k. × 157.47 c. =   3.15 c.
  "   "   steam to jackets . . . . 0.0324 k. × 496.56 c. =   16.09 c.

                     246.77 c.

Heat kept by steam leaving condenser . . . . . . 0.3679 k. ×   19.01 c. = −6.93 c.

 "   expended, Q_0 . . . . 239.78 c.
 "   rejected in condenser . . . . 21.8781 k. × 9.06 c. = 198.21 c.

                      41.57 c.

 "   in work done . . . . 28.97 c.
 "   external radiation . . . . 4.6   c.

                      ——— 33.57 c.

$$\text{Error,} \quad \frac{41.57 - 33.57}{246.77} = 3.2 \text{ per cent.}$$

The heat found in the injection water is too small, it should have been $239.78 - 33.57 = 206.21$ c.

The total heat brought to the engine per single stroke is 246.77 c., it represents a consumption of dry steam of $\frac{246.77}{654.03} = 0.3773$ k.

Weight of dry steam per hour per total H. P. . . . .   6.731 k.
"   "   "   "   "   " " ind. H. P. . . . .   8.273 k.
"   "   "   "   "   " " net H. P. . . . . .10.019 k.

C.—I. H. P.,215.7; revolutions per minute, 25.47; net on brake, 185.69; mechanical efficiency, 86.1 per cent.; back pressure work in per cent. of total work, 15.6; back pressure, 0.226 k. (3.2 ℔s.); expansion, 13; (boiler pressure, 70 lbs. above atmosphere).

Heat brought by dry steam. . . . . .0.5338 k. $\times$ 654.45 c. = 349.34 c.
"   "   " entrained water. . . . . .0.0304 k. $\times$ 158.88 c. =   4.83 c.
"   "   " steam to jacket. . . . . .0.0449 k. $\times$ 405.57 c. = 22.25 c

   Total . . . . .376.42 c.
Heat kept by steam leaving condenser. . . . . . . .0.5642 k. $\times$ 23.21 c.—13.09 c.

" expended, Q_0. . . . . 363.33 c.
" gained by injection water. . . . . .21.9136 k. $\times$ 13.48 c. = 295 39 c.
                                                                                 ————
                                                                                 67.94 c.
" in work done. 44.83
" external radiation. 4.6
            Error, $\dfrac{67.24 - 49.43}{376.42} = 4.9$ per cent.   ———— 49.43 c.

Heat found in condenser should have been. . . . . . . .363.33—49.43 = 313.90 c.
" brought per single stroke. . . . . .376.42 c.
Represents a consumption of dry steam. . . . .$\dfrac{376.42}{654.45} = 0.5751$ k.

Dry steam per hour per total H. P. . . . . .6.878 k.
"   "   "   "   " " ind. H. P. . . . . .8.149 k.
"   "   "   "   " " net H. P. . . . . .9.465 k.

F.—I. H. P., 149.53; revolutions per minute, 25.93; net on brake, 124.74; mechanical efficiency, 83.4 per cent.; back pressure work in per cent. total work, 17.5; back pressure on large piston, 0.175 k. (2.4 ℔s.); expansion, 25.

Heat brought by dry steam. . . . . .0.3652 k. $\times$ 654.03 c. = 238.85 c.
"   "   " entrained water. . . . . .0.0210 k. $\times$ 157.47 c. =   3.30 c.
"   "   to jackets. . . . . .0.0350 k. $\times$ 496.56 c. = 17.38 c.

   Total. . . . . : . . . . 259.53 c.
Heat kept by steam leaving condenser. . . . . . .0.3862 k. $\times$ 19.43 c. = —7.50 c.

" expended, Q_0. . . . . 252.03 c.
" given to injection water. . . . . .21.2674 k. $\times$ 9.89 c. = Q_1 = 210.33 c.
                                                                                 ————
                                                                                 41.70 c.

Heat in work done....................................30.51
"   " externa lradiation............................. 4.6
                                           —— 35.11 c.

$$\text{Error, } \frac{41.70 - 35.11}{259.53} = 2.5 \text{ per cent.}$$

Heat found in condenser should have been.......252.03 − 35.11 = 216.92 c.
Heat expended per single stroke.................. ....259.53 c.

Represents dry steam.................... $\dfrac{259.53}{654.03} = 0.3968$ k.

Dry steam per hour per total H. P...............................6.821 k.
"   "   "   "   " ind. H. P................................ 8.260 k.
"   "   "   "   " net H. P..............................9.898 k.

D.—I. H. P., 212.92; revolutions per minute, 24.83; net on brake, 183.67; mechanical efficiency, 86.2 per cent,; back pressure work in per cent. of total work, 14.9; back pressure on large piston, 0.218 k. (3 lbs.); expansion, 13; (boiler pressure, 70 lbs. above atmosphere).

Heat brought by dry steam..............0.5443 k. × 654.45 c. = 356.22 c.
"   "   " entrained water.........0.0310 k. × 158.88 c. =   4.92 c.
"   "   to jackets................0.0462 k. × 495.57 c. = 22.89 c.

    Total... 384.03 c.
Heat kept by steam leaving condenser,...0.5753 k. × 27.02 c. = −15.54 c.

" expended, Q_0.......... .... 368.49 c.
" found in injection water........18.0071 k. × 17.07 c. = Q_1 = 307.38 c.
                                             61.11 c.

" in work done....... ....45.39
" " external radiation............................. 4.6
                                        —— 49.99 c.

$$\text{Error, } \frac{61.11 - 49.99}{384.03} = 2.9 \text{ per cent.}$$

Heat found in condenser should have been....368.49—49.99 = 318.50 c.
Heat brought to engine per stroke ....384.03 c.

Represents dry steam per stroke................... $\dfrac{384.03}{654.45} = 0.5867$ k.

Dry steam per hour per total H. P................................6.983 k.
"   "   "   *   " ind. H. P.................................8.210 k.
"   "   "   "   " net H. P.............................9.517 k.

This Malmerspach engine is composed of two coupled on the same shaft, and experiments E and C were made on the left, while experiments F and D were made on the right-hand engine. We note that three of these experiments, E, F, D, check to 3 per cent. nearly, but C only to 5 per cent.; however the direct measurement is correct, being sensibly that of experiment D.

TABLE II.

	E.	F.	C.	D.
Expansion......	28	25	13	13
I. H. P., Ch. de V.........................	143	149	215	213
Dry steam per hour per total H. P., ks...	6.731	6.821	6.878	6.983
Per cent. back pressure work.........	18.6	17.5	15.6	14.9
Dry steam per hour per ind. H. P., ks...	8.273	8.260	8.149	8.210
Per cent. of mechanical efficiency........	82.7	83.4	86.1	86.2
Dry steam per hour per net H. P., ks....	10.019	9.898	9.465	9.517

Table II. sums our four experiments. The figures which are there, compared with Table I., permit us to decide if it is more advantageous to work with the throttle than with a cut-off in the small cylinder, or the reverse. If one is obliged to produce from an engine too small a power, either way is used, but for a careful comparison it is necessary to take if possible the work with the same difference in each. For example, Malmerspach Engine C and E; I. H. P., 215 and 143, being 3.2; expansions, 13 and 28; and the Münster engine, II. and III., I. H. P., 267 and 185, being nearly the same ratio, expansion 7.

In dry steam per hour per total H. P. there is a difference between 6.945 k., with 267 H. P., and 7.384 k., with 185 H. P. of $\frac{7.384 - 6.945}{7.384} = 5.9$ per cent. in favor of the larger power, both obtained by throttling.

If in the second engine we pass from expansion 13 to 28, the difference in dry steam per total H. P. is $\frac{6.878 - 6.731}{6.878} = 2.1$ per cent. in favor of the lesser power, 143 H. P.,; in these limits there is little to choose, for the difference is within the errors of observation.

It seems as if there was an economy of 5.9 + 2.1 = 8 per cent.; on the other hand, the 267 H. P. corresponds to the least consumption, 6.945 k. which has been obtained by throttling 1.342 k. at the cut-off (18.8 ℔s.). As this only differs $\frac{6.945 - 6.878}{6.945} = 0.9$ per cent. from that for 215 H. P., we conclude, as before, that it is unimportant.

We find ourselves here in the face of a contradiction which we can elucidate later after having given the complete analysis of these engines. For the time we have only to note how the heat of the injection water checks the consumption and fixes the degree of confidence which we should give to each experiment.

These remarks, based upon the amounts used per total H. P. per hour, only refer to the work of the steam itself in the cylinder. They are not affected by poor vacuum, nor the friction of the engine. The influence of these two elements is only felt when we consider the indicated work and the net work. Thus, in passing from experiment E 143. H. P., expansion, 28, to experiment C, 215 H. P., expansion 13, the consumptions differ per indicated H. P. 1.5 per cent. and per net H. P. 5.5 per cent.

This difference is in the reverse order of that for the total H. P.; it shows that practically there is 5.5 per cent. loss in changing from expansion 13 to 28. These same causes, back pressure work and friction, have brought for the Munster engine, with fixed expansion 7, stronger effects—increased to 16$\frac{1}{2}$ per cent. when throttle causes the work to fall from 267 H. P. to 185 H. P.

Upon the same engine at Malmerspach, and before the application of expansion gear, there had been made an experiment, with the object of defining the economy realized, which we will check as before.

B.—Indicated H. P., 201.64 H. P.; revolutions per minute, 24.18; net on brake, 172.80 H. P.; mechanical efficiency, 85.6 per cent.: back pressure work in per cent. of total work, 16.4; back pressure, 0.235 k. (3.3 lbs. per sq. in.); expansion, 6; (boiler pressure, 67 lbs. above atmosphere).

Heat brought by dry steam................	0.5823 k. × 654.03 c. =	380.84 c.
" " " entrained water.........	0.0312 k. × 157.47 c. =	4.91 c.
" " to jackets........	0.0330 k. × 496.56 c. =	16.38 c.
Total......................................		402.13 c.
Heat kept by steam leaving condenser.....	0.6135 k. × 22.73 c. =	13.94 c.
" expended, Q_0............................		388.19 c.
" found in injection water............	22.6234 × 14.50 = Q_1 =	328.04 c.
		60.15 c.
" in work done.........	....	44.14 c.
" " external radiation...............	....	4.6 c.
		48.74 c.

$$\text{Error } \frac{60.15 - 48.74}{402.13} = 2.8 \text{ per cent.}$$

The heat found in injection is too small; it should have been $388.19 - 48.74 = 339.45$ c. The heat per stroke is 402.13 c.

$$\text{It represents } \frac{402.13}{654.03} = 0.6148 \text{ k. dry steam.}$$

Dry steam per hour per total H. P....	7.402 k.
" " " " " ind. H. P..	8.847 k.
" " " " " net H. P.............................	10.301 k.

The result of this analysis, if we consider the engine in good order when the experiment was made, which we will suppose to be the case, compared with experiment C.

B.—Expansion 6, C.—Expansion 13.

$$\text{Per Total H. P. } \frac{7.402 - 6.878}{7.402} = 7.1 \text{ per cent.}$$

$$\text{Per Ind. H. P. } \frac{8.847 - 8.149}{8.847} = 8 \text{ per cent.}$$

$$\text{Per Net. H. P. } \frac{10.301 - 9.465}{10.301} = 8 \text{ per cent.}$$

by C over B.

I have valued the friction by the brake experiments of our Mechanical Committee. We shall see how far MM. Powell have obtained the same co-efficients upon their "Woolf" engines.

HORIZONTAL "WOOLF" ENGINE, BY ANDRE KOECHLIN, TRIED WITH BRAKE BY THE MECHANICAL COMMITTEE.

I.—I. H. P., 130; revolutions per minute, 39.37; net on brake, 112.08; mechanical efficiency, 86.1 per cent.; back pressure work in per cent. of total work, 20.06; back pressure, 0.253 k. (3.5 ℔s.); expansion, 6; (boiler pressure, 53 ℔s. above atmosphere).

Heat brought by dry steam.................0.2286 k. × 652.46 c. = 149.15 c.
"   "   " entrained water.........0.0079 k. × 152.17 c. =   1.20 c.
"   "   to jackets...................0.0263 k. × 500.29 c. = 13.16 c.

    Total...163.51 c.

Heat kept by steam leaving condenser.......0.2365 k. × 26.20 c. =   6.19 c.
" expended, Q_0... 157.32 c.
" found in injection water..............14.6202 k. × 9.20 c. = 134.50 c.

                                                 22.82 c.

" in work done.......................................17.45 c.
" in external radiation............................... 3.5 c.

                                   ———— 20.95 c.

$$\text{Error } \frac{22.82 - 20.95}{163.51} = 1.13 \text{ per cent.}$$

The heat gained by injection should have been 157.32 — 20.95 = 136.37 c.
Heat per single stroke......................................163.51 c.

Represents dry steam per stroke...................$\dfrac{163.51}{652.46}$ = 0.2506 k.

Dry steam per hour per total H. P.............................. 7.290 k.
"   "   " ind. H. P.............................. 9.120 k.
"   "   " net H. P..............................10.563 k.

There is only 1.3 per cent. difference between the consumption per total H. P., and that in experiment B; while for the indicated H. P. there is 3 per cent. in the other direction.

II.—I. H. P., 181; revolutions per minute, 39.67; net on brake, 161 H. P.; mechanical efficiency, 89 per cent.; back pressure work in per cent. of total work, 17.3; back pressure, 0.295 k. (4.1 ℔s.); boiler pressure, 54 ℔s. above atmosphere).

Heat brought by dry steam................0.3134 k. × 652.69 c. = 204.55 c.
"   "   " entrained water.........0.0134 k. × 152.96 c. =   2.05 c.
"   "   to jackets...................0.0271 k. × 499.73 c. = 13.54 c.

    Total...220.14 c.
Heat kept by steam leaving condenser......0.3268 k. × 23.90 c. =   7.81 c.

" expended, Q_0.. 212.33 c.

Heat rejected in injection water........... 14.5795 k. × 12.58 c. = 183.41 c.

$$212.33 - 183.41 = 28.92 \text{ c.}$$

" in work done.................................24.12

" in external radiation............................ 3.50

$$\overline{\qquad\qquad}$$

27.62 c.

$$\text{Error } \frac{28.92 - 27.62}{220.14} = 0.6 \text{ per cent.}$$

Heat brought per stroke......................................220.14 c.

Represents dry steam per stroke.......................$\frac{220.14}{652.69} = 0.3372$ k.

Dry steam per hour per total H. P................................ 7.328 k.

"   "   "   "   " ind. H. P................................ 8.878 k.

"   "   "   "   " net H. P................................ 9.975 k.

The consumption per total H. P. is nearly the same as for the preceding experiment, but for the indicated and net H. P. there is a marked improvement by better efficiency, and less proportion of back pressure work, although the vacuum is not so good. This is a fact which we have many times noted.

Finally, that we may not lack generality in our conclusions of the influence of expansion in the small cylinder, I will give the results of experiments made upon the engines constructed by MM. Powell. Little different from the preceding, they are designed with a view to an early cut-off in the small cylinder, but distinguish themselves by the excellent vacuum, 0.100 k. of back pressure (1.4 lbs.) on the large piston. We shall see that for 19 expansions the consumption per total H. P. is nearly the same as that we have found for 13 and 28 times.

"WOOLF" BEAM ENGINE BY POWELL, WORKING AT ST. REMY.—EXPERIMENT BY M. R. QUEM.

Expansion, 19 times; indicated horse-power, 137; revolutions per minute, 24.503; net on brake, 107.88 H. P.; mechanical efficiency, 78.7 per cent.; back pressure work in per cent. of total work, 9.9; back pressure, 0.102 k. (1.4 lbs.); (boiler pressure, 70 lbs. above atmosphere).

Heat brought by dry steam................0.3222 k. × 654.42 c. = 210.85 c.

"   "   " entrained water.......... 0.0110 k. × 158.80 c. =   1.75 c.

"   "   to jackets....................0.0412 k. × 495.62 c. = 20.42 c.

$$\overline{\qquad\qquad}$$

Total...233.02 c.

Heat kept by steam leaving condenser..........0.3332 k. × 27 c. = —8.99 c.

"   expended, Q_0... 224.03 c.

"   found gained by injection water......10.8511 k. × 18.24 c. = 197.92 c.

$$\overline{\qquad\qquad}$$

26.11 c.

"   in work done...29.79

"   in radiation.. 4.50

$$\overline{\qquad\qquad}$$

34.29 c.

$$\text{Error } \frac{26.11 - 34.29}{233.02} = 3.5 \text{ per cent.}$$

Heat found should have been..................224.03 − 34.29 = 189.74 c.
"   per single stroke .... 233.02 k.

Represents dry steam................................. $\dfrac{233.02}{654.42} = 0.356$ k.

Heat per hour per total H. P.......................................6.840 k.
"   "   "   "   ind. H. P.................................7.591 k.
"   "   "   "   net H. P....................................9.702 k.

The consumption per total H. P. of this last experiment, made with 19 expansions on the Powell engine, is exactly between the two experiments E and C, made upon the Koechlin engine with expansions of 13 and 28. These three consumptions are 6.731 k., 6.840 k., 6.878 k., differing among themselves 1.4 per cent. Upon different engines they prove, between expansions of 13 and 28, how little the effect of expansion is upon the good work of steam. The very good vacuum of the Powell engine, 0.102 k. (1.4 lbs.), gives it practically a marked superiority over the Koechlin engine, expanding 13 times, a circumstance remarkably exceptional for a "Woolf" engine, which demands justification by more numerous experiments ; it loses only 9.9 per cent. in back pressure work, in the place of 15 per cent., and we shall not be astonished to find there is

$$\frac{8.149 - 7.591}{8.149} = 6.8 \text{ per cent. in its favor.}$$

We had wished to join in these results those that were obtained by M. H. Roland upon the same Powell engines, tried at Bolbec ; but, as we shall see, their exactitude leaves much to be desired, and we only remark the excellent vacuum and the error committed, 9.9 per cent., which causes us to set aside the results.*

The results of the experiments C, D, E, F, of the Malmerspach engine, built by André Koechlin, with that on the St. Remy engine, by Powell, prove to us the small influence of an expansion from 13 to 28 ; in these limits the total H. P. cost varies only 2 per cent. in one case from the other. This fact acquired, we shall seek to render an account of the following anomaly, which we have already noted, between cost per total H. P. of experiments B and C of the Malmerspach engine. With expansion 6 and 13 we found 7 per cent. difference, which should represent the economy of expansion 13 ; but we should be too high, for it does not agree with the figures of C, D, E and F, nor with the results of the Powell engine. This difference is more when compared with II., 267 H. P., of the Munster engine, expanding 7 times, which gives the least cost as 6.945 k. per total H. P., when the expansion 13 gives 6.878 k.—difference of 1 per cent. We shall see if analysis will show us the cause of this irregularity.

ANALYSIS OF EXPERIMENT III.

Account of heat and cooling by condenser, per stroke:
Weight of fluid in small cylinder .... 0.5776 k.
"   " dry steam at cut-off................................. 0.4553 k.

---

*The computations are not transcribed.—C. A. S.

Weight of water at cut-off (21.17 per cent.)..................... 0.1223 k.
   "   "   " entrained .... 0.0145 k.

   "   "   " condensed up to cut-off........................ 0.1078 k.

Heat given to iron........................0.1078 k. $\times$ 516.77 c. = 55.70 c.

Weight of fluid in large cylinder........................... 0.5830 k.
   "   " dry steam at end of stroke .... 0.5399 k.

   "   " water at end of stroke (7.39 per cent.)............... 0.0431 k.

Internal heat at the end of admission, U_0.....................—290.12 c.
Internal heat at the end of stroke, U_1......................... 322.01 c.

$U_0 - U_1$.. 31.89 c.

Heat given by jacket.. 32.28 c.
   "   "   " condensation in small cylinder .... 55.70 c.

   " furnished during expansion .... 56.09 c.
   " absorbed by total work of expansion...............35.61 c.
   " radiated externally................................. 7.00 c.
                                            —— 42.61 c.

56.09 — 42.61 = 13.48 c. = Rc, cooling by condenser being 3.5 per cent. of the heat brought to the engine.

The final internal heat compared with the heat gained by the injection water furnishes a check on Rc.

Internal heat at end of stroke, U_1 .... 322.01 c.
Heat of back pressure work.................................. + 12.29 c.
   " remaining in cushion .... — 14.92 c.
   "   " after condensation........................... — 12.65 c.

                                            306.73 c.
   " gained by injection water............................... 322.80 c.

Rc .... 16.07 c.

The other method gave Rc = 13.48 c.; the error is only

$$\frac{16.07 - 13.48}{385.83} = 0.67 \text{ per cent.}$$

ANALYSIS OF EXPERIMENT II.

Account of heat and cooling by the condenser:
Weight of fluid in small cylinder.......... .... 0.7697 k.
   " " dry steam at cut-off .... 0.6603 k.

   " " water at cut-off (14.21 per cent.).................... 0.1094 k.
   "   "   " entrained................................. 0.0238 k.

   "   "   " condensed................................. 0.0856 k.

Heat given to iron up to cut-off........................ .... 43.40 c.

Weight of fluid in large cylinder................................. 0.7650 k.
"   " dry steam at end of stroke........................... 0.7237 k.
"   " water at end of stroke (5.39 per cent.)............... 0.0413 k.

Internal heat at cut-off, U_0.. 415.57 c.
Internal heat at end of stroke, U_1............................. 432.15 c.
$U_0 - U_1$... — 16.58 c.
Heat furnished by jacket...................................... 36.63 c.
"   "   " condensation in small cylinder.............. 43.40 c.
"   "   during expansion.... .... 63.45 c.
" absorbed by work of expansion.................... 49.80 c.
" external radiation................................. 7. c.
                                                  ———— 56.78 c.

$Rc = 6.65$ c.; Rc is a loss of $\dfrac{6.65}{505.43} = 1.32$ per cent. of total heat per stroke furnished engine.

Check on Rc:

Internal heat at end of stroke, U_1............................... 432.15 c.
Back pressure work.. + 14.53 c.
Heat remaining in cushion...................................... — 15.13 c.
Heat remaining in fluid after condensation...................... — 21.42 c.
                                                         410.13 c.
Heat gained by injection water................................. 419.57 c.
Rc... 9.34 c.

The other method $Rc = 6.65$; $\dfrac{9.44 - 6.65}{505.45} = .55$ per cent.

ANALYSIS OF EXPERIMENT I.

Account of heat and cooling by condenser, Rc:

Weight of fluid in small cylinder per stroke.................... 0.9847 k.
"   dry steam at cut-off................................. 0.8254 k.
"   water at cut-off (16.17 per cent.)...................... 0.1593 k.
"   water entrained .... 0.0290 k.
"   water condensed at cut-off.......................... 0.1303 k.
Heat given to iron at cut-off................................... 65.25 c.
Weight of fluid in large cylinder............................... 0.9691 k.
"   dry steam at end of stroke............................. 0.9051 k.
"   water at end of stroke (6.6 per cent.) .... 0.0640 k.
Internal heat at cut-off, U_0................................... 525.79 c.
"   " end of stroke, U_1............................... 543.19 c.
$U_0 - U_1$... 17.40 c.

Heat furnished by jacket... 43.89 c.

    "   "   by iron small cylinder........................... 65.25 c.

    "   "   during expansion.............................. 91.74 c.

Heat in total work done during expansion...................... 62.85 c.

Heat of external radiation...................................... 7.00 c.

                $Rc = 21.89$ c.; per cent. of heat furnished, 3.38.

    Check on Rc.:

Internal heat at end of stroke, U_1............................ 543.19 c.

Back pressure work..+ 15.37 c.

Heat remaining in cushion......................................— 14.60 c.

    "   "   fluid after condensing..................... 32.24 c.

                                                      511.72 c.

Heat gained by injection water................... .... 525.38 c.

Rc... .. .. 13.66 c.

    The other method gave 21.89:

        Error, $\dfrac{21.89 - 13.66}{645.52} = 1.26$ per cent.

        HORIZONAL "WOOLF," 130 H. P.; EXPANSION, 6.

    Account of heat and cooling by condenser Rc:

Weight of fluid per stroke in small cylinder......................0.2500 k.

    "   dry steam at cut-off..............................0.2220 k.

    "   water at cut-off (11.2 per cent.)......................0.0280 k.

    "   water entrained...............................0.0079 k.

    "   water condensed at cut-off.........................0.0201 k.

Heat given to iron at cut-off.................................... 10.30 c.

Weight of fluid in large cylinder.... ....0.2506 k.

    "   dry steam at end of stroke..........................0.2372 k.

    "   water at end of stroke (5.34 per cent.)................0.0134 k.

Internal heat at cut-off, U_0...................................137.85 c.

    "   "   end of stroke, U_1.............................141.48 c.

$U_0 - U_1$...—3.63 c.

Heat furnished by jacket........... .... 13.16 c.

    "   "   " iron above................................. 10.30 c.

    "   "   during expansion.............................. 19.83 c.

Heat absorbed during expansion, total work.................... 14.38 c.

    " external radiation.. 3.50 c.

    $Rc = 1.95$ c.; per cent. Rc of total heat furnished, 1.19 c.

    Check on Rc.:

Internal heat at end of stroke.................................141.48 c.

Back pressure work..+4.38 c.

Heat retained in cushion...................................—7.43 c.
"   "   in condenser...................................—6.19 c.

                                                             132.24 c.
"   gained by injection water.................................134.53 c.

Rc...   2.26 c.

$$\text{Error,} \ \frac{2.26 - 1.95}{163.51} = 0.1 \ \text{per cent.}$$

HORIZONTAL "WOOLF," 181 H. P.; EXPANSION, 6.

Account of heat and cooling by condenser Rc:

Weight of fluid per stroke in small cylinder............. 0.3459 k.
"   dry steam per stroke at cut-off.................0.3082 k.

"   water per stroke at cut-off (10.8 per cent.)............0.0377 k.
"   water entrained.................................0.0134 k.

"   water condensed at cut-off....................0.0243 k.
Heat given to iron.. 12.24 c.
Weight of fluid in large cylinder.............................0.3478 k.
"   dry steam at end of stroke.......................0.3324 k.

"   water at end of stroke (4.5 per cent.)..................0.0154 k.
Internal heat at end of admission, U_0...........................192.68 c.
"   "   "   " stroke, U_1..............................198.80 c.

$U_0 - U_1$...—6.12 c.
Heat furnished by jacket.................................... 13.54 c.
"   "   " iron above.................................. 12.24 c.

"   "   during expansion............................. 19.66 c.
"   absorbed during expansion, total work................... 14.50 c.
"   lost, external radiation................................... 3.50 c.

$$Rc = 1.66 \ \text{c.; per cent. of heat furnished} \ \frac{1.66}{220.14} = 0.75.$$

Check on Rc.:
Internal heat at end of stroke, U_1............................ 198.80 c.
Back pressure work... +5.10 c.
Heat retained in cushion.....................................—10.03 c.
"   "   condenser.................................... —7.81 c.

                                                             186.06 c.
"   gained by injection water.................................183.41 c.

Rc... 2.65 c.
The other method gave 1.66 c.

$$. \ \text{Error} \ \frac{2.65 - 1.66}{220.14} = 0.45 \ \text{per cent.}$$

The error appears to be $\dfrac{2.65 - 1.66}{220.14} = 1.9$. As the check on Rc gives — 2.65, the injection has gained less heat than was rejected.]

Experiment II. on the Münster engine and I. on the horizontal engine differ little as to proportions of final water and heat lost by the cooling due the condenser Rc. We have stated the difference $\dfrac{7.290 - 6.745}{7.290} = 4.7$ per cent. between the cost of a total H. P. It is due, part to the difference between 6 and 7 expansions, but more to the strong compression in the vertical engine which partially annuls the effect of the clearance.

The experiments, of which the analyses will follow, do not offer the precision of the two preceding series, of which the consumption checks within one per cent., nearly; also we will neglect the weight of fluid in the clearance when establishing the internal heats U_1 and U_0 and the difference $U_0 - U_1$. I did not proceed thus until I had rendered an account of the error which is committed.

With engine 267 H. P., $U_0 - U_1 = 16.58$ c.; when the clearance is taken into account, $U_0 - U_1 = 19.80$ c.; when it is neglected, there is an error of $\dfrac{19.80 - 16.58}{505.43} = 0.6$ per cent. For the horizontal engine, $U_0 - U_1$ will be 3.44 in place of 3.63 c., an error of $\dfrac{3.63 + 3.44}{163.51} = 0.1$ per cent.

Our second manner of procedure is thus justified above all in the practical experiments which check within 3 per cent. only, but we add again that this approximation is very satisfying and conducts us to some very remarkable results. [The error is always one way, and the comparisons are very accurate].

MALMERSPACH ENGINE, EXPERIMENT A—201 H. P., EXPANSION, 6.

Heat account and cooling by condenser Rc:

Weight of fluid in small cylinder	0.6135 k.
" " dry steam at cut-off	0.5350 k.
" " water " " (12.8 per cent.)	0.0785 k.
" " " entrained	0.0312 k.
" " " condensed at cut-off	0.0473 k.
Heat given to iron	24.09 c.
Weight of fluid in large cylinder	0 6135 k.
" " dry steam at end of stroke	0.5429 k.
" " water " " " (11.5 per cent.)	0.0706 k.
Internal heat at end of admission, U_0	384.86 c.
" " " " stroke, U_1	327.69 c.
$U_0 - U_1$	7.17 c.

Heat furnished by jackets.................................... 16.38 c.
"   "   " iron.................................... 24.09 c.
"   "   during expansion.............................. 47.64 c.
"   absorbed   "   "   by total work................. 34.60 c.
"   lost by external radiation............................... 4.60 c.

$Rc = 8.44$ c., being $\dfrac{8.44}{402.13} = 2.1$ per cent. of the heat furnished.

Check on Rc:
Internal heat at end of stroke, U_1............................. 327.69 c.
Back pressure work... 8.61 c.
Heat retained after condensation............................—13.94 c.

                                                            322.26 c.
Heat gained by injection water...............................328.04 c.

Rc... 5.68 c.
By the other method................................. .... 8.44 c.

Error, $\dfrac{8.44 - 5.68}{402.13} = 0.7$ per cent.

This engine differs from the horizontal one by a larger proportion of terminal water, 11.5 per cent. in place of 5.3 per cent. The cost of a total H. P. is also greater by $\dfrac{7.402 - 7.290}{7.402} = 1.5$ per cent.

The expansion 6 and the conditions of regulation are the same, but we see that the jackets are not working in the same manner as those of the horizontal engine condensing 10 per cent. of the steam, while the second is only 5.1 per cent.; there is then from this fact a loss which changes the internal heat and increases the heat lost by the cooling due the condenser.

Compared with Experiment II., 267 H. P., Experiment B gives us 4.7 per cent. less condensation in the jackets and a less cushion, which brings the Malmerspach engine $\dfrac{7.402 - 6.945}{7.402} = 6.1$ per cent. worse than the Munster engine. All these considerations should indicate where the economy really is rather than to a large expansion commencing in the small cylinder.

MALMERSPACH ENGINE—EXPERIMENT C., 215 H. P.; EXPANSION 13.

Account of heat etc., per stroke:
Weight of fluid in small cylinder............................ 0.5642 k.
"   " dry steam at cut-off.............................. 0.4303 k.
"   " water   "   " (23.7 per cent.)................. 0.1339 k.
"   "   " entrained...................................... 0.0304 k.
"   "   " condensed at cut-off......................... 0.1035 k.

Heat given to iron... 51.30 c.

Weight of fluid in large cylinder............................. 0.5642 k.

" " dry steam at end of stroke...................... 0.4632 k.

" " water " " (17.9 per cent.)........... 0.1010 k.

Internal heat at end of admission, U_0.......................... 283.55 c.

" " " " " stroke, U_1........................... 282.31 c.

$U_0 - U_1$.. 1.24 c.

Heat furnished by jackets................................... 22.25 c.

" " " iron....................................... 51.34 c.

Total heat furnished during expansion.................... 47.83 c.

Heat in total work done....................................... 38.79 c.

" " external radiation.................................. 4.60 c.

$Rc = 32.44c$, being $\dfrac{31.44}{376.42} = 8.3$ per cent. of the entire heat furnished.

The check on Rc is not as exact as before; but as we remember that in this experiment the error was 5 per cent., while in the others it was about 2.5 per cent., this is not surprising.

Internal heat at end of stroke, U_0.......................... 283.31 c.

Back pressure work... 8.48 c.

Heat retained in condensed water........................ — 13.09 c.

277.70 c.

" gained by injection water.............................. 295.39 c.

Rc.. 17.69 c.

The other method gave 31.44; $\dfrac{31.44 - 17.69}{376.42} = 3.7$ per cent. error.

The other experiments were much closer.

The cut-off in the small cylinder being much earlier, it is desirable to calculate the internal heat U_2 at the end of the stroke in the small cylinder.

Weight of fluid in small cylinder.............................0.5642 k.

" " dry steam at end of its stroke...................... 0.4901 k.

Internal heat, U_2... 305.84 c.

MALMERSPACH ENGINE—EXPERIMENT. D., 213 H. P.; EXPANSION, 13.

Account of heat, etc., per stroke:

Weight of fluid in small cylinder............................. 0.5753 k.

" " dry steam at cut-off.............................. 0.4328 k.

" " water " " (24.7 per cent.)........... 0.1425 k.

" " " entrained...................................... 0.0310 k.

" " " condensed at cut-off....................... 0.1115 k.

Heat given to iron... 55.31 c.

Weight of fluid in large cylinder.............................. 0.5753 k.
"   " dry steam at end of stroke......................... 0.4623 k.
"   " water   "   "   " (19.5 per cent)............ 0.1121 k.
Internal heat at cut-off, U_0.................................... 286.44 c.
"   "   " end of stroke, U_1.......................... 283.20 c.

$U_0 - U_1$... 3.24 c.
Heat furnished by jacket.................................... 22.89 c.
"   "   " iron.................................... 55.31 c.

"   "   during expansion............................. 81.44 c.
"   taken by total work of expansion........................ 39.04 c.
"   "   " external radiation........................... 4.06 c.
Rc.. 37.80 c.

$$\text{Per cent. of entire heat } \frac{37.80}{384.00} = 9.9 \text{ per cent.}$$

The check on Rc:
Internal heat at end of stroke, U_1........................... ...283.20 c.
Back pressure work.. 7.97 c.
Heat retained after condensation.............................. 15.54 c.

275.63 c.
" gained by injection water................................. ...307.38 c.
Rc.. 31.75 c.

$$\text{Error, } \frac{37.80 - 31.75}{384.03} = 1.6 \text{ per cent.}$$

At the end of stroke in small cylinder, U_2:
Weight of fluid... 0.5753 k.
"   dry steam... 0.4928 k.
"   water (1.43 per cent.)............................... 0.0825 k.
Internal heat at end of stroke in small cylinder................. 308.79 c.

These two experiments with the same expansion, 13, are made, one on the right engine, the other on the left, and give results little different.

The cost per total H. P. of C. is only $\dfrac{6.983 - 6.878}{6.982} = 1.5$ per cent. better than D.

The proportions of water for C and D respectively are at cut-off, 23.7 and 24.7 per cent.; at the end of the stroke in small cylinder, 13.1 and 14.3 per cent., and at the end of stroke in large cylinder, 17.9 and 17.5 per cent., following nearly the 1½ per cent. difference.

Rc differs 8.3 and 9.9 per cent., only 1.6 per cent.

We will take for comparison experiments B, expansion 6; C, expansion 13, and E, expansion 28, all made on the left-hand engine.

The last two experiments throw light upon a fact which should, above all, attract our attention. It is the great evaporation which takes place in the small cylinder during the first expansion. The introduction at full pressure has been carried to nearly half the stroke of the small cylinder, without preventing the evaporation of 10 per cent. of the fluid originally condensed, and a rapid augmentation of the internal heat of steam, 22.29 c. for C, and 22.35 D. (U_0-U_1). We see also that during expansion in the large cylinder a portion of the vapor, existing at the end of the stroke, in the small cylinder, has been condensed about 5 per cent., and the internal heat of the steam (U_2-U_1) diminished 23.53 c. C, and 25.59 c. D.

The number of calories returned by the internal heat during the stroke of the large piston is nearly the same as the work of expansion, 25 c. in the large cylinder; we could then conclude that the steam jacket has done nothing in this second expansion, in a word, does not perform its office.

Arriving at this conclusion will be denying one of the elementary principles of physics, for we know that the greater the difference of temperatures the more energetic the transfers of heat. During the stroke of the large piston the temperature of the steam in the jackets is much higher than that of the steam in the cylinders, it is then during this period that the transfer of heat should be best made—that the jacket should furnish more; this is really what takes place.

We will show later in treating of expansion how the passage of calories is made, and what is their occupation; we shall see that this phenomenon, which appears at first to be entirely abnormal, explains itself naturally; we shall see it become a very simple consequence of the principle of the transmission of heat which it seems at first to contradict.

We give then, to terminate the series of analyses, the two experiments E and F, made with expansions 28 and 25. We regret that we cannot join thereto the analytical story of the engine at St. Remy. Its consumption checks within 3 per cent. nearly, and it agrees closely with the Malmerspach engine, but it lacks the exact elements necessary in the indicator diagrams.

MALMERSPACH ENGINE, EXPERIMENT E., 143 H. P.; EXPANSION, 28.

Account of heat, etc., per stroke:

Weight of fluid in small cylinder				0.3679 k.
"	dry steam at cut-off			0.2214 k.
"	water	"	(40 per cent.)	0.1465 k.
"	"	entrained		0.0200 k.
"	"	condensed		0.1265 k.
Heat given to iron				63.08 c.
Weight of fluid in large cylinder				0.3679 k.
"	dry steam at end of stroke			0.3030 k.
"	water	"	" (7.6 per cent.)	0.0640 k.
Internal heat at end of admission, U_0				157.44 c.
"	"	"	stroke, U_1	183.32 c.
$U_0 - U_1$				25.88 c.

Heat furnished by jacket.. 16.09 c.
"   "   iron above................................. 63.08 c.

Total heat furnished during expansion.................... 53.29 c.

Heat in total work   "   "   "   .... 29.35 c.
"   "   external radiation................................ 4.60 c.
Rc.. 19.34 c.

Relatively to entire heat furnished $\dfrac{19.34}{246.77} = 7.8$ per cent.

Check on Rc:

Internal heat at end of stroke, U_1............................ 183.32 c.
Back pressure work... 6.63 c.
Heat retained in condensed steam.............................. 6.99 c.
                                                              _____
                                                              182.96 c.

Heat gained by injection water.................. .... 198.21 c.
Rc... 15.25 c.

Differing from the other $\dfrac{19.34 - 15.25}{246.77} = 1.6$ per cent.

U_2 at end of stroke small cylinder:

Weight of fluid... 0.3679 k.
"   "   steam end of stroke.............................. 0.2976 k.
"   "   water   "   "   (19.1 per cent.).............. 0.0702 k.
Internal heat   "   " U_2............................ 186.81 c.

MALMERSPACH ENGINE, EXPERIMENT F., 149 H. P.; EXPANSION 25.

Account of heat, etc., per stroke:

Weight of fluid in small cylinder............................. 0.3862 k.
"   dry steam at cut-off................................. 0.2471 k.
"   water   "   "   (36.1 per cent.)................. 0.1391 k.
"   "   entrained................................... 0.0210 k.
"   "   condensed................................... 0.1181 k.

Heat given to iron.. 58.83 c.
Weight of fluid in large cylinder............................. 0.3862 k.
"   dry steam at end of stroke.......................... 0.3180 k.
"   water   "   "   (17.8 per cent.)......... 0.0682 k.

Internal heat at cut-off, U_0............................... 172.10 c.
"   "   " end of stroke, U_1........................ 192.45 c.
U_0-U_1... —20.35 c.

Heat furnished by jacket..................................... 17.38 c.
"   "   iron above................................ 58.83 c.

Total heat furnished during expansion................. 55.86 c.

Heat furnished during external radiation...................... 4.60 c.
"   absorbed by total work............................... 29.93 c.
Rc.. 21.33 c.

being $\dfrac{21.33}{259.53} = 8.2$ per cent. of entire heat per stroke.

Check on Rc:
Internal heat at end of stroke, U_1............................. 192.45 c.
Back pressure work.. 346.43 c.
Heat retained after condensation............................ — 7.50 c.
                                                            ‾‾‾‾‾‾‾‾‾
                                                              191.38 c.
"   gained by injection water............................. 210.33 c.

Rc.. 18.95 c.

Differing $\dfrac{21.33-18.95}{259.53} = 0.9$ per cent.

Weight of fluid in small cylinder............................... 0.3862 k.
"   dry steam at end of stroke......................... 0.3147 k.
"   water (18.6 per cent.)............................. 0.0715 k.
Internal heat, U_2.. 197.46 c.

These two experiments E and F, give results which accord perfectly with expansions 28 and 25. We should also note in order the profound modifications to which the steam is submitted when the expansion is changed from 13 to 28. The internal heat which in C diminishes 1.24 c. during the expansion, changes to an increase of 25.88 c. for E, while for D and F there is for one a diminution of 3.24 c., and for the other an accession of 20.35 c. between expansion 13 and 25.

INFLUENCE OF VARIABLE EXPANSIONS UPON THE WORKING OF STEAM IN "WOOLF" ENGINES—THEIR UTILITY FROM THE POINT OF VIEW OF CONSUMPTION.

The exposition of the very complex phenomena which absorb us, the study of which should be made as clear and as easily grasped as possible induces us to give in Table III., page 254, a summary of the principal results which form the basis of our discussion.

The action of the iron upon the fluid which it incloses is so well established, and the result of Hirn's labors on heat engines is such that it naturally follows that variable expansions modify the nature even of the work of steam. We introduce into the cylinders different weights of steam, different quantities of heat, therefore it is not astonishing to see during expansion variations in the direction and amount of the changes of heat. But that which should be useful in practice is the experimental determination of these changes, followed by the results of their analysis, and their justification. We shall fall perchance on facts at first inadmissible like those we found for expansion 13, and find the natural explanation in the most profound study of the phenomenon, a purely physical study.

The paradoxical fact which we will recall is presented then in experiments C and D upon each of the Malmerspach engines working with expansion 13, and with full pressure more than one-half of the stroke in the small cylinder. During the expansion in the large cylinder a portion of the steam existing at the end of the stroke of the small piston is condensed—Experiment C., 4.8 per cent.; Experiment D., 5.2 per cent. The internal heat has diminished $U_2 - U_1 = + 23.53$ c. and 25.59. But the work of expansion in the large cylinder has demanded and absorbed 24.9 c. and 25 c., that is to say, nearly the same amounts for this period of work. There was no heat furnished from outside; the jacket appears to have yielded nothing; was it not working during this period of expansion?

This hypothesis is inadmissible, for we have seen that it contradicts a well-known principle, of physics relative to the transmission of heat; the exchange of heat across the sides of the cylinder should be more rapid with the greatest difference of temperature between the two surfaces, for one of them is in contact with the jacket steam at boiler pressure, and the other possesses the temperature of the cylinder steam at a much lower pressure. We would remark that the difference of temperature is not the only factor which can accelerate this transfer; the layer of water, which covers the internal surface has also its influence; it augments the rapidity with which heat is brought to the inner surface; it provokes a proportionally greater action in the jacket, as we will prove by the figures of Table III.

How can it be, then, since the jacket is in the best possible condition to furnish heat, that it appears to be inactive? This apparent anomaly has a very simple cause—the action of the surfaces at the commencement of the stroke of the large piston.

I established in my paper of 1878 that at the first tenth of the stroke of the large piston, a moment when the dry steam is nearly equally divided between the small and large cylinders, there is one-half at least of the fluid deposited as water upon the walls of the large cylinder; if we mark, then, that at the end of the first tenth of the stroke of the large piston the large cylinder contains more water than steam, that is, that the first part of this stroke the condensation has been very considerable, while the cooling due the condenser has been only 1.3 per cent. loss.

The same fact is presented for experiments C and D in stronger proportions yet; since by the cooling due the condenser the heat taken from the iron during exhaust is 8.3 and 9.9. It is upon this water which covers the surface that the jacket acts, and since it cannot evaporate a sufficient quantity, the internal heat at the end of the stroke is less than at the end of the stroke of the small piston. Such is the particular circumstance which the five experiments made upon the coupled engines at Malmerspach present to us; it is not the first time we have had occasion to remark it. I have already noted it in the experiments made on the Munster engines, 1876, working with little compression in the clearance spaces.

Let us indicate the modifications which a variable expansion brings to the transformation of steam and to the action of the jacket.

The three experiments, B, C and E, the first the result of a very slight expansion in the small cylinder where the steam has been admitted nearly all the stroke, with a total expansion of 6; the Indicated H. P. only reaches 201. To do this feeble work the steam pressure had to be throttled, for we have with thirteen expansions and full pressure, a work of 215 H. P., a greater load in spite of the less introduction.

In these conditions the weight of steam condensed during admission is small, 12.8 per cent., less the water carried, over 5 per cent. = 7.8 per cent. deposited upon the surface. The jacket yields proportionately less heat, for it only condenses 5 per cent. of the steam brought to the engine. We remark that in spite of the condensation which took place at the first stroke of the large piston, the proportions of water are within 1.3 per cent. the same at the beginning and end of the expansion, and that the cooling due the condenser is small enough, 2.1 per cent. of the entire heat brought the engine. In spite of these conditions, which appear advantageous enough, the consumption per total H. P. is 7,404 k., while those of C and E are 6,878 k., and 6,731 k., that is to say, by 7 and 9 per cent.

Is this the gain realized by the expansion? This we shall see.

Experiment C, with introduction of half stroke in the small cylinder, presents a condensation of $23.7 - 5 = 18.7$ per cent. during the admission, but the proportion of water which is found is partly evaporated

Passing to the results of experiment E, expansion 28, this modification is much more marked. The proportion of water at the end of an introduction of $\frac{1}{8}$ stroke of small cylinder is 40 per cent., and 21 per cent. evaporates during the first expansion, and the internal heat increases 29.37 c.; in short, we see that as the expansion in the small cylinder is increased the transfers of heat are increased.

On the other hand, the action in the large cylinder follows another law. We have seen, that with nearly full stroke introduction in the small cylinder, experiment B, the internal heat remains nearly stationary, diminishing by only 7.17 c., between the ends of the stroke of the small and large pistons. The same fact is found in experiment E, 28 expansions. But we have seen above that the intermediate experiments C and D show us a considerable fall of internal heat, a fall sufficient to furnish to the work of expansion the number of calories which it requires. Here there is, then, as in the small cylinder, an increase in the transfers of heat from experiments B to C, but a decrease follows the minimum, which appears toward expansion 13, to which is due that the internal heat U_1 is increased relatively to the final internal heat U_2 of the small cylinder.

By considering only the phenomena of the total expansion from the moment that it commences in the small cylinder to the end of the stroke in the large cylinder, we see that the differences of internal heat are continually reversed; this shows that the transfers of heat are greater and greater as the expansion is increased. Thus for experiment B the final internal heat U_1 is 7.17 c. less than U_0 at the end of admission; for experiment C this difference is only 1.24 c.; while for experiment E the difference is reversed, and the final internal heat is 25.88 c. larger than at the

TABLE III.

PER SINGLE STROKE.	MALMERSPACH ENGINE.			MUNSTER ENGINE.			HORIZONTAL ENGINE.	
	E.	C.	B.	III.	II.	I.	I.	II.
No. of expansions	28	13	6	7	7	7	6	6
Indicated horse-power on pistons	143	215	201	185	267	347	130	181
Dry steam per hour per total horse-power, kilograms	6.731	6.878	7.402	7.384	6.945	7.112	7.290	7.328
Back pressure work, per cent. of total work	18.6	15.6	16.04	24.10	20.52	17.43	20.06	17.30
Dry steam per hour per indicated horse-power, kilograms	8.273	8.149	8.847	9.730	8.739	8.614	9.120	8.614
Mechanical efficiency, per cent.	82.7	86.1	85.6	78.3	84.3	87.3	86.1	89.0
Dry steam per hour per net horse-power, kilograms	10.019	9.465	10.301	12.411	10.357	9.864	10.563	9.678
Per cent. priming or water entrained	5	5	5	2.3	2.9	2.8	3	4
" " steam condensed in jackets	8.5	7.7	5.1	10.4	9.0	8.6	10.0	7.5
" " water in steam at cut-off	40.0	23.7	12.8	21.17	14.21	16.17	11.20	10.80
" " end small cylinder	19.1	13.1						
" " end large cylinder	17.6	17.9						
Change of internal heat during expansion $U_0 - U_1$ calories	−25.88	+1.24	11.15	7.39	−5.39	6.60	5.34	4.5
" " in small cylinder $U_0 - U_2$ "	−29.37	−22.29	+7.17	−31.89	−16.58	−17.40	−3.63	−6.12
" " in large cylinder $U_2 - U_1$ "	+3.49	+23.59						
Rc or cooling due condenser in calories	19.34	31.44	8.44	13.48	6.65	21.89	1.95	1.16
Rc in per cent. total heat brought to engine.	7.8	8.3	2.16	3.5	1.82	3.38	1.19	0.5

end of admission. The qualities of heat furnished by the jacket, the proportions of steam condensed in the small cylinder during admission, which transforms the inner surface of the cylinder into a reservoir of heat, and the internal heat, all these values are intimately connected together, as we have already said many times: they depend the one on the other; and are in some sort the various manifestations of the same thing. We also see them changing in kind the condensation in the jacket and small cylinder during admission; increase with expansion, furnishing thus more heat in proportion than is measured by the expansion and considerably more.

This law appears to be general in "Woolf" engines, not only with variable expansions, but for fixed expansions and variable powers obtained by throttling the steam. The experiments upon the "Munster" engine show us that with 185 H. P. the final internal heat U_1 is 31.89 c. more than the initial internal heat U_0 at the end of the admission, while this difference is only 17.40 c. for the experiment with 347 H. P. Meanwhile examining more closely the figures of the two series of experiments at Malmerspach and Munster, we discover one point which merits being brought into light. The differences U_0-U_1 are close together for experiments I. and II.,—17.40 c. and 16.58 c., more alike than B and C, 7.17 c. and 1.24 c., which differ much from E, 25.88 c. This leads us to believe that in the limits of expansion and throttling of experiments I., II., B, C, the differences of internal heat remain nearly stationary; they only commence to increase rapidly when we go beyond 13 expansions and throttle below 267 H. P. of experiment II.

Finally we see for all the "Munster" eperiments of 1877 the final internal heat U_1 is greater than the initial internal heat U_0. If this fact is the reverse of what was produced upon the same engine in 1876, it is that at that time the engine was differently regulated, the compression in the clearance space being much less. The increase of compression diminished greatly the lead influence of the clearance. This realized an economy and the result betrays itself by an increase in the final internal heat. It is not necessary to believe that this is always the characteristic sign of a better working of the engine. We have in effect experiments C and E, of which the consumptions vary only 2.1 per cent. when the differences of internal heat U_0-U_1 are 1.24 c., and — 25.88 c. On the other hand, experiments I. and II. give $U_0 - U_1 = - 17.40$ c. and 16.58 c., and meanwhile the consumptions vary 2.4 per cent., the least being for experiment II. throttled to 267 H. P.

Summing the effects of a greater total expansion, commencing in the small cylinder and placing parallel to them the effects of the same kind produced by throttling, reducing the indicated work in the same proportion that the change of expansion did, the best experiments are C and E, expansions 13 and 28, and experiments II. and III., with the same expansion 7. The indicated horse-powers are nearly in the same ratio,

$$\frac{215}{143} = 1.5 \qquad \frac{267}{185} = 1.44$$

When the expansion changes from 13 to 28 the condensation in the small cylinder during admission increases from 23 to 40 per cent.; the heat given to the iron is increased. The jacket also gives a little more heat, but the greater part of this heat is restored in the small cylinder itself. It furnishes there more heat than is needed for the work of expansion, for the evaporation of 10 and 21 per cent. of the water deposited upon the surface. This is proved by the increase of internal heat by 22 and 29 c. at the end of the stroke of the small piston. In the same circumstances, throttling with nearly full admission in the small cylinder, experiments II. and III., the communication between cylinder and boiler is open also. The proportions of steam condensed only vary from 14 to 21 per cent., which show a very different kind of working. The steam passes then to the large cylinder; it is in this that the transfers of heat are found which did not take place in the small cylinder. The internal heat is increased during the expansion 16 and 31 calories; 9 and 14 per cent. of the water is evaporated. On the other hand, with 13 and 28 expansions, commenced with cut-offs at one-half and one-fifth in the small cylinder, the reverse action took place. The energetic changes are less in the large cylinder than in the small cylinder. This is a fact which will serve us later in comparing single and double cylinder engines.

Experiment B seems to contradict this law, for the internal heat diminishes 7 calories from the beginning to the end of the expansion, and the proportions of water are nearly the same, 12 and 11 per cent. This is due to two causes, the influence of a distribution with very little compression, and the less effect of the jacket, where there is only 5 per cent. of the weight of the steam condensed; but it is none the less true, that the heat furnished by the jacket has been during the expansion in the large cylinder. Before attacking the question from the practical industrial side let us seek to render an account of the advantages of expansion, considering only the work of the steam; that is to say, abstracting imperfections of vacuum and frictions of the engine.

In principle, theory has conducted M. G. Zeuner to recommend very prolonged expansions; M. G. A. Hirn, on the contrary, considering the practical conditions imposed on the engine, adopts moderate expansions. We shall see that these two opinions which appear contradictory are both sanctioned by our experimental researches when properly analyzed. The work of M. Zeuner supposed that the cylinder was non-conducting, and the closed cycle perfect, but it is clear that the cycle is interrupted by the conditions in which we place our "Woolf" engines. We should naturally expect to see the benefits of expansion considerably diminished by the transfers of heat to the internal surfaces; but the difference is great enough to allow us to affirm the law.

Commencing by comparing the cost per total H. P. of experiments I., II., III., C and E, experiment I., 347 H. P., expansion 7, has been made with an initial pressure near that of C and E, but it is experiment II., made with a lower pressure, which presents the minimum cost, 6.945 k. This is due to some particular circumstance which we have not been able to bring out, and which causes the cooling due the condenser to be least for experiment I., while to compensate this action we take for the consumption for 7 expansions the mean of I. and II., 7.028 k. The cut-offs for expansions 7, 13 and 28 are in the ratio of 1, $\frac{1}{2}$ and $\frac{1}{4}$; the costs are 7.028 k., 6.878 k.; and 7.731 k., a decrease of 2.2 per cent.; or an expansion four times as great procures 4.4 per cent. gain. The law of M. Zeuner is then found verified experimentally in "Woolf" engines. It is to be noted that the disturbing effect of the surfaces does not reverse this law, for in the method used to determine the cost this influence is fully accounted for. The cost for experiment III., 185 H. P., 7 expansions, is 5 per cent. inferior to that of I., II. Whence we conclude that it should have a marked advantage of about 10 per cent. in replacing by more expansion a too great lowering of initial pressure.

We have left to one side experiment B, made with the same engine as C and E, for two motives, which appeared to us ought to exclude it; in the first place the jacket did not yield enough heat. And then the valves are set with a compression not sufficient to help the clearance. But everybody knows that one of the effects of a prolonged expansion is to extenuate in part the pernicious effect of the considerable waste spaces of the "Woolf" engine.

The cost of a net H. P. brings us the modifications of the more or less perfect vacuum which falsifies the preceding law; thus experiments I. and II. differ in reverse order 1.4 per cent., and C and E, which vary 1.5 per cent.

Finally the cost of a net H. P., upon which the combined effects of poor vacuum and friction give the following results: Experiment I., 9.864 k.; II., 10.357 k.; III., 12.411 k.; C, 9.465 k.; E, 10.019 k. The least is experiment C, expansion 13; it only varies 5$\frac{1}{2}$ per cent. from E, expansion 28, and 4 per cent. from I, expansion 7, full pressure. This justifies the proposition of M. Hirn. There remains to calculate the dimensions to be given to engines and the frictions which result, the foreknowledge of the interrupted cycle and the moderate expansion. In a word he says: "For reasons of practical fact the steam engine with broken cycle and moderate expansion works better, *notwithstanding its faults*, than the engine working with the perfect cycle," without regard to first cost.

Experiment III., 185 H. P., expansion 7, pressure much reduced, differs 24 per cent. from the corresponding experiment, E, expansion 28, full pressure. This difference is due to the vacuum and friction. If the horizontal engine occupies the last rank, it owes it to the small compression, its vacuum and frictions. Its inferiority is only 2 per cent. relatively to the corresponding experiment II. and B, and 6 per cent. referred to the experiment with greatest power, I., 347 H. P.

The practical consequences of these collected researches upon the "Woolf" engine may be stated thus:

1. From the total point of view, considering only the best utilization of the heat brought to the engine, we can reduce the maximum work with 5 kilos. pressure. For example (70 pounds), expansion 7 to $\frac{1}{2}$, by

diminishing the initial pressure, and there results a loss of 5 per cent. of the cost of a total H. P.; while by reducing the introduction in the small cylinder, we can gain 4½ per cent. of the same cost.

2.   When one is obliged to reduce the work one-half, whether because of a change of load or because used with water power, we can make a practical gain of 10 per cent. at least by replacing the throttle by a variable cut-off in the small cylinder.   We suppose it well understood that the back pressure work remains the same in the two cases.   The friction is naturally the same, since the work is the same.

3.   The engine working near its full load, it is possible to vary the work 10 per cent. more or less, without any notable change in the economic régime due to expansion or change of pressure.   There follows the disposition we have already remarked; an expansion variable by hand and a governor throttle valve, which will answer all requirements, and is the most simple and durable.

INFLUENCE OF EXPANSION IN SINGLE CYLINDER ENGINES.

We proceed with this study as we did with the "Woolf" engines, checking first the consumption of the different experiments of which we make use.   These experiments are upon four valve engines with and without jackets.   They consist first of experiments made upon a horizontal "Corliss" by the Mechanical Committee of the Industrial Society in April and May, 1878.

The experimental process is that of M. Hirn often described in our *Bulletins*, and the direct results of observations are given in that for Dec., 1878.   I have checked and analyzed them, and added the experiments made in 1873 and 1875, upon the vertical engine with four valves of M. Hirn, without a jacket, and with and without superheating; it was also tried with a brake in 1865 by the Mechanical Committee.   We will commence with the results of the "Corliss:"

Corliss Engine by Berger, Andre & Co.

Tried with brake by the Mechanical Committee; check on direct consumption.

```
I.—Indicated on piston...................................105   H. P.
Revolutions per minute........................................ 50.41.
Net on brake................................................. 92   H. P.
Mechanical efficiency, per cent............................... 88
Back pressure work in per cent. total work................... 10
    "        "          .............................(2.1 lbs.)  0.148 k.
Expansion.................................................... 11
```

(Boiler pressure 68 lbs. above atmosphere.)

Per single stroke:

Heat brought by dry steam.................0.1306 k. × 654.24 c. = 85.44 c.
"   "   "   water entrained...........0.0043 k. × 158.18 c. =   0.68 c.
"   "   "   steam to jacket..   ....0.0094 k. × 496.06 c. =   4.66 c.

"   "   to engine........................ ....90.78 c.
"   kept to condenser......... ....0.1349 k. × 23.5 c. =   3.17 c.

"   expended, Q_0...87.61 c.
"   gained by injection water, Q_1.........5.4304 k. × 13.3 c. = 72.22 c.

                                                   15.39 c.
"   in work done...11.03 c.
"   radiated .... 1.50 c.
                                           —— 12.53 c.

$$\text{Error,} \ \frac{15.39 - 12.53}{90.78} = 3.1 \text{ per cent.}$$

Total heat is 90.78 c., it represents:

Dry steam per stroke .... $\dfrac{90.78}{654.24} = 0.1387$ k.

"   "   hour per total H. P.............. .. .. 7.188 k.
"   "   "   ind. H. P........................... 7.983 k.
"   "   "   net H. P... .. .. 9.071 k.

II.—Indicated on pistons... 137   H.P.
Revolutions per minute..................................... 51.12
Net H. P..135
Mechanical efficiency, per cent................................ 91
Back pressure work in per cent. total work.................... 8.8
"   "   ....$(2_{10}^{z}$ lbs.) —0.169 k.
Expansion.. 8

(Boiler pressure 66 lbs. above atmosphere).

Heat brought by dry steam.................0.1678 k. × 653.82 c. = 109.71 c.
"   "   "   entrained water........0.0075 k. × 156.74 c. =   1.16 c.
"   "   "   jacket.................0.0112 k. × 497.08 c. =   5.57 c.

Total.. .... 116.44 c.

Heat retained to condenser.................0.1752 k. × 27.65 c. =   4.84 c.

Q_0... 111.60 c.

Heat gained by injection water.............9.534 k. × 17.45 c. =   93.18 c.
$Q_0 - Q_1$... 18.42 c.

Heat in work done.................................14.25 c.
"   " external radiation.............................. 1.50 c.
                                           —— 15.75 c.

$$\text{Error,} \ \frac{18.42 - 15.75}{116.44} = 2.3 \text{ per cent.}$$

Heat per stroke, 116.44 represents:

Dry steam per stroke.......................................$\dfrac{116.44}{653.82} = 0.1781$ k.

  "   "   " hour per total H. P............................7.236 k.

  "   "   "   " " ind. H. P............................. 7.939 k.

  "   "   "   " " net H. P............................ 8.724 k.

III.—Indicated on piston.....................................158   H. P.

Revolutions per minute...................................... 49.54

Net on brake...142

Mechanical efficiency, per cent............................. 92

Back pressure work in per cent. of total work................ 8.1

    "   "   ....(2.6 lbs.) 0.184 k.

Expansion... 6

(Boiler pressure 68 lbs. above atmosphere.)

Heat brought by dry steam...............0.2015 k. × 654.24 c. = 131.83 c.

    "   " entrained water.........0.0112 k. × 158.18 c. =   1.77 c.

    "   to jacket...................0.0114 k. × 0.0114 c. =   5.65 c.

    Total...139.25 c.

Heat retained by condenser.................0.2127 k. × 29.57 c. =   6.29 c.

Q_0...132.96 c.

Heat gained by injection water Q_1...........5.7334 k. × 19.47 c. = 111.63 c.

$Q_0 - Q_1$.. 21.33 c.

Heat in work done......................................16.99 c.

  " " external radiation.......................... 1.50 c.

                     ————— 18.49 c.

$$\text{Error,} \quad \frac{21.33 - 18.49}{139.25} = 2.4 \text{ per cent.}$$

Heat per single stroke = 139.25 represents

Dry steam per stroke...................................$\dfrac{139.25}{654.24} = 0.2128$ k.

  "   "   " hour per total H. P............................. 7.307 k.

  "   "   "   " " ind. H. P............................. 7.955 k.

  "   "   "   " " net H. P............................ 8.646 k.

These three experiments check within 3 per cent., a very satisfactory result but, let us add, one difficult enough to obtain.

It is essential, as we have seen from a long practical experience in these researches, to attend to the most minute precautions to attain results which check to about 1 per cent., and we consider as purely accidental, circumstances which give closer figures, and believe the attempt to get them an illusion.

The consumptions of the "Corliss" engine with expansion of 6, 8, and 11, show us the limited influence of expansion upon the cost. I have already had occasion to note this fact when the "Woolf" engines were in question. There results from this that within the wide limits where we have operated, *and for jacketed engines*, the intrinsic work of the steam is scarcely influenced by a more or less prolonged expansion, this being defined by the cost of a total H. P.

The "Woolf" engines gained 4.5 per cent. by change from 7 to 28 expansions. The "Corliss" gains 1.6 per cent. by change from 6 to 11.

On the other hand, for the "Corliss" as well as the "Woolf," the differences which exist in cost change sign when we pass from the total work to the indicated work in which the back pressure makes itself felt; these differences are still more increased when we take the cost of a net horsepower, that is to say, the industrial consumption, which shows us that expansion 6 is 4.5 per cent. better than 11 for the "Corliss" engines, and for "Woolf" engines expansion 13 is 5.5 per cent. better than 28.

That which we have noted concerns only jacketed engines. Does expansion act differently without this adjunct?

The experiments made upon the vertical engine of M. Hirn will show us.

Hirn Engine.

Saturated steam, variable expansions. Check on consumption.

I. Indicated on pistons...107 H. P.

Revolutions per minute....................................... 30.41

Net on brake.. 95   H. P.

Mechanical efficiency, per cent............................. 89

Back pressure work in per cent. total work............. 11.8

"   "   .... (3 lbs.)   0.213 k.

Expansion... 7

(Boiler pressure, 56 lbs. above atmosphere.)

Heat brought by dry steam...............0.2604 k. × 652.48 c. = 169.90 c.

"   "   " entrained water..... 0.0030 k. × 152.25 c. =   0.46 c.

Total.. 170.36 c.

" retained to condenser...............0.2634 k. × 32.25 c. =   8.49 c.

Q_0.. 161.87 c.

Heat gained by injection water Q_1..........8.8131 k. × 15.72 c. = 140.38 c.

$Q_0 - Q_1$.. 21.49 c.

Heat in work done...................................... .....18.77 c.

" " external radiation................................... 2.50 c.

——— 21.27 c.

Error, $\dfrac{21.49 - 21.27}{170.36}$ = 0.1 per cent.

Heat per stroke, 170.36 represents

Dry steam per stroke................................... $\dfrac{170.36}{652.48}$ = 0.2611 k.

"   "   " hour per total H. P............................ ..... 7.822 k.

"   "   "   " ind. H. P............................... 8.837 k.

"   "   "   " net H. P.............................. 9.929 k.

II.—Indicated on piston..146   H. P.
Revolutions per minute.. 30.55
Net on brake...134   H. P.
Mechanical efficiency, per cent................................ 92
Back pressure work in per cent. total work.................... 9.2
"   .   "   ....(3.1 lbs.)   0.225 k.
Expansion... 4
(Boiler pressure 52 lbs. above atmosphere.)
Heat brought by steam....................0.3695 k. × 651.70 c. = 248.80 c.
"   "   " entrained...............0.0037 k. × 149.61 c. =   0.65 c.

Total ....   241.36 c.
Heat retained to condenser...............0.3732 k. × 33.65 c. = 12.56 c.

Q_0...   228.79 c.
Heat gained by injection water, Q_1..........92917 k × 21.82 c. = 202.75 c.

$Q_0 - Q_1$...   26.04 c.
" in work done..25.27 c.
" in external radiation............................... 2.50 c.
                                                          ———
                                                          27.77 c.

$$\text{Error}\quad \frac{26.04 - 27.77}{241.35} = 0.7 \text{ per cent.}$$

Heat per stroke, 241.35 c. represents

Dry steam per stroke,.................................... $\frac{241.35}{651.70}$ = 0.3703 k.

"   "   " hour per total H. P.. 8.449 k.
"   "   "   "   " ind. H. P................................ 9.307 k.
"   "   "   "   " net H. P.............................. 10.341 k.

These figures seem to prove that expansion has much greater effect when there is no jacket. Expansion 7 is 7.4 per cent. better than 4 for the total and 4 per cent. better for the net H. P. Is this kept up with superheated steam?

Superheated Steam—Hirn Engine.

I.—Indicated on piston.................................... 113   H. P.
Revolutions per minute.................................... 29.98
Net on brake... 102   H. P.
Mechanical efficiency, per cent.......................... 90
Back pressure work in per cent. of total work.............. 9.7
"   ....(2.6 lbs.)   0.188 k.
Expansion 7
(Boiler pressure 56 lbs. above atmosphere.)
Temperature of steam 196° c. (superheated 44.73° c.)
Heat brought by dry steam................0.2240 k.×652.48 c.= 146.15 c.
"   "   " superheating...........0.2240 k.×0.5×44.73 c.=   5.01 c.

Total...151.16 c.

Heat retained to condenser............................0.2240 k.×30.42 c.= 6.81 c.

Q_0.. 144.35 c.

Heat gained by injection water, Q_1............8.7384 k.×14.05 c. = 122.77 c.

Q_0-Q_1.. 21.58 c.

Heat in work done...19.97 c.

  " " external radiation .... 2.50 c.

                                                    22. 7 c.

$$\text{Error} \quad \frac{21.58 - 22.47}{151.16} = 0.6 \text{ per cent.}$$

Heat total per stroke, 151.16 c. represents

Dry steam per stroke..$\frac{151.16}{652.48} = 0.2317$ k.

Dry steam per hour per total H. P... 6.655 k.

  "   "   "   "   " ind. H. P....................................... 7.370 k.

  "   "   "   "   " net H. P.. 8.188 k.

  II.—Indicated on piston .... 154 H. P.

Revolutions per minute... 30.174

Net on brake...143 H. P.

Mechanical efficiency, per cent................................. 93

Back pressure work in per cent. of total work................. 8.3

Back pressure...(3 lbs.) 0.215 k.

Expansion 4

Temperature of steam 231°c. (superheated 80.85°c.)

       (Boiler pressure 55 lbs. above atmosphere.)

Heat brought by dry steam...............0.3065 k. × 652.79 c. = 199.92 c.

   "   "   " superheating....... .0.3065 k. × 0.5 × 80.85 c. = 12.39 c.

  Total...212.31 c.

Heat retained to condenser...................0.3065 k. × 31.3 c. = 9.52 c.

Q_0... 202.72 c.

Heat gained by injection water, Q_1............9.350 k. × 18.7 c. = 174.84 c.

Q_0-Q_1.. 27.88 c.

Heat in work done...27.08 c.

" in external radiation............................. 2.50 c.

                                                    29.58 c.

$$\text{Error} \frac{27.88 - 29.58}{212.31} = 0.8 \text{ per cent.}$$

Heat per stroke, 212.31 c., represents

Dry steam per stroke...$\frac{212.31}{652.29} = 0.3254$ k.

Dry steam per hour per total H. P... 7.000 k.

  "   "   " ind. H. P....................................... 7.633 k.

  "   "   " net H. P.. 8.207 k.

  III.—Indicated on piston................................125 H. P.

Revolutions per minute... ....30.306

Net on brake..114 H. P.

Mechanical efficiency, per cent...................................91
Back pressure work in per cent. total work......................8.9
    "   "   ....(2.7 lbs.) 0.190 k.
Expansion...2
Temperature of the steam 223° c.(superheated 73° c.)
       (Boiler pressure, 55 fbs. above atmosphere).
Heat brought by dry steam..............0.2822 k. $\times$ 552.25 c.   = 184.06 c.
   "   "   superheating........0.2822 k. $\times$ 0.5 $\times$ 73.00 c. = 10.30 c.

    Total...194.36 c.
Heat retained to condenser................0.2822 k. $\times$ 34.26 c. = 9.95 c.

    Q_0 ....184.41 c.
Heat gained by injection water, Q_1........8.5983 k. $\times$ 18.76 c. = 161.20 c.

    $Q_0 - Q_1$ ....23.11 c.
Heat in work done.....................................21.86 c.
   "   in external radiation............................... 2.50 c.
                           ——— 24.36 c.

$$\text{Error} \;\frac{23.11 - 24.36}{+94.36} = 0.6 \text{ per cent.}$$

Heat total per stroke 194.36 c. represents:

Dry steam per stroke.................................$\frac{194.36}{652.25} = 0.2979$ k.

Dry steam per hour per total H. P...............................7.874 k.
   "   "   "   "   " ind. H. P................................8.655 k.
   "   "   "   "   " net H. P................................9.511 k.

The experiments with superheating, expansion, 4 and 7, differ 4.9 per cent., without superheating 7 per cent. of the cost of a total H. P. Holding account of the superheating temperature 196° c. in the first case, we can say that between 4 and 7 expansions there is 7 per cent. difference with common and superheated steam. Introduction of $\frac{1}{4}$ probably passes below the limit above which the cost is nearly constant.

The superheater arranged to work with the normal conditions, returns less when the consumption is reduced, as is the case when expanding 7 times. It can produce a temperature of about 220° c. when the draught is not influenced by atmospheric conditions. We had a difference of 4 calories, and without, we should have had a gain of 3 per cent. more.

The experiment which best proves the influence of expansion when it passes certain limits is III., cut-off $\frac{1}{2}$, with superheating to 233°, giving 125 H. P. The cost of a total H. P. is 15.2 per cent. more than I., and this difference would have been greater if I. had the same temperature of superheating as III., 223°, instead of 196°.

But we say this experiment III. was made with a throttling of 1 atmosphere between beginning and end of admission.

We have seen that throttling is far from producing the effects and having the influence generally attributed to it. It only brought the "Woolf" engines, when the normal load was diminished one-half, an increase of 5 per cent. in the cost of a total H. P. Finally, an experiment of Hirn's, verified, gave, with the same introduction, one-half, and a load reduced to 100 H. P. gave the same cost as with 125, that is, with 20 per cent. less power.

Stating, then, a loss by throttle of only 5 per cent., there remains the fact that, with two expansions, there is an increase of 10 per cent. on the cost of a total H. P.

We have rapidly examined the principal facts which stand in relief on a first approach to the figures of consumption. A deeper study of the phenomena demands a verified analysis, which we will give.

CORLISS ENGINE—EXPERIMENT I., 105 H. P.; EXPANSION 11.

Account of heat, etc., per single stroke:

Weight of fluid at cut-off... 0.1370 k.
"   "   dry steam at cut-off......... .... 0.0848 k.

"   "   water   "   "   38.3 per cent..................... 0.0522 k.
"   "   "   entrained......................... .... 0.0043 k.

"   "   "   condensing admission........................... 0.0479 k.

Heat given to iron................... ....0.0479 k. + 499.77 c. = 23.93 c.
Weight dry steam at end of stroke............................... 0.1072 k.
"   water   "   "   21.7 per cent................. 0.0298 k.

Internal heat at cut-off, U_0...................................... 59.55 c.
"   "   "   end of stroke, U_1.......................... 65.87 c.

$U_0 - U_1$..... 6.32 c.
Heat furnished by jacket .... 22.28 c.
"   "   "   iron above... .... 23.93 c.

Heat furnished during expansion .... 4.66 c.
"   absorbed by total work of expansion .... 9.57 c.
"   lost by external radiation.............................. 1.5 c.
Rc............................ :.....................................22.28 − 11.07 = 11.21 c.

Rc, per cent. of total heat $\dfrac{11.21}{90.78} = 12.03$ c.

Check on Rc.

Internal heat at end of stroke..... .... 65.87 c.
Back pressure work.. 1.21 c.
Heat retained in condenser.................................... 3.17 c.
"   "   "   cushion.................................... 1.12 c.

62.79 c.
Heat gained by injection water................................ 72.22 c.

Rc.. 9.43 c.

Error. $\dfrac{11.21 - 9.43}{90.78} = 1.9$ per cent.

CORLISS ENGINE—EXPERIMENT II., 137 H. P.; EXPANSION, 8.

Heat account, etc., per single stroke:

Weight of fluid present	0.1775 k.
" " dry steam at cut-off	0.1211 k.
" " water at cut-off (31.7 per cent.)	0.0564 k.
" " " entrained	0.0074 k.
" " " condensed during admission	0.0490 k.
Heat given to iron ... 0.0490 k. × 499.93 c.	= 24.49 c.
Weight of dry steam at end of stroke	0.1434 k.
" " water at end of stroke (19.2 per cent.)	0.0341 k.
Internal heat at cut-off U_0	82.25 c.
" " " end of stroke U_1	88.17 c.
$U_0 - U_1$	− 5.92 c.
Heat furnished by jacket	5.57 c.
" " " iron (above)	24.49 c.
" " " during expansion	24.14 c.
" absorbed by total work during expansion	11.50 c.
" lost by external radiation	1.50 c.
Rc ... 24.14 − 13.00	= 11.14 c.

Rc in per cent. of total heat furnished $\dfrac{11.14}{116.44} = 9.8.$

Check on Rc:

Internal heat at end of stroke	88.17 c.
Back pressure work	1.38 c.
Heat retained in condenser	− 4.84 c.
" " " cushion	− 1.23 c.
	83.48 c.
" gained by injection water	93.18 c.
Rc	9.70 c.

Error, $\dfrac{11.14 - 9.70}{116.44} = 1.2$ per cent.

CORLISS ENGINE—EXPERIMENT III, 158 H. P.; EXPANSION 6.

Account of heat, etc., per single stroke:

Weight of fluid	0.2151 k.
" " dry steam at cut-off	0.1608 k.
" " water " " (25.3 per cent.)	0.0543 k.
" " " entrained	0.0112 k.
" " " condensed at cut-off	0.0431 k.

Heat given to iron...........................$0.0431 \times 498.64 =$ 21.49 c.
Weight of dry steam at end of stroke...........................0.1753 k.
   " " water   "   "   (18.5 per cent.)..............0.0398 k.
Internal heat at cut-off U_0.......................................106.30 c.
   "   "   end of stroke U_1..............................108.13 c.

$U_0 - U_1$...—1.83 c.
Heat furnished by jacket .... 5.65 c.
   "   "   " iron (above).................................. 21.49 c.

   "   "   during expansion............................. 25.31 c.
   " absorbed by total work of expansion...................... 12.66 c.
   " lost by external radiation .... 1.50 c.
Rc...25.31 —14.16 = 11.15 c.

Rc. in per cent. of total heat furnished.......$\dfrac{11.15}{139.25} = 8$.

Check on Rc.

Internal heat at end of stroke U_1..............................108.13 c.
Back pressure work.. 1.51 c.
Heat retained in condenser.... .. ..—6.29 c.
   "   "   " cushion ....—1.21 c.

                                               102.07 c.
   " gained by injection water................................111.63 c.
Rc..... .... 9.56 c.

Error, $\dfrac{11.51 - 9.56}{139.25}$ = 1.1 per cent.

The results of the analysis of these three experiments upon the "Corliss" engine at different loads follow in order as remarkable as regular. The increase of final internal heat U_1, compared with initial internal heat U_0 varies with the water present at cut-off and with the expansion.

There is an important circumstance which we shall utilize later in comparing single and double cylinder engines. In spite of the radical difference in the principles of construction of the "Corliss" and "Woolf" engines, we see that with 13 expansions for the "Woolf" and 6 for the "Corliss" the weight of water at the beginning and end of the expansion and the cooling due to the condenser are very close.

"Woolf" engine, initial water, 23.7 per cent.; final 17.9 per cent.; Rc.8.13 per cent. Expansion 13.

"Corliss" engine, initial water, 25.3 per cent.; final 18.5 per cent., Rc. 8 per cent. Expansion 6.

With expansions 28 and 11 there are greater differences.

"Woolf" engine, initial water, 40 per cent.; final 17.6 per cent., Rc. 7.8 per cent. Expansion 28.

"Corliss" engine, initial water, 38.3 per cent.; final 21.7 per cent., Rc. 1.23 per cent. Expansion 11.

Account of heat, etc., per single stroke:

Weight of fluid.. 0.2634 k.
   "   " dry steam at cut-off............................ 0.1656 k.

   "   " water   "   "   " 37 per cent............... 0.0978 k.
   "   "   " entrained....................... 0.0030 k.

   "   "   " condensed at cut-off...................... 0.0948 k.
Heat given to iron........................0.0948 k. × 507.35 c. = 48.10 c.
Weight of dry steam at end of stroke..................... 0.1707 k.
   "   " water   "   " 35.2 per cent.............. 0.0927 k.
Internal heat at cut-off U_0.................................... 114.19 c.
   "   "   " end of stroke U_1............................ 109.07 c.

    $U_0 - U_1$... 5.12 c.
Heat furnished from iron (above). .... 48.10 c.
   "   "   during expansion........................... 53.22 c.
   " absorbed by total work................................. 13.70 c.
   " lost by external radiation................................ 2.50 c.
Rc..53.22 -- 16.20 = 37.02 c.

      Rc in per cent. of heat furnished $\dfrac{37.02}{170.36}$ 21.6 c.

Check on Rc.

Internal heat at end of stroke U_1............................. 109.07 c.
   Back pressure work....................................... 2.43 c.
   Heat retained in condenser..............................— 8.49 c.

   Rc.. 37.37 c.

        Error, $\dfrac{37.02 - 37.37}{170.36} = 0.2.$

Account of heat, etc., per single stroke;

Weight of fluid.. 0.3722 k.
   "   dry steam at cut-off......................... 0.2571 k.

   "   water (31 per cent.)......................... 0.1161 k.
   "   " entrained.......................... 0.0037 k.

   "   " condensed at cut-off...................... 0.1124 k.
Heat given to iron...........................0.1124 × 513.76 c. = 57.73 k.
Weight of dry steam at end of stroke........................... 0.2792 k.
   "   water (25.2 per cent)........................... 0.0940 k.
Internal heat at cut-off, U_0.................................. 173.92 c.
   "   "   end of stroke, U_1............................ 175.79 c.

    $U_0 - U_1$ .... —1.87 c.

Heat furnished from iron (above)................................ 57.73 c.

  " "   during expansion.... . ... 55.86 c.

  " absorbed by total work of expansion........................ 15.83 c.

  " lost by external radiation............................ .... 2.50 c.

  Rc..55.86 — 18.33 = 37.53 c.

    Rc in per cent. of heat furnished, $\dfrac{37.53}{241.35} = 15.4$

  Check on Rc:

Internal heat at end of stroke, U_1................................ .... 175.79 c.

Back pressure work...... ".... .... 2.58 c.

Heat retained after condensing....................................—12.56 c.

                      165.80 c.

  " gained by injection water................................ 202.75 c.

  Rc... 36.95 c.

    Error, $\dfrac{37.53-36.95}{241.35} = 0.1$ per cent.

These two experiments offer a peculiarity which is worthy of attention; we find equal weights of water at the end of the stroke 0.0927 k. and 0.0940 k. and the values of Rc, 37.02 c. and 37.53 c. The cooling due the condenser is, we know, the heat carried by the water on the surface which it covers, re-evaporating and going to the condenser; the agreement with the weight is remarkable.

This fact is not found with the "Corliss" engine, for Rc is the same, 11.21 c. and 11.15 c., while the weights are 0.0298 and 0.0398 k. for expansion 11 and 6. We believe then this is due to the jacket, for the same phenomenon reversed is met in the "Woolf" engine; the weight of water present at the end of the stroke of the large piston is 0.0413 k. and 0.0431 k. nearly the same for experiments 267 and 185 H. P., while Rc is 6.65 c. and 13.48 c. respectively.

HIRN ENGINE—STEAM SUPERHEATED TO 196° C.; EXPERIMENT I. 113 H. P.; EXPANSION 7.

Account of heat, etc., per single stroke.

Weight of fluid... 0.2240 k.

  " " dry steam at cut-off.................................. 0.1688 k.

  " " water " " (24.6 per cent.)...................... 0.0552 k.

Heat given to iron ....0.0552 × 506.5 = 27.96 c.

Weight of dry steam at end of stroke............................ 0.1761 k.

  " " water " " (21.38 per cent)............. 0.0479 k.

Internal heat at end of cut-off, U_0............................ 110.22 c.

  " "   end of stroke, U_1........................... 108.56 c.

  $U_0 - U_1$.. 1.66 c.

Heat furnished by superheating................................ 5.99 c.
"   "   " iron (above)................................. 27.96 c.

"   "   during expansion.............................. 35.61 c.
" absorbed by total work of expansion..................... 14.31 c.
" lost by external radiation............................ 2.50 c.
Rc ....35.61 — 16.81 = 18.80 c.

$$Rc \text{ in per cent. of total heat furnished } \frac{18.80}{151.16} = 12.5 \text{ c.}$$

Check on *Rc:*

Internal heat at end of stroke, U_1............................. 108.56 c.
Back pressure work.. 2.14 c.
Heat retained after condensation........................... —6.81 c.

                                                                        103.89 c.
Heat gained by injection water............................. 122.77 c.

Rc.. 18.88 c.

$$\text{Error, } \frac{18.80 - 18.88}{151.16} = 0.05 \text{ per cent.}$$

HIRN ENGINE—STEAM SUPERHEATED TO 231° C.; EXPERIMENT II., 154 H. P.;
EXPANSION 4.

Account of heat, etc., per single stroke:

Weight of fluid.. 0.3065 k.
"   " dry steam at cut-off................................. 0.2866 k.

"   " water   "   " (6.5 per cent.)..................... 0.0199 k.
Heat given to iron.............................0.099 × 504.42 10.04 c
Weight of dry steam at end of stroke .... 0.2698 k.
"   " water   "   "   " (12 per cent.).............. 0.0367 k.

Internal heat at cut-off, U_0.............................. 176.81 c.
"   " at end of stroke, U_1............................. 164.44 c.

$U_0 - U_1$.. 12.37 c.

Heat furnished by superheating.............................. 13.22 c.
"   "   " iron (above)......... .... 10.04 c.

"   "   during expansion.............................. 35.63 c.
" absorbed by total work of expansion..................... 16.52 c.
" lost by external radiation............................ 2.50 c.
Rc...................................... ....35.63 — 19.02 = 16.61 c.

$$Rc \text{ in per cent of heat furnished } \frac{16.60}{212.31} = 7.8 \text{ c.}$$

Check on *Rc:*

Internal heat at end of stroke, U_1............................. 164.44 c.
Back pressure work.. 2.45 c.

Heat retained after condensing............................ ..   9.59 c.

                                          157.30 c.

"   gained by injection water...............................   174.84 c.

Rc..   17.54 c.

$$\text{Error } \frac{16.61 - 17.54}{212.31} = 0.4 \text{ per cent.}$$

HIRN ENGINE—STEAM SUPERHEATED TO 223° C.; EXPERIMENT III., 125
H. P.; EXPANSION 2.

Account of heat, etc., per single stroke.

Weight of fluid...   0.2822 k.

Weight of dry steam at cut-off.................................   0.2866 k.

       "   water at cut-off (superheated)....................... —0.0044 k.

       "   dry steam at end of stroke..........................   0.2449 k.

       "   water at end of stroke (13.2 per cent.)..............   0.0373 k.

Internal heat at cut-off, U_0...................................   169.93 c.

     "   "   end of stroke, U_1..............................   149.42 c.

$U_0 - U_1$..   20.52 c.

Heat furnished by superheating................................   11.56 c.

     "   "   during expansion........................ ....   32.68 c.

     "   absorbed by total work of expansion.....................   9.24 c.

     "   lost by external radiation.................. ....   2.50 c.

Rc............................. ....32.08 — 11.74 = 20.34 c.

$$Rc \text{ in per cent. of heat furnished } \frac{28.34}{194.36} = 10.5 \text{ c.}$$

Check on Rc

Internal heat at end of stroke................................,....   149.42 c.

Back pressure work...   2.17 c.

Heat retained after condensing................................. —9.49 c.

                                          141.64 c.

"   gained by injection water............................. ..   161.30 c.

Rc..   19.66 c.

$$\text{Error } \frac{20.34 - 19.66}{199.36} = 0.3 \text{ per cent.}$$

The three values of Rc, 18.80 c., 16.61 c. and 20.34 c., vary little; we can therefore state that these figures do not agree with the weight of water at the end of the stroke. Thus for experiments II. and III. the final weights of water are 0.0367 k. and 0.0373 k., very near each other, while Rc is 16.61 c. and 20.34 c. We recognize here the effect of superheating, for under the same conditions saturated steam gave equal weights of water and equal values of Rc. It is to be remarked that the highest cooling by the condenser corresponds to the lowest work and the longest admission $\frac{1}{2}$ superheated.

With jacket, on the contrary, the largest value of Rc is with the longest expansion, 11, of the "Corliss," or to the least work, 185 H. P., of the "Woolf" engine. The reason is that the jacket gives up heat during exhaust proportionally to the difference of temperature, while with superheating and saturated steam the heat is stored in the surface. Also we see that the difference 16 to 20 c. is much less than for the "Woolf" engine, 6 to 13 c., while for equal values of Rc, 11 c., we have in the "Corliss" 0.0298 and 0.0398 k., varying 3 to 4, while with superheating the values of Rc vary 4 to 5.

Finally, we see the proportion of steam condensed during admission diminish rapidly, with the expansion passing from 24.6 to 6.5 to 0 in experiments I., II. and III., while in this last case we find, if we calculate by volume and weight the steam at cut-off, we get more than that given by the direct measurement. The steam occupying the volume at cut-off possesses an excess of heat, which is betrayed by the greater pressure than would be given by the same weight of saturated steam occupying the same space.

It is then incorrect to say that superheated steam falls to the condition of saturated steam *always*, and partially condenses on arriving in the cylinder; it is also wrong to attribute to the initial condensation all the loss of pressure observed between the boilers and cylinders. These losses of pressure are mainly due to restrictions in the pipes and passages; this is proved by this experiment where the steam at cut-off is superheated and where the condensation cannot be the cause of such loss of pressure.

Influences of various expansions upon single cylinder engines—their utility from the point of view of cost.

Uniting in a single table (on opposite page) the results of our analyses we shall render the discussion easier.

The general effect of a prolonged expansion appears the same whether it be a question of one cylinder or two; whether jacketed or not. It is to be remarked that the phenomenon is much more regular when the expansion is produced in the same inclosure, the order of transfers of heat is continuous, while the large cylinder of the "Woolf" engines gives birth to singular modifications in the thermic action of the surfaces. This peculiarity we have had occasion to note for the experiment with expansion 13, and introduction of one-half the small cylinder.

The increase of expansion always causes an increase in the proportion of steam condensed during admission, and a decrease in the amount of dry steam per total H. P. per hour; but this double action is more or less energetic as the engine is provided with a jacket or not, and according as saturated or superheated steam is used, which the figures of Table IV will prove to us.

Notwithstanding the reputation of the "Corliss" and its derivatives we have studied them as a single cylinder jacketed, with four-valves.

TABLE IV.

| | CORLISS, WITH JACKET. | | | HIRN WITHOUT JACKET. | | | | |
| | | | | Saturated. | | Superheated. | | |
	I.	II.	III.	I.	II.	I. 196°	II. 231°	III. 223°
No. of expansions....	11	8	6	7	4	7	4	2
Force indicated on pistons, H. P..............	105	137	158	107	146	113	154	125
Dry steam per hour per total H. P., ks........	7.188	7.236	7.307	7.822	8.449	6.655	7.000	7.874
Back pressure work per cent. of total work...	10	8.8	8.1	11.8	9.2	9.7	8.3	8.9
Dry steam per hour per Ind. H. P., ks.........	7.983	7.939	7.955	8.837	9.307	7.370	7.633	8.655
Mechanical efficiency, per cent...............	88	91	92	89	92	90	93	91
Dry steam per hour per net H. P., ks.........	9.071	8.724	8.646	9.929	10.341	8.188	8.267	9.511
Per cent. water carried over...................	3	4	5.2	1.1	1.0			
Per cent. water condensed in jacket......	6.5	6	5.3					
Per cent. water contained at cut-off..........	38.3	31.7	25.3	37	31	24.6	6.5	*
Per cent. water contained at end of stroke...	21.7	19.2	18.5	35.2	25.2	21.4	12	13.2
$U_0 - U_1$ during expansion, cs..............	−6.32	−5.92	−1.83	+5.12	−1.87	+1.66	+12.37	+20.52
Rc loss by cooling due condenser, cs........	11.21	11.14	11.15	37.92	37.53	18.80	16.61	20.34
Rc in per cent. of total heat furnished........	12.03	9.8	8	21.6	15.4	12.5	7.8	10.5

Without doubt the arrangement with circular valves and the releasing gear are very ingenious and offer a certain interest, but practically we much prefer flat valves with right line movements moved by cams or eccentrics; they always close tight in consequence of the very nature of their working. We have seen "Woolf" engines with the valve seat in perfect order after twenty years' working. The Hirn engine with four slide valves, with seats smooth and close to the cylinder, presents no defects after twenty-five years. This reservation made, we will pass to the examination of the three cases of the single-cylinder jacketed engine with four valves.

The expansion changing from 6 to 14, the proportion of initially condensed water increases from 25 to 38 per cent., a change of 13 per cent. At the end of the stroke the difference is less marked, from 18 per cent. to 21 per cent. This proves a greater evaporation for the greater expansion. The heat required is drawn from the jacket and surface which has received it during the admission. But I do not insist upon this series of phenomena discovered by M. Hirn and described by him, for I have treated them at sufficient length in an elementary form in my paper of

*Superheated.

25th October, 1876 (*Bulletins* for March, April, May, 1877), concerning the experiments executed under his direction.

That which we should remark, however, is that this progress crosses the difference U_0-U_1 between the internal initial and final heats, the latter becoming greater as the expansion is increased. The "Woolf" engines with variable expansion and jacket have already presented the same phenomenon. Is it then one of the effects of the expansion? or is it an effect of the jacket? The study of the Hirn engine permits us to decide.

We have seen that the proportion of water at the end of the stroke for the "Corliss" differs 3 per cent., while the weight of water is 0.0298 k. for 11 expansions, 0.0341 k. for 9, and 0.0398 for 6; the value Rc is also a function of this weight of water, since the loss Rc is the amount of heat required to evaporate a portion of water on the surface and return it to the condenser in the shape of steam. How is it then that the three values of Rc are equal to 11 calories, when the weights are as 1, 0.85, 0.75? The same phenomenon presents itself with the "Woolf" engines, but in a manner reversed: in that we have different coolings with the same weights at the end of the stroke. Thus for B and F, expansion 6 and 25, the weights are 0.0706 and 0.0685 k. of contained water, while the values of Rc are 8.44 c. and 21.33 c. Is this still the effect of expansion? But then in the same expansion equal weights of water should give equal values of Rc., and we should not have with the Munster engine, expanding 7 times, values of Rc, 6.65 c. and 13.48 c., when the weight of terminal water is 0.0413 k. and 0.0430 k. for 267 and 185 H. P. Still, a question to which the experiments on the Hirn engine will give a solution.

The intrinsic values of the different expansions are fixed as we have said by the cost of a total H. P. The economy realized by the work of steam is 2.15 per cent. between expansion 6 and 11 for the "Corliss" engine; but this benefit does not exist industrially, the most economic being expansions 4.6 per cent. better than 11. We can state here again, for single-cylinder engines, the fact that our analyses established for "Woolf" engines jacketed that prolonged expansions are far from being economical in practice.

The Hirn engine, without jacket, consuming saturated steam with expansions of 4 and 7, offers initial condensations of 31 and 37 per cent.; with the latter the terminal value is nearly the same, 35 per cent., while the former has evaporated 6 per cent., which is the reverse of jacketed engines. In these, a large expansion gives a larger evaporation; the superheating also gives a large evaporation with a less condensation for the expansions which augment it. With expansions of 2, 4 and 7, the steam remains superheated for the first, and for the two others condenses at the end of admission, 6 and 24 per cent. at the end of the stroke. The proportions of contained water are 13, 12 and 21 per cent. For the first case the superheated steam becomes saturated and then condenses 13 per cent. during the expansion, for the second the proportion of water increases 6, and for the last only 3 per cent. to the end of the stroke.

With regard to the surface condensation and evaporation, the super-heating acts partly as a jacket. Its influence upon the internal heat U_1 and cooling due the condenser Rc should present the same analogies, for these quantities of heat are in intimate relation with the weights of water present at the commencement and end of the expansion ; but the study of U and Rc will show us that the action of superheating is less energetic upon them than a jacket, but that it conducts to an economy at least equal if not greater upon the consumption of steam.

If we work the Hirn engine with saturated steam, the internal heat U_1 grows less with regard to U_0 when the expansion is increased. The difference $U_1 - U_0 = -1.87$ c. with 4, and becomes 5.12 c. for 7 expansions. The jacketed engines gave a reversed difference; the final internal heat is there increased with regard to the initial, when the expansion was prolonged. The jacket is then the only cause of this accession of internal final heat following the order of expansion. This is also the manner of action with superheating, for we see the difference $U_1 - U_0$ pass from 20.52 c. to 12.37 c., and to 1.66 c. when the expansions are 2, 4 and 7.

The remarkable action of the jacket upon different expansions, and the analogous but less strongly marked effect of superheating, are more especially characterized by the successive values which the cooling due the condenser Rc acquires. The Hirn engine without superheating, with expansions 4 and 7, presents the same weight of water, 0.0940 k., and 0.0927 k. at the end of the stroke, the values of Rc are 37.53 c. and 37.02 c. Note well that it is not necessarily thus, that the thermic conditions of the surfaces could and should differ with expansions 4 and 7. This remarkable fact proves to us that without a jacket and with saturated steam the weight of final water decides the value of Rc. If, however, we give to the steam an excess of heat and superheat it, we see that with equal weights of water at the end of the stroke, 0.0373 k. and 0.0367 k. with expansions 2 and 4, we have values of Rc, 20.34 c. and 16.61 c., differing 3.7 c., when with saturated steam they were equal; but it is with jacketed engines that the difference is greatest. Experiments B and F on the Malmerspach engine, expansions 6 and 25, have, as we have seen, values of Rc, 8.44c. and 21.33 c. for weights 0.0706 k. and 0.0682 k. The Munster engine offers Rc, 6.65 c. and 13.48 c. for 267 and 185 H. P., the weight of water being 0.0413 k. and 0.0431 k. Finally, the "Corliss," with $Rc = 11$ c. for expansions 6 and 11, has terminal water 0.0398 k. and 0.0298 k.

There is a particular mode of working, which, singular and energetic as it seems, should find its natural explanation when carefully studied. The cooling by the condenser Rc is, as we have many times said, the heat drawn from the surface by the evaporation of a part of the water which covers it, and the passage to the condenser of the water as steam. This heat furnished by the iron surface is given in two ways, according as the engine is jacketed or not. If saturated steam arrives in a cylinder without this improvement, it partially condenses during admission, giving up thereby a certain quantity of heat to the metal, which restores it during expansion and exhaust. We have stated that in this case and in the limits in which we have operated, the values of Rc are equal for equal weights of terminal water. Substituting superheated steam for saturated steam, the heat furnished the iron surface during admission will be differently restored during the exhaust. Equal weights of terminal water give different values of Rc, a loss of 3.7 c. more corresponding to the greater expansion. But it is with the jacket that the loss Rc increases with the expansion for equal weights of terminal water; here the heat is not only stored in the metal surface during admission, it is furnished from without across the thickness of metal by steam from the boiler condensing on the cylinder. This condensation is greatest when the difference of temperature is greatest between the steam in the cylinder and the jacket, that is to say, during exhaust. This transfer of heat accelerates the evaporation of the water which lines the interior surface, augmenting the value of the loss Rc. Such is the cause which in most cases renders the jacket less effective than superheating moderately; that its action appears at first sight more energetic we should remember that it makes the difference of heat that it gives the expansion and the waste heat that it gives the condenser a larger quantity than is given by superheating.

The influence of a greater or less expansion appears to be more with unjacketed engines, at least this is the case with the Hirn engine between 4 and 7 expansions. With saturated steam the costs of a total H. P. are 8.449 and 7.822 k. which differ 7.4 per cent. The same costs with superheated steam are 7.000 and 6.665 k.; at the same expansions they differ 4.9 per cent., being less than for saturated steam. But we should hold account also that the steam has not been obtained at the same temperature in these two experiments. If the superheating had been the same, the difference would have been 2 per cent. more, or 7 per cent., whether the engine works with or without superheating. Is it then only an effect of the absence of a jacket, or should we consider it as caused by an introduction already too great in the cylinder? We are brought to believe that these causes both act, for with superheating and introduction of one-half there is a difference of 15.2 per cent. more than in the experiment with 7 expansions, a difference which would have been still greater if the temperature of the steam in this last experiment had been 223° C. instead of 196° C.

We see from the cost of a total H. P. which fixes the value of the intrinsic work of steam, and to which we could give the name of generic cost, offers a marked advantage for the prolonged expansion 7, as well for saturated and superheated steam. This advantage diminishes in practice, the back pressure and friction not varying with the useful work. That is with superheated steam the cost of a net H. P. is the same 8.188 k. and 8.207 k., when the generic costs differ 4.9 per cent. for expansions 7 and 4 with saturated steam, and the same expansions the generic economy 7.4 per cent. becomes a practical economy of 4 per cent. We found with the "Corliss" that the generic economy of 2.15 became a practical loss of 4.6 when the expansion changed from 6 to 11.

These results bring us to the conclusion we have already stated for "Woolf" engines jacketed, they confirm experimentally the *theoretic* advantage of large expansions established by M. Zeuner; at the same time the *practical* advantage of moderate expansions, preconceived by M. Hirn.

COMPARISON OF EXPERIMENTAL VALUES FOR DOUBLE AND SINGLE CYLINDER ENGINES—CONCLUSIONS.

Before stating the figures which serve for this study let us recall some principles which it is indispensable to keep well in mind during the course of the discussion.

We have determined for each experiment the number of calories brought to the cylinder per stroke, as well as the consumption of dry saturated steam that it represented. This calculation had for its object to bring all the engines to the same unit of comparison. Thus all the engines which we have examined, whether jacketed or not, whether using superheated steam or not, consume a certain number of calories per stroke, which can be represented by a weight of dry steam produced by the boiler at the pressure of the experiment. By operating in this manner we preserve a rigorously exact unit, while approaching the old valuation which established the consumption of steam taken by the cylinder with more or less water and even superheated.

It is not necessary to say that this weight of dry steam is not that which we study in the cylinder; in all the analyses we naturally hold account of the weight really existing in the engine.

This consumption of dry steam is then presented in three forms, embracing each a particular order of facts. The cost per hour of a total H. P., of an indicated H. P., and of a net H. P.

The first supposes a perfect vacuum, and we get rid of the construction of the engine, and sometimes of the system adopted; in a word, we have the intrinsic value of the work of the steam. In comparing them, we are in a manner studying the use of the heat—of the heat brought to the engine.

The second holds account of the back pressure work, which varies from one experiment to the other upon the same engine with different loads. It is the cost referred to the measure of the area of the indicator diagrams.

Finally the cost of a net H. P. takes into account the friction of the engine and is the industrial value, more or less economic, of the engine ; it corresponds to the force measured by the brake.

To each of these three kinds of consumption corresponds a method of working characteristic of engines with one or two cylinders. This mode of working we will define, and join therewith the different results which indicate the kind and value of the transfers of heat.

In the series of our eighteen experiments we find two experiments of which the figures are closely alike ; they can only be distinguished by the cost, and are eminently suited for an exact comparison of single and double cylinder engines.

These are the experiments upon the " Woolf," expanding 13, and the "Corliss," expanding 6. The proportions of contained water differ little, 25.3 for the beginning and 18.5 for end, for the "Corliss"; 23.7 and 17.9 per cent. for the " Woolf."

The internal initial and final heats are nearly constant, 106.30 c.-- 108.13 c. $= -$ 1.83 c. $= U_0 - U_1$ and 283.55 c. $-$ 282.31 c. $=$ 1.24 c. The " Woolf " presents a peculiarity which we have already noticed. During the expansion in the " Corliss " engine a continuous evaporation of 6.8 per cent. took place. In the " Woolf " engine the phenomenon is not so simple. We have in the total expansion an evaporation of 5.8 per cent.; but, because of the arrangement with two cylinders and the introduction to half stroke in the small cylinder, the expansion is broken into two portions, in each of which the transfers of heat in a manner differ.

The expansion in the small cylinder during the last half of the stroke gives rise to an evaporation of 10.3 per cent. of the water inclosed with the steam, the internal heat is augmented $U_0 - U_1 = 283.55$ c. $-$ 305.84 c. $=$ $-$ 22.29 c., much more rapidly than in the corresponding experiment with the "Corliss," and is with 13.1 water. When the mixture passes to the large cylinder at the end of the stroke, the weight of the water is 17.9 per cent., there has been 4.8 per cent. of the fluid condensed in the second part of the expansion.

The modification of the thermic phenomena by an expansion commenced at half the small cylinder is radical, as we see ; it seems to prove the inaction of the jacket. We have seen that the jacket counteracts in part the energetic condensations which are produced at the commencement of the stroke of the large piston.

The fact which we note, joined to the values of the cooling, by the condenser, for the two experiments should reduce to their just value the edifying considerations, outside of experimental grounds, which show the superiority of " Woolf " engines.

The too widely diffused opinion still is that for stationary as for marine engines the double-cylinder jacketed engine is actually that which gives the best economic return in the production of motive power.

" In these engines the steam acts first with or without expansion in the small cylinder, then with expansion in the large cylinder. This latter is then alone in communication with the condenser. By this disposition a portion of the force produced escapes the cooling action of the condenser and the cylinder condensation.

" Further, because of the jackets in which the two cylinders are placed in the midst of steam from the boiler direct, the expanding steam in the large cylinder is at a much lower temperature than that of the jacket, and consequently is easily warmed and the cylinder condensation notably lessened."

These deductions, which appear so logical that I myself believed them rational enough (1874-75), receive the formal condemnation of experience.

This proves once more that it is impossible, as M. Hirn has said, to establish *a priori* anything that shall be tolerably exact concerning steam engines. "A correct theory can only be established *a posteriori*, that is to say, after the experimental study of each special system of engines." We shall see at the same time that it is important to collect together the discoveries that M. Hirn calls by the name of the "practical theory of the steam engine." This theory will enable us to establish on a certain basis and with the most minute details the comparative experimental values of the different systems of steam engines.

It is generally admitted, we will say, that the arrangement with two cylinders ought to withdraw a portion of the force produced from the cooling action of the condenser; how is it then that we have Rc 8 and 8.3 per cent. for the "Woolf" and the "Corliss"? This same arrangement, where the expansion is made in the large cylinder with a steam jacket which warms it easily, should diminish the condensation. Whence comes then the condensation of 5 per cent., which we have found, when, on the contrary, the "Corliss" and the small cylinder present evaporations of 7 and 10 per cent. during the expansion. Two hypotheses which appeared to have a certain basis are annulled by the analysis; they should put us on our own guard against all researches which are not purely experimental and verified.

The two experiments which we compare have the same proportion of initial and final water, 25 and 18 per cent., the same loss by the condenser, 8 per cent., for both the internal, initial and final heat are nearly constant.

The consumption of dry steam should then fix for us the relative value of single and double cylinder engines with jackets, but they should not be admitted without preliminary discussion.

The consumption of dry steam per total H. P. gives, as we have said, the intrinsic value of the work of the steam; it is 6.878 k. for the "Woolf," expanding 13, and 7.307 k. for the "Corliss," expanding 6, being 5.9 per cent. in favor of the "Woolf." This figure fixes at 6 per cent., the intrinsic economy realized by expansion in a separate cylinder; if it was not submitted to two important corrections in passing from the domain of theory to the realm of industrial practice, it would seem to give reason to the partisans of this system.

But before making these two corrections, we should notice that these two experiments have been made, with all their similar features, with different expansions. An expansion of 13 gave with the "Corliss" an economy of 1.5 per cent., and we can affirm without committing sensible error, that an expansion of 13 would give 2 per cent. improvement, which reduces to 4 per cent. the generic economy of expansion in the large cylinder. It is not large, as we see, and this disappears completely, giving place to a considerable increase in practice.

In a note presented to our society (session Aug. 26, 1874) and appearing in the *Bulletin* in 1875 I studied the variations of back pressures in steam cylinders, with the values of negative work in terms of total work.

This study proved that the negative work absorbed 15 per cent. of the total work in "Woolf" engines, and 7 per cent. only in "Corliss" engines, the back pressure work being the same—0.210 to 0.217 in the two cases (2.9 and 3.0 ℔s.). These results were established where the proportions of total work absorbed by the back pressure remained constant. The two experiments which occupy us have not the same vacuum, that of the "Corliss" is a little better than the "Woolf," 0.184 to 0.226 k., making 8 per cent. instead of 7 per cent. for we are within the stated limits; with a back pressure of 0.226 k., the negative work of the "Corliss" would have been 9 per cent. It is thus proved that with the same vacuum of 0.226 k. by the fact of adding a second cylinder to prolong the expansion we create a serious loss; this loss destroys the genuine economy that we have established for double-cylinder engines from the consumption per total H. P.

We shall not be astonished then that the "Corliss" leads 2.3 per cent., when we compare the cost per indicated H. P., over the "Woolf."

Finally, the last brake experiments by our Mechanical Committee have proved that there is a notable difference in the power absorbed in friction of the moving parts in two horizontal engines, of which one had a single cylinder while the other had two cylinders, "Woolf" system. This inferiority adds its influence to the negative work and brings the two following consumptions per net H. P.; "Corliss," 6 expansions, 8.646 k.; "Woolf," 13 expansions, 9.465 k. Such are the weights of dry steam valued on a Prony brake; they represent the quantities of heat expended in the industrial cost of the motor, their difference is $\dfrac{9.46 - 58.646}{9.465} = 8.7$ per cent.

in favor of the engine with one cylinder, coming to the point of the principle which I stated at the session of January 30, 1878, concerning jacketed engines, viz.:

That it is always possible to construct a vertical beam engine with one cylinder and four valves, consuming saturated steam that shall be at least as economical as the "Woolf" beam engine.

We have compared the two experiments which are alike in most of the transfers of heat, etc. There are also others which should conduct us to more rigorous conclusions. Let us see, meanwhile, what will result from the whole of our verified experiments, to which we will add the results upon the compound of the French Navy, which I published in my last memoir.

Our readers may perhaps find that we fall into fastidious repetitions; but the figures inscribed in Table V. shows us once more that it is impossible to draw conclusions if one is not in possession of a sufficient series of experimental studies, not only of one system or other, but even from one experiment to another upon the same engine. What is the use of seeking the law of expansion, of substituting a curve of the hyperbolic family, of comparing adiabatic curves and others with the indicator diagram, when it is impossible to deduce from one verified experiment the results which we shall obtain when we impose other conditions upon the engine? The *practical theory*, the verified analysis of numerous experi‑

TABLE V.

	Ind H. P.	Expansion.	Dry steam per hour per total H.P., ks.	Back pressure, ks.	Negative work in per cent. of total work.	Dry steam per hour per ind. H.P., in ks.	Mechanical efficiency, p. c.	Dry steam per hour per net H.P., in ks.	Difference of internal heat $U_0 - U_1$ in calories.	Cooling by the condenser, Rc in p. c.
DOUBLE CYLINDERS.										
I. "Woolf" vertical jacketed............... {	143	28	6.731	0.181	18.6	8.273	83	10.019	−25.88	7.8
	215	13	6.878	0.226	15.6	8.149	86	9.465	+1.24	8.3
II. "Woolf" vertical jacketed .... {	185	7	7.384	0.234	24.1	9.730	78	12.411	−31.89	3.5
	347	7	7.112	0.293	17.4	8.614	87	9.864	−17.40	3.4
III. "Woolf" horizontal jacketed............. {	130	6	7.290	0.253	20.1	9.120	86	10.563	−3.63	1.2
	180	6	7.328	0.295	17.4	8.878	89	9.975	−6.12	0.7
Compound vertical jacketed.................	690	5	7.510	0.216	13.4	8.671	89	9.975	+40.32	5.7
SINGLE CYLINDERS.										
"Corliss" horizontal jacketed............ {	105	11	7.188	0.148	10.0	7.983	88	9.071	−6.32	12.0
	158	6	7.307	0.184	8.1	7.955	92	8.640	−1.83	8.0
Hirn vertical unjacketed, superheated 196°.....	113	7	6.655	0.188	9.7	7.370	90	8.188	+1.66	12.5
Hirn vertical unjacketed, superheated 231°......	154	4	7.000	0.215	8.3	7.633	93	8.207	+12.37	7.8
Hirn vertical unjacketed, superheated 223°......	125	2	7.874	0.190	8.9	8.655	91	9.511	+20.52	10.5
Hirn vertical unjacketed, superheated 220°......	99	2	7.763	0.178	10.4	8.063	88	9.844	+16.82	14.1
Hirn vertical unjacketed, saturated steam	107	7	7.822	0.213	11.8	8.837	89	9.929	+5.12	21.6
Hirn vertical unjacketed, saturated steam	146	4	8.449	0.225	9.7	9.307	92	10.341	−1.87	15.4

ments, can alone give us the solution of problems to which they still apply formulæ which are only experimental in name. This law which M. Hirn has stated, and which my preceding memoirs have confirmed, makes us consider the formulæ called experimental of expansion and work as algebraic distractions, perhaps interesting, but having, from a practical point of view, a utility hardly worth contesting.

For us the true theory of the steam engine created by M. Hirn completes itself every day that new experiments, entirely checked and analyzed, are made public and added to those which we have published after him.

Have I not compared the results of pure experience in determining the influence of the vacuum, of throttling, of expansion, of the addition of a separate cylinder? And still in this case before placing the principle let us leave a sufficient margin for the minor irregularities which it is difficult to avoid practically.

All that we have said concerns only those researches which are entitled "experimental researches." By the side of the practical theory the generic theory of the employment of steam as an intermediate in the employment of force retains its special value. The fine work of Zeuner, for example, conceived in the purely theoretic manner, remains a model of the method to be followed when the hypothesis is that the surfaces transmit no heat; but what it is necessary to shun with the greatest care is the mixture of generic theory with the practical theory of which the starting points are diametrically opposed one to the other.

The successive analyses have already given all the remarkable peculiarities; in each of the experiments we have used them to determine the influence of expansion upon the transformations of the steam. We shall also ask of Table V a collected view of the costs and the circumstances which influence them.

A part of the interesting results which we shall note concern the "Corliss," expansion 6, and the horizontal "Woolf" with the same expansion. They present the relative value of single and double cylinder engines in a different form from that which we have examined when we consider only the parallelism between the transformations of steam. Thus, with the same expansions the cost of a total H. P. corresponds, 7.307 k. for the "Corliss" at 158 H. P., and 7.290 and 7.328 k. for the "Woolf" with 130 and 180 H. P. But we have already said that this latter had an insufficient compression in the clearance; if this compression had been properly regulated the cost would descend to 7 kilos. of steam per total H. P. We should then find an intrinsic difference of 4 per cent. in favor of expansion in a separate cylinder, a difference which confirms the principle that we have stated concerning the generic economy of this kind of engine.

What becomes of this benefit of 4 per cent. when we pass from the total work to the indicated and the net work; that is to say, when we occupy ourselves with only the industrial work usefully realized.

The negative work of the "Woolf" engine absorbs 20 per cent. at 130 H. P. and 17 per cent. at 180 H. P., while the "Corliss" only loses 8 per cent., which brings the "Corliss" 6 per cent. ahead of the "Woolf" under its best conditions at 180 H. P. If we compare the cost of a net H. P., valued by a brake, we find $\dfrac{9.975 - 8.646}{9.975} = 13.5$ per cent., which a sufficient compression will reduce 4 per cent., and there remains a practical gain in favor of the "Corliss" of 9.5 per cent., working at the same expansions.

We see that the cost of a total H. P., 7.307 k. and 7.328, are equal for the "Corliss" and horizontal "Woolf" for 6 expansions, 158 and 180 H. P. A well-known construction would give the same vacuum, 0.184 k., to the "Woolf" as the "Corliss;" but the negative work would be 8 per cent. and 11 per cent. at least. A difference of 3 per cent. should be added for friction, being 92 and 89 per cent. respectively.

The total, 6 per cent., could be reduced by 4 per cent. by proper cushion and there remains at the end of our account an inferiority of 2 per cent. for the "Woolf" working at the same expansion as the single-cylinder "Corliss." In conditions easily realized in practice the consumption of the "Woolf" per net H. P. would be 8.8 k. This is the lowest we should expect from this kind of engine. In my preceding paper I had fixed this consumption at 9 k. deduced from the vertical "Woolf" and the "Hirn" engine with superheated steam.

With different expansions, 13 and 6, but with equal transformations of steam, the costs per total H. P. vary 5.9 per cent. against the "Corliss" with the same vacuum 0.184 k.: for the two engines the back pressure work would have been 8 per cent. for the "Corliss" and 13 per cent. for the "Woolf," being 5 per cent. the other way; there remains only about 1 per cent. advantage, comparing by the indicated H. P. Industrially this advantage disappears and there is a loss of 5 per cent. against the "Woolf," the friction being such that we obtain 86 per cent. being 6 per cent. worse than the "Corliss" at 92 per cent. mechanical efficiency.

We have then the right to conclude that the single-cylinder engine is at least the equal of the double-cylinder, although to this day with different consumption more favor is shown the double-cylinder engines.

A number of other interesting results are presented by our table. I will point out those given by superheating without going into details on the subject, the question having been many times treated in our *Bulletins,* then the effect of throttling reducing from 347 to 185 H. P. For the other experiments the small difference in generic cost is the other way and may be neglected.

We can push all these comparisons very far into the most intimate details of the working of the engine, following the elementary method, which consists simply of examining all the results of our verified experiments. We believe that we are rendering a service to our readers in leaving to each the particular study of the experiment which interests him. Our duty should be to point out the path to be followed; to give a sufficient number of verified experiments to permit the engineer to find the points for future researches. My end in writing this paper has been above all to confirm by a sufficient number of verified analyses the principle of the equality of double and single cylinder engines in point of consumption, to determine the degree of influence of a more or less prolonged expansion, to verify again the influence of a reduction of passageway or throttling the steam entering the cylinders.

CONSUMPTION OF DRY STEAM PER HOUR IN DIFFERENT ENGINES.	Expansion.	Total H. P. per kilos.	Negative work per cent.	Ind. H. P. per kilos.	Efficiency per cent.	Net H. P. per kilos.	Coal per net H. P. kilos.
Woolf engines, jacketed........	13	6.8	14	7.9	87	9.8	1.14
" " "	7	7.1	13	8.2	88	9.3	1.16
" " "	6	7.3	12	1.3	90	9.2	1.15
Compound engines, jacketed...	5	7.5	12	8.5	90	9.5	1.19
Single cylinder................							
Corliss, jacketed..............	6	7.3	8	7.9	92	8.6	1.08
Hirn, superheated.............	7	6.6	9	7.2	90	8.0	1.00

All these actions we have seen are in a restricted circle; we can fix for the builders the lower limit of consumption, a limit which we should seek to attain by good designs. We can give at the same time the corresponding consumption of coal, but we warn the reader that this valuation should never be taken as a unit of comparison, the calorific power of coal being as variable as their localities. We will admit, however, that from the numerous experiments made by the Society of Mulhouse upon boilers, a weight of dry steam, eight times the weight of the coal can be produced by medium coal (Ronchamp). This is the figure on which we will give the fuel required.

The consumptions of dry steam per hour for indicated and net horse-power, are deduced from the total horse-power found experimentally· They have a real base, a definite point of departure essentially certain in practice.

The back pressure work varies from 0.200 k. to 0.220 k. for the double-cylinder engines and 0.180 to 0.200 k. for single cylinders, values which it is always possible to secure by proper arrangements of the exhaust.

Concerning the mechanical efficiency, three of them have been obtained directly by brake. The others have been deduced from these same experiments by comparing the indicator diagrams. We have seen that there cannot be an error of 1 per cent. The net power is then exact. It is that which represents the industrial work.

In this form, which only differs from Table V. by the uniformity of the back pressure work, we perceive clearly the influence of an expansion prolonged from 7 to 13, a generic gain of 4 per cent., which industrially is 2 per cent. The compound engine comes after the "Woolf."

The horizontal "Woolf" and horizontal "Corliss" have the same generic consumption for the same expansion. This disappears and the "Corliss" is 6.5 per cent. better than the "Woolf," industrially.

Finally the steam per total horse-power for the "Woolf" expanding 13 times is within 3 per cent. of the Hirn unjacketed with steam heated to 200° C., which becomes 12 per cent. in favor of the superheating, when we compare the net horse-power, while the "Corliss" is only 7 per cent behind the Hirn.

In presence of these results have we not the right to ask what discoveries have been made since the day that Watt created the engine?

Without speaking of the well-balanced mechanism of the beam engine we can say that this man of genius had produced the heat engine complete in its three parts; the separate condenser, the steam jacket, an expansion prolonged as useful, leaving to those who came after to seek the attainment of high pressures, the construction of boilers at his time prohibiting him from following the complete realization of the principles of expansion which he had stated.

Also is there not in the series of improvements in the construction of engines that we have been studying, a marked discovery in the history of the heat engine, bringing another order of ideas, born nearly at the same time as thermodynamics, of which it is one of the best applications?

Each of my readers has always understood that I refer to the discovery made by Hirn and stated in our *Bulletins* for 1855, for it was at that time that he demonstrated the thermic influence of the metallic surface of the inside of the cylinders upon the inclosed steam. This discovery, analyzed, discussed and completed by twenty years of continual research in which he has kindly associated me, has conducted him to a method of analysis that he has called the "Practical Theory of the Steam Engine." We have not insisted upon the exact character and almost elementary simplicity which is one of the remarkable features of this practical theory. As to its importance, it is, I think, placed beyond doubt by the value of the facts that it has permitted us to define in the course of this paper.

CHAPTER VI.

STEAM HEATING.*

INTRODUCTION.

The subject of Steam Heating will be presented in this Chapter under the following heads:

A.—The theory of steam heating, the laws of the transmission of heat and the coefficients used in reducing this theory to practice.

B.—A description of the various systems in use in the United States, with a note on the magnitude of the works employed up to 1881.

C.—A detailed description of the apparatus used and the experiments made under the direction of the writer.

D.—The project of heating a cotton mill with steam, and a comparison of the cost when condensing and non-condensing engines are used to drive the mill.

A.—The Theory of Steam Heating.

The transfer of heat takes place by three processes: Radiation, Conduction, Convection.

In heating a room, for example, with an open grate fire, the heat in the room is mostly radiant heat. The heat of the fire is given to the gas and air in the flue and is carried away by convection. With radiation we have little to do, as in all heating apparatus the heat is brought to and delivered from some intervening solid body by fluids and passed through the solid.

The rate of conduction through a plate is expressed by a well-known formula (Rankine's "Steam Engine," p. 260.)

$q = \dfrac{T' - T}{\sigma + \sigma' + \rho x}$ where T and T' are the temperatures of the fluids on either side of the plate, σ and σ' are the coefficients of conductivity from the fluids to the plate, and x the thickness of the plate, ρ the conductivity of the plate itself.

For British units with x in inches $\rho = 0.0043$ heat units per square foot per hour for iron plates, a quantity which, with ordinary thicknesses, is so small that it may be neglected for iron plates.

The terms σ and σ' depend entirely upon the nature of the surfaces and upon the rapidity with which the fluids are circulated and the heat brought to and removed from the plate or surfaces in question. What is required

*A paper read before the Engineers' Club of St. Louis, June, 1882, by the Author.

for us as engineers is to determine the limits which appear in practice, leaving to the physicist the general investigations of the laws of the subject.

It has been suggested (*v.* Rankine's "Steam Engine," p. 260) that for iron plates $\sigma + \sigma'$ may be put equal $\dfrac{a}{T' - T}$, and then $q = \dfrac{(T' - T)^2}{a}$ and $a = \dfrac{(T' - T)^2}{q}$, and he further states that for air and water in a furnace and boiler a is from 160 to 200 for q in British units.

When the fluids are steam and air, we should expect from the greater mobility of steam than water, a greater rate of conduction, and we are not disappointed.

From many experiments in the open air, the steam condensed per square foot of pipe surface of $\frac{1}{8}$ inch thick wrought iron is found to be $1\frac{3}{8}$ pounds per square foot per hour when $T' = 220°$ F. and $T = 20°$ F.

In British heat units, the heat given up per pound of steam is 969 units; but as the water temperature is not given and is usually from 180° F. to 200° F., we shall make no large error by taking in this and in other investigations the heat delivered by condensing 1 pound of steam as 1,000 heat units; we then have.

$$a = \frac{(T' - T)^2}{q} = \frac{200 \times 200}{1375} = 29 \text{ nearly.}$$

Experiments made by the writer, which will be described hereafter, give values of a as great as 100. As experiments were made under the usual usage, and are more nearly in accordance with practice, the results, moreover, giving for the larger values of a a less rapid transmission of heat, they are obviously the safer to follow in designing heating surface. The great difference is to be attributed entirely to difference in the circulation of the air by which the condensation was effected.

By experiments made in the United States Navy, see page 63 of "Treatise on Boilers," by Engineer-in-Chief Wm. H. Shock, the transfer of heat is stated to be in proportion to the difference in temperature, instead of the square of the difference as taken by the writer.

The experiments there given appear to give the same quantities as those noted above in the open air, but would be reduced to $q = 2.6(T' - T)$ by the writer's experiments under the practical conditions commonly found, and this seems to agree more closely with the usual practice in the United States, and we shall therefore use this formula in preference to the other and more scientific one.

The heat required in any given building will depend upon the heat transmitted to the external air around the building and the amount of air carried through the building or the ventilation. The former effect is measured by the same formula, $q = \dfrac{T' - T}{\sigma + \sigma' + \rho x}$, where of course the constants have different values, and the latter, by the quantity of air used in ventilation and the amount of heat given to the air.

The constants σ, σ' and ρ vary very much with the materials of the walls and roofs, and the kinds of surfaces; but the most important cause of variation is the rapidity with which the heat is removed from the outside by the action of the wind, and the variation found here is so great that the minor changes become less important. The effect of ventilation is easily computed from the weight and specific heat of air when the quantities are known.

The values of ρ and $\sigma + \sigma'$ are given by some writers on heating and ventilation, but our safest course, as engineers, will be to seek the practical limits given by experience, and we find the limits pretty wide.

According to D. K. Clark ("Manual for Mechanical Engineers," p. 488), M. Peclet found that for $T' - T = 36°$ F. each square foot of wall would transmit 26 British units per hour, and that the glass windows passed heat at the rate of 30 units in place of 26. The same author gives, on the authority of Mr. Hood (*Idem.*, p. 481), the rate of 1.4 units per square foot per hour per degree of F. of $T' - T$ for glass windows, or for $36°$ $q = 50.4$ units, and the further statement that q varies with the square root of the velocity of the wind. From experiments by the author on large buildings, the transmission varied from 0.67 to 1.25 units per square foot per hour per degree F. of $T' - T$ for the whole surface of walls and windows. The larger values were produced by wind action, and are the ones that should be taken in practice. The effects of a liberal ventilation are included in the above results. The experiments will be given later.

Summing up these results we find that the transfer of heat from steam to air may be expressed as $q = a (T' - T)$ where T' and T are the temperatures of the steam and air on each side of a thin iron surface, and q is the rate of heat units per unit of surface per hour.

For T' and T in degrees F. and q in British heat units, $a = 2.6$ for 1 square foot per hour.

For T' and T in degrees centigrade and q in calories per square metre per hour, $a = 12.48$.

For the external surface of a building, including walls, windows and roof together, and taking no account of the material for the maximum transfer of heat, $q = c (T' - T)$.

For q in British heat units per square foot per hour $c = 1.25$ for F°.

For q in calories per square metre per hour, $c = 6$ for C°.

For the surface of a steam boiler as ordinarily constructed $\dfrac{(T' - T)^2}{a}$

For British heat units and F. per square foot per hour, $a = 200$.

For French heat units centigrade degrees and meters, per square meter per hour in calories, $a = 23.14$.

$$\frac{1}{a} = 0.0432.$$

For keeping any building permanently warm we must have a steady flow of heat from the furnace to the boiler, from the boiler through the heaters to the air in the building and from the walls to the external air. The same number of heat units per hour must be transferred in each case, whence it becomes easily possible to find the heating surface and boiler surface to warm any given building, taking, of course, the most unfavorable cases, and allowing for losses between the boilers and heaters, and for the ventilation.

Another method of expressing the transfer from heaters to building is by the number of units of volume which can be warmed by a unit of heating surface, and this, of course, varies with the proportions of the building and the range of external temperature, but the application must be to buildings of ordinary proportions, and though more commonly used, is really less reliable in its results.

With the practice of the Dubuque Steam Supply Company, at Dubuque, Iowa, we find that with the external air ranging to 0° F. or — 18° C., 1 square foot of heating surface warms a number of cubic feet as follows, in columns 2 and 4.

	When Heaters are in Same Rooms.		When Heaters are in Basements and Warm Air.	
	Cubic ft. per sq. ft.	Cubic metre per square metre.	Cubic ft. per sq. foot.	Cubic metre per square metre.
Dwellings...........................	50	15	40	12
Stores, wholesale..................	125	37	100	30
" retail......................	100	30	80	24
Banks...............				
Offices............................	70	21	60	18
Drug stores...........				
Dry goods.........................	80	24	70	21
Hotels, large..........	125	37	100	30
Churches..........................	200	60	150	45

To reduce these numbers to cubic metres warmed per square metre we multiply by 0.3, obtaining columns 3 and 5.

B.   Various Systems in the United States.

In the United States the application of steam for heating was begun in 1842, by J. J. Walworth and Joseph Nason, and the first building heated by steam was a cotton mill in Portsmouth, N. H. The exhaust steam from the engine was used very successfully, and from that time to the present there has been a steady increase in the number and magnitude of the works constructed for this purpose. This has been owing to the severity of the climate and the large number of new buildings erected in the rapid growth of the country. The business of the Walworth Manufacturing Company, of Boston, Mass., in constructing steam heating plant is now $1,500,000 per annum, and there is in the United States a business estimated by competent authorities at $6,000,000 per annum, which has for the past 30 years averaged $2,000,000 per year. In other words, there is now invested in the United States about $60,000,000 in steam heating apparatus, so that in this subject there is no lack of precedents for many kinds of apparatus.

There are two classes of plant used, as was indicated by the columns 2 and 4 for the table above.

When the heaters are placed in the rooms to be heated, the heating is said to be direct. When the heaters are used to warm air in separate chambers, which air is then transferred through flues to the rooms to be warmed, the heating is called indirect.

The choice between these systems is to be governed by other conditions. Where the air is not renewed frequently, or where the space to be warmed is large in plan but not in height, the direct system appears preferable; but where large ventilation is required, or the building is lofty, the indirect method offers many advantages. It appears necessary to provide more heating surface by the latter method; but the labor and expense of fittings is often much reduced thereby, while with improved arrangements there is little difference in the surface required. Usually the movement of the air by which the indirect system heats a building is effected by gravity, but in some instances fans have been employed, requiring, of course, power to drive them.

In regard to the different forms of heaters used in the United States there is great variety, from the single line of large pipe and the manifold lines, where the steam flows through several pipes side by side, to the elegantly finished work used in all the large hotels, and the complicated heaters used with the indirect method.

Within the last three years preceding 1881 steam heating has assumed a new form, by the use of long lines of pipes underground, thus placing the subject upon the basis of a gas or water supply. Companies for this purpose have been formed and works put in operation in many places in the United States. The table opposite gives some information concerning these works. This list is being rapidly extended, and after passing its experimental stage the subject can be placed upon a good financial basis. At the present time, although the matter is a success from the physical standpoint, yet rates and charges are still in an unsettled condition, and the owners by no means satisfied in most of these places.

From experiments with pipe laid and protected, as such companies protect them, a loss of heat of the pipes is found at 50 British heat units per square foot per hour with steam at 258° F., the ground at say 58°, 0.05 pounds per square foot per hour being the condensed water by weight. Experiments by the writer gave the same value, but in long lines a further loss takes place by leakage and by imperfect traps, a very essential part of the system. In fact the experience at Dubuque is that about one-half of the steam made is wasted, according to the statement of the superintendent.

Steam for heating is carried at all pressures in the United States, and while, as well known, no economy in fuel can result from the use of high pressures, yet a smaller plant can be made to do the work, and, in fact, the first remedy in cold weather for cold rooms is to raise the steam pressure until the increased energy of transmission of the heaters produces the desired result.

City and State.	Pipe Underground.	Remarks.
Lockport, New York	3 miles.	
Dubuque, Iowa	800 feet 6 inches 1,960 " 5 " 3,818 " 4 " 4,441 " 3 " 205 " 2 " 2,073 " 1½ " 2,508 " 1¼ " 643 " 1 "	Heats 3,500,000 cubic feet space; has 100 consumers Boiler capacity 25,000 lbs. water per hour, from 40° F., at 280° F. evaporation.
Auburn, New York	1 mile.	Heats 6,000,000 cub. ft.
Detroit, Michigan	5,000 feet 6 inches 2,000 " 8 " 5,000 " smaller than 6 in	
Milwaukee, Wisconsin	585 " 10 inches 2,540 " 8 " 5,156 " 6 " 875 " 5 " 5,195 " 4 " 1,300 " 3 " 6,900 " smaller pipe.	Heats 5,000,000 cubic feet and runs 10 engines.

Boilers for steam heating are of all sorts and kinds, and the only point which is vital in designing them is to keep in mind the range of action to which they will be subjected. For the work of a boiler in making steam for heating is more like that of a locomotive boiler than anything else. Every degree change of temperature, and every change in the wind is felt by the men with the shovels, and quickness of steaming and capacity of furnace for burning fuel is essential. Grate surface enough must be provided to do the work in the coldest weather; and this grate will be too large for economic evaporation in milder weather; and while large boiler surface is a good thing it is not judicious to invest in a boiler large enough to work at a high economy of evaporation during a few days only in a year of the hardest work. It is more economical to crowd the boilers at the expense of the fuel at such times, and a boiler must be provided which can be crowded hard.

C.—*Apparatus and Experiments Made by the Author.*

In the winter of 1878 the writer placed before the directors of Washington University in the City of St. Louis, Missouri, a plan for heating a portion of the buildings belonging to the University by steam, which plan was adopted by them and built.

The central group of buildings consists of the Academy, the Museum of Fine Arts, the Manual Training School, the University, Laboratory, and Gymnasium; the three latter are called collectively the University. To the west is the Mary Institute, with its own boiler, and to the east the Law School, occupying the old building erected for the Mary Institute; the future of this building being uncertain, it has not been connected for steamheating. The Mary Institute heating apparatus is mainly indirect,

and consists of heaters hung in the basement in small air chambers connected by flues to the different rooms.   The air heated is taken either from
the basement or from out-doors as desired.   The operation is quite satisfactory; the steam is at present supplied by two boilers in the building,
but it is probable that it will be connected to the central group and operated from the main boiler house in a short time.   It has now been in use
for four years.   The condensed water returns directly to the boilers.
The heaters of cast-iron are corrugated castings short and placed horizontally.

The Academy and Museum of Fine Arts are heated by fittings put in
by the Walworth Manufacturing Company.   In the Academy cold air is
taken through openings in the walls close to the heaters, and the foul air
passes through flues from the rooms to the top of the building and
escapes.   The steam and return mains are led around the basement, and
vertical steam and return pipes rise through the buildings with one heater
connected to them on each floor.   As little horizontal pipe is used as possible, and that is kept in the basement.   The steam pipes rise all the way
and the return pipes fall all the way.   The horizontal steam main must
be kept dry and the return main full of water in order to prevent
what is known as "snapping" a phenomenon sure to attract attention
when it does occur, and which is sometimes dangerous to the joints of
the pipes.

"Snapping" is caused in this way: when any of the condensed water
finds its way into steam that is warmer than itself, it causes a sudden condensation, and the steam closes up so rapidly that a shock and violent
sound result.   With large pipes and well-defined currents of steam the
water condensed remains at the temperature of the steam and is swept
along with it.   To illustrate more fully, if, in the Academy building, a
heater on the upper floor is shut off, steam will condense in the upper
portion of the vertical stand-pipe, and there being no current in the upper
portion and not much below, the water stands in drops on the iron cooling and accumulating till it falls into the hotter steam below.   A sound
like the crack of a rifle is the result.   The remedy is to open the heater
on the summit of this pair of pipes, or to connect the stand-pipes themselves; a better but more expensive way is to put in a pair of vertical pipes
for each heater from the mains in the basement, with the valves at the
bottom.   The greater portion of the University buildings is heated by
tubular heaters in the basement, the warm air being led to the various
rooms by flues in the walls and moved only by gravity.   The old heaters
were of cast-iron heated by fires made in them, and the new heaters were
applied to the same system of flues.   The heaters were described in a
paper by Mr. Chas. F. White before the Club, and printed in *The American
Engineer*.   Certain rooms in the upper floors are unprovided with wall
flues and are warmed by direct heaters; as these heaters are connected to
a pair of horizontal pipes of considerable length, the condensed water does
not drain properly.   The drying tables and sand baths in the chemical
and physical laboratories and one small heater is placed in a small room

on the first floor of the south wing, and one on the upper or second floor
of the Laboratory building. The Gymnasium is to have heaters of the
kind in the upper floor, with horizontal mains in the basement. At the
west end of the University building, the heating surface is not sufficient
to make up the loss from the walls, and the upper floors draw off the heat
from the lower rooms. This could be prevented by controlling the area of
the flues which carry away the warm air, but will be remedied by placing
heaters in the lower room. With the exception of two rooms the heating
is ample in the coldest weather.

The Manual Training School is heated in part by direct and in part by
indirect radiation. The two lower floors with the four workshops are
warmed by 4 lines of 2-inch pipe along the foot of the walls under the
benches, and the upper or school-room floor by a pair of tubular heaters in
the basement, and one room has two lines of pipes on three sides. The
steam is taken either from the steam main or from the exhaust steam of the
non-condensing engine used for running the tools in the workshops. The
air from the heaters in the basement is conveyed to the upper floor by metal
flues passing through the floors.

The dimensions of the buildings and surfaces met with are given
for the central group in the following table with French and English
units:

APPROXIMATE DIMENSIONS OF BUILDINGS IN THE CENTRAL GROUP.

	Academy.	Manual Training School.	Museum of Fine Arts.	Gymnasium	University.
Volume, c. f.	450,000	225,000	500,000	100,000	750,000
Volume, c. m	12,600	6,300	14,000	2,800	21,000
External surface in sq. ft.	36,000	20,000	36,000	13,000	80,000
External surface in metres.	3,348	2,418	3,348	1,200	7,440
Heating surface in sq. ft.	3,500	1,870	3,300	500	6,000
Heating surface in metres	323	174	307	46	552
Volume c. f. to 1 sq. ft. heating surface	129	120	152	200	125
To 1 sq. ft. of wall	12.8	11.2	13.9	7.7	9.4
Cubic metres to 1 sq. metre heating surface	30	36	45	60	38
To 1 sq. metre wall	3.8	3.3	4.2	2.3	2.8
External surface to heating surface	10.3	10.7	10.9	26.	13.3

The boilers are three in number, set independently, two being used at
once. They have each 768 square feet of heating surface, and 24 square
feet of grate. The stack is 12.25 square feet aperture at the top, and is 105
feet above the grate bars.

All fuel is weighed, and all water, fresh or return, is measured either
by metre or weight as desired. The coal used is bituminous, from the
neighboring mines in Illinois, and has a chemical composition capable of

evaporating 12 units of water by 1 unit of coal by weight, from and at
212° F.; ash, 12 per cent.

Experiments of March, 1880. Fuel and water weighed for one week;
one boiler; maximum coal per square foot of grate, 38 pounds; mean evaporation from and at 212° F., 6.49 pounds; priming, 2 per cent.

Experiments of October, 1880. Coal weighed and water by meter
(Worthington) for one week; two boilers; mean evaporation for the week,
7.1 pounds; maximum for 24 hours, 7.9 pounds.

As the meter was a piston meter, the results are not likely to be in excess of the truth on that account. The weight was charged each time, full
and empty barrel of water, and the time noted.

The priming by the method of Hirn. The work done was exceedingly
varied in the March experiments; it was found that at that time the work
from 6 A. M. to 12 noon was double that done in the other 18 hours.

Experiments upon the transmission of heat have been made upon the
Academy and University buildings only, the quantity of water condensed
being noted, with the steam pressure, the temperature of the external air,
the air in the buildings and of the return water.

With external temperatures from 10° F. to 45° F., and the buildings
from 60° F. to 75° F., steam from 260° F. to 280° F., the values already given
for *a* were found. The duration of the experiments was from three
to eight hours, taken during the ordinary operation of the works. The
return water was usually from 190° F. to 210° F. The experiment for
underground condensation was made in the same way, and lasted five
hours.*

The construction of the boilers was shown in the paper by Mr. White
above referred to.

There is one element, not yet mentioned, and that is the time in which
the buildings must be warmed. In the experience of the writer at the
University buildings the Academy can be warmed in cold weather in three
hours, and in fact the steam is only supplied for twelve hours out of the
twenty-four. The University building with the indirect heaters has to
be kept warm all the time, and in cold weather takes ten or twelve hours
to get warm throughout. For rapid heating, the direct system with ample
surface appears best adapted; but for steady heating, with purity of air,
the indirect is to be preferred.

D. Designing a System.

Suppose that it is required to design the heating apparatus for a
large building. This will include the boilers, the heaters and their disposition, and the choice of a system direct or indirect, and the use of exhaust steam from an engine.

---

*In the experiments with the buildings the ample ventilation was not interfered
with. The other buildings have just been completed, and the experiments made with
them are only preliminary.

To fix our ideas let us consider the case to be that of a cotton mill with the following dimensions:

In English measure, 328 feet long, 40 wide and three stories of 13 feet in height, making 40 feet say as the height, rectangular in plan, having a volume of 524,800 cubic feet and a surface of 42,560 square feet.

In French measure, 100 metres long, 12 metres wide and 12 metres high, having a volume of 14,400 cubic metres and a surface of 3,888 square metres.

Such a mill will contain 10,500 spindles, 225 looms and the proper proportions of cards, with the other machinery belonging to the manufacture of cotton.

Let the lowest external temperature be assumed at 5° F. $= - 15°$. C., and let the minimum internal temperature be assumed at 59° F. $= 15$ C., values which would be likely to suit most localities in the United States, and even if exceeded would not be very often passed. The range of wall transmission will then be from 59° to 5° $= 54°$ F. $= 30°$ C., and the quantity of heat transferred may reach 54 × 1.25 units per square foot per hour or 30 × 6.0 calories per square metre per hour—67.5 English or 180 French units.

$67.5 × 42,560 = 2,872,800$ heat units per hour, or
$180 × 3,888 = 699,840$ calories per hour.

To decide upon the amount of heating surface the temperature of the steam must be known. The choice of the direct or indirect methods will probably be made from the form of the building, which covers a large area and is not very high, and the magnitude of the rooms, supposed to be not more than two to a floor, as direct surface; and the kind of heaters by economy only, to be pipes laid along the foot of the walls, or rather along the walls near the floors.

The temperature of the steam will much depend upon where it comes from, from a separate boiler or from the exhaust of an engine, and we will examine three cases:

1. A separate boiler.
2. A non-condensing engine.
3. A condensing engine.

With a separate boiler we are not limited as to pressure except by convenience, and we will assume 50 pounds per square inch above the atmosphere, 65 pounds absolute, or 4½ atmospheres, the temperature of the steam being 297° F., or 148° C. $297° - 59° = 238°$ F. $= T' - T = 148° - 15° = 133°$ C., $q = \frac{(T' - T)^2}{100} = 566.44$ heat units per square foot per

hour $= 1,528$ calories per square metre per hour.

The slight difference in these results is due to a neglect of decimals and is of no practical value.

The boiler, to give this amount of heat, will have to evaporate 2,873 pounds of water per hour, or say 3,000 pounds, and will require, at 4 pounds of water evaporated per 1 square foot per hour, an amount of heating surface = 750 square feet. As this is the maximum capacity, we find that 24 square feet of grate, with coal evaporating 6 pounds of water per 1 pound coal, burning 500 pounds per hour, or about 22 pounds coal per square foot of grate, is an ample provision. A smaller grate, with careful firing, would give better results for fuel, but would not be as easy to work on cold days.

The cost of such a boiler set in the United States would not be far from $1,300, including everything ready to use, but not counting any out-lay for buildings to put it in. The cost of the pipe in place to make 4,460 square feet of surface for 1-inch or 2-inch pipe would be about 40 cents per square foot, or $1,856. Total cost, $1,856 + $1,300 = $3,156, and including contingencies, say $3,200 at 5 francs per dollar, 16,000 francs, of which the boiler cost 6,500 and the pipes 9,100 francs.

Suppose the steam had been at 212° F. or 100° C., 212°—59° = 153° F., in place of 238° for $T' - T$, but the transmission is now reduced, and the surface must now be increased 1.55 times to 7,192 square feet, say 7,200 or to a cost of 13,950 francs; total, say 31,000 francs. The steam temperature is now at the lowest possible in a non-condensing steam engine; and if such an engine, using 2,800 pounds of steam per hour, be at hand, the only outlay involved is the pipe surface of 14,000 francs, say; but with the more active circulation of the steam there will be found an increase in the radiating effect, which, however, we will not consider here.

We have then a decrease in the cost of the plant of 400 dollars, or 2,000 francs, which is equivalent to say 40 dollars or 200 francs per year interest and repairs, and we should, of course, recommend the use of exhaust steam.

There remains to be considered the use of a condensing engine, with the exhaust steam at say 100° F. = 38° C.

It would be possible, by the use of a very large amount of pipe surface and a very carefully arranged drainage, to return to the air pump; but the great cost of pipe surface and the practical troubles of making pipe joints hold in vacuum would cause us to reject this idea as impracticable, and there remains the use of a separate boiler, or the running of our condensing engine as a non-condensing engine during the winter months.

For ordinary condensing engines the increase of fuel would be in pro-portion to the increase of work on the forward stroke, rendered necessary by the increase of back pressure, and in such cases it would be desirable to use a separate boiler, as the fuel used would be great; for example, the engine using 400 I. H. P., with 4 pounds of coal per H. P. per hour, or 1,600 pounds of coal per hour. The increase of fuel may be measured by the increase of forward work, which, of course, depends upon the engine used; but if the forward mean pressure had been 30 pounds and the mean back pressure 3 pounds per square inch when running condensing, the forward pressure will now be raised to 43 pounds, and the back pressure to 16 pounds, the fuel from 1,600 to 2,292 pounds, or say 700 pounds per hour increase, between three and four francs per hour, say 40 francs per day for the maximum work in heating, but this must be kept up for 100 days, or a cost per year of 4,000 francs.

When we compare this with our separate boiler we have an excess of 2,000 francs to begin with, but also the cost of the fuel in addition, which cannot be taken less than 1,800 per year, as estimated below, making together, say 2,000 francs, and we should in this case use the separate boiler and engine.

When, however, we have the mill in good order, and have the best engine in use, that of M. Hirn, using superheated steam, we find that the power is not over 250 horse-power and the fuel 2 pounds per hour per I. H. P., or 500 pounds per hour in place of 1,600, the increase $500\frac{43}{30} - 500 = 217$ pounds, which costs about one franc per hour, or say $200 to $230, or 1,000 to 1,200 francs per year, on the above basis of 100 days of 12 hours.

The cost of the fuel alone for the separate boiler on the basis given above of a maximum of 500 pounds, and say an average of 300 pounds of coal per hour, would be from 30 to 40 cents, or $1\frac{1}{2}$ to 2 francs, say for the 100 days of 12 hours; $360, or 1,800 francs, as estimated above, which, with the cost of the boiler, would leave us $160, or 800 francs per year in favor of this plan.

We find then that with non-condensing engines and the best class of condensing engines, the use of exhaust steam is desirable, while with ordinary condensing engines a separate boiler is to be preferred.

The pipe surface for 7,200 square feet can be arranged to take the exhaust steam from the engine through an 8-inch or the 10-inch exhaust pipe to the top of the building, and to open into 2-inch pipes on each floor, in two directions, uniting in a descending 10-inch pipe carried to a hot water tank, and the exhaust to be either circulated or turned loose into the air without going through the building.

Seventy-two hundred feet would require 14,400 feet of two-inch pipe and as we can easily place 300 feet in one line and 600 feet in the two lines, we have twenty-four lines, or four lines of 2-inch pipe on each of the two main walls. The end walls and vertical pipes will make up the amount. Twenty-four lines of 2-inch pipe will present the same resistance that one line of 10-inch, and we need fear no great increase of back pressure above that assumed. (Two-inch pipe is 0.05 m. diameter.) The wall pipes should fall uniformly 1 in 200. Each line of pipe should have its own valve connections, and when most of them are closed the steam allowed to flow directly into the air, as well as through the building, to avoid back pressure. One and one-quarter inch pipe is usually preferred to larger sizes, as being easier to bend without fracture.

In the above recommendation of the use of exhaust steam by discarding the condenser of an engine, it is, of course, supposed that both boilers and engine can do the required work under the new conditions with entire safety and satisfactorily. This can only be ascertained in the particular instance by a careful and complete examination of the conditions under which the engines are now working, and the change should not be made until the result is clearly foreseen, for the example supposed the best state of things, and for all but the best kind of condensing engines and mills in the best order, we shall not find it advantageous to make so novel a departure, and shall use the separate engine and boiler.

To get the pipe surface three lines of 2 inch pipe in each floor may then be employed.

In the United States the cost of a given surface of pipe is about the same for 1-inch and 2-inch pipe, the labor making up the cost to the same amount. With the larger sizes the cost increases, but for the use of exhaust steam the larger pipe is to be preferred, unless more than one line be used at once in the example above.

[NOTE.—The conclusions of the above paper have been borne out by the experience of the winters 1880–81 and 1881–82.—C. A. SMITH.]